So Long, Vietnam

BY

Brian King

Cover image of soldiers:
originally published in *Liberated Barracks*, vol. 2, courtesy of
James Lewes. With thanks to David Zeiger of Displaced Films
and his documentary *Sir! No Sir!*.

Cover image, 'jungle': © FabVietnam_Photography via istockphoto

Book and Cover Design: Vladimir Verano, Third Place Press

Edited by Teresa Selfe

ISBN: 978-0-615-83984-4

Published by
THIRTY SECOND STREET RACCOONS PUBLISHING

To contact the author, or obtain copies of the book, visit:
www.solongvietnam.com

This book is dedicated to my grandchildren,
Fiona and Gabriel King, ages 7 and 4.

May they live in a healed world without the
threat of Global Warming, where everybody
has a decent job, and no one has to live under
the fear of war.

To Stan & Joyce,
I hope you guys enjoy this as
much as I enjoyed "Uncharted Sky!"
I sure do love Riley, he can
come any time!

Brian

AUTHOR'S NOTE

Many events in this book are autobiographical. The Army adventures including the D Company meeting of Bros and Heads (just before the invasion of Cambodia) are told pretty much as they occurred. After the meeting the book enters the arena of fiction. As my friend, a veteran of the Cambodian invasion said, it could have happened. And we all would have been much better off.

SO LONG, VIETNAM

PROLOGUE

March 6, 1968

THREE AMERICAN SOLDIERS

THE WARM, PRE-DAWN AIR SMELLED OF AVIATION GAS AND TOBACCO smoke, giving the young airwarriors reason enough for quickened pulses. The three men stood together on the flattened grass of their airfield near Quang Ngai, Vietnam, as ground crews scurried about, hurrying to finish topping off the fuel tanks on the helicopters that would be flying into battle that day. It wasn't quite time to launch yet, still a little dark. Daylight, it turns out, was the best friend American soldiers had in Vietnam. Way too easy for the Viet Cong to take a shot and duck back in the bush when the sun was down. But when the day turned bright, it was so much harder for the bad guys to hide. Scare 'em into taking a shot, then call in the big boys and blow 'em straight to hell. That was Warrant Officer Hugh Thompson's job and, for the most part, he loved it. At least the flying part, that is.

"What's up today, Hugh?" Sergeant Glen Andreotta asked. "Otta" was crew chief for the three-man team assigned to the small OH-6 "Scout" helicopter they would be flying that day. He was expected to make sure the chopper was ready to fly and then take care of any equipment problems that might arise during flight. Andreotta was twenty-one years old, from Cincinnati, Ohio, and had volunteered for helicopters, despite the danger involved. "Nothing like soaring with parrots in the steam of the jungle-almost makes the fuckin' war worth it," he often said.

Thompson took a long drag on his Camel, squinted to look at his watch, then glanced at his clipboard. "When it gets light enough to see, we'll read our orders, and then we'll all know what's up." He exhaled casually, and gave the younger Andreotta a generous grin that was easy to see, even in the half-light. Hugh Thompson spoke with a mellow twang, picked up from his childhood in Stone Mountain, Georgia. "…and maybe see where we're flyin' besides," Thompson added. He took another lazy drag on the Camel. The fireball on the end of the cigarette glowed enough to reveal his handsome unwrinkled twenty-four-year-old face. Hugh Thompson was at six foot three inches, a little tall to squeeze himself into a Scout's cockpit. But his flying skills were superb and his courage in battle unsurpassed. No one ever complained when receiving an assignment to Thompson's crew, except maybe about his long legs and knobby knees in the confined seating area of the little Scout helicopter, or "bubble."

Minutes later, Thompson read their orders for the day.

"Pinkville," Thompson grumbled.

Andreotta and Colburn looked away from each other in ill-concealed disgust.

"Squack!" went the radio in the bubble. "Here we go, guys." Thompson flipped his smoke and crushed it underfoot. He pulled on his helmet and listened for a few moments to the radio coming thru the attached mike. "Right." Then a nod to Andreotta and his machine gunner, Specialist Fourth Class Larry Colburn. Thompson next motioned "thumbs up" to the crews of the two gunships that would be flying with them that day. Helmets and flack vests on, the three young men took their places in the bubble. Thompson was at the controls, Andreotta next to him riding 'shotgun', and Colburn right behind them in front of the open cargo door with his M60 machine gun.

After spooling up the turbine, Thompson gently pulled up on the collective control stick and the little bird gracefully rose from the grass. He flew a lazy arc to the north of the field until his two Huey Gunships were airborne and had separated about a thousand feet in altitude, heading south. Thompson then took up his customary position between the two Hueys. The three helicopters formed a vertical column: high gunship, bubble, low gunship.

Thompson then shoved the cyclic forward a little, pushing the bubble to its top speed, about 160 mph. Colburn turned his attention to his M60, which hung from a stout bungee chord in the open starboard door of the chopper. He jacked a round into the chamber and fired a few into the rice paddies below, splashes barely visible in the pre-dawn light.

Minutes later, Thompson tapped each of his now-sleeping crew members on the shoulder and pointed to the port side of the chopper where the sun had just risen. Heat would be building soon, but for now, things were almost indescribably beautiful. The soft morning sun reflected off the paddies beneath them, emphasizing the shapes of the dikes, water buffalo, and the occasional farmer toiling in the ancient fields below. Misty clouds of vapor wafted up and past the bubble, bringing with them the smells of agriculture mixed with those of the nearby jungle. In the distance, the vast blue of the South China Sea gently rolled. *Almost worth the fuckin' war*, Andreotta caught himself thinking again.

"All right, you guys remember Rule Number One, right?" Thompson said while looking straight ahead.

Colburn spoke up, "When you're flying with Thompson, or anybody else in this fuckin' gun-company for that matter, you make sure you see a weapon in the little son-of-a-bitch's hand before you fuckin' zap him."

"That's it, guys." Thompson smiled and looked to port, then starboard, constantly verifying his flight path with familiar landmarks. "We stick to Rule Number One and everything stays groovy."

Andreotta took a pack of Doublemint gum from his pocket and offered sticks to his buddies. They began chewing, almost in unison. The three men settled into silence, excited and scared as they looked ahead to the day's combat. Each man trying very hard to show neither feeling.

"There they are!" Colburn called out as he locked and loaded. He was looking at the characteristic aerial view of battalion-size combat in Vietnam. Transport helicopters, "slicks," setting down with bunches of bobbing helmets disgorging from them. *Like mama salmon laying eggs in a stream*, Colburn, who had grown up in the Pacific Northwest, thought, and smiled. Ahead of the slicks in a line of trees, more helmets with rifles pointing at a village. Puffs of smoke emerged from the peasant dwellings as the troopers in the treeline laid more and more heavy fire down on the sleepy huts.

On the road leading out of the village, a couple-hundred peasants were moving quickly out of harm's way. Thompson swooped in low to have a look. "Heading to market," he said.

"Empty baskets," Andreotta said, agreeing with Thompson.

"Let's see what kind of shit we can stir," Thompson said as he banked the bubble toward the other end of the village and a treeline behind it. The high and low gunships followed Thompson's lead, staying back a little and waiting for word from the bubble that a target had been sighted. Thompson checked his radio switch to make sure it was on and that he had communication with his two gunships. The radios in the choppers could not connect with anyone on the ground.

"Got something!" Colburn screamed as he let loose a burst from his M60 directed into the treeline behind the village.

"'Gunny low', you see that?" Thompson said over the radio.

"Bubble, I do see that," Warrant Officer Danny Watkins answered as he maneuvered his ship into position and let loose a fusillade of machine gun and rocket fire upon the same area.

"Hey, looks like 'Goodnight, Irene' for those motherfuckers," Colburn said as he offered thumbs up to Andreotta.

Thompson put the little chopper into a dive over the area they had just attacked. Smoke was rising from the area they had fired upon, making vision to the ground a little difficult.

"Got three dead ones down there," Colburn called out, "and looks like two.... three AK's." (AK-47's; the standard Russian made rifle used by the Viet Cong)

Thompson nodded slightly, then pulled the helicopter into a wide turn and headed back toward the road and the main area of fighting.

Ninety seconds later, Andreotta called out, "Whoa!" as he looked at a ditch next to the road where they had sighted the large group of peasants minutes before. "Looks like they made all those gooks lie down in the ditch next to the road."

Colburn looked at Andreotta, perplexed. "What the fuck...?" he said.

Thompson said nothing as he banked the bubble around for another look. As they approached the ditch where Andreotta had spotted the peasants, the first thing they saw was a dozen troopers standing around with their M16s at the ready, muzzels in the air. Standing guard?

"Hey, Hugh, aren't we a little low?" Colburn voiced a common concern in Vietnam; always avoid hovering at less than a hundred feet. It rendered the bird and its crew extremely vulnerable to groundfire.

"Oh Jesus...," Andreotta said, his voice barley audible above the rotor. "The fuckers shot the kids."

"Yeah." Thompson said and went still lower as they surveyed the grisly results of the morning's "battle." Bodies piled on top of each other; children, women, old people. He moved the little chopper along above the ditch as the three soldiers took in more horror than they ever expected to come upon, even in Vietnam. "Fuckin' body count," Thompson muttered.

"Hugh, that guy's still alive!" Colburn called out.

Thompson put the bubble in a stationary hover at about ten feet and turned to Colburn. "Put some green on him, Colby." Green smoke on a wounded person would bring the medics to help.

Thompson slowly moved the chopper along the ditch, giving Colburn and Andreotta a chance to locate any additional signs of life. When they found people moving, they marked them for the medics and moved on. After they marked the tenth wounded peasant, one of the guards walked over to the semiconscious woman next to the smoking, green canister. Captain's bars were visible on his helmet as he cupped his hands in front of his mouth to shout up to Thompson.

"What the hell do you think you're doing?" Screamed Captain Joseph Barnes, commander of Charlie Company, 1st Batallion, 20th Infantry, 11th Brigade (Light), of the 23rd (Americal) Division.

"She's hurt," shouted Colburn above the roar of the rotors, "so we put smoke on her."

The angry officer kicked the half-conscious woman in the stomach, stepped back, and killed her with a burst from his M16 to her head. Thompson swung his chopper around and flew back along the ditch in time to see other troopers on the ground finishing off the wounded.

"Goddamn, Hugh!" Andreotta called out, "it's like we marked 'em all so they could finish 'em. Jesus!"

Thompson worked his way along the ditch looking straight ahead. His face had turned beet-red and his jaw was quivering.

Seconds later, Colburn tapped on Thompson's shoulder and pointed to a dike about one hundred-and-fifty yards away. At one end of the dike a dozen or so Vietnamese were running toward a cave. At the other end, a squad of American soldiers was racing to catch them.

Thompson turned the bubble toward the dike and nosed over, pushing it up to max speed. "It don't take a genius to figure out what's going to happen if those GIs catch those poor little fuckers at the other end of that dike," he said.

Thompson hovered the bubble for a second near what looked like the mouth of a cave at the end of the dike, where the small group of Vietnamese had disappeared from sight. He brought the helicopter down, placing the little chopper between the troopers and the villagers.

"Colby, take your gun off the bungee and stand down over there between us and those guys comin' this way." He paused for a second and shook his head to clear his thoughts. "Don't let 'em get past the bird, Colby."

Colburn looked at Thompson and didn't move. "But Hugh..."

"It's all right Colby." Thompson pointed to the doorway and nodded his head. "We're just gonna make sure nobody else gets hurt here today, okay?"

"Okay, Hugh." Colburn reached for the snap holding his gun to the bungee chord.

The squad of eleven GIs had stopped ten feet from the bubble and were standing around looking confused. Colburn hopped to the ground holding his machine gun with its muzzle pointed down and a two-foot belt of ammo dangling from the magazine. He did not lock and load. The big gun was not yet ready to fire.

Thompson followed Colburn down and stood in front of the American troopers. A lieutenant in the group stepped forward with a glower on his face.

"Was that you landed the chopper here, between us and that bunch of VC we was chasing?" snarled Lieutenent Boyd Dowler.

"Sir, we got this situation under control," Thompson said as he turned around and motioned toward the cave with his head. "That group was all friendlies, far as I could see." He turned back toward Dowler. "We'll get 'em outta there, Sir. Take 'em somewhere safe. Away from the fighting, okay Sir?"

Dowler pulled a hand grenade from a clip on his packstrap. "Look here," he squinted to read Thompson's nametag, "Thompson, is it?" He held the grenade out toward the lanky helicopter pilot. "All it takes is one of these, and them gooks will be outta that cave, smartly."

"Just let me see what I can do for a second," Thompson spun around moving toward the cave entrance, "okay, lieutenant?" he called out over his shoulder as he walked. He stopped for a moment and spoke quietly to Colburn. "If they try to get past you, Colby, shoot 'em." Then he headed into the cave.

"He talks Gook," Colburn said to the assembled GIs between chews on his Doublemint. "Really. He'll have em outta there in a sec. You guys'll be amazed." Colburn smiled and winked at a couple of grunts in the front of the group. He still had not locked and loaded, nor did he point the machine gun at his fellow GIs. Lt. Dowler stood to the side, angrily squeezing and massaging the hand grenade he had shown Thompson.

"Fuck this shit!" Private First Class Forrest Schrader, a six foot five inch black GI from Detroit said, as he threw his M16 to the ground and spat to the side. He turned around and walked with a strong, ambling gait back toward the Charlie company command post. "I'm going to go get some chow. Anybody comin' with me?" Two more of Lt. Dowler's men, a white and a black soldier, dropped their rifles and followed Schrader.

Platoon Sergeant "Buck" Snider walked up to Lt. Dowler. A grizzled, twelve year Army veteran, Snider usually knew when it was time to help a young lieutenant with his decision making. "Sir, I expect everybody's a little hungry by now." He motioned his head toward Schrader and the other two, who were now halfway back across the dike. "Why don't we get these guys over to the command post before Schrader eats all that good food the cooks have fixed for us."

Without saying anything, Dowler rehooked the grenade onto his pack strap and took off, following Schrader back across the dike. The rest of the group began moving behind them.

"Whittington," Snider said, pointing to the three discarded M16s, "I believe Schrader and his buddies forgot their weapons. Would you please police them up for me and return them to those fuck-ups?"

"Aw, Sarge," Whittington groaned as he leaned over and retrieved the guns.

Minutes later, Thompson stood in front of a terrified group of eight: old men, women and children. "Bin tinh, moi thu deu on—calm down, everything is all right," he said gently pushing on the air as he spoke. The villagers stood very close together, clutching one another and watching Hugh Thompson intently. Two of the women were crying.

Thompson turned and walked back to his helicopter, reached in and picked up his helmet. He took a step back from the chopper, placed the headpiece on, and spoke into the microphone.

"Hey Danny, I'm sorry to ask you to do this," he said over the radio to the pilot of his low helicopter gunship, "but I need you to bring your bird down here and pick up some friendlies before they get killed."

"Hugh," Watkins' voice came over the radio, "you lost all your marbles, or what?"

"I know we're taking a pretty big chance here with two birds on the ground, but Bill can keep an eye out from high chopper. And I really need you to do this, Danny."

"Roger that, bubble." Watkins' reply came over the radio. "Keep us in your cross hairs, William."

"Roger that, Danny." the pilot of the high gunship responded.

Thompson and his two crewmen stood in the downwash of the helicopter gunship as it powered up and off the dike, their hair dancing in the breeze of the whirling rotor. It was about the only time anybody on the ground in Vietnam ever got a chance to cool off a little during the heat of the day.

"Where they taking 'em, Hugh?" Colburn said, his voice raised above the noise of the crowded, climbing chopper.

"They're going to Brigade Medical in Quang Ngai, Colby," Andreotta said, and then wiped dust from his mouth with a bare arm. Helicopter crews in Vietnam often wore flak vests without shirts under them. Arm muscle rippled under sunburnt reddish-brown skin. "Same as us, right Hugh?"

"Well, not exactly, Otta."

Andreotta and Colburn looked at each other seriously with, "What's Hugh up to now?" expressions.

"You guys ever get a chance to have a little chat with a bird colonel?" Thompson asked.

"Oh shit," Andreotta and Colburn both said, practically in unison.

"Aw, it's gonna be great, fellas." Thompson had regained his normal countenance of taciturn cockiness, with an occasional slice of wry humor. "I think the colonel needs a little review on Rule Number One," Thompson was smiling broadly as he spoke, "don't y'all?"

✶ ✶ ✶

Dust enveloped the little helicopter as it landed fifty feet from the entrance to the headquarters tent of Task Force Barker, 23rd (Americal) Divison, II Corps, US MACV (Military Assistance Command, Vietnam). Four armed MPs came running out of the tent to challenge these intruders on the tranquility of Colonel Frank A. Barker, commanding officer of Task Force Barker. The MPs had taken their side arms out of their holsters and were pointing them upward.

"We're here to see the colonel." Thompson spoke softly.

"Colonel Barker's kinda busy today, Sir," an MP sergeant said to Thompson, "and I'm going to have to ask you to move your helicopter to somewhere more appropriate, okay Sir?"

"Not okay, fella," Thompson said and walked past the sergeant with Andreotta and Colburn following him. The MPs watched the trio walk into the tent, and then reholstered their 45's, shaking their heads at the foolhardiness of Thompson and his crew.

Once inside the tent complex, Thompson stopped and looked around for a moment, trying to locate the colonel's office. The three were quite a sight in the normally clean and tidy environment of Task Force Barker's battalion headquarters. Between the blood mixed with dust and sweat on their clothing, and their wild windblown hair above the fierce expressions on their faces, they gave a strong impression of troops just returning from some terrible battle. Not the kind of guys one would choose to mess with.

"What can we do for you, gentlemen?" Command Sergeant Major Richard Hurley asked crisply as he walked up to the three weary airmen. "Thompson, huh?" Hurley read Thompson's nametag. "We've heard your name a few times around here, young man. The grunts are always glad when they hear it's your group flying scout for us."

"Thank you, Sergeant Major, but we need to speak with the colonel about a situation we just came from out at Pinkville," Thompson said.

Hurley was a third generation Army man from North Dakota. He had been in for twenty-eight years and believed rules should be followed, especially in a war zone.

"Well, Thompson, I'm afraid I can't get you in to see the colonel looking like you do right now." He arched an inquisitive brow and looked at Colburn. "Son, where did all that blood come from? Are you wounded?"

"No Sergeant Major," Colburn responded. "The blood's from a little gook kid we grabbed out of a ditch full of dead friendlies back in Pinkville."

"Sergeant Major, we really have to speak to Colonel Barker on an urgent matter...," Thompson began.

"Is this child alive, Colburn?" Hurley asked, interrupting Thompson.

"Yes Sergeant Major, he is alive." Colburn self-consciously rubbed his pant legs, trying to clean his hands. "He wasn't wounded himself, all the blood was from dead people on top of him, including this woman he was clinging to, probably his momma. We dropped him off in Quang Ngai with some nuns before we flew over here."

"Sergeant Major...," Thompson began, and then proceeded to tell the story of what they had seen and done that day.

When Thompson was finished, Colburn related his own story of their landing to pick up the last survivor in the ditch. "And after I snatched the kid away from his momma, I looked over and saw Hugh arguing with one of the guys who'd been shootin,' the friendlies." He looked at Thompson, "What was that lieutenant's name you were hollerin' at over there?"

"I don't know." Thompson scrunched his face, trying to remember. "Callen, maybe Calley. Somethin' like that."

"Anyhow, Sergent Major, I yelled at Hugh that we had to get going. And I'm glad I did, cause it looked like those two were ready to start swingin' fists." He took a deep breath and let it out. "So here we are, Sergeant Major."

Hurley stood silent for a full minute. "Wait here," he said. He then whirled about and walked smartly thru an open doorway up to a man seated at a desk. When Thompson moved a little closer, he saw a nameplate that identified the man behind the desk as Colonel Barker. After a brief conference with Hurley, Barker picked up the phone on his desk and spoke with someone for a minute or two.

Hurley came back. "You three come over to the radio communications area with me." He turned toward another doorway and marched off, the three following him. "There's something I want you men to hear." Without breaking his pace toward the radio room, he said to the desk clerk, "Redman, get an av-gas truck over here and have that scout chopper on our front lawn filled up. Otherwise, we'll probably never get rid of these guys."

"Right away, Top!" Redman fired back.

As Hurley and the three helicopter men entered the radio room, the operator was writing out a message on his log sheet that everyone in the room could hear. "Attention, Pinkville!" came the authoritative voice over the radio, "This is Division speaking: Stop the killing! I say again: Stop the killing!"

✷ ✷ ✷

"Hey, Hurley was pretty cool," Colburn took a deep drag on the Camel cigarette he had just bummed from Thompson. The three airmen stood a respectful distance from their chopper as it was being fueled.

"What was the name of that place we were at today?" Thompson puffed on his Camel and exhaled the smoke in a luxuriant cloud.

"Something like," Andreotta began, "Song Lai or Mai Lai. My Lai, that was it."

"Like, me lie down and go to sleep, huh?" Colburn offered.

"Yeah," grunted Thompson, and raised his cigarette to his lips.

CHAPTER 1

May 20th, 1969

0600 HRS

TOM KELLY DID LOVE THIS. HE WAS SITTING IN A RATHER AWKWARD lotus position, inside a claw foot bathtub. Soothing, warm water sprinkled down from the shower onto his shoulders. He bowed his head and let the water massage the tension from his neck. *There. Maybe*, he thought, *I can actually make it through this fuckin' day.*

His thoughts bounced through his life since high school. A couple of former girlfriends he wasn't exactly on speaking terms with, studying for college classes, voter registration for the Civil Rights movement in Mississippi and Florida and participation in the Anti-Vietnam War movement flowed through his mind. The images were vivid, if not always pleasant. He hadn't really been successful at any endeavors so far in his young life.

Suddenly, Tom was rudely interrupted by one of his trademark "grizzly bear" farts. Just as he was congratulating himself on the force and tonal quality of his flatulence, the cloud of odor hit his face at full strength. Rising quickly, he made good his escape. *Oh well*, he thought. *Time to face it, anyway. Might as well get this over with.*

"It" was riding a bus fifty miles from San Jose to Oakland, CA, and getting inducted into the Army. What would happen for the next couple of years, after, "taking the oath," wasn't very clear to Kelly.

Rebecca "Becky" Frankel stood in the doorway of their bedroom, watching Kelly fumble around for his clothes. *What a target*, she thought. He stood a little over six feet tall and had what she regarded as a pleasant build, if you overlooked the love handles that seemed to come and go with each new moon. "He's so slow," she had confided to a friend, after he received his draft notice. Tom Kelly was probably the slowest guy to make the varsity basketball team at his high school. "When the shooting starts how is he going to get his head down in time?" If that wasn't bad enough he was also a bit of a dreamer, not always completely tuned in to his immediate surroundings. "He'll probably try to talk the Viet Cong into not shooting him, for God's sake!" Becky said to her friend.

As Tom was buckling his belt, Becky walked over and put her arms around him. *God, how I'm going to miss him while he's gone,* she thought. "How's it going, HB?" she asked. "Honey Bun", seemed to fit this affectionate Irishman, pretty good in bed, potentially a decent father, but definitely not much of a fighter.

"I guess it's going OK, so far," he replied. He kissed her, and they walked to the kitchen to try and eat some breakfast, something neither of them had much interest in. "Might as well get going," he mumbled. "Bus leaves in twenty minutes."

"Shit," Becky replied, "I suppose you're right. You wouldn't want to be late for your first day, huh?" She looked at the half-asleep young man across from her, "Hey, back off a little on the anti-war organizing for awhile, OK?"

Becky thought back to her first meeting with Kelly on the San Jose State College campus. Springtime was demonstration time. The freshly blooming mimosa trees contrasted with the shiny helmets of the riot police, floral smells and acrid tear gas mixing. The cops came charging out of a building entrance the students were trying to blockade. Becky found herself unceremoniously squashed under one Tom Kelly, a worried look on his face.

She quickly got to her feet and helped Kelly up. He introduced himself and invited Becky to dinner that night, which she thought was a little presumptuous. But then, she looked him over and decided she rather liked what she saw.

Kelly was a little more than a foot taller than Becky, with an unkempt head of auburn hair. He had a sprinkle of freckles across his nose and a warm, Irish smile. *Well, he does have a pretty cute mustache,* thought Becky. He was wearing blue jeans, Sears work boots, and a blue work shirt; a student movement uniform, of sorts. The effect of the outfit was a little spoiled by a small foodstain just below one of his shirt pockets. *What the heck,* she thought. "Sure, why not?" she had said, brushing dirt from her jeans.

That had been six months before Kelly received his notice to report for induction into the Army.

"C'mon Beck, why not organize? I got to do something fun to pass the two years, don't you think?" He cracked a little smile. "Especially in Nam, right?

"No." She gave him a stern look and pointed a finger at him. "Especially NOT in Vietnam!"

Becky drove down to the bus station. At Tom's request, she dropped him off in front of the terminal. Kelly leaned into the driver-side window of the little car, "You don't want to come in and hang around bored while the bus driver takes a leak and then say good-bye in front of a bunch of grinning 18-year-olds, do you?" She smiled weakly, giving him a little wave of her hand. Back home a lonely sadness settled over her as she pulled into their driveway.

"Clang!" went the heavy, metal latch on the main cellblock door. Two men, one white and one black, stepped through the opening. Willie Tuggins was dressed in white muslin pants and shirt, with a large black "P" on the back. The white man wore the uniform of a Hampton County Deputy Sheriff. He held Tuggins' arm, guiding him along the jail corridor that stretched between occupied prisoner cells.

"Take care, Bro," said a voice from one of the cells, followed by others wishing Tuggins well as he made his way to the jail's release room. He acknowledged each greeting with a small nod. His stride was easy and athletic. His handsome, cleanshaven face conveyed little emotion.

"You a popular boy, Willie," said the overweight deputy, his words interrupted by his heavy breathing as he struggled to keep up with his prisoner.

Tuggins looked back at Deputy Willits as they walked, and smiled, ever-so-slightly. Willits turned a doorknob and motioned Tuggins into a well-lit, air-conditioned workspace. The sound of a typewriter blended with an unintelligible voice coming from a small radio.

"Box over yonder has your stuff in it." Willits pointed to a worn and dirty cardboard box. "You can use the men's room to change." The deputy nodded in the direction of a door marked 'COLORED.' "Just leave your jail clothes in there. There'll be a gal along to clean up."

Tuggins carried the box and pushed open the door with his back.

"Your daddy's out front waitin' on you, so get a move on, boy!" Willits called out.

One week later, on the evening of May 19, 1969, a huge gathering of the close-knit Tuggins family took place in Varnville, South Carolina, a small farming community located in Hampton County, about fifty miles east of Charleston. The local economy had been based on crops of melons, corn, and vegetables since before the Civil War. The local population in 1969, including "county" people, hovered around 8000, about sixty-five percent black. There was a strong sense of change and progress in Hampton County these days. The mood at the dinner table in the Tuggins home in part reflected this spirit of optimism.

"Daddy," Willie Tuggins said quietly in his place at the dinner table next to Reverend Joseph Tuggins, "you still gonna run for mayor?"

"I think so," the reverend answered. "What with all the Civil Rights activiy, we got the worst of the crackers on the run, don't you think?"

"Yeah, but I was worried that all the trouble I've been through lately, maybe...."

"Don't you worry about that, son. Your only job for the next two years is keeping your head down." The reverend smiled and leaned to whisper in Willie's ear. "If anything, you'll help me with the young ladies' vote, right?"

Wille looked down at his plate, shook his head and laughed.

Politics wasn't the reason for this gathering of thirty-six members and four generations of the Tuggins clan. The family had come together to say goodbye to the current "apple-of-it's-eye," twenty year old Willie Tuggins, son of the Reverend Joseph and Helen Tuggins. Willie had a date the following morning to report for induction into the Army.

The food that night, prepared by Helen and her sisters, was the kind that helps a person forget, for a while, every resolution ever made about watching their waistline-Southern fried chicken, brown and brittle with just enough red pepper to give you a warm feeling inside; pan-fried okra, fragrant and gooey with bits of bacon; steaming cornbread; warm, crispy French fries; fresh picked, melt-in-your mouth, early string beans smothered in butter; and the kind of fragrant sweet potato pie that makes you wonder if, just maybe, everything might be all right after all.

From the corner of her eye, Willie's sixteen-year-old sister, Cynthia, noticed that her brother was pushing his food around his plate, not eating much. She admired his handsome face and his bright, thoughtful eyes. Willie had a powerful, athletic build inherited from his mother's side of the family. He wore his hair in a trim 'Afro' and dressed in a neat, casual style.

Cynthia recalled how he'd been a year before, forced to stand trial on charges stemming from his political activities at school. Although the jury had found him 'not guilty,' he was expelled and lost eighteen pounds. Now, after his most recent round of trouble, Willie was facing another terrifying threat, Vietnam.

This Army stuff has him worried, Cynthia thought.

"I'll tell you how you can help me," Reverend Tuggins said, continuing the conversation with his son.

"How's that, Daddy?" said Willie.

"You can show up in your soldier's uniform at a couple of my rallies this October."

"Aw, Daddy...."

"I know," said Reverend Tuggins, "You ain't exactly lookin' forward to doin' what the uniform represents."

"Daddy," Willie whispered, " I just don't wanna go to Nam."

"Black folks are very proud of our young men who put on the uniform." Reverend Tuggins waved his chicken leg. "Nobody's gonna think you support the war, necessarily," he raised his eyebrows for effect, "just that you are doin' your duty and you support your Daddy." He broke into a large, warm smile, "How 'bout it?"

"Aw, if I'm around, you know I'll do it."

A couple of years earlier, Willie had organized a chapter of the Black Student Union at Charleston State College. Later, he had been expelled on trumped-up trespassing charges after leading a BSU-sponsored sit-in against representatives of the US Marine Corps.

The Marines came to convice students to join and in Willie's words, "to recruit fresh meat for the war." One of the issues the students felt strongly about was the high rate of combat deaths suffered by black soldiers in

Vietnam. The Marines seemed like a logical target for a protest, considering their reputation for sky-high casualties suffered in futile battles.

One year after being expelled from college, Willie was visiting friends in the black section of Charleston and had suffered the common misfortune among many young black men of looking a little too much like somebody else. Evidently, the fellow he resembled had just robbed a liquor store a few blocks away, on the border between the white and black parts of town. The police knocked on the door where Willie was visiting and in a matter of minutes young Mr. Tuggins was handcuffed and sitting in the back seat of a police cruiser.

Willie had taken a ride on "the only well-functioning railroad in the country, the American judicial system," as Reverend Toggins liked to say. The day he was to receive his sentence, Willie stood in court not expecting any favors. The presiding magistrate, Judge "Brown the Clown," had a reputation of showing little sympathy for defendants who were part of the Black freedom movement.

Judge Brown cleared his throat and looked down on Willie from his elevated perch. His brow was deeply furrowed and his cheek twitched under his left eye. Brown scolded the young man imperiously, emphasizing the disgrace brought upon Willie's family by his activities in the BSU the previous year.

At that point, Rev Tuggins brought his feet under himself and looked like he was about to rise and physically challenge the eighty-two year old judge. Mrs. Tuggins laid a hand on her husband's arm. He should restrain himself, for their son's sake. The reverend leaned back with a look on his face that could have frozen an erupting volcano.

Willie was then offered a "choice" of three years in prison or two years in the Army. Three years in prison would almost certainly ruin the young man's chances for any kind of decent life. He assured Judge Brown that he would "volunteer" for the draft. Just to make sure Willie Tuggins understood the seriousness of his situation, Judge Brown ordered the young man to be held in the county jail "until such time that a representative of the Army can be found to sign him up."

So, Willie felt a little "olive drab" on the night of his send-off party. After dessert, he excused himself from the table and stepped outdoors to mull over his situation. A dog approached him with his tail wagging and tongue dangling.

"Good boy, Ralph." Willie scratched the dog's head as they both sat down and allowed the warm, thick South Carolina night to wrap itself around them.

"Well, look who I found," said Dorothy, as she walked up. Dot was Willie's girlfriend and political soul mate at Charleston State. She sat down next to Willie and patted Ralph between the ears, "Cynthia told me you was out here. I thought you might enjoy a little company-after you get through with your contemplation, that is."

Dot was, in Willie's opinion, a most remarkable woman. The young man was about as crazy in love with her as he could be. He looked at Dorothy and enjoyed the effect she had on him.

She was gorgeous. Dorothy was wearing a bright orange necklace that emphasized her lovely, chocolate-brown complexion. Her loose skirt came to her mid thigh. She was an athletic black woman with long, slender legs; a strong, well-proportioned torso; ample bust, and a derriere that made Willie feel sorry for white guys, "cause those white girls all got such puny butts. Nothin much to grab onto."

Neither one of the two were thinking much about politics at the moment.

"Girl, what you got that blanket for? It must be eighty degrees out here," Tuggins said with a smile. Dot looked down at the neatly folded quilt and giggled softly. Turning toward him, she took his hand in hers and replied, "Just thought it might come in handy, you know, in case it gets cold tonight."

Tuggins stood up and shoved his hands into his pockets. He looked up at the beautiful South Carolina night sky. Dot walked up next to him, placed her hand in the small of his back, and whispered in her boyfriend's ear, "I'm going to take a little stroll, maybe wind up at that old hay barn. You comin'?"

Tuggins said nothing and kept his eyes fixed on the stars overhead.

"Or maybe I should find somebody else to keep me company on your grandma's quilt tonight," she said as she nibbled on his ear.

Tuggins followed her like a puppy. Dot spread the quilt on a pile of soft hay. The young couple undressed, lay down, and wrapped their arms around each other. In the warmth of their embrace, they both forgot, for a while, the troubles they were facing.

Afterward, the happy young man wondered out loud, "Man, how can life be so good and so bad, all at the same time?"

Dot smiled and kissed him on the lips.

While strolling back to the house, Tuggins started to feel a little guilty about not using "protection" while they made love, but chose not to mention it. Caution had seemed like something they both decided to dispense with that night, a first for them.

Along with expressing her love and affection for Willie, Dot had been doing a little thinking ahead at the hay barn. Getting pregnant might not be such a bad thing. She figured it could turn out to be a way to protect her young man, or at least give him a little breathing room when he really needed it. She reasoned that, if there was anything the Army would feel obliged to make allowances for, a new baby would have to qualify.

Willie turned to Dot, "Look, maybe this won't be as big a deal as we're makin' out. A lot of guys have gone to Nam and made it back okay. Most of 'em that's gone, matter of fact." He stopped, took her by the shoulders, and looked into her eyes. "I definitely will not be taking unnecessary chances. I promise. I'll be back, we'll get married, and we'll live to be obnoxious old folks with grandchildren crawlin' all over us, just like them at dinner tonight."

Hand in hand, the young lovers slowly strolled back to the house. A red hot game of "rise and fly" bid whist was in progress and Dot informed the card players that she and Willie would play the next winners, if no one else was waiting. The adults at the table all politely pretended that they hadn't noticed Dot and Willie's absence.

As the night wore on folks began to grow sleepy, one by one, people said their goodbyes and wished Willie good luck. It gave him a warm feeling to receive these gentle reminders of his family's love and support. He would carry the memory of this night with him through the next couple of years. No telling when he might really need it.

Dot was the last to leave. Mother Tuggins came up to her, as the young woman found her car keys in her purse. She gave Dot one of her famous Mother Tuggins' total immersion hugs. Dot was crying.

The two women said goodnight to each other and Willie walked with Dot out to her car. "They'll let me come home for a week or two before I go to Nam," he said.

Dot grasped Willie's arm, "Maybe you'll go someplace like Germany, instead," she said hopefully.

"Yeah, you never know, maybe they'll need a few guys on the moon," he replied and chuckled. They kissed briefly, and Dot started the car. Willie clenched his fist, in a "Black Power" salute, and Dot broke out one of her knock-you-over smiles, which she knew would leave the poor guy weak in the knees as she put the car into gear and headed home.

Next morning, Tuggins rose early as was his usual practice. Sun-up was his favorite time of day, with everything fresh and full of life, especially this time of year.

Willie's mother was the other early riser in the Tuggins family. Mother and son always enjoyed their time together in the early morning, before the rest of the family was up.

"Son, what are you and Dot gonna do?" Willie knew what his mother meant. She had accepted Willie's young lady as one of her own and she was anxious for the two of them to be married. A couple of grandchildren would certainly not displease her.

"Mom, we need to get this Army thing out of the way."

He's afraid he won't make it back in one piece, thought Helen.

There was an uncharacteristic tension in the Tuggins' kitchen that morning. Mother and son felt their way carefully through the complicated emotional atmosphere, each one extra careful of the other's feelings.

"What time you got to be there, Willie?"

"The letter said eight o'clock, but I guess they can hold on for a few minutes, since they seem to want me so bad."

Helen frowned, worried that something might happen to cause the law to become interested in her son again.

Willie picked up on her concern as he dug into the meal of eggs, grits, bacon, toast, and coffee. "Don't worry Ma, I got this fella pickin' me up in a few minutes. His brother is going in today too, and he said I could ride with 'em to Charleston."

Right then a car horn sounded. He wiped his mouth, got up, and went to the bedroom where he and his two brothers slept. Bending over their bed, he kissed each one, without waking them. Walking back into the hall, Willie nearly ran into his father who had just emerged from his room, rubbing the sleep from his eyes. Their relationship had been somewhat difficult in recent years, but both father and son were determined to make this morning a happy one, in consideration of what might lie ahead.

Reverend Tuggins stood in the middle of the hall, dressed in his favorite long-johns, complete with several strategically located missing buttons and holes in the knees. The old man wore a grin that morning that could light a fire. He took his son in his arms and softly cautioned him, "Keep your head down, boy. I'm counting on you getting through this business in one piece. You know we'll be praying for you every day while you're gone."

"Okay, Daddy." The young man turned to his mother, giving her a hug and a kiss. On the porch, he looked back at his parents and said with a wink, "You all try to stay outta' trouble while I'm gone, OK?"

Tuggins hopped in the waiting car. On the road, they quickly relaxed into the easy bantering and bragging young men the world over seem to fall into when there aren't women or older men present to keep the conversation a little closer to reality. Willie and Ben Turner took turns boasting about how they were going to breeze through their hitches, considering it a point of honor to not disclose any of their apprehensions about what might be in store for them.

The early morning air was pleasantly fresh, washing in through Willie's open window. As the car cruised the empty highway toward the induction center in Charleston, Willie decided that he should be extra cool, and see what happens. Probably a wise choice for the brash young "freedom fighter": let the Army make the first move.

The night before Willie Tuggins reported for induction in Charleston, Frank Dunlop and seven of his close friends lounged together in a secluded spot on the bank of the American River, just east of Sacramento, California. The place was perfect for a gathering of old pals, some from as far back as grammar school days. The hot "Sack of Tomatoes" sun had been down for a couple of hours and the temperature next to the water had dropped to an almost pleasant seventy-eight degrees.

There was a gentle breeze coming across the river on that night of May 20, 1969. The sound of water lapping at the river's bank mingled easily with the voices of Dunlop and the others. Darkness surrounded the group. From ten feet away, all that could give away their presence were the pulsing flashes of their doobies, as Dunlop and his friends took their tokes and passed them along. From a distance, the gathering could easily have been mistaken for fireflies dancing next to the river.

Dunlop was often described, to his mild irritation, as a "regular guy." He wasn't short or tall and he never seemed to carry much bulk. He had let his blonde hair grow down to his shoulders in the current fashion, which he hoped made him look like a Viking warrior, or maybe a rock star. He wore jeans, tennis shoes, and a green t-shirt this night. His steady blue eyes, the strongest feature of his face, projected an easy-going sincerity. His ready smile and laugh made people want to be around him. Women found him quite attractive, describing him as cute, trustworthy, and sometimes even cuddly.

He felt content that night, which surprised both him and the others. After all, Frank Dunlop was the first member of his friends to get nailed by the draft. Those days around Sacramento, everybody put it off as long as possible. Tonight's gathering was the gang's sendoff for him. Tomorrow morning at six he would be joining sixteen other poor souls from Sacramento who had received their summons to duty that week. They would board a bus and begin the journey to Oakland and to basic training, and then on to Vietnam.

To Frank, the war was a case of "pure and simple bullshit." He and many of his friends had reached this conclusion by simply watching the evening news and seeing one politician after another trip over their words. His plan was "to get it the hell over with." He certainly wouldn't have to worry about getting drafted anymore.

After graduating from high school in Sacramento, California's state capital, Frank had joined the legions of state workers as a clerk for a couple of years. Frank's experiences with the state left little room for illusion in the young man's mind. Fast-talking members of the 'establishment' didn't impress him.

"Hey, this is pretty good shit," Frank opined exhaling a cloud of thick, pungent marijuana smoke. He turned to Elena Canby with a grin on his face and passed the joint to her. Elena, Frank's sweetheart took a toke. She held her breath for a moment, then exhaled and lay back against Frank with a look of satisfaction on her face. The doobie continued its way around the group of old friends, pausing while each made it glow bright for a moment.

It was good dope. The highly potent marijuana had arrived from South East Asia with a returning serviceman. It was, so far as Frank and his friends could determine, the very best, not for sale anywhere in Sacramento.

Jeffery, a long time member of the "River Rats" as the bunch at the river referred to themselves, had a brother in the Marines who had just returned from Vietnam. When Jeff's brother was told about the going away party, he had given him a couple of lids of high quality, water buffalo grass, straight from the Nam.

"Have the guy smoke some of this, it'll take his mind off what he's in for," said the jaded lance corporal

At the river, a baritone voice called, from out of the dark, "Hey Frank, you better bring some of this stuff with you when you come back."

"You mean *if* he comes back", interjected a second voice. It was meant as a joke, but the silence that followed showed the disappointment, frustration, and fear that lingered within the tapestry of the night's gathering. Would this be the last time all eight of the old pals were together?

Frank broke the silence, "Dennis, you asshole, you know I'm coming back. Actually, I'm a little worried about how you'll do while I'm gone. I should probably get somebody to make sure you shower at least once a week and check to make sure you're fly is zipped before you go to work in the morning. Anybody interested?"

Everybody seemed to relax and "get into" the evening after Frank's reply. If he could be cool about the situation, so could they. The stars were sparkling, the wind soothing. It was truly enough to make a person glad to be alive, even if only for this one night.

"Hey Frank," Dennis called from the rock he was seated on, "what do you want me to do with the rest of the inventory?"

"What's left?" said Dunlop.

"Oh, let's see," said Dennis. "Five stereos, nine TV's, a couple of fancy Swedish cameras, and a motorcycle, er, with sidecar."

"Frank," Elena exploded, "where did all these things come from?" She turned and looked directly at Dunlop. "It's going to be a race to to see who gets you first, the cops or the Army!"

"Really, sweetheart, it all came from a state warehouse," Dunlop said. " We're not ripping-off any of the little people."

Dunlop turned back toward Dennis. "Get a good price, sell the stuff, and send me half." Dunlop made the doobie glow as he inhaled. He held his breath, and when he was ready to exhale, said, "I'll send you an address soon as I have one."

"Frank," Elena said with a note of worry in her voice, "you promised. No more rip-offs, right?"

"Aw, Elena," Dunlop said, "We just gotta sell what's left, and then we're done, okay?" He let out a laugh and said, "Besides, shit, I'll be in the Army, so I gotta behave myself, right?"

The group laughed together for a moment, then fell silent as another marijuana cigarette was passed around.

The next day at 6:30 AM, Frank Dunlop's mother, Julia, was at her morning battle station in her son's bedroom doorway. She firmly told him that he absolutely had to get up. "You're lounging time is done, Buster." The words caught in her throat as she realized what a change they were facing. From here on in he would have to fend for himself. She couldn't be there anymore to urge him on, or catch him when he faltered.

Dear God, please let him survive the next two years and come back to us in one piece. The thought seemed strange to her in a way. She hadn't prayed or gone to church for as long as she could remember.

Frank followed his standard routine of rising from bed at the last possible minute. He grabbed an apple, holding it between his teeth as he buttoned his shirt while hurrying toward the front door. Julia intercepted him as he turned the handle.

Mother and son looked at each other for a moment. "Your father had to leave early for work, but he said to tell you good luck." Dunlop and his dad weren't exactly on the best of terms.

"Don't cry, mom." He raised his hand to her cheek and wiped a tear with his thumb.

Julia ruffled his hair in the same manner she had done since he was a baby and said, "Make sure you don't get that cute little ass of yours blown off, OK? There are a number of young ladies around here who would be quite disappointed."

Frank smiled, took a bite out of his apple, and mumbled, something to the effect that he would be sure to see her after his training, "before I go to Nam."

Elena waved to Frank's mother as he climbed into her car. River Rats Jeffery and Dennis were in the back seat, asleep and snoring. Elena smiled as she explained, "They insisted on me picking them up so they could see you off at the bus."

Dunlop shook his head and said, "It doesn't look like they'll be seeing anybody off this morning."

At the bus station Dunlop walked around the car to Elena's window and leaned forward. He was close enough to smell his girlfriend's perfume mixed with her breath. He closed his eyes for a moment and smiled. Dunlop said, "Look, I'm just going to get this the fuck over with. Know what I mean?"

Dunlop leaned in a little more and kissed Elena on her nose, one of his favorite spots when he couldn't reach to pat her butt. Off he went, with his characteristic bounce, saying hello to a couple of guys he recognized.

Off to war, she thought. She sighed as she watched her young man climb on the bus, sit down and launch into animated conversation.

CHAPTER II

May 20th, 1969

1400 HRS

BY THE TIME TOM KELLY AND FRANK DUNLOP CROSSED PATHS AT the Oakland Armed Services Induction Center, their transformation into soldiers was well under way.

Kelly stood in line with the rest of the new soldiers about fifteen places away from Dunlop. Each recruit held his induction paperwork in one hand, his jacket or sweater in the other. Sheets of paper occasionally fluttered to the floor as guys shifted around to try and gain a little comfort, or maybe scratch an itch. They had been standing together like this for almost an hour since the last of them finished their physical exams. Mumbled curses, chuckles, and an occasional fart provided momentary diversions from the general atmosphere of boredom. Being a regular bunch of fellows, they all just wanted to "get on with it."

"Haller! Lopez!" boomed a voice.

"What's going on?" Kelly whispered to the guy standing next to him.

"Williams! Defreeze!" the voice continued.

Kelly leaned out from his position in line to get a better look. A rather bedraggled representative of the U.S. Marine Corps called out names in no discernible order from a sheet on a clipboard. The light blue trousers with large red stripes down the sides were a dead giveaway:

"Thompson! Washington! Schram!" On he went, the look on his face suggesting that though he personally bore no ill will toward the persons whose names he was calling, he would react unkindly to anything but speedy compliance. Finishing the list, he flipped the sheets on his board back to the front page in a way that indicated he had done this before and liked to add a little panache to an otherwise dreary duty."My name is Gunnery Sergeant Jenson and I'd be most grateful if the fourteen men I just called would fall out and come with me," he bellowed.

"Shit!" muttered Kelly. "He's calling guys to draft em' into the fucking Marines." He had heard the Marine Corps was having trouble finding volunteer recruits. Lack of support for the war on the home front coupled with the Marines' reputation for frequent displays of foolish bravado in combat, caused many potential leathernecks to look for other ways of becoming real men. So here was Sergeant Jenson summoning draftees to fight the next battle of Hamburger Hill.

Jenson wrinkled his nose as six forlorn fellows stepped forward. His facial expression conveyed a world-weariness born of broken dreams, lost battles, and the certainty that, judged by even the most generous standards, his military career had been less than stellar. He tried to suck in his belly as he demanded, "I just called fourteen names. Now can anybody tell me why I see only six future Marines standing tall in front of me?"

No one spoke up. Someone near Kelly whispered something about a "fucking death warrant." From further up the line Kelly thought he heard someone whisper "motherfucker." Sergeant Jenson either couldn't, or chose not to, hear the comments. "I'll read the names one more time so you sleeping beauties will not miss this opportunity to serve your country. After that, I'll just turn over the names of anybody missing to the FBI."

Kelly held his breath. Maybe he hadn't heard the whole list the first time and Jenson would call his name now. The Sergeant read the names again, stopping after each one until the unlucky person stepped forward. Jensen's face relaxed as the last name on the list joined the small group gathered in front of him. Neither Kelly nor Dunlop had been called. They, along with everybody else in the Army line, heaved a small sigh of relief and reflected on their good fortune. Several of the fellows started horsing around again.

"Follow me, men." The group of fourteen walked off behind the Sergeant. Kelly felt a little sad that his good luck was at the expense of others.

Things seemed to go quickly after the encounter with the Marine. A Captain came out to administer the oath of induction, and congratulated the young men on becoming the newest members of the U.S. Army. Finally, another Sergeant informed the group that everybody already had their plane tickets in blue envelopes inside folders marked Transport. "Your bus is waiting gentlemen, right outside that door. The quicker you get moving, the more time you'll have to smoke and joke at the airport." He pointed to a door under a sputtering *EXIT* light and the fellows began to file outside, moving with the common athletic swagger of young men everywhere. They boarded the bus for the ride across the San Francisco Bay.

Upon arriving at the airport, the brand new soldiers found themselves at the terminal gate with two hours to spare untill their plane left for Fort Lewis, Washington. Some of them wandered off to the gift shop while others, including Kelly and Dunlop, made themselves comfortable near their gate and got acquainted.

Not long before departure time, Kelly noticed a soldier waiting for a plane at the next gate. Judging from his uniform, Kelly guessed that he was probably on his way home from Vietnam. A black enlisted man, a sergeant, he probably had a few stories to tell and maybe a little advice for a scared white guy.

"How's it going?" asked the nervous Kelly. Big smile from the experienced guy. Relief spread over Kelly's face. "You just getting in from Nam?" he asked.

"Yeah," the guy nodded

"Where you headed now?"

Another smile. "Georgia. Be home in Pellan, a little after midnight." Kelly couldn't quite put his finger on the vibes he was getting from this fellow. Happy, content, excited, all seemed inadequate to describe what was coming from this sergeant as he smiled at the world.

Survived Nam, Kelly thought. *That's it. Now he has his whole life in front of him. No draft, no early death or dismemberment. Just one adventure after another stretching out in front of him as far as he can see.* "What's it like over there, man?" Kelley asked.

"It all depends on your job," replied the sergeant. "If you a grunt, it's kinda rough. Clerk, cook, supply, not so bad. You figure on going to Nam?"

Kelly pointed to the others in his group, waiting for their plane. "We're all headed to Fort Lewis tonight. Basic Training."

"You're thinking maybe you won't make it, aren't you?" said the black vet to the white greenhorn. "Over there, I could usually pick out guys who weren't comin' back. I never told nobody, but my feelings were usually pretty close to what happened. You gonna make it, man."

The flight to Seattle was announced for boarding. Kelly shook hands with the sergeant and joined the other draftees. On his way through the gate, Kelly looked back and saw the soldier pick up his bag and hurry off to his flight. *Nice guy*, he thought, as he walked up the ramp with a renewed spring in his step.

Much to the surprise of the new soldiers deplaning in Seattle, Basic Training started at the airport where a smartassed Specialist Fourth Class was waiting for the group. The moment he saw the California recruits he began hurling insults, yelling at them to "line up or else!"

Taking the path of least resistance, Kelly, Dunlop, and the others did as they were told.

The Spec IV called the roll and, satisfied that all were accounted for, grunted and marched off, mumbling to a couple of guys at the head of the line to "follow me." The group was led to a waiting bus, which they boarded for the thirty minute ride to Fort Lewis.

CHAPTER III

Fort Lewis

"PLATOON!" THE SERGEANT IN THE BARRACKS DOORWAY CALLED OUT at 0600, Kelly and Dunlop's first morning at Fort Lewis. "Atten-hut!"

Kelly was startled awake and slowly climbed down from his top bunk. Dunlop, in the bottom bunk, jumped up and came to an approximation of the "attention" position next to Kelly in the barracks walkway. *When are they gonna run out of these guys?* Kelly wondered.

"My name is Sergeant Holcomb and I need you pieces of shit to shut your yaps and pay attention." Sergeant Holcomb's fatigues were starched enough to crack. His Army baseball cap was pulled down to hide his eyes, and he held copies of paperwork for Kelly and the rest to fill out. "Since most of you are going to be dead within six months, the Army wants you to have some life insurance."

Jesus, Kelly thought, *this guy is number five since we got here yesterday. How do they keep comin' up with ways to insult us?* He looked at Dunlop, and they both shook their heads.

Holcomb moved among the new troops, handing each a form as he passed. "Oh yeah," he snarled, "you want my advice, put your mommy's name down for beneficiary. Your girlfriends and wives are probably already makin' it with the 4F guy across the street that didn't get drafted."

Kelly looked at Dunlop and mouthed, "Un-fucking-believable."

A couple of guys from Turlock, California always seemed to understand what the Army wanted, and Kelly was happy to follow their lead. The Turlock guys sat down on their footlockers and began to fill out the insurance forms. Kelly and the rest did the same.

Haircuts were done on Wednesday, their second full day at the Fort. As the group filed in, the barbers were complaining to each other about having to work on guys from California, "the land of the long hairs." Dunlop smiled as he climbed into the chair, realizing that the fellow with the clippers would have to clean up once they were done. The barber moved swiftly. Dunlop glanced down and watched his beautiful blonde hair, the symbol of his independence and manliness, hit the floor and mix with everyone else's precious locks. The transformation in Dunlop and the others was remarkable. They were headed for something light-years different from their former lives.

Later at the mess hall, Kelly pushed his lunch tray along and picked up a salami sandwich, fruit salad, juice, milk, and chocolate chip cookies. *Maybe they really mean it when they say the Army runs on its stomach,* Kelly thought.

The guys wolfed down their food down and drifted back to the barracks. They talked quietly in small groups, mostly speculating on what was to come in the days ahead. By this time the guys from Turlock were thought to have some kind of inside knowledge of the Army's plans. People would check out rumors with them and follow them around like puppies.

After lunch, Kelly stretched out on his bunk for a couple of minutes until he heard the sounds of several guys jump off their bunks and their boots hitting the floor. He looked to see what was up. The man standing in the barracks doorway seemed different from the procession of jerks that had come before him. Up to now, the Army's representatives had come off more foolish than intimidating. This guy radiated confidence along with a predatory energy. Kelly thought he was a little scary and said so to Dunlop.

"I think he's going to be our DI, you know, our drill instructor" Dunlop said to Kelly and a couple of other guys who were listening in. Kelly whispered, "That guy looks like a cross between Jim Brown and Atilla the Hun."

"Gentlemens!" The sergeant called to the men in the barracks from under his 'Smokey the Bear' hat. The Army's drill sergeants wore these odd, wide-brimmed hats in order to signify near-complete authority over fellows like Dunlop and Kelly.

Physically, the sergeant was impressive. He stood a little under six feet tall and was well proportioned with a powerful chest and broad, strong shoulders. His fatigues were flawless and starched enough that if killed in battle, he could be painted and left as a statue where he died.

"My name is Drill Sergeant Dunnigan."

What's he smiling about? wondered Kelly. The pure white of the man's teeth contrasted strongly with his glistening, deep black face. His nose and eyes were like everything else about the guy, strong and determined.

Sergeant Dunnigan was smiling because he truly enjoyed what he did for a living. He was a good soldier and proud of it. He had been to Vietnam, been wounded a couple of times, and had several boys like the ones now in front of him, die in his arms. He had proven himself to be fiercely courageous in battle. The grunts--infantry soldiers--under him were always grateful that he was on their side rather than fighting for the Viet Cong against them. He figured the boys in the barracks were fortunate to have him as their DI. He would show them, as well as anybody could in this army, how to survive the next couple years of their lives.

"Everybody get enough to eat?" This drill sergeant resonated with authority. Murmurs of agreement as to the adequacy of noon chow arose from the group.

"You gentlemens need to learn to answer your Drill Sergeant properly. First, I ask y'all a question; y'all get enough to eat? Then, since I ask everybody, y'all answer together, YES DRILL SERGEANT!" Dunnigan shouted and resonated.

Upon being given a second chance, the fellows did well enough to restore the smile to Sergeant Dunnigan's face.

"Y'all are now members of the United States Army. To be exact, you are the Third Platoon of D Company, Third Battalion, Second Basic Training Regiment here at Fort Lewis, D-3-2 for short. I will be your drill sergeant for the next nine weeks. You will come to know me very well. As my name says, everything you need to learn to become one of the worlds' finest fighting mens, will be done. If not done properly, it will be done again."

Dunnigan chuckled at his little pun, and cracked a smile big enough to melt an iceberg.

Kelly mouthed the words to Dunlop "I can't believe this guy." Dunlop rolled his eyes then returned his attention to the end of the barracks.

"Gentlemens, this afternoon we going to start acting like soldiers. To help y'all feel more like soldiers, we're going to put y'all into some fighting men's clothes. Get y'all out of that silly civilian shit you got on and into the OD." OD stood for olive drab, the theme color of the Army, as it were.

"I want y'all to gather up your things, form two lines and, walk out the door in an orderly fashion and onto the bus waiting outside. You will not be returning to this barracks, so make sure y'all don't leave anything. Do it, now!"

The newly formed Third Platoon followed Sergeant Dunnigan's instructions and, after a twenty minute ride, filed into an enormous warehouse that resembled an empty airplane hanger. Long tables stacked with green clothing took the place of aircraft. The cavernous room smelled of new cotton, wool, and mothballs. *We're in the Army now, for sure,* Kelly thought.

He felt humiliated, which was exactly how he was supposed to feel. The Third Platoon had passed by the stacks of uniforms and been issued their fatigues for basic training, along with a small cardboard box for their civvies. The men changed clothes together and placed the remnants of their pre-Army lives in boxes, addressing them to be mailed home. A sympathetic young private collected the boxes, assuring everyone that the packages would reach their destinations safely.

Just look at all of us, thought Kelly. New, baggy, green uniforms, and bald heads. *We're like a bunch of Beetle Baileys without hair.* He looked down at himself and wondered if the Tom Kelly he had been could possibly still be inside. Sergeant Dunnigan stood off to the side, looking like a proud but concerned new father in a hospital waiting room who had just been told he had become the father of twenty-two healthy boys.

As the last of Third Platoon was finishing the addresses on their boxes, a commotion arose on the other side of the warehouse. Kelly moved closer for a better view. What he saw he wouldn't forget, a defining moment he would carry with him through his stint in the Army.

A returning group of Vietnam vets, fresh off the plane, hooted and jostled each other as they burst into the warehouse. Their jungle uniforms were ripped and muddy and, for a moment, Kelly thought he saw bloody spatters on a couple of their shirts. Their faces were sunburnt and their bodies were lean. These guys were definitely a bunch of grunts, fresh from the war. They reminded Kelly of a victorious football team storming into their locker room and headed for the post-game showers. The war returnees were full of energy and looking forward to their next game in life, they had made it home.

Suddenly, the vets became quiet as they looked across the room and saw the Third Platoon, a reflection of themselves from what must have seemed like a couple of lifetimes ago. A stillness descended upon the space as Kelly, Dunlop, and the others looked respectfully, even enviously, upon the battle-hardened fellows across from them. The vets returned their silent gaze. Morgan, one of the Turlock guys, summed it up, "They made it through the war. That's a proud feeling."

"Hey man, don't worry, they'll let you grow your hair when you get to Nam!" one of the vets called from across the room. The grunts all laughed and went back to their business of picking up fresh uniforms for their upcoming leaves. Dunnigan spotted an old buddy among the returnees. The two men slapped and pushed at each other affectionately while they talked, obviously delighted to see one another alive and back in the world. If Dunnigan had impressed the platoon up untill then, they were now completely in awe of their drill sergeant.

On the way to their new barracks, Dunnigan told the bus driver to make a stop at the PX to allow the men a chance to purchase any personal items they needed. The guys bought letter writing materials, candy, cigarettes, toothpaste and cigarette lighters. The lighters the men came away with were like the one John Wayne used in war movies to light up a last smoke before charging up a well-defended hill. They opened and closed with a flick of the wrist and a resounding click. The flame was a couple of inches high if you used enough lighter fluid.

Standing in formation and playing with their new lighters while waiting for the bus, the newly formed Third Platoon reminded Kelly of photographs he had seen of GIs setting fire to peasant's huts in Vietnam. Like the one accompanying the infamous statement by a battle-weary platoon leader, "We had to destroy the village to save it."

How am I going to get these guys to risk anything to stand up to the Army, and go against the war? Kelly thought. The other guys in the group seemed to be going hook, line, and sinker for how the Army wanted them to act. He shook his head as he lit a cigarette and snapped the lighter closed with a resounding click.

CHAPTER IV

Basic Trainees

THE GUYS IN THIRD PLATOON SETTLED INTO BASIC TRAINING. UP at 5:30 every morning, their routine consisted of lots of heavy exercise, incredibly boring military classes, too much food, and weapons practice. The days were scheduled right down to the minute from when they got up till lights out. If a guy was really unlucky, he had to get up in the middle of the night for an hour of barracks Guard Duty.

The only topics interesting enough to catch a trainee's attention dealt with death or dismemberment. Land mines, punji stakes, poison gas, bullets, bombs, and rockets, were all covered in detail. *What, can a guy do to get through all this shit in one piece,* thought Kelly one day as the platoon arrived for one of their early morning classes.

As the guys were filing into the classroom and sitting down, Kelly noticed that Sgt. Caton was cradling a two-by-four. Kelly leaned over and whispered to Dunlop, "What the fuck is that for?"

Dunlop shook his head. "Nothing surprises me about this place any more," he whispered.

This morning's class was Systems of Military Rank and Command and was so dry that most of the men only heard a sentence or two before they let their minds wander. Long, arduous days of training with little time for rest began to have an effect. Seated in the back of the room, the two guys from Turlock laid their heads down on the table using their arms for pillows.

Kelly was getting pretty sleepy himself when, out of nowhere, came a sound like a rifle firing in the room. Everybody looked around anxiously trying to determine the source of the explosion.

Dunlop nudged Kelly and pointed to the back of the room where the dour-faced Sgt. Caton stood behind the wide-awake guys from Turlock. "Man I thought that was a fuckin' shot," said Dunlop. Caton had slammed the piece of wood onto the table between the two recruits, waking them more quickly than their mothers ever did.

"Drop and give me twenty!" The red-faced Drill Sergeant Ranger came so close to Kelly's face that he bumped him with the brim of his hat.

"Yes, Drill Sergeant," a dispirited Kelly replied as he got down and knocked off twenty push-ups then returned to the dinner chow line.

Later, Kelly complained to Dunlop, "It's not so bad when they're yelling at all of us, but that guy was so close I had to wipe his spit off my face before I could eat."

"I know," replied Dunlop. His face brightened, "But just think, those push-ups are gonna save your ass in Nam. You know, more sweat now, less blood later." Dunlop raised his eyebrows and nodded at Kelly.

"Shit, I guess..." groaned Kelly.

"Ranger's the worst," Dunlop added, lighting a cigarette and leaning back in his chair.

"He's a former semi-pro boxer and a murdering braggart," Kelly said.

Dunlop started laughing in the middle of a long drag on his smoke, which made him cough. He reached for his water glass and drank till the coughing subsided.

"Ranger loves to let everyone know that he can't wait for his next assignment to Nam, where he can resume killing to his evil heart's content," Kelly threw in with a look of disgust.

The guys always had a good time hustling to the Mess Hall in the morning, pouring out the door at a trot. Before going in for breakfast, each soldier was expected to perform the difficult task of going hand-over-hand for twenty feet on the overhead bars. Dunlop, a compact and powerful fellow, always finished the entire length. On the other hand, Kelly had never made it more than halfway before dropping from the bars and walking the rest of the way to the Mess Hall door. This morning, Kelly made it further on the bars than ever before, three-fourths of the way.

"Nice going on the bars this morning." Dunlop smiled at his buddy as they sauntered into breakfast.

Kelly noticed his arms were shaking as he set his tray down and started to eat. When he was almost done with his food, he strode over to the coffee urn for the one luxury of his daily routine; a morning cup of the potent Army Java.

"That looks pretty good," said Dunlop, "I believe I'll have one of those myself." The two fellows sat and relished a moment's peace amid the hum of conversation in the room, slurping their morning coffee.

Kelly half-noticed the room had become quiet. A moment later his chair flew out from under him without any warning, kicked away by Sgt. Ranger who had called the men in the mess hall to attention. Kelly, not noticing the command, had not responded. As the dazed Private Kelly picked himself up off the floor and came to a loose version of attention, he looked around and saw a few grins on his buddy's faces. Ranger just grunted in contempt as he turned and walked away. The Third Platoon had some good laughs over that one for a few days. When his pride had healed abit, Kelly had to admit that it had been pretty funny.

A group of Third Platoon members sat on the barracks steps smoking cigarettes, polishing their boots, and exchanging raunchy jokes.

"Hey," Kelley said to the rest of the group, "anybody know what's up for tomorrow?"

"I think…" Dunlop said as he took a final drag on his smoke and tossed it into the gravel next to the steps sending a small shower of sparks as it hit the ground in the near darkness. "it's gonna be one of the ranges."

"Great." said Kelly, "We get to take a few more chips out of the Fort Lewis rock collection.

Rifle ranges at Ft. Lewis are windswept, rustic, cool and cloudy in the early summer. Kelly liked that he could get away from a lot of the silly parts of Army life during target practice. The DI's avoided screaming at trainees while they held loaded guns.

The next day the Third Platoon went to one of the ranges to fire their M14's. Since there were only enough shooting positions for half the platoon at once, everybody else spent about half their time waiting, while the other half of the group finished each exercise.

Not wanting to waste the Army's valuable time, Kelly thought it would be fun to build something while he was standing around. Fort Lewis is covered with rocks, six-eight inch rocks, a legacy of many volcanic eruptions of nearby Mt. Rainier.

He began carrying a few of the larger rocks over to a small clearing about fifty yards from the firing positions where the rest of the platoon was blasting away. Arranging the stones in a large circle, a dozen or so other guys pitched in to help. It was cold for the young men standing around, and carrying a few rocks seemed like a good way to warm up.

A party atmosphere developed as the guys realized they were working together on a project that had not been assigned from some Drill Sergeant's clipboard. Whatever they were making, it would be theirs, not the Army's.

Realizing the other guys were watching him to see what he would decide to build, inspiration struck Private Kelly. "Hey guys, we're going to make a signal for airplanes passing over. You know, like if we get separated from our unit in Nam and want to let the searchers know where we are."

"What's it going to say, Kelly?" huffed Ricky Anderson from Lodi, California as he rolled a boulder almost half his size into place.

"FTA," Kelly declared, barely able to contain the grin on his face. Cheers and laughter came from the soldier-stonemasons.

Fuck the Army or FTA summed up the average soldier's opinion of the Green Machine. A genuine enthusiasm for their mission set in among the laboring soldiers as they worked. Sweat broke out on brows and a cloud of dust arose at the site from the rocks hitting the ground.

The ground-to-air message was finished in a few minutes. Rocks were arranged in a circle about twenty yards in diameter. Inside the stone enclosure, the Third Platoon had removed the brush and written FTA in bold, ten-yard high letters made of white rocks

The fellows stood off to one side, brushing the dirt from their clothes and admiring their work, while the staccato cracks from the M14s firing by the other half of the platoon continued in the background. "Looks great!" exclaimed the cherubic Anderson as he began to catch his breath. "Fuckin A," said Munson, the shorter of the two Turlock guys, as the rest of the group congratulated each other on a job well done, laughing and joking about what the Army pilots would see as they passed overhead.

Kelly noticed a white stone slightly out of place in the message and strolled over to set it properly. As he was bending over, he noticed a familiar silence from his chattering buddies. *Oh shit*, he thought as he looked through his legs. *It's Ranger!* Standing in front of Kelly's friends with his hands on his hips and a scowl on his Nordic face, Drill Sergeant Ranger didn't have to say a word. Ranger was obviously pissed so Kelly just dropped the rock and assumed his very best version of attention. Actually, Kelly had learned this ancient position of military submission while in the Boy Scouts, and he was reasonably good at it when he wanted to be.

"I'll see you at Drill Sergeant's board tonight, Kelly." Ranger then turned to the rest of the guys and snarled, "I want this shit cleaned up, now!" There wasn't any confusion as to what he meant. The men busied themselves rolling the rocks around until the area had more or less returned to its natural state.

When the troops had finished for the day, they assembled in the dusty parking lot near the buses waiting to take them back to the barracks. The clanking of steel equipment mingled with the murmur of the young soldiers talking and arranging their packs and rifles. Kelly was one of the first from Third Platoon to grab a seat on the bus. He settled in feeling a little glum and apprehensive about the DI board he would be facing after dinner.

Kelly harbored no illusions about making a successful military career for himself. He just wanted to organize GIs to stand together with his friends in the anti-war movement to somehow put an end to the terrible conflict in Vietnam. Still, he was just as subject to embarrassment as the next fellow. He didn't know what was in store for him at the Drill Sergeant's board but suspected it would involve some form of humiliation, like crawling around in the sandpit next to his barracks for a couple of hours after everybody had gone to bed. Kelly leaned against the window and closed his eyes, thinking he might catch a nap on the way back from the range.

When he had almost fallen asleep, Kelly felt a nudge on his shoulder. Anderson sat next to him.

"If you have to go to that board thing tonight, I'm going with you," Anderson said.

Kelly's eyes brightened, "Geeze, man. Thanks. I guess I could use some company."

The rest of Third Platoon continued to file on the bus. As they passed Kelly's seat, half of them stopped to say they'd be glad to accompany him to the board that night.

When Kelly, Dunlop, Munson, Anderson and the rest of the fighting Third Platoon filed into the Mess Hall for dinner that night, they all seemed to have a bit of a bounce in their step. Perhaps, they were a little less intimidated by their new lives as soldiers.

After he finished dinner and left the Mess Hall, Kelly ran into Sergeant Dunnigan. "What do you think, Sarge? Am I in for it tonight at that Drill Sergeant's board?"

Dunnigan gave Kelly one of his enigmatic grins and said, "Don't sweat it, Kelly."

There was no summons for Kelly, or anyone else that night. The Third Platoon stayed awake in their bunks for a couple of hours after lights out, regaling one another with tales of bravery in confronting Ranger and sticking by their buddy Kelly. The whole thing seemed like a lark now that they had been victorious over the despised Sergeant, and taken no casualties.

On Thursday evening of "FTA" week, Kelly stood in his GI boxer shorts brushing his teeth at one of the bathroom sinks when he noticed a commotion at the doorway leading to the entry porch of the barracks. Several of the guys were gathered at the door looking out toward the Second Platoon barracks, across the street.

"Look at that crazy fucker!" said Munson. "

"What the hell's he doing out there?" asked Dunlop, getting on his tiptoes for a better look.

"That's Thiebeaux, he's in Second Platoon," said Marty Jackson in a matter-of-fact tone. "He thought maybe they'd let him out of the Army if he slashed his wrists. They took him to the hospital, sewed him up, and then they recycled him. Assigned him to D-3-2 for another complete round of Basic Training."

Anderson commented, "They don't care what you do to fuck yourself up, they got ways of making sure they get what they want in the end."

After pulling on his pants, Kelly stepped outside and sure enough, there was Thiebeaux, crawling in the sandpit next to Second Platoon barracks. There didn't appear to be anyone supervising the poor bastard's punishment, so Kelly walked over and squatted in front of the crawling, filthy troop. Thiebeaux stopped and looked up at the freckle-faced Irishman from California.

"Hey man, what the fuck are you doing?" Kelly asked kindly as he noted the confusion and fear in the eyes of the veteran basic trainee.

"Sergeant Ranger told me I had to low crawl until he came back."

Kelly looked at his watch and said, "It's 10 PM, fella. Ranger ain't comin' back tonight."

Thiebeaux began crawling around Kelly who stood up, then reached down and gently grabbed him under the arms and lifted him to his feet. As he brushed some of the sand off his fellow soldier, Kelly noticed an angry, dark red scar on one of his wrists.

"If Ranger hassles you about this, tell him Kelly, from Third Platoon, gave you a direct order to go to bed." Kelly stood back and looked Thiebeaux over. "I'll talk to him, so don't sweat it, man. Really, go on and get some sleep."

The confused lad's face relaxed as he mumbled agreement and walked back towards the barracks to clean up and, hopefully, forget his demons, long enough to get a little rest.

It was a fine Sunday afternoon at Fort Lewis. The Third Platoon was taking it easy writing letters and playing pick-up basketball. A few of the guys were catching up on some of the sleep they had missed during the long week of training.

Kelly was lounging on his bunk, reading a week-old newspaper he had scrounged off one of the clerks in the orderly room. He enjoyed catching up on what was happening out in the world, even if it wasn't exactly what you'd call hot off the press.

Fred Munson walked up to Kelly's bunk and stood there for a second until Kelly looked up from his paper. "There's a guy at the door asking for you, man."

Kelly sat up. "A guy? What's he look like?" He wasn't expecting anyone and felt a little paranoid about how the Army might react to his anti-war and socialist beliefs. Maybe this guy spelled trouble for the activist turned private.

"He's just a guy, Kelly. Looks kinda like an officer, maybe, only in civvies."

Kelly wrinkled his brow, "Guess I better go see what he wants." He tossed the newspaper onto his bunk. "Thanks, Munson."

The fellow waiting outside did look something like an officer, or maybe a college student. He smiled generouly, as he extended his hand to the somewhat bewildered Private Kelly. "Hi, I'm Denny Dixon, from Progressive Labor Party."

About all Kelly could think to say was "Huh?" When the pleasant, clean-cut fellow repeated himself as they shook hands, Kelly said, "No shit?"

Dixon laughed and asked, "Can you get away from the barracks for a few minutes? My car is parked out by the Mess Hall, and someone's out there I think you'll be glad to see."

"Sure," Kelly said.

As Kelly walked away from Third Platoon's quarters, the consensus on the porch was that he was a lucky stiff to have a visitor. He would probably get a chance to do something really great, like get drunk or maybe stoned in the guy's car.

I guess I'll talk to this guy, Kelly thought, as the two walked past the barracks. *Maybe I'll get a chance to find out if they meant all that stuff they said about making the anti-war movement a real mass movement, not just for students.* Dixon set his hand on Kelly's shoulder, and Kelly looked at the hand. The look meant to say, "You're not my friend—yet. Take it down." Dixon removed his hand.

As Kelly and Dixon rounded the corner by the mess hall, a late-model civilian car came into view. A man and a woman were seated inside, but he couldn't quite make them out. "That your car, man?" Kelly pointed to the gray Dodge.

Dixon nodded in the affirmative as a door opened and Kelly's girlfriend, Becky Frankel, hopped out. At that moment, Pvt. Kelly could have been knocked over by a feather. With huge smiles and tears in their eyes, the young couple embraced in a most unlikely place, right next to the D company mess hall.

"How'd you get here, Becky?" A dumb question, but about all the flabbergasted Kelly could think of at the moment. "Well, we got on the plane, then we got off, then we rented a car, then..." Becky trailed off her tongue-in-cheek account of the trip as Kelly wrapped his arms around her and buried his face in her hair. The two of them cooed softly at one another as they embraced.

Dixon hustled the lovebirds into the car before they could be seen by any nosy sergeants. He knew it was the time of the week when most of the lifers were away from the basic training companies. Even guys like Sgt. Dunnigan needed some time away from their Army duties every once in awhile.

One of the Progressive Labor Party's West Coast leaders, Paul Rosen, was also in the car. The four of them relaxed and had a pleasant conversation. Kelly understood that the two PL guys were sizing him up, seeing if he could be trusted to be part of a loose-knit group of like-minded guys who had recently been drafted into the Army.

Kelly was doing a little sizing up as well. He was wondering how sincere these guys really were. Some of the PL leaders he had met had seemed a little pompous to him, *but these two seem ok*, he thought.

After visiting for about an hour, Dixon suggested that it was probably time to go. Kelly and Becky agreed and, after a quick kiss goodbye, Kelly hopped out of the car and waved as they pulled away.

Kelly had agreed to stay in touch with the PL guys. They had some good ideas for organizing GIs and besides, Kelly felt a whole lot stronger about his beliefs, knowing there was a group like theirs supporting him. Dixon, a recently discharged Army private himself, had impressed Kelly with his easy-going enthusiasm for what they were all trying to accomplish. Everybody had enjoyed his story about the FTA rocks and Sgt Ranger.

As he climbed the steps of the barracks entry porch, Kelly thought about Becky. Seeing her was wonderful. A warm sensation filled him as he recalled her parting words, "Hey big guy, keep your head down, will you?"

By the seventh week of Basic Training, the fellows seemed to be carrying themselves much more easily as soldiers. They were starting to look, and act, a little like the vets group they had encountered the day they got their uniforms. They had acquired a certain swagger. Kelly had been particularly impressed a few days before when the company set out on a march one evening in full battle gear. The feeling of power and confidence that comes from being part of a large group of heavily armed men had been surprisingly intoxicating for the anti-war activist from San Jose. As he marched with the ninety men of D-3-2 he thought, *wouldn't it be great if we were headed somewhere to do something right?*

Kelly was no pacifist. Actually, he had become something of a Civil War history buff since participating in voter registration drives in Mississippi and Florida during the summers of the mid-1960's. He had taken a particular interest in the pivotal Battle of Gettysburg, and was a great sympathizer with the Union Army's struggle to abolish slavery and preserve the Union.

He let his mind drift as the company route-step (battle) marched along an old logging road through the beautiful Northwest forest at twilight. The sound of the soldiers' footfalls, together with their clanking gear, joined with the caw of a nearby raven.

He imagined his company to be part of the corps hurrying toward the sound of cannon-fire at Gettysburg to relieve gallant cavalry troopers. At that moment, the Union Cavalry had been locked in a deadly embrace with vastly more Confederates near the little Pennsylvania town, fervently hoping for the deliverance that was soon to come.

"Hey Kelly! Slow down boy, we got all night. You're crowding the guy in front of you. Don't forget to maintain your spacing, troop. You step on a mine, we don't need any more guys down because of your bad luck." Dunnigan brought the daydreaming Kelly back to the reality of the war he would soon be facing.

"Sorry, Drill Sergeant." Kelly replied as he reestablished the proper distance between himself and the man in front of him.

With only a little more than a week left to go in their Basic Training the Third Platoon fellows began to seriously consider what would be next for them after they graduated from D-3-2. Kelly desperately hoped it would not be an assignment to an infantry training company, which would be a one-way ticket to deadly battles he wanted no part of.

During Kelly's time at Fort Lewis the topic of advanced training assignments was often mentioned by trainees and their sergeant trainers. If you received orders for eleven bravo that meant another nine weeks of weapons training and then a quick plane ride to Vietnam. Kelly figured his chances of ending up hamburger over there were pretty good. Infantry training prepared guys to be grunts, and that's what the Army seemed to do with all the two-year draftees, like Kelly and Dunlop. Safe jobs were reserved for guys who signed up for a third year, something that was hard for most guys to stomach.

One evening during their eighth week, Dunlop, Kelly and several of the other fellows sat on their barracks porch, shining the heavy black boots they wore every day. "Look at that "strac" troop shine his shoes!" exclaimed Anderson, pointing to the spit shine Kelly was applying to the toes of his field boots.

"I was in Boy Scouts, you know, and uh, we used to shine them like this before meetings," explained the radical from California. "When you get a really deep shine on them, they're more comfortable, they shed dirt and dust, and it waterproofs them. Besides, they look kinda nice."

Dunlop addressed the group, "Hey, anybody know what's up for tomorrow?"

"We're goin' back to Range twenty-two" answered Marty Jackson, Third Platoon's acting, trainee-Sergeant.

A groan, peppered with a few curses arose from the group. Range twenty-two was not their favorite place. "It was cold as shit out there today and besides, that range lieutenant is a real yo-yo," said Dunlop. "I mean, why did he have to tell that stupid fuckin' story about eating his dog?"

Morgan chimed in, "I could have done without that, right before lunch, man."

Kelly rubbed the toe of one boot and turned to Dunlop. "Hey man, we stand a good chance of going to clerk school, don't you think?" a little of the dread he felt at the possibility of being assigned to the Infantry leaked into his tone despite an effort to appear nonchalant.

Dunlop replied, "Yeah, sure, guy. Why not?" Dunlop always humored Kelly when he brought up the eleven bravo thing. He was a little amused at how the anti-war Kelly wanted so badly to avoid the very situation where his efforts might pay off, among the GIs doing the fighting. Kelly's mood lightened up considerably, as it always did when Dunlop reassured him. "Kelly, you just look like a clerk to me. Besides you're too fuckin' slow to be a grunt. You'd just put everybody else in danger cause they'd have to carry you out after you got shot, man."

Kelly had become known in D-3-2 as one of the stragglers at the rear during their long daily marches. He had an ankle problem that caused it to ache miserably after a couple of miles of stumbling over the Fort Lewis rocks. If somebody wanted to find him, he would be at the rear, limping noticeably, straining to keep up.

Kelly agreed with Dunlop that it would be foolish to have such a slowpoke in the Infantry where quickness and agility on everyone's part involved was necessary for survival of the group. But over the last two months, Kelly had seen the Army do many foolish and stupid things. He would just have to wait with everybody else until next week to see his orders

Jackson spoke up, "Hey guys, time to crash. We got a full day ahead, and I don't want anybody puking when that Range Lieutenant tells one of his fucked-up stories tomorrow." One by one the fellows on the porch gathered their things and went inside. After giving everybody a few minutes to wash up and get in bed, Jackson posted the first shift of the nightly fire watch, and then turned out the lights. The young fellows closed their eyes and drifted off to sleep, with thoughts of home and girlfriends to ease them on their way.

Week nine, the Third Platoon's last week of Basic, arrived. It came as a tremendous relief. But still, here they were, short-timers now, making plans for what would be coming next. No matter how difficult, it couldn't possibly be as bad as what they had just been through for the last eight weeks.

Orders for advanced training assignments were handed out when D-3-2 returned after a final day at one of the rifle ranges. All the draftees in the company, except for one lucky fellow who was assigned to cook's training, found out they would be headed across the parade field to one of the Advanced Infantry training companies, AIT--eleven Bravo.

Kelly and several of his Third Platoon buddies figured that their assignment to the Infantry called for a celebration, but it didn't seem like much of a party would be possible. For the last two months, the men had been Army-induced tea-totalers. During Basic Training, the Army had confined its trainees to company areas; usually four barracks, a mess hall and an orderly room. Not much room for mischief.

Across the quarter-mile parade field, however, was another story. The Infantry training companies had their barracks over there and, rumor had it, a beer hall for the advanced trainees. Anderson spoke up as half a dozen Third Platoon guys lounged around their entry porch after dinner, working up to their nightly bull session.

"You guys want to get drunk tonight?" the glint in Anderson's boyish eyes seemed to convey the message that he had a plan.

"And just how are we supposed to manage that?" wondered Kelly aloud.

"Simple," said Anderson, "we get ourselves into a military formation and march across the parade field. I met this guy from one of the AIT companies last week and he told me how to find the beer hall."

The fellows looked at one another as Dunlop said, "Shit, it might work."

Kelly was a little reticent. "I don't know, we might get busted and..."

Dunlop put his hand on Kelly's shoulder and counseled his buddy, "Fuck, man. What can they do, send us to Vietnam?" Anderson picked up on Frank's line of reasoning and loudly declared, "Hey man, they're already doing that!"

At that, the entire group, including Kelly, erupted in laughter as Anderson called out, "Okay, fall the fuck in!"

Quickly, the size of the group swelled to approximately twenty, including a guy from another platoon who later said he thought it was a required formation. Standing in front, Anderson ordered the men to make sure they each had a few bucks. A couple of guys without money were given cash by those who had a little extra. Everybody waited for Anderson to begin the evening's operation.

"Alright, men," Anderson sounded out in his best imitation of a drill sergeant's command. "Tonight we're calling upon you to volunteer for a clandestine and highly dangerous mission. If you choose to complete the task at hand, you may not return in any condition to see your mother for a day or so. Well, are you with me?" A cheer arose from the group, along with enough "fuckin' A's" to convince Anderson it was a definite go.

"Left face!" The group responded smartly to Anderson's command and off they went, looking like any of a dozen groups marching from pillar to post around Fort Lewis at that moment. The fighting Third Platoon, D-3-2, made their way across the wide parade field, calling out their cadences smartly and enjoying themselves for once while playing soldier.

Anderson put his buddies into route step as they neared the beer hall. "Is that it, Andy?" asked Dunlop. Anderson answered, "Sure is," and the boys climbed the steps, went inside, and made themselves comfortable with huge paper mugs of Army beer.

The brew served to Infantry trainees was flat and tasteless, but to the Third Platoon lads, it might as well have been champagne. Everyone, including the initially skeptical Kelly, drank with youthful gusto.

Kelly looked around the packed room at all the fellows who, like himself, were headed for grunt duty in Vietnam. The room was electric with the spirits of the young men. Everybody seemed to be genuinely enjoying the beer, and the company. The jukebox filled the room with the Booker T and the MGs song 'Time is Tight.' It contributed perfectly to the general atmosphere of fellowship and good cheer. *Hey, fuck the Army*, Kelly thought.

Kelly began to feel at peace with his fate. Sitting among these guys, he felt like he might just be able to handle being a grunt in Nam.

When it came time to leave, he was the only one of his group sober enough to line everybody up outside and march them off across the parade field back to the company area. Anderson had to be carried, until Dunlop discovered that yelling march cadences in his ear kept him going until he was safely back at the barracks and in his bunk.

Standing in line for chow the next morning, Kelly asked Dunlop, "Your leave all set?"

Dunlop nodded "yes," as he puffed on a smoke. The two had concocted a brilliant scheme to secure a week at home for themselves after Basic.

The Army was reluctant to grant leave at this early stage of a soldier's career, preferring to have its young men complete AIT before letting them go home for a week just before shipping out to Vietnam. Realizing this, the two boys had separately informed their commanding officer, Captain Remney, that their girlfriends were pregnant and were worried about starting to show if they had to wait another nine weeks to get married, when guys were done with eleven bravo training.

Being a standard Army-issue lifer, Remney went for the utterly false tale hook, line and sinker. The Army loves to attend to the needs of its soldiers, when those needs don't interfer with the soldier's development into an efficient and committed killing machine. Besides, it gave Remney the chance to engage in some great PR, while helping a couple of his obviously fertile and manly troops out of a jam.

Dunlop exhaled a long puff. "I talked to the Chaplain yesterday. He was a little suspicious at the similarity in our stories, but he's going to recommend leave for me. How about you, man?"

"I'm all set" Kelly replied, as he thought of the plane taking off and smiled.

"Funny thing," Dunlop said, "we really are going to get married."

Kelley chuckled, "Us too. Becky will get some money from the Army that way, and we'll be able to afford getting together when my leaves happen. Those plane tickets really add up, you know? Hey, let's ride home on the plane together, what do you say?" Kelly suggested.

"That's cool," replied Dunlop. "Maybe we can get together that week. You could meet Elena and I could meet your girl, uh, what's her name again?"

Kelly smiled and replied, "Becky. Maybe I should write her name on the back of your hand. Think that would help?"

The final week was filled mostly with classes that were even more useless and boring than usual. D-3-2 had completed its firing range training, so the fellows were stuck with classes like "The Advantages of Early Purchase of Life Insurance" and "Seven Ways to Catch Venereal Disease and Not Realize it." At least Sergeant Caton had given up the use of his exploding two-by-four, since just about everybody in the company had learned to sleep sitting up.

On the way back to the company area for evening chow on Thursday Kelly was letting his mind wander when Dunlop said, "If this keeps up, we're going to have to dust off our hairbrushes pretty soon." Tom quipped, "You are looking pretty shaggy there, troop." It had been a couple of weeks since the company had been taken to the barbers for the dreaded #1 haircuts. Each time they had gone, the treatment had been the same, clippers raked across the young men's heads to give that bald look the Army seemed to think was so military.

The hope in Third Platoon was that Captain Remney would let the men grow their hair a little in anticipation of their completion of Basic Training. That way, it would be easier for the guys from D-3-2 to ease into their advanced training companies without being so obviously new, with the awful burr haircuts.

That hope was forlorn. "Companeeeeee, halt!" came the command from the head of the column. "Shit, it's the barbershop," Munson said with dejection.

"Maybe it'll only be a trim," offered Kelly, the eternal optimist in these matters.

"No way, man," said Munson, the pessimist from Turlock, California, who often differed with the guys from other parts of California on these kinds of things. "It'll be Number Ones, for sure."

Dunlop pointed to the first platoon guys as they emerged from the rear door of the barbershop, their haircuts complete. "Looks like Munson's right, guys."

The fellows returning to the formation reminded Kelly of how they had looked that day long ago at the Log center when they had picked up their uniforms. Only now the fatigues they wore were a bit faded from the miles of dust and sweat they had accumulated over the last two months. *We really do look a little better now, even with the damn buzz cuts*, thought Kelly.

Kelly relaxed in his first-class seat on the plane as it accelerated down the runway, rising into the south wind, headed for California, and Becky. Soldiers in uniform were allowed to fly for half-price on a stand-by basis, so he thought it was a little funny to be seated with all the wealthy businessmen, but his had been the last seat available before take-off.

As the plane rose toward cruising altitude, they swept past snow-covered Mt Rainier, then banked to the West. Kelly asked the stewardess for a bottle of champagne and a couple of glasses. He was, after all, seated in first class, and he might as well make the most of it. After she returned with the bubbly, he took the bottle and glasses and headed back to the coach section.

As Kelly stumbled through the curtain dividing the two sections, Dunlop looked up and grinned. "This is going to be an okay plane ride," said the soldier from Sacramento, as Kelly handed him a full cup.

CHAPTER V

A Little More (Advanced) Training

"HEY TUG, WHAT'S UP WIT YOU TONIGHT, MAN?" THE FRIENDLY expression on Henry Carter's face was inviting and Pvt Willie Tuggins knew he was expected to join in a game of bid whist in the barracks that night. Carter pointed hopefully to a deck of cards in his hand.

Tuggins and Carter had been through Basic Training together. They were two of a dozen guys from their company at Fort Gordon, Georgia to receive orders to Fort Dix, New Jersey, for Advanced Infantry Training. All twelve, nine black and three white, had been assigned to the same training company, where they tended to seek one another out in their free time, like old friends anywhere.

"Sorry, Carter. I'm gonna try and get this letter done. You guys go ahead." A knowing smile came across Carter's face as he commented, "Must be somebody special to pass on whist, man."

"Ain't I told you 'bout Dot?" asked Tuggins.

Carter put the cards in his shirt pocket and pulled out a cigarette. "Yeah, you told me about Dot. Maybe a hundert times." Carter was exaggerating, but not by much.

"Maybe tomorrow night, whadaya say?" said Tuggins.

"Sho, Bro." The two friends slapped fists in an abbreviated version of a greeting that black GI's called "dap", and Carter strolled off toward the card game. Tuggins turned his attention to the blank sheet of paper in front of him.

August 26, 1969

Dear Dorothy,

It's a little after 8 in the evening here, and man, am I beat! I wonder what you're doing as I write this. Maybe you're just finishing up with the dishes from dinner, or maybe you're settling in for the evening with a book, getting ready for class this fall. Whatever it is, I hope you give me a thought every now and then. Let me tell you, I can use any soul assistance that's available, and your thoughts pack a heavy spiritual punch with me (smile.)

AIT is definitely easier than Basic. They don't run us or stay on our backs with harassment the way they did at Ft. Gordon. We get plenty of sleep, the food's a little better, and your free time is really yours to use as you see fit, even if it's only a couple of hours in the evening and then all day Sunday, unless you got guard duty or KP.

No, girl, I'm not going to Sunday services. I don't see much point in starting that again. Besides, it would feel kind of phony, like I was doing it because I was afraid of Nam. I pray to the Lord in my own way, every day, and I hope He's satisfied with what I've got to say.

I'm going to become quite an expert in the manly art of war while I'm here, or so I'm told. Dot, you would find it hard to believe the amount of firepower each lowly grunt carries around with him in Vietnam! Rifles, machine guns, rockets, mines, hand grenades, it's hard to imagine those poor VC's standing up to us. But they sure enough keep coming back for more! There's a lot of fellas back from the war, teaching trainees here, that's got nothing but respect for old Charlie. I know I do. This boy's head is definitely staying down as close to the ground in Vietnam as he can get it!

Tell Momma I'll be home for a week around the end of Ocober. We can have an early Thanksgiving dinner, then it's off to the jungle for your South Carolina boy. Once I'm there it'll be cool, because then we can start marking off days for real till I'm done with this stuff. Hey girl, you got any plans for a year from this November? I was thinking I might want to get married to somebody, and if you're still available, maybe we can work something out (smile.)

Tell Daddy I'm okay and looking forward to some of his good preaching when I come home. Tell Cynthia I love her and tell the boys to behave themselves. Love to your Momma, Poppa, and Grandma.

That's about all, Dorothy.

From the one who loves you so,
Willie

TWO WEEKS EARLIER

It was not unusual at this particular Safeway food store on the east side of San Jose, California for a group of kids standing in line at the check-out counter to act a little silly. This group, however, seemed a little old for the uncontrolled giggling that rolled over them in waves. The gray-haired checker smiled at the four youngsters waiting to pay and speculated to himself while he tallied their purchases. Perhaps it was marijuana making his current customers so giddy.

Weed was a good guess, but since Kelly and Dunlop were wearing hats to conceal their lack of hair, how could he have known that they were soldiers on leave, letting off some steam? Chemical mood enhancers were not necessary for this group on a fine summer evening in California's Santa Clara Valley.

"Did we remember everything?" asked Elena as the group stumbled toward their car in the parking lot. Like everything else that night, the question seemed incredibly funny and the four chums burst into gales of laughter, holding their sides and falling into the car, Becky landing in Elena's lap while Kelly fumbled for the keys to the car, finally getting it started and driving to a large, new apartment complex.

"What do you guys think we should be celebrating?" asked Kelly. They were seated around the kitchen table where Becky and Tom were staying.

5

Friends of theirs from Students for a Democratic Society had loaned the apartment to them for the week of Tom's leave.

"Tell you what," said Elena, "first, let's toast the fabulous four newlyweds." Beer bottles rose in unison and clinked together in recognition of their new lives begun that week. Hearty cheers and a belch or two followed the generous imbibing as the bottles returned to the table. "Then," continued Elena "I think we ought to congratulate all the pregnant people here!" Silence.

A very surprised Becky looked at her new friend, and asked, "What do you mean, pregnant?"

"Last time I checked, pregnant only means one thing," replied Elena, a satisfied grin on her lovely Italian face.

"Shit, what are you going to do?" Becky was genuinely concerned. For girls of their generation, pregnancy could be eagerly anticipated or it could be dreaded. It all depended on the circumstances.

Kelly stood up and lifted his nearly empty bottle, "Well, I can tell you what I'm going to do. I'm going to offer a toast to this soon-to-be member of our happy little group." Kelly's voice lowered in pitch and increased a little in volume, as he adopted his best impression of a commanding presence. "To the newest Dunlop. May he, or she, be blessed with health and vigor, and may this child live a decent and secure life without fear of the scourge of war."

Around the table, all nodded in agreement and finished what was remaining in their bottles. Frank looked happy and relaxed as he dealt the first hand of pinochle. The evening proceeded, a little subdued, but quite pleasant.

After Frank and Elena left for their return drive to Sacramento the next morning, Becky seemed pensive to Kelly. "What's on your mind, Babe? Having second thoughts on the guy you picked to marry?"

Becky looked at Tom and managed a weak smile. "You guys have to go back to the Fort tomorrow," she reminded him.

"Yeah, I know. But it won't be forever."

Becky sighed. "This is starting to look awfully serious to me, you know?" She placed her hand on his arm and said, "Look, I don't think it will matter to me if you organize every guy in the Army to be against the war, if you come home in a bag." The light in her eyes became very intense and stern as she looked into his eyes and said, "Don't take any unnecessary chances, okay? I want my healthy Irishman back, not some dead anti-war hero."

Unable to come up with a reply, Kelly put his arms around his new wife, and the two held each other, forgetting for a moment the struggles they would be facing in the coming months.

The barracks buildings looked dark and deserted as Kelly and Dunlop walked up the street of the Infantry Training Center. Both boys bent a little under the weight of their duffel bags. Kelly set his load down and squinted at the sign in front of him. "Is this it?" he said.

Dunlop walked over for a closer look. "E-2-3. Yeah, that's what the orders say. Let's go down to the orderly room and let 'em know we're here." Dunlop looked at Kelly disapprovingly. "But first, Kelly, will you please hide that Goddamn peace symbol?"

While saying goodbye at the airport, Becky had pinned the simple geometric design to the lapel of Kelly's uniform. She had worn the penny-sized symbol since her senior year in high school. It felt like a shield now to Kelly, representing his love for Becky and his commitment to the beliefs they shared.

"No shit, man. I nearly forgot about it." He dropped the pin in his pocket and climbed the orderly room stairs, knocking on the door until he heard noise indicating someone moving around inside.

"What's up, guys?" A bedraggled Private First Class stood in the doorway with sleep in his eyes and a .45 pistol holstered on his hip.

"We just got in from San Francisco." Frank handed him their orders.

"A little late, aren't you?" queried the night guard, more awake now.

"We got hung up catching a stand-by in San Francisco." Dunlop glanced at his watch. It was 12:30 AM and their orders clearly stated that they were to have reported by 9PM, 2100 hrs military time.

The PFC studied the paperwork for a couple of minutes while Dunlop and Kelly fidgeted on the porch. Finally, the clerk in the doorway looked up at the rumpled new arrivals. "Shit, as far as I'm concerned, it's now 2045 hrs. Maybe my watch is a little slow or something. And I don't want to hear any more about this, right?"

Tom and Frank grinned at him and nodded in agreement.

"There's one bunk over in Second Platoon and one open over in First." The sleepy PFC pointed to the different buildings. "You guys take your pick. You can get processed in after chow in the morning.

"I guess I'll go on down to First Platoon", said Dunlop with a yawn.

Kelly started up the path to the Second Platoon barracks, then turned toward his friend. " See you tomorrow, Dad."

Kelly and Dunlop soon discovered that Advanced Infantry Training was quite different from the routine followed during Basic. This came as a bit of a surprise to them after watching AIT companies marching around the Fort along the same roads. They expected little more than a continuation of their first two months of Army life, but after a couple of weeks of AIT, Kelly, Dunlop and the rest of the young soldiers training with E-2-3 were fairly relaxed, compared to when they had first arrived. A little sleep and considerably fewer insults per hour, had brightened spirits considerably.

One evening in week three, several trainees gathered around a plain formica table at the beer hall up the street from their company area, the same place where Dunlop, Kelly, and their friends from basic had been a month before. No longer fugitives from across the parade field, the young guys felt at home, as they consumed their share of the Army's weak brew for that evening. Across from Kelly, Leonard Baden spoke in a rich baritone voice, "The Army has to get down to business sometime. I mean, if they kept up that harassment shit forever, nobody'd ever learn how to fight the war, know what I mean?" Baden spoke in-between gulps of his beer and puffs on a Camel. He was from Sacramento and had attended the same high school as Frank Dunlop when they were freshman. Everybody seemed to like Baden's down-to-earth approach to the affairs of Army life, considering him something of a military philosopher..

"You're probably right, Lenny," replied Kelly. "All's I can say is I'm grateful for any let-up in that DI-in-your-face routine. It was getting kinda old. Speaking of learning how to fight the war, what do you guys think it's going to be like when we get over there?"

"It's going to be a real pile of shit, if you ask me." Baden said. He stood up, belched, and took his cup up to the counter for a refill. He walked slowly with abit of a wobble, but still managed to swagger.

While Baden was drawing his beer, Dennis O'Connor, a tall red-headed son of a mill worker from Lewiston, Idaho looked at Kelly with a mischievous grin. "Kelly, I think I can tell you with some assurance, that Nam is going to be a bitch." O'Connor was a stout fellow. He had broad shoulders, with big freckled biceps. The Army had allowed him to grow his curly hair the way he liked it so that a small swirl fell down on his forehead.

Kelly's expression became serious as he began to formulate a reply to O'Connor, but Dunlop gently cut him off, "Down, boy! There'll be plenty of time for the Revolution after we get to Nam." Kelly broke into a smile, as everybody else had a little laugh at the know-it-all, anti-war GI who sometimes didn't know exactly when to shut his yap.

Joey Maynard commented in his twangy Oklahoma drawl, "I don't know what it's going to be like over there, and I don't exactly care. I just flat-assed don't want to go." Everybody expressed general agreement with Maynard's sentiments, drained their cups and wandered back to their respective barracks to get some sleep.

During the Vietnam years, AIT focused almost completely on the weapons and combat techniques soldiers would be using in South East Asia. The hope was that a minimum of on-the-job training during firefights would give the guys a fair chance of living through their year.

The tools of their trade were few. Every trainee infantryman was expected to gain a working knowledge of them, if not complete mastery. Taken as a whole, these weapons provided enough firepower for a squad of eight or nine Vietnam-era grunts to hold off the might of all Caesar's legions, at least until their ammo ran out.

The US infantryman's basic weapon, the M16 is an automatic rifle made of a light, strong aluminum alloy and black plastic. Kelly, Dunlop and the other trainees were each assigned an M16 of their own which they were expected to carry on all field exercises. A frequent comment Kelly heard among the new soldiers was that it reminded them of a Christmas toy buried in a closet back home under board games and teddy bears.

"Some plaything," he thought. "It can spray bullets from a twenty-round magazine faster than a machine gun."

Kelly, being the guy who wanted to know what was happening, could list the rest of the weaponry. Guys carried hand grenades and M79 grenade launchers. The M79 allowed a soldier to place a murderous blast up to 200 yards away, with enough accuracy to kill a sniper or small concentration of enemy soldiers. Each squad typically had one man carrying a belt-fed M60 machine gun and one guy with an M79. Miscellaneous weapons included shotguns, .45 pistols, and LAWs--light anti-tank rockets that were carried on straps over a man's shoulder. A grunt could carry half a dozen LAW's, which had replaced the World War II bazooka, along with his rifle and pack.

AIT was organized around these weapons. First, the trainees would be given lectures explaining how one of them worked. Then came practice in the field for a few days, including live fire.

Week six was designated for machine gun training. The eighty-three trainees filed into an open-air classroom next to a range designed for firing .50 caliber machine guns. No one sat down. Kelly and his mates waited for the range instructor to make his appearance.

The energetic murmur of young men vibrated through the bleachers. A pungent cloud of tobacco smoke mixed with sweet smelling after-shave lotion hung above the group. Some strained for better views of the huge guns they would be firing that day.

The half-dozen '50's' were lined up, each in its own sand bag bunker, crouching on tripods with long belts of enormous ammunition hanging down from their firing chambers. Pointed up-range menacingly, they waited for the trainees to put them into action. To Kelly the guns looked like a row of monster metallic grasshoppers, ready to spit fire and destruction. He butted his smoke and raised his voice enough for the guys near him, "Hey troops, looks like we'll be doing some blasting today."

After a few minutes, the instructor stepped up to the lectern, looked out at the young soldiers before him and called, "Ready....SEATS!"

Kelly and the rest of the men responded to this ritual challenge by yelling in unison, "E-2-3! WHERE EVERY MAN'S A TIGER! A BIG FUCKIN' TIGER WITH A DICK THIS LONG!" and stretching their arms to full wingspan.

Having assured the range instructor that they were indeed anatomically qualified to defend their country, the fellows of E-2-3 were then allowed to sit. This ritual occurred before each class.

Class began and, as usual, within a few minutes about a third of the company was peacefully asleep. They were packed together tightly enough in the bleachers so that the sleepers remained upright and appeared to be concentrating very hard on what the instructor had to say. These men had definitely learned at least one survival skill during Basic Training; the graceful art of sneaky unconsciousness.

After lunch, it was time for live fire. Kelly approached his assigned firing position cautiously, as though the iron monster might turn on him if startled. The Spec IV in the bunker with Kelly grinned at the tentative trainee, took him by the arm, and settled him into a prone firing position behind the gun. He grasped the control handles firmly in both hands, his right thumb on the button firing mechanism. The concrete target that he was about to pulverize stood two hundred yards up-range.

Kelly felt a gentle pat on his shoulder.

"Any time you're ready, pal, fire away."

The anti-war activist from San Jose pressed the trigger and the machine gun exploded into life. It quickly became obvious to the young private that aiming was the last thing to worry about. More important was just hanging on to the monster. The overwhelming noise and heat from the bucking machine felt like he was on an erupting volcano. When the ammo belt was expended and the gun finally fell silent, Kelly opened his eyes and heaved a quiet sigh of relief. He had absolutely no idea what, if anything, he had hit.

The trainees in Dunlop and Kelly's company walked away that afternoon a little dazed. The Army had not taught them much about using the weapons, but everybody did leave the range impressed with the gun's destructive power. That was, of course, the real lesson the troops were supposed to learn that day.

"Wake up, man. He's got a rabbit down there." Kelly pointed to the stage in front of the bleachers where the company was seated for a class to prepare them for a special night training exercise. This was one of the outdoor classes that like others, was next to a firing range.

Dunlop jumped a little as he awoke, then looked up to where his friend was pointing, eyes squinting against the light on stage. "What's up, Kelly?" Dunlop yawned and stretched, knocking the cap from Joe Maynard's head, seated next to him. "Sorry, partner," Dunlop leaned over, picked up the hat, and handed it back to Maynard.

The soldiers were assembled for what had been billed as the ultimate educational experience the Army had to offer its infantry soldiers: Search, Escape, and Evasion.

The plan was for the guys to take off on their own, simulating an escape from a POW camp. They would break up into small groups of five or six, hike in the dark across a three mile wooded course of river crossings, up and down a series of four steep ridges, and then to a clearing in the woods where they would be declared "home free." Those who made it to the clearing without being captured, would be allowed to relax on warm buses while they waited for the rest of the company to make their way over the long and difficult course.

The lifers went to great lengths to make this night exercise seem realistic. Ninety troops from another training company were assigned to play the part of enemy soldiers who would try to capture the E-2-3 guys. The enemy all wore blue vests and helmets, and carried three-foot-long poles to intimidate those they captured.

At the moment, the twenty-five captors assigned to guard duty were assembled in full view of the E-2-3 fellows. Many of them were brandishing their poles like riot police. To Kelly, the whole set-up seemed to have a sinister air of unreality about it. A light mist fell from the thick Puget Sound cloud cover that had blanketed the Fort for the past two days. No moon this night, it was going to be dark and damp as a dungeon out there.

The burly Sergeant holding the rabbit grinned as he stroked the animal to keep it calm. Next to the man with the rabbit, an instructor explained the need for resourcefulness when making your way through enemy lines.

"You will have to depend on animals that you can catch and kill for your food." The man spoke with a pronounced German accent. "Any creature can give you the nourishment you need to survive." He seemed to enjoy himself as he addressed the training company. "Cats, snakes, squirrels-all these can make excellent items on your jungle menu. And of course, bunny rabbits must be included on our list."

As the sergeant said the word "rabbits," the man holding the helpless animal killed the poor creature with a swift and powerful stroke to the back of its neck. Blood spurted from the dying animal's mouth as a collective groan came from the stands.

"I really can't fucking believe this." Kelly spoke loudly enough to be heard at the stage.

A few seats away, O' Connor placed his head between his knees and puked up his dinner, commenting when he was through that it didn't "look a whole lot worse now than when they served it for supper."

As the instructor's calm and measured tones relayed the necessity of avoiding fires after escaping, the assistant holding the dead rabbit quickly butchered it with his pocketknife. Opening its chest cavity, he tore the still-beating heart from the animal's body, plopped it into his mouth and swallowed it as an evil grin spread across his face. Rabbit blood dripped from one corner of his mouth as he wiped his chin on his sleeve.

The sergeant with the German accent ended the class with a warning: "If you are captured before you complete the course tonight, we have prepared an interesting little reception for you. If you conceal yourselves well, this will be an easy night. Good luck!"

"Allright! I want a company formation ten yards in front of the bleachers!" Sergeant Enright of E-2-3 bellowed to the troops in his impressive command voice, pointing to where he wanted them to assemble. "Let's move quickly, gentlemen, before the enemy has a chance to get themselves organized."

The company departed the bleachers for the assembly point, and lined up in their usual squads and platoons. "Hey guys, let's take off." Kelly spoke from his position in third squad

The descending darkness made it difficult to detect the faces of the sergeants and officers in front of the company. They were silhouettes floating back and forth in front of the men, barking orders, trying to establish control before they released the company to the night's field exercise. Kelly added, "I mean, we're supposed to fucking escape, aren't we?"

From behind Kelly, Maynard asked, "Have they told us we can leave?"

Kelly turned around, "Hey man, like, we're prisoners. Are we supposed to wait for the bad guys to tell us when we can go?"

Dunlop cracked up, "Come on, let's get outta' here." His laughter caught on as half the thirty-man platoon drifted out of formation and went with Kelly and Dunlop. They took off at a trot across a field toward the safety of a tree-line, in jubilant defiance of the shouted demands from their officers to return to formation.

The group of escapees with Kelly and Dunlop had swollen to twenty-five, roughly a quarter of the company. They quickly moved about a mile into the forest crossed a rain-swollen stream, coming upon a meadow of thick grass where they had decided to stop and rest. The men huddled under their ponchos to stay dry. Within a few minutes, all but O'Connor had fallen asleep.

The clearing was about twenty yards wide and surrounded by hundred-feet-tall Douglas Fir. The early-fall, night air was damp and heavy with clouds. The temperature was about sixty degrees. Across from the lounging soldiers, an owl hooted from time to time.

The men had been sleeping for an hour or so when a question broke the silence. "Well, what do we do now, fellas?" O'Connor sounded a little worried. Coughing and stretching their muscles, the young guys awoke to face their current problem.

"No sweat, Conman. All we have to do is cool out here for a while longer, then we split up, and make our way to the buses." Baden said.

"Yeah, but what if some of us get caught?" O'Connor wasn't convinced. "A fellow I know told me that they're pretty rough on the guys they take prisoner."

Dunlop said, "I heard they put you head-first into a fifty gallon drum and then they beat on the sides with those poles they're carrying. A fellow from another company told me they discharged a couple of guys a month ago with hearing loss."

Maynard turned toward Dunlop, "Hey, if it gets us out of going to Nam, what're we waiting for? Let's turn ourselves in, and volunteer for the barrel!" A chorus of guffahs and boo's followed Maynard's tongue-in-cheek proposal.

Kelly propped his head up on the rock behind him. "Look, the barrel's not all they got in that compound. I heard about these two-by-fours they make you balance on like your doing push-ups, one for each foot and one for both hands. They keep you up there, screaming insults, until you drop. Then they start kicking and punching you until you get back up on the boards."

Frank Dunlop stood up and walked across the clearing to a pile of tangled branches left by a tree blown down during a long ago storm. He searched for a few moments, then bent over and picked up a branch the size of a large baseball bat. He walked back to the group, stopped near Kelly and took a few practice swings. The whooshing sound of the branch cut the air and added emphasis to the determined look on Dunlop's face.

"Hey Dunlop, what's the war club for, man?" Maynard asked.

"I ain't going to no POW compound tonight." There was a hard edge in the voice of the clerk from Sacramento.

Kelly raised his hand, "Hey you guys, I got an idea." Quiet descended on the clearing; everybody seemed willing to listen to the company commie."Look, there's about twenty-five of us here now, right?" Murmurs of agreement came from several in the group. Kelly got up on one knee, coughed, and cleared his throat. "If we stick together, protect one another, there's no way they can herd us all into that fuckin' torture compound."

A voice several yards from Kelly commented, "Yeah, but what if they decide to bust us for not playing the game the way they want us to?" said Keith Erickson, a first squad guy from Montana.

"Erickson's got a point." O'Conner said. "We could be in some really deep shit if they decide to come down on us."

"Hey, look, you guys." Kelly said. "We're supposed to work together on this deal. The lifers didn't tell us we couldn't kick a little butt. All we're doing is being resourceful, like they told us."

Maynard chimed in, "I'm with Dunlop and Kelly. If we hang as a group, we can walk on in. Those blue guys won't hassle this big a bunch of us."

"Okay, then. Troops, let's move out!" Kelly stood as he spoke. "If they try to grab any of us, we kick a little ass." He was on a bit of a roll now, speaking with some fire in his voice. "Just like if we were really in a war. When they see we're serious, they'll leave us alone."

"Hey, who farted?" one of the first squad guys called out. "Goddamn, they'll track us down easy with those gas attacks fuckin' Kelly keeps launching."

"Hey man, we're going to have to put a cork in your butt." Dunlop leaned on his war club and laughed as he admonished his friend. "Otherwise, you might make some of these guys here consider surrendering without a fight. They ain't used to it, man, like those poor guys in your barracks."

"Dunlop's right, Kelly." Maynard said, adjusting his poncho. "You gotta try and control yourself, man. It's for the good of the operation tonight, you know?"

"Hey, I'm a sick man. You guys ought to show a little mercy." Kelly pleaded to his mates as they started off toward the other side of the clearing and on into the forest.

A couple of hours later, Kelly pointed to a dirt road running across an open meadow and a treeline in the distance. "Well, there it is." Everyone could see a point where the road disappeared into trees approximately a mile away. They stood on a rocky ledge about twenty feet above the road. "The buses are just beyond those trees, the other side of this little valley. Right, Maynard?"

"You got it, gas man." Maynard always seemed to know where he was in the grand scheme of things. Kelly was confident the buses would be there if Joey Maynard said so.

The cloud cover had lifted, leaving a three-quarter moon to light their way. The night had grown much cooler, so that the rhythmic exhalation of the young soldiers turned into a light mist as they stood looking out across the valley. The escapees waited for Dunlop and Kelly to lead the way down to the road, and possible capture.

"Remember," Kelly said, "Everybody stick together. And under no circumstances does anybody get taken without a fight, OK?"

"Hey, General Kelly," Lenny Baden called out, "let's get the fuck going for those buses, man. I'm freezing my ass off up here!" Baden was at the other end of the line of troopers. His prodding was met with general agreement from the group.

"No time like the present..." Dunlop plunged down the ridge, using his big stick for balance. The rest of the guys followed him, cheering and catcalling as they picked their way down the loose, rocky slope.

The E-2-3 group was all but daring the blue guys to try and capture them. Their smokes glowed in the night, and their chatter was frequently punctuated with robust laughter. They could easily have been on their way to a football game or a dance, back in their hometowns.

After Kelly and his friends had covered about half the distance to the treeline, a group of eight blues surprised them, jumping onto the road from behind trees. The blue soldiers informed the unruly E-2-3 guys that they were now prisoners and must follow them to the POW compound. A chorus of threats, curses, and abuse erupted from Kelly, Dunlop, O'Connor and the rest. A few pushing and shoving matches erupted as the blues attempted to enforce their demand for surrender.

Finally, the sergeant in charge of the blue squad ordered his men to pull away. He had apparently decided that a bloody brawl would not be in his, or the Army's, best interests.

"I guess we're in it all the way now," Erickson said, adjusting his steel pot as he walked. "That was a fuckin' master sergeant back there." He spoke with more than a trace of pride in his voice. The rest of the E-2-3 troopers formed a line of two's and three's, about fifty yards in length, strung out along the road. Their gait was relaxed, and the rich murmur of their voices was interrupted from time-to-time by laughter and hooting. Kelly and Dunlop were in front while Baden stayed in the rear, making sure stragglers kept up with the group.

"Hey Erickson, we got 'em by the balls, man," Dunlop said, as he reached into his pocket for a smoke. "They told us to figure out some way to avoid getting caught, right?" He flicked open his zippo, lit a cigarette, and took a long, purposeful drag. "Now, how the hell are they going to tell us we weren't supposed to put up a fight?"

Dunlop patted the younger Erickson on the shoulder. "Besides what can they do?" Taking the cue, several nearby fellows recited with Dunlop, "Send us to Vietnam?" Everybody, including Erickson, had a good laugh at what had become a favorite slogan for Vietnam era GI's. No punishment the Army was likely to administer could be anywhere near as painful as what they already had planned for the young soldiers, sending them to Vietnam.

Kelly and Dunlop's group were among the early members of the company to make it back to the pick-up point, and they enjoyed themselves thoroughly in the warm confines of their idling bus. O'Connor called out, "Hey Dunlop, we saw you out there with the cow. Bet you thought we were all asleep, huh?"

Dunlop turned toward O'Connor with a big smile, "Aw, that cow reminded me so much of Kelly's sister, I couldn't help myself, man."

The bus slowly filled as the bantering continued. Some of the new guys recounted their experiences in the prisoner compound. It wasn't as bad as Kelly and the others had feared. There were no serious injuries, and nobody complained of hearing loss. Perhaps the recent scandals surrounding the rough treatment had gained the attention of the training center's commanding general. And then again, maybe the stories that Kelly and Dunlop had related earlier that night had been blown out of proportion as they were passed from soldier to soldier.

When the last young man took his seat, quiet came over the bus. At the front next to the sleeping driver, stood Sergeant Enright. He was holding his clipboard and looking a little glum.

Kelly leaned over toward O'Connor and spoke softly. "I guess this is when we find out how pissed they are." O'Connor didn't reply, keeping his eyes on Enright and his clipboard.

Dunlop leaned forward toward Kelly and O'Connor. "Just stick to the story; we were only following orders, avoiding capture, okay?"

O'Connor grunted.

His face absolutely expressionless, Enright made his way up the aisle, checking off the name of each soldier he passed by. Coming to Kelly and O'Connor, he stood and glared at them for a moment before he placed a check next to their names on the roster, and moved on.

Kelly slumped down in his seat and closed his eyes. A warm feeling of relief spread over him. *I can't believe we got away with it*, he thought. He pulled his steel pot down over his eyes and began to drift off to sleep. Behind him, Dunlop chuckled.

When Sgt Enright finished recording the names of those on the bus, he walked to the front, pausing briefly to speak to the driver, then left the bus. The driver pushed his cap back, coaxed the gear shift forward, and the sleepy GIs settled in for their ride home.

Kelly figured he had lucked out, even though he had been assigned KP on the last day of the training cycle. Since it was a Saturday, only two meals had been served in the Mess Hall, before the cooks closed up the place. The trainees who pulled duty that day had been sent on their way with half the afternoon and the entire evening left to fool around.

On his way up the street toward the barracks, Kelly walked slowly to take time to stretch his back and to admire Mt. Rainier. The enormous mountain towered serenely above the Fort on this crisp and cloudless fall day, its massive glaciers an icy pink in the lengthening sunlight of mid afternoon. It seemed that a guy could just about reach out and touch the peak, though it was eighty miles from where he stood.

Despite his gimpy ankle, Kelly had a distinct spring in his step as he climbed the stairs to his squad's section of the barracks. And why not? At formation the previous evening, everybody, including Kelly, had received orders for Fort Hood, Texas, instead of Vietnam.

Maybe things really were winding down over there. What with the peace talks in Paris and weekly announcements of small-scale troop withdrawals, it seemed possible that the Army might just forget about him and his buddies down in Texas until their two years were up. Everybody had received three hundred dollars travel pay and five sweet days before they were to report. Things were definitely looking up.

Rounding the corner into his squad's sleeping area, Kelly noticed that the room was empty, except for eighteen neatly, made bunks and closed lockers. The newly waxed floor glistened, without any footprints. No one had been here since morning formation.

He stepped into the latrine area to relieve himself. It was odd, everybody being gone at a time on Saturday when many of the fellas would normally be getting ready for a night on the town. It was always fun to be around the ever-hopeful single guys as they shaved, showered, and drenched themselves in cologne.

Kelly walked over to his locker and grabbed a book. He stretched himself out on his bunk and opened the mystery novel he had picked out the week before at the PX. After reading the first sentence three times, he sighed, tossed the book back in his locker and folded his arms beneath his head, gazing up toward the ceiling.

Kelly had noticed a spider's web at the top of the wall above his bunk when he had first arrived in E-2-3. The insect's home was in a perfect position for him to keep an eye on her daily activities.

Hey, looks like a pretty fat fly you caught yourself last night, he thought as the creature busied herself wrapping the new food cache in layer upon layer of carefully woven web strands.

Kelly watched the spider for half-an-hour as she busied herself, working with a sense of purpose he admired. As the spider was finishing with her catch, the clumping of boots on the stairs at the other end of the room drew his attention back to the human world. *Sounds like the troops. I wonder where the hell they've been*, he thought.

Baden, O'Connor, Maynard, and Erickson along with the squad's other six guys, came into the room quietly. Each guy headed for his own bunk area fumbling with his locker or staring out the window. There was none of the usual back and forth between the guys as they busied themselves in their own areas. Kelly started to feel a little strange.

Kelly broke the silence; "Hey, Denno, what's happening, man?"

O'Conner closed his locker door and walked over to Kelly's Bunk. "Don't worry, guy. We covered for you."

"Covered me for what, Dennis?" Kelly was a little confused. He sat up and looked quizzically at his squad mate.

"Well, uh,..." O'Connor looked a little sheepish as he chose his words carefully. "They, uh, had a special formation after breakfast, where they had all the guys from our squad fall out and go to the Day Room. Sergeant Enright was in there with these two guys in suits."

"Suits? You mean civilians with ties?" Kelly leaned on an elbow. "What were they doing here? Where were they from?" He looked intently at his friend.

"They said they were from the Pentagon."

"The Pentagon?" said Kelly. "Fuck...."

"Anyway, these guys asked each of us, one at a time, about you, man."

"Me?" Kelly dropped an unlit cigarette from his lips.

"Yeah." O'Connor scratched his nose. "They said they're considering you for some top secret deal back in D.C."

The rest of the squad members drifted over to Kelly's bunk and arranged themselves in a circle around him and O'Connor, jostling each other in the small space.

"Don't worry, Kelly," Maynard chimed in, "we told him you'd make a great secret agent. No shit!"

"That's right," Baden said. "Everybody figured it was none of their goddamn business about you being a fuckin' commie and all."

With Baden's crack, the room erupted in robust laughter, as everybody relaxed and competed for the chance to describe their own experiences with the suits from the Pentagon.

Kelly felt a little embarrassed, but grateful. "You guys are okay. And I really want to thank you for covering me. Only thing is, now they'll be sure to want to keep me in the Army, cause you all told 'em what a patriotic motherfucker I am!"

The group had a good laugh at the thought of Kelly as a Patriot.

"Hey man," O'Connor said "If we told 'em what a political asshole you are, they'd probably have us all up on charges for letting you live so long."

"That's right." Maynard elbowed his way next to the bed. "Since they're sending us to Nam to kill Charlie and all, they'd probably figure we should sneak over to your bunk some night and practice."

"Yeah," O'Connor waved his finger at Kelly, "and then who would we get to cover your KP, huh?"

The group had a good laugh, and Kelly shook his head.

"Hey, what's happening tonight?" Maynard spoke up. "We gotta' do something to celebrate the end of all this training shit. It's been four months, man! Anybody feel like going up to Seattle and partyin'?"

Saturday night turned into quite a blowout. E-2-3's proud graduates were in rare form. They wouldn't be going to Vietnam for now, and they were through with being punk trainees. Reason enough to get roaring drunk and do a little hollering at the moon.

The following Monday morning dawned overcast and cool. A brisk wind whipped across the quarter-mile-wide parade ground next to E-2-3, bending the sparse tufts of grass down to the rocky ground. After breakfast, with most of the soldiers already on their way to their distant hometowns, the barracks of E-2-3 stood empty in the gloom. An occasional window was open, curtains flapping softly in the breeze.

Tom Kelly and Frank Dunlop stood together in the company formation area/parking lot. Conversation was a little awkward between the two men. Dunlop was wearing dress greens, ready to hop on a bus that would take him to the Seattle-Tacoma airport for his flight to Sacramento. Kelly was wearing rumpled work fatigues.

Dunlop swung his duffle bag off his shoulder and set it on the ground between them. "Hey trooper, you don't look like you're going anywhere today."

"No shit? Now whatever gave you that idea?" Kelly reached down and tried to smooth his shirt under his belt.

You heard any more about that business with those guys from the Pentagon?"

"Just that I get to stay here in E-2-3 for the next one hundred years or so. I don't think they know what they want to do with me."

"Hey, it's better than going to Nam, isn't it?"

Kelly raised his hat and rubbed his head, still looking for the hair the Army had shaved off six months before. "All the same, I wouldn't mind going down to Fort Hood with you guys. Hood might be in Texas, but it's a damn sight better than Vietnam. And it'd be a nice change from this fuckin' place."

Dunlop lit a Marlboro, puffed a couple of times, then flicked the ash. "What about O'Connor and those other guys from your squad? I didn't see any of them at breakfast this morning," asked Dunlop.

"They all took off as soon as they could after formation, - planes to catch. Christ, Maynard was so excited about getting back to Oklahoma and seeing his parents, it took him three tries to get his shirt buttoned right."

Dunlop chuckled. "Oh, by the way, I've heard that getting assigned stateside might not keep us out of the war after all. A couple of guys I know thought they were all cozy at this fort in Oklahoma."

"Fort Sill?" Kelly stuck his hands into his pockets.

"Yeah, that's the one. Anyway, they were assigned there after AIT, just like us. After a month their names came down on a levee for Nam, and BOOM, off they went!"

"Hmm. Well, you have a good week down in California with Elena. How's she doing, by the way? She must be getting really pregnant by now."

Frank's facial expression turned serious. "I don't know about Elena. I think she's a little pissed at me these days. You know how it is. She's stuck at her parent's house, getting bigger every day, and she thinks I should be making more of an effort to be there with her."

"But man, you can't just tell the Army to go fuck off. They'll put you in jail, and then where'll she be?"

"I know." Dunlop butted his smoke and placed the unused portion behind his ear. He picked up his duffle bag and swung it over his shoulder as the small bus for main post turned into the area. "Hey Kelly, try to stay out of trouble, will you?"

"I'll do my best." He nodded as he said it.

Both men smiled and shook hands. Dunlop started up the stairs of the bus, then turned around and flashed a smile and a two-finger "V" peace sign. Kelly gave his buddy a crisp military salute, then shoved his hands into his pockets and slowly headed back up the hill toward the barracks. The lonely sound of the bus accelerating through its gears faded, and silence descended on Kelly and the surrounding company area.

Well, what happens now? Kelly wondered. He plodded up the walkway past his empty barracks, and headed over to the Mess Hall. Entering the warm building, he was greeted by the sounds and smells he associated so closely with Army life: stale coffee, greasy and sweet food cooking, the banging of pots and pans and, above all, the voices of young men working together.

Kelly drew a cup of strong brew from the giant urn at the end of the dining room. He added just enough cream and sugar to leave a hint of the taste of burnt coffee, settled at one of the empty tables. In-between slurps, he gazed through a dirty window at an American flag snapping in the breeze in front of the company orderly room.

"Hey troop!" thundered Carmello, the Italian cook from the Bronx. "Off yo ass and take out the trash!" Teddy Carmello was a draftee soldier, only a few months ahead of Kelly who had lucked out and drawn stateside duty. He was also a fairly decent poet with a head of thick black hair that fell into his eyes demonstrating to the trainees just how long he had defied his Sergeant's demands that he go to the barber. Everybody liked the guy, even when he made his poetic demands upon them during KP.

"Aw, man!" Kelly drained his cup and followed Carmello out to the kitchen, chuckling and shaking his head.

CHAPTER VI

On to Vietnam

THREE THOUSAND MILES TO THE EAST OF FORT LEWIS, ON THE following Sunday in November, Private Willie Tuggins stood with his family and a group of his friends on a sidewalk just outside the Charleston Airport. Since he couldn't think of much to say, he kept his hands in his pockets and shifted his weight back and forth from foot to foot, grinning a little whenever his eyes met those of another.

Tuggins wore dress greens for this flight to New Jersey, where he would catch a Seattle-bound plane. His orders directed him to report to the Overseas Replacement Station, Fort Lewis, Washington, then board a flight that would take him to the war.

His sister Cynthia stared at him adoringly. She was sure there was never a soldier in uniform as handsome as her brother. Four months of arduous physical training had hardened Willie's physical features. His sharp angular jaw, broad shoulders, and almost non-existent waistline made him look like a black Sergeant Rock, ready and willing to smite his country's enemies.

Looks, however, can be deceiving.

His girlfriend Dot slid her arm through Willie's, leaned over and spoke softly in his ear. "It's up to you, baby. If you decide you want to make a run for Canada, just let me know where to meet you. I'll be there." She placed her other hand on his chest. "The border's so close up where you're going. I really think we'd be all right."

Willie looked into her eyes and realized, for at least the tenth time that week, that she was serious. "Dot, I just want to get this stuff behind us. Our life is here in South Carolina, not in some ol' cold place we never been before." He reached down and picked up his bag. "Like I tol' you last spring, I'll keep my head down. One year ain't that long and then I'll be back. Same Willie Tuggins, I promise."

As two tears slowly fell from Dot's eyes, he kissed her cheeks catching the salty liquid with his lips. "Now go on over and see about momma while I say goodbye to these fellas from school."

She walked over and stood next to Helen Tuggins. Willie's mother hugged the young woman, doing her best to reassure both of them.

Willie walked over to three young black men standing a polite distance from his family. They were engaged in a quiet conversation of their own, but fell silent as Willie neared them. Members of the Black Student Union Chapter at Willie's former college, the young men offered quite a contrast to the Tuggins family. Each wore his hair long in the current Afro style. Two of them wore t-shirts with clenched fists stenciled on the front, displaying their commitment to Black Power.

The four young men greeted one another with a brief slap to each other's open palms. A phenomenon of the Black movements of the 1960's, Dap was the name of a variety of greetings practiced by many young Blacks who felt that shaking hands in the traditional way favored by whites was too businesslike, or maybe just too white.

Joseph, the tallest of the group, smiled and nodded at Willie. "Hey, dude, you look impressive."

"Aw, c'mon man." Tuggins gave Joseph a firm jolt on the arm setting off hearty laughter from the group.

Recovering his balance, Joseph placed a hand on Willie's shoulder, "Seriously, you do look pretty sharp in them soldier threads."

"Well, I wish I felt sharp." Tuggins took off his cap spun it around in his hand. "I have to wear this silly green shit to get half-price on my plane ticket. If it was up to me, I'd be looking just like y'all." They all fell silent a moment.

Tommy, who divided his time between playing defensive tackle and sergeant-at-arms duties at BSU meetings, spoke up, "How's Dot doing with all this?"

"She's okay, man." Tuggins turned his head and looked over at his mother and Dot standing together. A soft, worried smile crept across his face. "She wants to split for Canada."

"Might not be such a bad idea, Bro." Joseph looked directly into Willie's eyes as he spoke. "Things can get pretty rough over there, especially for Brothers."

"I know. But I figure I'll just keep my head down... and pray a lot." Willie put his hat back on, "Who knows, maybe I'll get lucky. You know, get some valuable work experience walking around in the jungle for a year. Never even hear a shot."

Peter Williams, the short and wiry member of the group, cast an arrogant nod at Willie. "Say Bro, what you gonna do if the Man tells you to blow innocent folks shit away for him?" Just like Brother Peter to ask an obnoxious question for the maximum negative impact. Peter stood with his hands on his hips and his jaw thrust out, waiting for an answer.

Truth was, Peter's father was a dissolute rogue who had abandoned his wife when Peter was six. The boy's grandmother, who had raised him, didn't care much for the angry lad. Tuggins figured that his antagonistic stance at the moment probably had more to do with his belief that Willie had stolen Dot from him, than it did with any genuine concern for people in Vietnam.

Willie looked at Joseph, shook his head and smiled. Turning back toward Peter, he said, "I'll miss your lectures while I'm gone, Bro. But I can tell you this, I won't be doing the Man's job for him over there. I'll do what I always do, fight for good over evil and protect the innocent the best I can."

"Willie!" Reverand Tuggins called to his son.

"I know, Daddy." It was time for the younger Tuggins to say his final goodbyes. He slapped hands again with his three friends then walked back over to his family. Before being allowed to walk into the terminal where he was hugged and kissed by the half-dozen people there leaving him a little rumpled, but smiling warmly.

Dot and Willie left the others outside and walked together towards the Departure gate. "Your daddy doesn't care much for Joseph and them, does he?" Dot said.

"It's Peter, mostly," he said. "Daddy blames him for subverting me into the BSU, which he figures led to all this other stuff." He pointed to the single stripe on his uniform sleeve.

Dot kissed her fingertip, then touched Willie's nose. They put their arms around one another for what Willie feared could be the last time. He held Dot away from him a little, gave her one of his grins he knew she could not resist, winked and then sauntered through the gate and onto the plane.

*   *   *

DECEMBER 5, 1969

AN KHE, VIETNAM

In the eyes of the young American soldiers sent there to Vietnam, it was a strange, scary, and often beautiful place. Dunlop had never imagined so many brilliant shades of green, one after another, blending into the jungle canopy as he rode along the seemingly endless dirt road that brought him and the other replacement soldiers to the Fourth Division Base Camp at An Khe.

He was used to the heat from his days growing up in Sacramento. But here everything was like a Louisiana swamp, soggy with a jungle odor that often smelled like a giant garbage dump. The air was so heavy it felt like being in a wet sauna. His clothes began sticking to him a half-an-hour after he dressed.

Dunlop's first couple of nights in country were spent at the Replacement Depot in Saigon among a couple of thousand other GIs armed with clipboards and manila envelopes trying to get their paperwork completed.

"You noticed yet?" Dunlop was sitting on the steps of one of the many offices the American soldiers were sent to. Seated next to him was Private First Class Munster from Florida. Munster continued, "There's two kinds of guys, here at the repo depot-them just arriving, and them's done with their year and headed home." Munster leaned toward Dunlop and lit a cigarette. "It don't take long to figure out who's who." He took a long drag on his smoke and exhaled a grand cloud. "The ones smiling and joking are headed back to the States. Them with the serious, worried looks, they got their year in front of 'em."

The two days at the depot in Saigon had been long, hot and boring enough for Dunlop to be glad that he had been assigned to the Third Battalion of the Eighth Light Infantry Regiment, Fourth Infantry Division, headquartered three hundred and forty miles up north, in Pleiku.

After a two-hour plane flight in an old propeller-driven C-130, Fourth Division headquarters turned out to be a small Army office complex of one-story prefab buildings plunked down next to a sleepy Vietnamese market-town. More forms to fill out, a few more hours waiting in line, then Frank and the other new guys climbed aboard waiting trucks destined for Fourth Division base camp, sixty miles toward the coast next to the small town of An Khe.

The trip to An Khe amounted to four hours on the open back of a two-and-a-half ton army truck, seated on a hard bench. The gravel and dirt road had enough bumps and holes to keep even the most determined sleepers awake.

Frank worried about the possibility of an ambush since none of the forty-two replacement soldiers had been issued weapons. But the fellow next to him pointed to two helicopter gunships cruising overhead. "Wouldn't be worth it to the VC. Choppers'd really fuck 'em up." Typically, this guy acted like he knew what he was talking about, but Dunlop suspected that he probably knew as little about the situation as any of the other FNG's (Fucking New Guys) on the truck. After seeing the gunships, Dunlop relaxed a little and settled into the rhythm of the bumpy trip.

His first night in base camp became permanently etched in his memory. Not much sleep as he tossed in his bunk under a wool blanket. An Khe was cooler than Saigon but the war felt closer and hotter. Along with the other Fourth Division replacement soldiers, he spent most of the night wondering what the hell he was doing there.

The surrounding Night-sounds emphasized the sense of danger and decay he had felt since arriving in Saigon. Water dripped like falling hailstones on leaves outside his screened window. Insects came in for a lazy bite buzzing his ear and making him itch in more places on his body than he thought possible. And for a chilling few moments, he heard the distinct staccato of an M60 machine gun; death cracking in the darkness.

Dawn finally came to the new Fourth Division troopers, bringing a sense of relief and renewed hope. After all, everybody knows that bad things happen at night, not in the gentle light of the morning sun.

This illusion of safety was quickly dispelled. A loudspeaker right outside Frank's window suddenly blared reveille, the tune barely discernible through the static. Soon after, the tent flap opened and in stepped a neatly dressed soldier in jungle fatigues carrying a clipboard.

"Hey, you fuckers! You better get up and get going, cause you got some nasty shit to eat! Then I got a day's worth of processing for you before they can have your young asses for the war. Come on now!" Spec IV, William Lister stared at the stubborn, nearly-motionless young men.

Dunlop focused on Lister's thoughtful black face. *Not scowling*, he thought, *just doing his job. Waiting for his year to be over like everybody else around here. Probably hated this part of his assignment. Making sure everybody has wills, recording blood types so transfusions will be ready before arms and legs are blown off, bellies torn open. He has to get the paperwork straight before we hit the sticks.*

The new troopers rose from their bunks with groans, curses, and a few sonorous farts. Lister heaved a sigh of relief, spun around on his heel and called out over his shoulder on the way out, "See you guys after breakfast."

✦ ✦ ✦

DECEMBER 8, 1969

Three days later, the Third Battalion of the Eighth Light Infantry Brigade, Fourth Division was moving out with barely enough time to assign the new guys their bunks. Dunlop got up early that morning to pack his rucksack. He tried to think of everything he might need while they were out on patrol. The resulting pile of stuff turned out to be more than enough for three packs. He culled the pile down to the bare essentials and stuffed them in his rucksack.

After a breakfast that he hadn't felt much like eating, Frank grabbed his gear. He found the other guys in Third Platoon, Second Squad, assembled in the shade of their Mess Hall, waiting for the slicks-transport helicopters-to pick them up for the planned operation

FNG (fucking new guy) Frank Dunlop stood among a group of seven grunts in jungle fatigues, puffing nervously on his third cigarette in twenty-five minutes. He was starting to feel a little dizzy from the nicotine. Today, December 8, 1969, marked the end of his first week in Vietnam. He was as shiny and new a trooper as could be found in this part of the Central Highlands today. But being new around here usually wasn't a very good thing.

Dunlop's jungle fatigues were deep green without even a frayed area to alter the 'new guy' impression. He hated that he looked like such an inexperienced ignorant kid fresh from the World. He averted his eyes from the guys lounging by the Mess Hall as he scratched and fidgeted, fearing they might notice the admiration in his gaze. They were all such grizzled veterans, leaning, squatting and sitting in the shade with their gear stacked casually in front of them. They all seemed lost in thought, confident in their ability to survive the murderous battles they would face in the coming weeks.

The Third Battalion was preparing itself for an operation that would keep it out in the rolling hills of Central Vietnam for at least the next month. All the officers and senior sergeants of the four companies assigned to the extended field maneuver seemed to be frenetically checking details, hollering at subordinates, looking and talking tough for each other. The grunts by the Mess Hall found this spectacle mildly amusing, if they noticed at all. *It's going to be one fine Christmas this year*, Dunlop decided. He wondered with a chuckle if Santa would bring them presents if they were still out on Christmas Day.

Dunlop squatted alone amidst his stacked gear and began tightening the laces on his boots. *I'm not sure exactly how I feel right now*, he thought. *But I think it's some version of scared shitless of going to war.*

Sgt. Roland Peterson, leader of Second Squad, Third Platoon, "D" Company gave up his favorite shady place under the mess hall window and strolled over to where Dunlop was standing.

"You better rub some dirt into that new boot leather you're wearing, troop." Peterson stood in front of Dunlop with his legs spread in a casual athletic stance and took off his bush hat, wiping the sweat from his brow with his forearm. "Those toes are so fuckin' shiny you might as well be wearing mirrors. Attracts the wrong kind of attention out there, know what I mean?"

Rollie Peterson looked like a guy running a highway construction crew in California's central valley. The tall sergeant was handsome and confident, and always on the alert for the possibility of disaster. Dunlop had heard from sources around Third of the Eighth that Peterson was the best squad leader in the battalion. Frank flipped his cigarette on the ground as he hunkered down and began rubbing some of the local red mud onto the toes of his boots.

"You from California, Dunlop?"

"How'd you guess?" The new troop looked up, smiling at the question.

"Aw, forget that steers and queers shit, man. There's been a lot of new guys in the battalion from Cal lately. That's enough."

"Huh?" Dunlop looked confused for a moment. "Oh, yeah." He stood up and looked down at his toes.

"Now you're starting to look like something besides fresh meat for Victor."

"Victor?"

"Victor Charlie. The guy in the black pajamas who wants to make your wife glad you took out that extra life insurance policy before they dropped you into this shit hole."

"Oh, that Victor." Frank smacked his lips, feeling a little dry in the mouth.

"Now, if it's okay with you, let's have a look at what you got in that rucksack."

Peterson squatted and, before Dunlop could respond, opened the bulging pack and pushed the top items aside. He looked up and gazed into the distance for a moment, his brow furrowed, jaw set. Then he tipped the pack upside down and shook till all its' contents were on the ground between the two men.

"Sorry, guy." Peterson gave the astonished Dunlop a comforting nod, and then went to work sorting the gear into two piles.

Frank cast a furtive glance over his shoulder toward the rest of the squad still lounging in the shade, cigarettes dangling from their expressionless faces. They were watching Peterson's inventory of Dunlop's things, and they all seemed to be at least mildly interested in the show.

"Hey, Rollie, give you a good price for his stash when you find it." PFC Bill Vandyne, known as "Lizzard", rocked on his steel pot, took a puff on his smoke, and laughed at his own joke. Vandyne always seemed high on something or other. When he wasn't high, he was usually pretty nervous, tapping out the beat to some song only Lizzard could hear.

Vandyne wasn't what you would call a popular soldier. Several of his fellow squad members had accused him, on different occasions, of stealing from their footlockers. None of the thefts had been proven, but Peterson believed it would only be a matter time before the guy got nailed. Upon his arrival he had informed some of the squad that he had escaped a Breaking and Entering charge by joining the Army. Besides, it was widely believed that the slimy Vandyne cheated at whist.

"Say, new guy, you look like you're going to the prom, man." PFC Frank Burkowski, from St. Louis, stood and pointed to the gear in front of Dunlop. "Anybody with that many pairs of pants must be planning on dancin' with the Gooks. And let me tell you man, that ain't what they got in mind for your young ass!"

Peterson looked up at his squad, frowned, and said, "Why don't you guys just shut the fuck up? Can't you see I'm tryin' to get the guy squared away?"

Sergeant Peterson went back to sorting the last few items while Dunlop made like he wasn't much concerned. Actually he was beginning to think that fighting the VC might not be so bad, if it would keep the attention of the squad on something else.

Letting his mind wander, he imagined himself gravely wounded after a heroic effort in a fierce firefight. Blood soaking his shirt, these same guys who were now enjoying themselves at his expense would be gathered around him and murmuring things like "brave... hardcore... hang in there troop!"

"Dunlop!" Peterson said for the third time, waking Dunlop from his reverie.

"Oh, yeah," he started, then looked directly at Peterson.

"Look, this shit's fine," Peterson pointed to the smaller of the two piles. "Put it back in your rucksack. This other, put it in a bag and leave it off at the supply room." He stood up and stretched his arms while Dunlop busied himself placing the gear back in his pack.

"After you leave your shit off at supply, get a couple dozen cans of c-rations and then go over to the Armorer and pick up a dozen clips for your M16, three maybe four frags, and a couple Laws." Peterson stroked his mustache for a moment, "Oh yeah, stick a Claymore in there, okay?"

"Then add a dozen eggs, stir it good and bake it for a couple a hours, man. You'll have yourself a nice little death omelet. No shit!" Spec IV Eddie Miller, "Fast Eddie", spoke with his standard wry grin. Miller considered himself the squad comedian. He also liked to get in his digs at the war effort whenever the opportunity presented itself.

Peterson turned to his unruly squad. "Listen up! Six hours from now any one of you could be beggin' this guy for help. You all know that, so why fuck with me while I'm trying to get him squared away?" He turned back to Dunlop. "You understand what I want you to get?"

"Yeah, sure." Frank finished repacking the rucksack and stood up. "All right if I run over to the Mess Hall and get a bag for this other stuff?"

"OK, but be back here in 30 minutes with a full pack and ready to roll."

Dunlop hustled away, glad to be finished with his time on the spot in front of the second squad cut-ups. *They didn't seem like such a bad bunch, not really. And Peterson, he was all right. Except, he seemed a little nervous. Every once in a while he'd jerk his head a little, like he couldn't control it. That kind of thing could spoil your aim. Well, if that was all that was wrong with him, hey, no problem. Better to have a guy in charge who treats you right and can't shoot, than the other way around,* he thought.

After forty-five minutes of running around trying to figure out how to find the items that Peterson had told him to bring, Frank wound up at the company Weapons Room. He made himself comfortable leaning on his elbows across a wide, olive drab, metal counter top. An electric fan whirred at the counter, pushing the hot air over Dunlop, which he found mildly pleasant. The armorer, PFC Darryl Wilbik, strolled up and looked blankly at Dunlop.

"I need this stuff to take on patrol." Dunlop held up a list he had jotted down on a torn piece of paper. Wilbik took the paper, then turned around and disappeared without a word into a shelving area. Dunlop relaxed on his elbows again, positioning himself to get as much of the airflow from the fan as he could, and let his thoughts wander to home and Elena. Things hadn't gone so well with her during his two week leave between Fort Hood and Viet Nam. *Maybe she'll mellow out after the baby's born,* he thought.

He turned away from the counter and walked over to the doorway and looked in the general direction of a distant roar in the sky. Nothing much up there, not that he could see anyway. "Hey, new guy! Here's your shit!" Wilbik slapped the cardboard box and its deadly contents down on the countertop.

"Let's see: twelve clips, four frags, two light anti-tank weapons-- everybody calls em' LAWS," he looked up at Dunlop to see if he understood, "and a Claymore. That about it?"

"Close enough, man."

"Groovy, then. Just sign here, and you're on your way."

Dunlop picked up the pen attached to the clipboard next to the box and signed where Wilbik indicated. He tossed his bag of c-rations in with the ammunition and wrapped his arms around the box as though to pick it up, but stopped and looked up quizzically. His brow furrowed as he moved his head around trying to locate the source of a roaring sound, which now seemed to be directly overhead. A concussive force added to the noise as though giant construction workers were passing overhead, jackhammering the air.

"That's your ride, troop." Wilbik shouted with his hands cupped to his mouth.

"Huh?" Dunlop mouthed toward the weapons clerk.

"Choppers, man." Wilbik looked a little disdainful as he belted the words across the countertop. "You best get your ass in gear, troop. Your squad'll be loading in a couple of minutes."

"Oh shit!" Frank grabbed the box and flew out the door. He looked over at the Mess Hall and saw that second squad was on their feet with packs on and rifles in hand. His rucksack sat forlornly off to the side where he and Peterson had packed it, his rifle leaning across the bag.

Dunlop knelt down on one knee and set the box down next to his pack. He looked from the box to the pack, pawing at each, without really moving anything. Eddie Miller, a California surfer boy turned soldier, walked over carrying two canteens in holders and squatted next to Dunlop. Miller had been in Vietnam a little over six months, and was regarded highly by his fellow grunts for his soldiering skills.

"Don't worry, man." Miller set the canteens down next to Frank's pack. "They ain't going nowhere without us." He reached down and opened the pack and started rearranging things.

"Now, stand up and let's get you set." Dunlop stood and Miller hoisted the rucksack, making sure the straps were adjusted properly on Frank's shoulders. "I got you a couple of extra canteens for your belt. You're gonna be glad to have the water after ten klicks or so."

"Thanks, man." Frank held his arms a little out from his side as Miller fit the two canteens onto the web belt Dunlop wore around his waist. "Say uh, what's ten klicks?"

Miller proceeded to arrange the various weapons and ammo on Frank's pack straps. "Klicks are kilometers, about two-thirds of a mile. You'll get used to it, like military time." He slid the straps for the Law anti-tank missiles over Dunlop's shoulders and across his chest. The Bandoliers of

M16 clips went next to the Laws in the same fashion. The Claymore and the c-rations went into the rucksack, where his extra pants had been. Frank did his best to appear nonchalant while Miller put him together.

"Here's a good place for your smokes, man." Miller shoved Dunlop's pack of ciggs into the elastic band surrounding the base of his helmet. "Oh yeah, don't forget this stuff." He took a plastic squeeze bottle of the white goo called LSA, and placed it next to the cigarette pack. "It looks like mayonnaise when you squeeze it out. Keep a coat of it on all the metal parts of your 16. It helps cuts down on jamming. Let's go, grab your gun, man." Dunlop picked up his M16 and trotted off toward the chopper. As he ran, Dunlop looked back for Miller, who was right behind him. Miller pointed to the helicopter they were headed for and nodded.

CHAPTER VII

December 11, 1969

HUMPIN' THE BOONIES

THREE DAYS INTO THE PATROL, DUNLOP HAD FALLEN INTO A RHYTHM. One foot in front of the other, and keep up with the guy in front of you. But not too close, in case he might step on something nasty. It was best to keep moving. Rest breaks only made him sleepy and less alert, which was not a good way to survive the next hour, stumbling into stuff that can kill you.

Dunlop was pleased to discover that he was getting used to the heat and humidity. The Central Highlands was not quite the steam kettle as the soggy Mekong Delta, three hundred miles to the south.

The night before, Miller had conducted a short "seminar" on the state of the war for Dunlop and another new guy, Benton, just before the three fell asleep in their ponchos. According to Miller, the war had become a little less furious since the Tet offensive in January of '68, almost two years before Dunlop arrived in country. Since Tet, the Army's strategy for the Fourth Division was to keep out on the trails of the Central Highlands as much as possible. Most of the supplies from the North and many infiltrating North Vietnamese soldiers passed along the same route that Dunlop's company currently patrolled. The goal of the North Vietnamese Army was to reach the Mekong Delta, and build up its forces for a renewed offensive that would cut off Saigon from its food supply, and finally defeat the Americans, or so went the U.S. theory.

✦ ✦ ✦

"So, that's where you are right now troops." During a rest for Delta Company along the trail, Miller took off his helmet (steel pot), and, in-between sips of water, continued last night's discussion of their geo-political situation along with the rest of the American Army in Vietnam.

"This whole area is part of what they call the Ho Chi Minh Trail." He pulled a handkerchief out of his pocket and rubbed his hair where the inner band of the helmet rested. Like the rest of his body and clothing, his head was soaked with sweat.

"Basically, we've been humpin' Injun Country since the slicks dropped us off." Miller put his helmet back on and Dunlop took the cue. "We haven't had any kills for a few weeks now, our side or theirs. But that don't mean they ain't out there. We been finding signs of bad guys all along-things like rice bags and dead cooking fires. Shit, they might be watchin' us right now, maybe have an ambush laid up a couple klicks."

"So, what do you do when they spring one?" Dunlop tried to look and sound as cool as he could.

"Hey, didn't they cover that in AIT? You know, advanced ambush control 1-A." Miller smirked and took another swig on his canteen. Dunlop chuckled.

Miller's young face was hardly the image one might expect of a U.S. soldier. He had grown a small goatee that made him look like a seventeenth century pirate, and his brown hair tumbled out two inches below his helmet in back. Sweaty strands dangling on his forehead over dark brown eyes that always seemed to be at least half-smiling. He invariably offered a good-natured apology to Sgt. Croix, the career enlisted man in charge of Third Platoon, whenever Croix asked him about his appearance. The Sergeant had never pushed it beyond that

Miller wore a small pin on his packstrap with an image of a crow's foot peace symbol next to a dangling hand grenade. He always had a pack of Bugler tobacco, which he claimed to prefer to regular cigarettes because he liked to "stay in practice". The Bugler also offered a cover when one of the lifers saw him rolling marijuana joints. They could easily tell themselves it was just tobacco, since they saw him rolling his own cigarettes all the time.

Miller was a fast accurate shot with his M16, quick with a joke, and he could roll joints like the wind. Word was that when it was time to party, he could have four guys smokin' and jokin' in less than a minute. Everybody liked the dude.

"Anytime," Miller said, "you hear somebody yell something, anything, you hit the ground and make like a mole. Fast as you can, get flat. Same thing goes for any loud sound that could be shots, just get the fuck down, man." Dunlop and Benton sat motionless. Frank didn't want to miss a single word uttered by this wiley combat veteran. "Once you're down, count slowly to three, then look up without raising your head. Okay, now you just do whatever you see the other guys doing, the ones that are still moving that is."

Smiling a little, Miller took a drag on his Bugler, then went on. "If you're lucky, it's over and you're cool. You just earned your Combat Infantryman's Badge (CIB) and you can whack off that night just thinking about how sweet it is to be alive. If, on the other hand, the Gooks are still at it, do NOT run away from them. They'll drop you before you take two steps. If they're only on one side of you, stay as low as possible and back away from the trail slowly while keepin' up your return fire. If you're surrounded, just jack a fresh clip into your sixteen and run over the little cocksuckers. But everybody's got to do it all at the same time for it to work. Got it?"

The two green troopers looked at Miller in reverent silence with their eyes wide and mouths slightly open. Then Freddie Benton from Madison Wisconsin, who had been a failing English Lit student at the University only six months ago, spoke softly. "Uh, you been in one of those things, Eddie?"

"Yeah, a couple a times." Miller spoke with conviction, but tried not to overwhelm the new guys. Benton and Dunlop exchanged a glance, each raising their eyebrows a little. "It ain't as bad as it used to be, from what I heard, before I got here. Maybe it's winding down some." He seemed to want them to understand what they were in for, so they wouldn't lose their heads when it was their turn in the frying pan.

"How long you been here, man?" Dunlop asked.

"Way to ask that is how long I got to go. As a matter of fact, I just passed six months, which makes me a bit of a short-timer. I got one-hundred and eighty-two days left before the ol' freedom slick will be coming for me." He took off his helmet and pointed to a crude calendar on the outside. "This here's my short timers charm. I'm on months now." He pointed to a row of letters representing six months. "When I get to next June, I'll go to numbers for each day till I get to thirty, then I'm gettin' the fuck outta here, man."

"Say, Miller." Benton asked, "What's that 'Thousand Yard Stare' thing about?"

Miller grinned, "Where'd you hear about that, man?"

"Some of the AIT instructors at Fort Hood used to talk about it." Benton shifted to his other knee and looked respectfully at Miller. "I was just wondering."

Miller chuckled. "I heard about it, too. It happened a lot around here before Tet, or so I'm told." He finished rolling a cigarette and lit up. "Still does down in the delta where they see more action than we do up here." He puffed on his smoke, then went on, "One of the grunts gets an empty look in his eyes, like he's staring at something isn't there, people call it a thousand yard stare."

"Why a thousand yards?" asked Dunlop.

Miller looked serious. "'Cause that's how far it usually takes before the guy gets medivac'd out," Miller flicked the ash off his smoke, "or stuffed into a bag."

"Oh...." Benton and Dunlop responded in unison.

Dunlop spotted an exotic, fluffy white spider next to his boot. The two-inch furry creature seemed undecided about how to relate to this invader of her territory. The spider approached Dunlop's toe twice, each time retreating before she finally mustered the courage to leap up onto his boot. Dunlop grinned and reached down to flick her off. He looked at Miller. "Say, that peace pin you're wearing reminds me of a guy I trained with at Fort Lewis. He was wearing one on his greens the night we reported to our AIT company. Fuckin' Kelly, wonder what he's up to now."

"You were at Fort Lewis for AIT?" Miller asked.

"Basic, too," Dunlop reached down and flicked the persistent spider from his boot again.

"Hey, my family lived in Seattle for a while when I was a kid, before we moved to California." Miller's face broke into a smile. "You probably went by my old house on your way to town for weekend passes. Shit, small world, huh?"

Bill Vandyne approached the group. "What's up, gentlemen?" He unslung his rifle and leaned back on it. Vandyne had a nervous face, like he was worried somebody might be sneaking up behind him. He glanced around, not making eye contact with any of the fellows talking with Miller.

"Hey Lizzard, I thought Peterson had you out on the flank for the break." Miller looked right at Vandyne as he said it, without smiling.

"Aw man, there's nothin' out there. I cruised around a little and besides, we're mounting up here in a second." Lizzard pulled a Winston from his pocket and lit it with his Zippo, taking great pains to make the lighter snap shut loudly.

"Troop, you best get your ass out there where Peterson put you and watch that flank 'til we move out." Miller waited a second, then said, "I mean it, pal." Fast Eddie Miller stood up and faced Lizzard.

"Aw man." Vandyne threw his smoke on the ground and crushed it. He picked up his M16 and tramped noisily back to his position, twenty yards out.

"Asshole." Miller muttered as he stretched. Dunlop flipped the spider off his shoe for the fourth time and the three men broke into laughter at the sight of the bug positioning itself for yet one more assault on Dunlop's boot.

"Hey, Dunlop, that spider has a thing for you, or your boot at least." Benton rose and adjusted his rucksack.

Peterson bounded up the trail to where Miller, Dunlop and Benton stood. Rollie caught Miller's eye and raised his arm a little with his thumb pointed in the direction the company was headed. Miller nodded to Peterson, who trotted back to his position at the front of the squad.

D Company moved along the trail like a centipede. Sixteen squads, four platoons, one-hundred and twenty-two guys including lifers, lieutenants, and the CO, Captain Richard Welby. The main sound was the swishing of pants as the soldiers moved and the squishing of mud underfoot. Their eyes were alert, faces taut, rifles at the ready. The tall broadleaf plants alongside the trail filtered the sunlight and brushed the soldiers' fatigues as they passed, mixing dew with sweat.

Dunlop reflected as he walked that he and the other guys had avoided stepping on the little white spider as they left her territory. *She might be jumping on some Viet Cong guy by now*, he thought.

Without talking, the soldiers proceeded deeper into an area where the Army hoped they might encounter enemy soldiers. Dunlop felt a knawing tension that reminded him of waiting in his bedroom for his father to come and beat him when he had done something to really piss the old guy off. Only this feeling in the pit of his stomach went on for hours. Bad guys could be lurking behind a row of trees, or under some bushes to the side of the trail, or just about anywhere. Or you could step on a mine. And when you forgot to be scared for a minute, boredom almost killed you. *This Vietnam shit is hard to take*, he thought.

Twenty yards behind Dunlop, the distinctive cracking spray of one of the company's M16's exploded the silence. Dunlop was on the ground, feeling the moist dirt of the trail on his cheek even before he heard the yells to take cover.

After counting to three a couple of times, he looked around. Everything was very quiet. Miller was up on one knee, rifle to his shoulder aimed in the direction of the shots. Muffled voices relayed the message that everything was OK, and that they had a kill.

From his vantage point after he stood up, Dunlop could see the dead Vietnamese guy, his body splayed in a twisted, painful posture. Blood soaked the back of the man's black shirt, a conical hat covered most of his face.

"He was comin' up on us from that little side trail over there," said Miller.

"Jesus," muttered Benton.

After dark, with their night time defensive perimeter established, the young men near Dunlop stared into the darkness and kidded him about the spider, warning him that it might come back that night.

"Hey, Miller." Dunlop whispered.

"What's up, Spiderman?" Miller spoke softly in a rich baritone from his position, five feet away from Dunlop.

"You see that dead guy today?"

"Yeah."

"What'd he have on him?"

"Rice, some maps and what looked like a journal. Had a picture of some gook chick in the diary."

"No gun?"

"Naw, but that don't matter. Only reason for him to be out here on that trail is to fuck with us."

"Hmm." Dunlop grunted to indicate that he understood.

"Whole thing sucks, Spiderman." Miller concluded.

By the ninth day of the operation, Delta company marched much longer than usual in an effort to catch up with Alpha and Charlie companies in order to secure its' own flanks. The going was hot, humid and very tense. Thick plant cover made it difficult to see more than ten yards in any direction.

"Hey, Miller, you hear that whistling?" Dunlop spoke in a husky whisper, his eyes darting back and forth as he tried to keep track of his surroundings while he walked. "Sounds like two birds talking to each other, don't it?" He spun his rifle toward another longer whistle. "Hear that?"

Miller turned and faced Dunlop, walking backwards with his rifle pointed upward. He held his hand palm out and signaled Dunlop to stay calm, then brought his finger to his lips and motioned for silence. He pointed with his thumb in the general direction of the whistling and raised his eyebrows twice. He then turned back on the trail to face forward, locked and loaded a round into the chamber of his M16, and clicked the safety off. Dunlop followed suit and heard the distinctive clicking and metal sliding of several other weapons belonging to the guys near him.

The ambush hit like a sudden, bloody thunderstorm. Suddenly, there was so much noise it was nearly impossible to think. Dunlop reacted quickly; *Get down, locate Miller, do whatever he does,* he thought.

Guys up in first squad screamed. "Medic! Medic!" One guy yelled he didn't want to die, "Not today, please not today." Something popped, like a machine gun from a tree line thirty yards out, thwacking in the leaves just above Dunlop. If he had been standing, he'd be dead for sure. Some sergeant, probably Moore, screamed at his men to "Get some fuckin' fire on that fuckin' tree line!" Someone about fifteen yards from Dunlop cried and called for his mother. *Good luck, pal,* Frank thought.

Miller crawled backwards away from the trail and Dunlop followed. The rest of the company moved in the same direction, dragging several wounded GIs. After crawling away from the ambush, Dunlop stopped to return fire and saw men off to his left get to their feet and run in a crouch for a tree line. He looked at Miller, who nodded and motioned to him to hurry up and follow the others.

Miller and Dunlop passed several guys already in prone-firing positions. Moments after they turned around and hit the ground, the company opened up on its former positions. Dunlop could see the wisdom of placing the company in this much more defensible position.

"What happens now?" Dunlop shouted to Miller.

"Just keep those fuckers pinned where they are." Miller popped an empty clip out of his rifle slamming in a full one from the bandolier he wore across his chest. The fighting filled the air with deafening noise and the acrid smell of burnt gunpowder. Dunlop fumbled with a full clip, trying to load his M16. "C'mon, man! Keep up your fuckin fire! They'll lose interest pretty soon, now that the surprise is over. But we gotta hit 'em hard, or they'll think they can take us."

Finally getting the fresh clip into his weapon, Dunlop sprayed bullets into the enemy tree line, and began to felt a bit pleased with himself for getting the hang of it.

Fast Eddie Miller shifted his position. He was on his fifth clip and Dunlop was having trouble getting the second empty out. Fire, fire, fire, it was mind-numbing giving nobody, including Dunlop, time to worry about getting hit. Dunlop noticed a couple of guys in first squad shooting without even looking, their faces buried in foliage and their rifles over their heads and extended in front of them.

A deafening explosion went off thirty yards from Dunlop and Miller close enough for them to feel it's concussive force. Screams and curses came from the struck section of the company's line. Dunlop looked over at Miller. "What the fuck is going on?"

"Jesus Goddamn Christ!" Miller screamed, "Somebody must have fumbled an egg when he tried to toss it at the gooks! It looks like it landed right on top of Silverman over there. Fuck!" Miller rose quickly to his feet and turned toward Dunlop. "Keep an eye on that tree line over there, man. If you see so much as a leaf quiver, fuckin' waste it! "

Dunlop nodded and Miller was off at a trot.

The ambush was over and the NVA had withdrawn, probably before the grenade landed in the middle of Second Squad. The company pulled its defensive perimeter tight around its three dead and four wounded. Dunlop saw the CO moving around as he gave orders, trying to sound confident and authoritative but his voice was much too high and weak to carry any authority in a situation like this. Everyone seemed to be going about their grim business and ignoring him.

Silverman and another guy lay still, with ponchos covering their heads and their feet sticking out below. Dunlop looked at the boots below one of the ponchos and thought about the guy lacing up that morning. *And there they were*, he thought *still tied just the way he liked them.*

Minutes later, Miller had tears in his eyes when he came back to where Dunlop and Benton lay in the grass, their M16's pointed outward waiting for a possible second attack that would almost surely not come. Miller sat down against a tree, his rifle across his lap. He rubbed his face with his hands, then looked into the distance.

"What's up, man?" Dunlop said.

"Silverman," Miller said softly

"Yeah, Eddie, we seen him." Benton sat up and faced Miller.

Miller turned toward the two new guys he was keeping under his wing. "He must have been stoned or something." Miller took a deep breath. "Grenade he dropped killed him, but his radio was okay. Ain't that a bitch?"

"Sorry, Miller," Benton said.

"Man had thirty-four days left in country. He was a good guy, fun to do some smoke with, know what I mean? I think he was gonna get married when he got back to the world." Miller pulled his Bugler out and rolled a smoke. He looked up, "You guys want one?" They both nodded.

The decision was made to remain in place for the night. By the time the dust-off (medivac helicopter) left with the dead and wounded, the day was fading, and Captain Welby issued orders to set out claymore mines and dig in.

Miller, Benton and Dunlop finished their dinner of c-rations out of little OD cans; beans and franks, rolls, topped off with a deluxe dessert of fruit cocktail and chocolate chip cookies. It was somewhat extravagant, having both cookies and fruit cocktail, but Miller assured Dunlop and Benton that they'd earned the extra chow that day. "So what happens now?" Benton wondered out loud.

"Same old shit, only deeper." Miller shook a c-ration can upside down till the last cookie plopped into his hand. His face became serious as if he were saying a prayer. He took small bites, chewing slowly, until half the cookie was gone. "Did you think they were gonna bring us back for a parade on account of what happened today?" He pushed the remaining cookie into his mouth and a satisfied grin spread across his face.

"I just thought maybe...." Benton's voice trailed off.

"Shit, man. Them fuckin' generals at Division love this kinda stuff." Miller rubbed a crumb from his goatee. "The CO gets on the radio and pumps up his body count, and they all go, 'Right on! Right on!' It worked exactly like it's supposed to work today. Nothing went wrong, not for them." He rolled a cigarette and let it dangle from his lip, unlit.

"But we're down seven guys! And that grenade hitting first squad..." Benton paused to think a second. "I can't believe they're going to leave us out here short like that. The CO just can't let that happen!"

Miller spat at the mention of the company commander. "That little tweek, all he cares about is makin' major. He'll get as many of us killed as it takes for his promotion." He lit his cigarette and kept it carefully cupped so as not to make their position a target. "Listen Bent, leaving us out here is exactly what they're going to do." Miller took a drag and let the smoke drift slowly from his mouth and nose as he spoke softly. "We're nothing but bait, my man." Dunlop and Benton looked at each other through the descending darkness. "The fuckin' Army dangles us in front of Sir Charles 'cause they know he can't resist." Miller finished exhaling the smoke and scratched his cheek. "We're a big fat company of American GI's. If Charlie could wipe us out all at once, it would be on the news back in the world that night and then there'd be shit in the streets the next day, maybe a few more congressmen wanting to pull out."

Miller went on, "But the Army's betting that ain't gonna happen. They figure we can get enough fire down on 'em before they get that many of us. Usually works, too. They always seem to run out of ammo first. The body count keeps growing, so they must figure there's some magic number of dead gooks to pile up and all of a sudden the rest of 'em will run up a white flag." Miller sighed. "Maybe they're right," he said with more than a little resignation in his voice.

"What was that?" Dunlop said and looked in the direction of a sound in the trees.

"Sounds like monkeys. There, up in that tree, can you see him, Spiderman?" Miller extended his arm and pointed his finger.

Dunlop squinted and looked as hard as he could, without success.

"This is the jungle, man." Miller chuckled. "There's all kinda weird animals here. Now if that had been Mr. Victor, the sound would have been at ground level. And then again, we probably wouldn't have heard a thing until he opened up on us." Miller chuckled again, joined this time by both Benton and Dunlop.

The dark was complete now, allowing the events of the day to fade into the young men's memories. The night-sounds were constant, and at times, intense; it depended on how many cicadas were hissing, how many early nightbirds screeched. The monkeys in the trees near Delta Company sounded like they were having either a terrible argument, or a great party. The air was still, cool, and damp. Dunlop noticed his forehead was wet with perspiration, and wiped with his arm. Almost Christmas, and it was going to be another sticky night.

"I'll take first tonight." Miller ejected the clip from his M16 and made sure it was full. "You guys try and get some sleep for a while, okay?"

"Sounds good to me." Dunlop turned over and brought his rucksack under his head. "Only make sure you wake me up if I start snoring too loud. I wouldn't want to disturb those monkeys, they might decide to attack."

Dunlop settled onto his poncho, which he had laid out in the shallow foxhole they had dug for the night. "Hey, Benton," he said.

"Yeah?"

" Hey, man, don't come rolling on top of me again tonight, okay?"

"Aw, I'm sorry, man." Dunlop listened to Benton's voice in the darkness and bit his lip to keep from laughing. "It's just that I'm used to sleeping with my brothers at home. Know what I mean?"

"Not exactly." Dunlop started laughing. "You mean in the same bed, or what?"

Dunlop and Miller had a good laugh at Benton, who turned over and became quiet. Dunlop turned on his side and closed his eyes.

CHAPTER VIII

A New Use for Av-Gas

It was still dark as Tom Kelly dressed for the work day at Fort Lewis. December was usually dark, cold, and wet in Tacoma, especially at 6:30 in the morning. He had to locate his clothes mostly by touch.

"What time is it, Tom?" asked Kelly's new wife, Becky.

"I was trying to let you sleep, babe," he said, then dropped one of his boots with a resounding clunk. "Goddammit," Kelly muttered.

"Maybe you should turn the light on, sweetie."

"OK." The light revealed a pile of olive drab clothes and a pair of black boots next to Kelly on the edge of their bed. He grunted and pulled on his pants.

"Do you have time for breakfast?" Becky sat up. "I can fix you something."

She's such a cutie, Kelly thought as he checked his pockets for wallet and keys. *Especially that sweet butt*, he mused.

"Thanks, but it's 6:30 already, so I'll just go on in and get some coffee in the Mess Hall, before formation," Tom said as he laced his boots.

Becky had come up to Tacoma from California the week before, after Kelly decided it was a good bet that he would be staying at Fort Lewis for a while. It was looking more and more like the Army had decided not to send him to Vietnam. Kelly suggested that perhaps he had become too valuable as a garbage man to risk losing him in Vietnam. The newly-married couple found a nice apartment off base that was a short commute to his company barracks.

"What are you up to today, Becky?" asked Kelly.

"Well, I'm going to try and get to the laundromat," she said as she parted her long brown hair and pulled it back away from her face. "Then I've got an appointment with the nursing school director that I told you about."

"Oh yeah," he said. He pulled his Army cap on and zipped up his fatigue jacket. "Good luck at the nursing school, Beck."

"Thanks," she said and smiled. "I'll probably have a pretty good idea if they're going to accept me or not after I talk to them today."

"Let's fall in, gentlemens!" Sergeant Swanson called out to the ninety-six olive-drab-clad young men. The men, as usual, ignored Swanson's first few orders to assemble before he cut loose with his Army-command voice. Until then, they circulated among their squads, telling stories of hot dates, settling debts and sharing the latest news and jokes about the Army.

Many of the soldiers wore gloves, and those who didn't blew into their cupped hands to stay warm. Rain fell gently on the porch roof sheltering the soldiers, and the first weak light of dawn was barely visible in the cloudy sky.

"GENTLEMENS!!" Swanson bellowed. That did it, each soldier assumed his rightful position in the 543rd Supply Company's formation. "Before y'all go to work this morning, I got a couple announcements." Swanson waited a few seconds 'till everyone was absolutely quiet. The E-7 Sergeant looked over his troops. His appearance, in stark contrast to the other soldiers was impeccable. From his gleaming boots to his starched Army baseball cap, Swanson was an impressive sight; one strac sergeant.

"Your battalion commander, Major Hadley, wants y'all to know that losses at the logistics center, your place of work, are increasing at an unacceptable rate." The sergeant paused for a moment and glared at some fellows in Kelly's platoon who were playing a little 'grab-ass.' When the offenders noticed they were under the sergeant's scornful gaze, they quickly ceased the disturbance. Swanson returned his eyes to the front of the company. "Last month alone, two million dollars worth of parts and tools mysteriously disappeared from their rightful owner, the United States Army." Swanson hardened his gaze. "Gentlemens, THIS MUST STOP TODAY!"

Swanson stood and glared at the men for a full minute, while most of them quietly laughed and giggled at the plight of the "Green Machine" losing track of its tools.

Swanson took a breath and began his second announcement. "Your brigade commander will be visiting the 543rd tomorrow, Saturday, for an inspection at 0900!"

Groans, curses, catcalls and a few caustic remarks came from the group in response to the news. Everybody's Saturday would be pretty much ruined.

Over the chorus of disappointment, Swanson went on. "This will be a full inspection, gentlemens. Dress greens and weapons, no exceptions!"

When Swanson left, Kelly walked out to the parking lot behind the barracks where the shuttle bus waited to carry the soldiers to their duties at the Logistics Center.

Gunner Fernley, a member of Kelly's platoon, came up to him.

"Kelly, you lucky son-of-a-bitch, you're going to your family housing job tomorrow instead of standing inspection, aren't you?"

"Every day, Gunner." Kelly smiled at his black friend. "Gotta pick up that lifer garbage, keep their yards clean, you know."

"Sheeit!" said Fernley.

"Hey, say hi to the Colonel for me, will ya?" Kelly smiled and spun around to start his walk of six blocks, to report for work at the post family housing office

Kelly and his work partner, Benny Lester, met daily at the housing office. They had a route thru the family housing area on the base to collect trash. Kelly liked Benny and thought he was quite a character. Benny was the current AWOL champion at Fort Lewis, having left post without permission sixteen times in the thirteen months he had been there.

"Benny, what's wrong?" asked Kelly as he approached the desk of their boss, Sergeant Major Dennison.

Lester looked at Kelly and quietly said, "Busted."

Oh shit, Kelly thought. *They figured out what we've been doing, playing around and not picking up any garbage.*

"Private Kelly," Dennison said, and looked up from the paperwork on his desk. "I have no idea what you two have been doing with the Army's truck every day, but I can tell you what you haven't been doing," he slammed his fist on the desk, "and that's your job!"

"Yes, Sergeant Major," Kelly meekly replied.

"Kelly, Lester," Dennison angrily looked from one to the other, "You men are to report back to your companies." He paused for a moment, his lip quivering. "You are both fired!"

"Sarge, I don't know if this is such a good idea," Kelly said.

"Kelly," said Sergeant Greenly, "You're a good, strac troop, and I've got faith in you to come through on this for me." Greenly was Kelly's current platoon sergeant. A likable man, Greenly was fifty-two-years-old, and had been in the Army for twenty-eight of those years. He possessed a kind face with just a hint of the red nose and sunken cheeks that come from too many years drinking the Army's cheap beer at the NCO (non-commissioned officer's) club after work.

"You're sure there isn't some job I could do instead of the inspection?" Kelly pleaded with his sergeant. Greenly had been very cool about Kelly being fired, not letting the news rise any higher in the leadership of the company than himself. "Sarge, I'm about as far from being ready for inspection as a guy can be!"

"Kelly," Greenly said over his shoulder as he started to walk toward the orderly room, "formation is at 0700 tomorrow, and inspection is at 0900. I'm counting on you, soldier!"

Kelly stood in place for a few moments, shaking his head. "Fuck," he muttered.

Kelly felt a strong sense of dread. His brigade commander, Colonel Longmire, a full bird colonel, was inspecting a guy two places from Kelly in the line. The rain had stopped and the sun had come out making the brass and silver on the Colonel's uniform glisten. *I am so fucked*, Kelly thought. And then, boom, Colonel Longmire was standing in front of him, resplendent in his dress greens. The silver eagles on his shoulders conveyed the tremendous authority he had over the sad sack troop in front of him. He was about the same height as Kelly, and looked him right in the eye. The disdainful expression on Longmire's face greatly heightened the unpleasantness of the moment for Kelly.

Kelly looked terrible. His uniform was dirty, wrinkled and fit poorly. He had cut himself while shaving, and Becky had to chase him out the door that morning with a piece of tissue paper to stem the bleeding. Kelly felt himself wilting under the Colonel's glare.

"Let's see that weapon, soldier!" barked the Colonel.

Oh God! Kelly thought, and handed his M16 to Colonel Longmire.

As he looked into the barrel, Longmire's face turned beet red. "Private Kelly," he screamed, "When was this weapon last cleaned?"

"I… I don't recall, sir," Kelly stammered.

"Oh, private, you don't recall?" Longmire raged. "Well, it may interest you to know, soldier, that there is no light visible through the barrel of this weapon." He lowered his voice and looked at Kelly with complete disgust. "It would not surprise me if the next time this weapon is fired, it exploded in your face, you miserable excuse for a human being!"

Longmire threw Kelly's M16 at him and turned to the 543rd commander with the rifle clattering to the ground. "This inspection is over, Captain Wilcox!" Longmire stormed off, got into his waiting car, and left.

Kelly picked up his M16, while his commander, Captain Wilcox, and all the lieutenants and sergeants from his company glared at him.

"Greenly says it's OK for you to take off now, Kelly," said PFC Jacob "Jake" Weydemeyer.

He'd been in the Second Squad, Third Platoon of the 543rd since Kelly had arrived from his training company two months before. Kelly liked the guy, who was from Minnesota and always seemed ready for a prank or a joke. His black-rimmed GI glasses framed intelligent eyes that always seemed to glint mischievously.

"Eight o'clock, huh?" Kelly looked at his watch. "Becky's going to think I got sent to Nam or somethin'."

"Didn't they let you call and tell her you were going to be late?" Weydemeyer asked.

"No, man." Kelly shook his head. "They just told me to come up here and wait." He pulled a cigarette out of his pocket and lit up. "I figured I might be goin' to jail," he said and exhaled the smoke from a generous puff.

"Jail?" Weydemeyer said with a grin, "Nah, they just want to pretend like it didn't happen, man." He reached down and pulled a cigarette out of Kelly's pocket. "Really, Kelly, I could not fucking believe it when the Colonel looked down the barrel of your M16." He laughed out loud. "I thought he was gonna have a heart attack or somethin', right there!"

"Shit," Kelly said, "I'm sure the guys I rode in with this morning are long gone."

"Ah, don't sweat it, man, I'll get you home." Weydemeyer lit up the cigarette he had bummed off of Kelly. "Go call your wife, and tell her to give us a half hour or so." He puffed on his smoke with a satisfied grin. "We gotta stop and get some gas on the way to your place."

"This the way to the gas station?" Kelly asked. They had turned away from the Fort's main gate where the only on-post gas station was located, and were now heading toward the sprawling Fort Lewis Air Field, home of three helicopter squadrons and two fixed wing groups.

"It's the way to <u>my</u> gas station, Kelly." Weydemeyer said, as he rolled past the airfield guard station and tooted his horn. The fellows up in the tower both waved and Weydemeyer waved back. "I knew all those chopper guys in Nam." He pulled up to a large fuel-storage reservoir and hopped out. Opening the trunk of his car, he then placed the nozzle from a hose attached to the fuel reservoir into a tank inside the trunk.

Five minutes later, Weydemeyer put the nozzle back on its holder, hopped back in, and started the engine. "That's a two-hundred gallon tank in my trunk. I filed down the heads and timed the engine for av-gas." Stopping by the towers as they left, he beeped and waved at his buddies and continued out the gate of the airfield. "I can make it from here to New York, without stopping." He looked over at Kelly with a grin. "Whadaya think, man?"

"Weydemeyer, I gotta say, this tops anything I've seen since I've been in the Army."

"Just wait, man," Weydemeyer said as they cruised onto the freeway. "You ain't been to Nam, yet."

CHAPTER IX

An Ancient Village

AFTER THE FIREFIGHT, THINGS SETTLED INTO A DULL ROUTINE FOR Delta Company. Alpha and Charlie Companies had doubled back on their routes for a day and assumed their positions protecting Delta's flanks. It wasn't possible for Dunlop, or anybody else in Delta, to see the guys from the other two companies in the battalion, but the knowledge of their presence was comforting.

On Christmas Day, division flew in a bunch of c-ration cookies and pound cake with little red ribbons tied around them. Word was that the Donut Dollies, women volunteers with the Red Cross, had brought Christmas to the troops in the field, tying each of the ribbons by hand. Dunlop thought it was kind of nice and enjoyed the extra cookies while everybody made fun of the little ribbons.

Lizzard said that he would much rather have one of the dollies wrapped in a red bow, since he had already eaten more than enough c-rations to last him the rest of his life. "But, you can't never get enough snatch," Lizzard said.

The battalion's route proceeded north from An Khe, up the Song Ha River Valley. The plan, according to Third Platoon Leader Lt. William Winston III, was to continue upriver about fifteen miles and then turn southeast toward Kontum, another ten miles overland. They expected to arrive in Kontum around the end of January, where they would get on trucks and drive south to Pleiku and then west over Route 19 and back to An Khe for a week's stand-down at Fourth Division base camp.

★ ★ ★

DAY TWENTY-SIX

According to Fast Eddie Miller, Winston was not such a bad guy. For a lieutenant, that is. He was Third Platoon leader, in overall command of First, Second, Third, and Fourth Squads.

Rollie Peterson and Winston walked back to Miller's section of the company line to march with Second Squad. The four platoons of the company had separated for the day, each following a different tributary of the Song Ha River.

"How's it goin', Winnie?" said Miller with a nod. "Hey Rollie."

"Okay if I join you guys?" said Winston.

"My favorite lieutenant's always welcome in Second Squad, far as I'm concerned," said Miller.

"Sounds like it's time to shove off, fellas." Miller stood and adjusted his pack straps. He picked up his M16 and commenced his daily slog. The others followed.

"So, Winnie," Miller looked backward toward Winston for a second, "what's this I hear about you bein' a college boy, huh?"

"Well," said Winston, "I went to Santa Clara University for three years, but I never finished my degree." He ducked under a low branch hanging over the trail. "I took a trip to Europe during my senior year, and then the Army grabbed me." He brushed some of his long, dark brown hair out of his eyes and back under his helmet, revealing his handsome, boyish face.

"So how did you wind up an officer?" asked Dunlop, from behind Winston.

"I finished the ROTC course, and the Army really needed second louies. So…"

"Gotcha," said Dunlop.

"Anyway," continued Winston, "I figure I get a year's paid vacation in sunny exotic Vietnam." He chuckled. "I just love this shit, don't you guys?"

Dunlop, Benton, Peterson, and Miller joined in the laughter, but they all tried to hold the noise down so as not to alert any bad guys nearby.

"So if we only gotta hike about twenty-five miles, and we make three or four miles a day, how come it's gonna take us six weeks to get where we're going?" Benton asked as he walked, directing the question to Winston.

Leave it to Benton, the only guy in the platoon still fat after four months training and a month in Vietnam, Dunlop thought. *All he's worried about is how far he's gotta walk.*

Miller chuckled at the new guy's ignorance of Army ways.

"Hey Bent, turn the volume down a little, will you?" Dunlop turned around and faced the young man from Minnesota, his M16 pointing upward. "We should be trying to be a little quiet, don't you think, sir?"

"Shit, I don't know. Why ask me, I'm just the fucking L-T." Peterson elbowed Winston, grinned, and shook his head. "Look Benton." said Lt. Winston. "Here's the deal. We're out on patrol. That means we're looking for trouble. We're sort of following the river, but every time we come across a tributary with a trail along side, we follow it and see what we can flush out." Winston leaned to cross over a tree trunk that was blocking the trail. Once on the other side he turned back toward Benton. "We'll probably end up humping a couple hundred clicks, at least one hundred and twenty-five miles, by the time we reach Kontum. Serpentine, get it?"

"Yeah, I guess so." Benton didn't sound too happy, but then his lightly-freckled, pudgy face brightened. "Hey, when are we stopping for lunch?"

Dunlop rolled his eyes.

An hour later, the line came to a halt. Miller, Winston and Peterson looked serious and alert, their eyes scanning the jungle cover for signs of danger. Winston pointed to Peterson and silently signaled him to get up to the CO and find out what was going on. Peterson nodded and was off, gracefully vaulting rocks and limbs in his path. Rounding a bend in the trail, he placed a hand on the arms of some troops as he passed, then disappeared from sight.

"What's going on?" Benton whispered. Winston looked at Benton and raised a finger to his lips.

"Probably a vil." Winston looked ahead. "We'll sit tight till we hear from Rollie."

Vandyne, Dunlop, Benton and Miller stood guard at the downriver edge of Ak Minh, a small village of rice farmers who worked the fields. Their assignment was to watch the trail and make sure they weren't being followed by bad guys. Winston and the rest of the company continued into the center of the little river hamlet, then fanned out in groups of three or four searching for evidence of VC activity. Dunlop could see the green helmets of the Delta soldiers, bobbing up and down as the soldiers scoured the area.

"What do you guys think?" Benton said to no one in particular.

"About what, Freddie?" Dunlop asked.

"Well, here we are at an enemy village."

"We don't know this fuckin' vil is VC." Miller cut in.

"Well," Benton said nervously, "it might be, and if it is, we could be hanging way out on a limb here if something started. What makes you think it's safe, Miller?"

Eddie Miller inhaled deeply, pushed his helmet up off his forehead. "Look guys, this vil has probably been here a thousand years or so. That's a long time before any VC might of showed up, right? Besides, we just saw some boys down by the river old enough to fight. They'd be off getting ready to ambush us somewhere, if the place was VC. Ever since Tet a couple years ago, there's been a lot less activity around here. What I heard from guys leaving when I first got here was we killed just about the whole Viet Cong during that fight. Pretty much all that hits us now is NVA, like last week."

"I hear they got a lot of our guys too, during that Tet thing." Benton folded his arms and warmed to the topic. "One of our AIT instructors told us about a company-sized patrol that left base camp one night where only two guys made it back, and one of them was wounded pretty bad."

"What do you think, Miller?" Dunlop scanned a tree line near the trail, shading his eyes with his hand. "We heard some of that same stuff at Fort Lewis. You think they were bullshitting?"

"When I first got here, it was pretty fresh in everybody's mind." Miller pulled out his pack of Bugler and rolled smokes for Dunlop and Vandyne. Benton, who wasn't hooked yet, declined Miller's offer. "What I noticed was, even the most hardcore guys had gained a lot of respect for Sir Charles. The way they told it, the VC fought like the craziest sons-of-bitches you ever seen. They held their positions and kept shooting until somebody finally blew their fuckin' heads off. They might have been exaggerating a little, but I don't think they were bullshittin'." He took a long drag off his cigarette, savoring the cheap smoke like it was the most expensive cigar you could buy.

Peterson came down the trail at a trot. He breathed heavily from his run through the village in the mounting heat of the day as he carefully surveyed the jungle in front of them, then turned to Miller. "How's it going, Bro?"

"Pretty quiet, Pete."

"OK if I grab Benton and Dunlop? CO wants the new guys to get some experience at interrogations."

"Don't see why not." Miller extended his Bugler package toward Peterson.

"You rolling?"

Miller chuckled and began rolling Peterson a cigarette. "The Lizzard and I can hold the fort here, right Lizz?"

"Fuckin' A, man." Vandyne kept his eyes on the area in front of them, his M16 at the ready. His hands were shaking a little, but his jaw was set.

"Okay, Benton and Dunlop, you guys come with me. And stay alert on the way, okay? You never know when we're gonna come across something."

"Right." Dunlop and Benton answered, nearly in unison.

As the three men walked through the village, Dunlop felt excitement and curiosity, but also slightly embarrassed. It reminded him of when he was at a party back in Sacramento one time and he wandered off to a part of the house where he really wasn't supposed to be. These were people's homes they were passing, open for his viewing with nobody around to maintain their sanctity or guard their treasures.

The huts, or hooches, were arranged at irregular intervals along a narrow curved trail that paralleled the river about two hundred feet away from a steep bank that fell to the water. Chickens and ducks wandered among the huts and across their path, getting underfoot to the point of tripping Benton, his arms and legs flailing amidst much squawking, quacking and clucking, and not a few ruffled feathers. A couple of squealing pigs cut across the trail in front of Peterson, the larger one chasing a small one and nipping at the little guy's butt, drawing blood. The little pig dove beneath a log for safety and Dunlop smiled at the narrow escape as he reached to help Benton regain his feet.

Many of the hooches had untended cookfires smoking, with bubbling pots held over them on tripods. The pleasant odors of fish, vegetables, and oil tantalized the young men, reminding them it was almost lunch time for them, too.

After they had passed half a dozen dwellings, the center of the village came into sight. The rest of Delta Company, except for those posted as guards around the outer perimeter, had gathered next to one hooch along with about twenty villagers who had been found at their homes that morning. Most of the soldiers were standing in small groups, smoking and leaning on their rifles. A couple of the groups were enjoying bullshit sessions, laughter erupting at regular intervals.

The villagers were clad in traditional peasant garb: loosely fitting black pants and tops that looked like pajamas to the American GI's, along with the wide-brimmed conical hats farmers in Vietnam wore to protect themselves from the relentless sun. There appeared to be an equal number of very young and fairly old. Men, women and kids were lined up in front of a group of Delta Company's senior soldiers. The faces of the villagers told Dunlop little of what they were thinking or feeling. They all seemed to be gazing somewhere in the distance and not having anything much to do with one another.

Sergeant Richard Potter, the first sergeant of the company, stood next to Captain Welby and Lt. Winston. Potter, Winston and Welby conferred in low, serious tones a few steps in front of the sullen villagers. Sergeant Frederick Moore, the staff sergeant for Second Platoon, was talking to an elderly Vietnamese man with one hand on the man's shoulder, and the other holding a paper with what looked to be messy, hand-written notes on it. The old man was looking at the ground, his chest heaving with each breath he took.

Dunlop leaned toward Benton and said quietly, "This doesn't look like it's going to be a lot of fun, man."

Benton raised his eyebrows and shook his head back and forth a couple of times.

Just then, a loud eruption of laughter came from under a banana tree a few yards from where Dunlop and Benton were standing.

"That Sergeant Flowers, he's a real comedienne, isn't he?" Benton said to Dunlop.

Sergeant Damon Flowers, leader of Third Squad, First Platoon, stood with six men from his squad under the banana tree a few yards away from the interrogation area. Flowers had been in Vietnam for nine months. He was a big guy, and extremely popular in the company. He was a fine soldier and a kind man who had received his sergeant's stripes because of courage and competence under fire, as well as his natural leadership ability.

Flowers entertained his buddies with a steady stream of jokes they seemed to enjoy immensely. Third Squad had become the place in the platoon where most of the black soldiers, including Sgt Flowers, had gravitated. Cigarette smoke hung above them in a cloud beneath the canopy of the banana tree, giving the appearance of an impromptu GI jungle party.

"Hey, Flowers!" Sergeant Moore held the sheet up near his mouth to cup his voice as he shouted. "Your squad is supposed to be guarding these people while we conduct interrogations." Moore was a by-the-book soldier who kept his hair cropped short, and always had clean and pressed jungle fatigues to wear every day, even in the boonies. He never seemed to miss the opportunity to bully any Vietnamese people he encountered.

"Yeah, Sarge!"

"I hate to be a party-pooper, but would you please be kind enough position your men near these prisoners so that if one of them tries something, it might be noticed and acted upon before one of us gets killed?" Moore spat the words, barely containing his contempt for the Third Squad revelers, who weren't exactly under his command, since they were in another platoon. Sweat dribbled down his red face in large drops, causing him to squint as he shouted. Dunlop tried to imagine one of the cowering farmers in front of him "trying something" and let out a small quiet chuckle.

"Right, Sarge!" Flowers shouldered his M16 sling, and the other men from his squad followed suit with ample grumbling and muffled comments. Without haste, Third Squad moved out from under the tree and over to the villagers waiting silently in the sun. Flowers positioned his men at intervals around the group of Vietnamese and took up a position himself, near Sgt Moore. The tall athletic sergeant spread his feet slightly and held his M16 pointing up with the butt of the weapon resting on his canteen as he stood facing the villagers. Dunlop thought he saw Flowers roll his eyes when their gaze met for a second.

"Dunlop, come over here, please." Moore pointed to the ground in front of him, as though Dunlop, a mere PFC had to be shown where "here" was. Dunlop walked over next to Moore and waited.

"Here, take notes for me." Moore handed Dunlop the paper and pencil from his pocket. "Find something to write on."

Dunlop looked back at Benton to ask for help, but Benton raised his hands and shook his head as he took a step backward. Dunlop looked toward Peterson, but Peterson's attention seemed fixed on something down by the river. Dunlop shrugged his shoulders, squatted and laid his M16 across his lap so he could use the rifle butt as a small table to write on.

Satisfied, Moore turned back to the old peasant who had begun to shake and breathe even harder. He grabbed the man's shoulder again and began shouting questions at him in rapid succession. "How many VC? Where VC now? When VC here?" The peasant grew more agitated with each question and began moaning. He looked up fearfully at Sgt Moore, who towered over him by close to a foot. Moore removed his helmet and used his sleeve to wipe his sweat-soaked forehead as he considered his next move.

Dunlop busied himself with writing down Moore's futile questions when he heard the unmistakable sound of flesh striking flesh as all the villagers began wailing and moaning. He looked up from his paper to see Moore's arm raised over the old man, ready to strike again. The old man was now kneeling in front of Moore and appeared to be begging the Sergeant to release him. Blood was dribbling down the man's chin as he repeated a Vietnamese phrase, over and over, and clutched at the bottom of Moore's shirt.

Moore looked angry, confused and frustrated. His face was red, and he had begun to shake a little. He turned as Sgt Potter approached him. "Top, you got any suggestions? All this guy does is keep muttering some Gook bullshit at me. Maybe you can get him to talk."

Sgt Potter, or "Top", the customary nickname for company first sergeants throughout the Army, was a wizened veteran of the Korean war and an early hitch in Vietnam, back in the Kennedy days. He had retired to a reserve unit in 1964, but then decided to return to active duty in 1967 after finding civilian life not much of a challenge.

Top was respected by everybody in the company. Draftees and lifers, officers and enlisted, everybody had something nice to say about Sgt Potter. Miller liked to tell the story about when his mom was sick in the hospital and Top had gone against regulations to get him back to California to see her before she died. It would have been the end of Potter's long career if Miller hadn't returned to the company before they left for a planned mission. He made it back in time, and Top never asked for anything in return.

Top smiled softly at Sgt Moore as he placed his arm around his shoulders. "Listen, Sarge. I really don't think we're going to get anything out of these people. None of them speak English or French, and the place just gives me the feeling that nothing much is going on. What do you say we just pass out a few packs of cigarettes, and march on out of here with the alliance intact?" Moore hung his head and nodded in agreement.

That evening after the platoons had rejoined and Delta had set up its perimeter for the night, Dunlop, Peterson, Miller and Benton huddled under their ponchos, eating the last couple of cans of chocolate cookies that Miller had magically produced from the bottom of his rucksack. They had humped for three hours after leaving Ak Minh when Captain Welby called a halt for the night. It had been a little early to stop, but everybody's butt was dragging in the rain, and the men were grateful for the break.

"Man, I sure wish I could have hopped on that slick back to An Khe with ol' Top this afternoon." Sgt Potter had been called back to An Khe to handle something that had come up. Dunlop wiped cookie crumbs from his mouth and looked over toward Miller who was keeping an eye on the tree line along the river a hundred yards away, his rifle at the ready. "Eddie, are all the patrols like this one? This really sucks, you know what I mean?"

"Yeah, Spiderman, I know." Miller's tone was flat, and he kept his gaze on the tree line. Warm drizzle had started just as D company left Ak Minh, and it didn't look like it was going to let up any time soon. The temperature would probably drop enough that night to chill the soaked troopers.

Delta Company's soldiers were bone-tired. So far, the operation had amounted to twenty-six days of constant walking in eighty-degree heat with sixty pounds on their backs, followed by chilly, damp nights. Gnawing fear gave Dunlop a constant feeling like a lump of burning coal, deep in his gut.

Up to this point, there was little to write home and brag about. They had lost three dead, one of them from friendly fire, and four wounded. The last serious wound had happened to another poor devil from First Squad. The guy stepped on one of the dreaded anti-personnel mines the VC left like deadly calling cards all over the place. His left leg was blown off at the knee and his right leg and groin hadn't fared much better. Ironically, this same guy had taken over the radio after the grenade incident that killed Silverman, the last radioman.

"That was bullshit back in the village today." Benton said

"What's the matter, Bent? Don't you realize what a dangerous enemy that poor old fucker was?" Miller looked away from the river and towards Benton. "Just be glad we got guys like ol' Moorsie, who aren't fooled by that innocent old peasant disguise the VC likes to hide behind."

"I thought I was going to puke when I heard him whack the old guy." Dunlop took a long, deep drag on the heroin-laced cigarette he had purchased from Lizzard that afternoon. This was his second time smoking heroin, the first being a week ago. He promised himself not to do it every day, and certainly not to become addicted. But the high he experienced from inhaling the heroin smoke was pleasant and relaxing, and got his mind completely away from the war. It was hard to resist.

Dunlop wrapped his hands around his bent knees and leaned back against the tree they had chosen for shelter. "I think I got a spatter of the old man's blood on my shirt for Christ's sake." He reached around to point to a small brown patch on his sleeve above the folded cuff. Taking another drag on the cigarette, he closed his eyes and drifted off to a deep and pleasant sleep, far from Vietnam.

"Hey Spiderman, wake the fuck up, will you?" Benton was leaning over close to Dunlop's ear so he wouldn't have to raise his voice. Peterson, Benton, and Miller had decided to let Dunlop sleep in, since they figured he'd be pretty groggy from the drugs he had done the night before. But it was getting toward time to mount up, and he was still in his poncho, snoring like an old dog.

Dunlop began breathing more quietly and started to stir. All of a sudden, he sat up and pushed his poncho away with one arm, using the other arm to rub the sleep from his eyes. "What's happening, guys?" Dunlop looked around and saw that the others had their gear all packed and were ready to go. "Did I miss breakfast?"

"Old Man sent word to be ready in fifteen. You best get a move on, troop." Peterson pulled back the bolt action on his M16, checking the firing chamber for debris and the slide for proper lubrication one last time. He then released the safety, held the weapon in the air and pulled the trigger. As he heard the resounding click of a well-functioning mechanism, he nodded with satisfaction then reached down and picked up a c-ration can of cookies. "Here you go, man. We kept a can of your favorites out so you could munch while we hump." He smiled, extending his arm and making a throwing motion to gain Dunlop's attention, then tossed the can, which Dunlop caught with both hands.

"Thanks, Pete." Dunlop placed the cookies down on the ground next to him and began quickly folding his poncho. "Where's Fast Eddie and Lizzard?"

"They went to get some more clips and grenades. Had a supply drop, first light this morning." Peterson said, picked up the clip in front of him, blew the debris off the top rounds and slammed it home into the rectangular magazine on the bottom of his rifle.

"So, what's up for today?" Dunlop asked as he lit a cigarette, took a deep drag, and set it down on a rock next to him. He continued to gather his things. The rain had stopped and the sun was out, giving Dunlop a renewed sense of hope about life.

"You know, SOS--Same Old Shit, only warmed over and piled higher just the way we like it. They're gonna put us on slicks this morning." Peterson rubbed his bristly chin and Dunlop thought he noticed a tic in the sergeant's face again, like when he was helping him pack at the beginning of the operation. "They want to drop us a few miles up river. God knows why. And, oh yeah, I heard they decided to cut the operation off a little sooner than we expected. We should be back to An Khe for standdown in about a week."

"Peterson, that's great fucking news!" Dunlop's eyes brightened as he cinched the strap on the top flap of his rucksack, lifting it over to stand against a tree next to his M16.

"Yeah, if we can just get everybody through the next week in one goddamn piece." Peterson stood and stretched, then picked up his steel helmet and put it on. "You watch your ass for the next few days, will you partner? I've seen guys get a little overconfident after a few weeks out here, then bam! They never knew what hit 'em cause they got careless when they thought they had it all figured out."

"Don't worry about me, Pete." Dunlop reached down and picked up his morning smoke, flicking off the ash at the end. "I know I'm still green as the jungle here, so I'll be paying careful attention to you and Miller whenever you got something to say to me."

"Well, what I'm saying to you now is, 'Keep your head up all the time, man.'" Peterson slung his M16 over his shoulder with the barrel pointing down and out a little. "And you might want to think about laying off those funny cigarettes, at least 'till we're back in base camp.

Dunlop looked down and said, "Yeah, you're probably right about that."

CHAPTER X

January 9, 1970

"MAY GOD HAVE MERCY ON HIM AND HIS MEN…"

SIX DAYS AFTER AK MINH, D COMPANY HALTED FOR THE NIGHT on a ridge a thousand feet above the Song Ha River Valley. Word was they were up there to find a good landing zone (LZ) for the slicks to come in and pick them up for the ride back to An Khe. The water below was a distant roar and the air was noticeably cooler than the soldiers were accustomed to while plodding along the valley trail. The operation was coming to an end within the next day or two, and between the relief in temperature and the anticipation of being back in the relative safety of base camp, the troops felt almost like they were heading back to the world.

"Winston says the Old Man is gonna send out an ambush tonight." Lizzard showed up just as the necessary digging for their perimeter position was finished.

"Hey Lizz, how do you always manage to make yourself gone until we get the work done?" Dunlop asked, a note of exasperation in his voice. Benton, Dunlop, Miller and Peterson were covered with dirt except for rivulets of sweat on their faces, arms, and bare chests

"Planning, Spiderman, careful planning." Lizzard gave his buddies an ingratiating smile and sat down on his steel pot.

"So what the fuck is this about an ambush on the last night of the patrol?" Dunlop wiped the back of his neck with a filthy cloth from his rucksack as he directed his question to Peterson.

"The CO needs to get his body count up or he's got no chance of making Major next year," Peterson said. "He's already been passed over for promotion once. If he flunks again, the Army will send him home to his momma in civvies and he'll have to find himself a real job."

"I thought we killed a whole bunch back in that firefight a couple weeks ago." Dunlop said.

"We only found firm evidence of half a dozen kills that day, and Captain Welby has to share credit with Alpha Company," Peterson said.

"Alpha!" Dunlop exclaimed. "Where the hell did they come from? I thought they were way out of position, nowhere near us that day."

"Fuckin' A," Miller joined in, "but we wouldn't want the CO's little buddy in Alpha to get in trouble for being lost, would we?"

"So, when it comes right down to it," Peterson said, "Welby's only got one scalp to drag back into base camp. Remember that Gook we wasted on the trail? And shit, that guy probably didn't even have a gun on him." The sergeant spat to the side and picked up his rifle.

"So poor old Captain Welby. He wants to get his promotion, and we have to go out and maybe get our asses shot off tonight," Dunlop said waving his hands for emphasis, then looking around for a moment, 'till he found his shirt and put it on.

"Well, not exactly," Lizzard said. "Third Squad's got the bush tonight, and Flowers ain't in no mood for much walking around. He says he's going to take us out a couple hundred meters, then call in after a while and say he's out about eight clicks, waitin' for Sir Charles."

Lizzard looked behind to make sure no one else was close enough to overhear, then lowered his voice to a whisper. "It's going to be partytime out there, gentlemen. I got some really fine hash, and a few of those fancy ciggs. Why don't you guys volunteer to come along? We can celebrate the end of the patrol properly, if you know what I mean." He grinned and looked at each of the fellows in turn.

That night, the perimeter was set up and the ambush was out. D company's soldiers were settling in for a last night of tension and watchfulness before standdown back at base camp the next day.

"Did you guys hear that?" Spec IV Sam Brubaker whispered to his three buddies at firing position three on D Company's defensive perimeter.

Brubaker was from Pittsburg, PA and very near the end of his year in the war. He was so damn short, he never tired of reminding anyone who would listen, that he had to reach up to tie his boots in the morning. Twelve days and a wake-up, then he was out of Nam and back to the world. It was understandable that he was a bit jumpy on this, the final night of his final patrol.

"Powers, get over to the CO and let him know we got some possible bogies out about two hundred, maybe two hundred and fifty meters." Brubaker spoke quietly, with confidence and force. "Shit, there it is again. Man they're slippin' in here to give me a fuckin' send-off, I can feel it." He checked the belt feeding his M60 and found plenty of extra ammunition with every fourth round a tracer to direct his night fire. "For Christ's sake, Powers," he whispered, "don't just stand there like some FNG, get going and be quick and quiet about it!"

Five minutes later, Powers was back at position three. "Gelhorn from position two was at the Command Post when I got there. They heard it too." Powers stopped a moment to catch his breath.

"So what's the deal?" Brubaker turned away from his machine gun and looked at Powers without smiling. His face and fatigues were filthy. He leaned over slightly and spat.

"Captain Welby's all fired-up and ready to unload on whatever's out there. But Lt. Winston's saying it might be the ambush screwin' off instead of being out where they're supposed to be."

"Aw, fuck...." Brubaker reached down and checked his extra ammo belts again.

"Winnie's trying to get the guys out on ambush over the radio. CO says to hold our fire till we hear position one's 60 open up. Then we're supposed to give it all we got, out to where we heard them noises."

Brubaker turned back to his weapon, placed his finger in the trigger guard and looked into the blackness in front of him. "So, I guess we just sit tight for now."

The ambush party halted for the night about two hundred meters away from D Company's perimeter. Flowers led them down a gently sloping ravine through thick jungle to a small creek that looked like it emptied into the Song Ha River two or three klicks downstream. They set up for the night next to the stream in dense growth that Flowers thought would provide cover for the ten weary soldiers, four men from Third squad and three from First, along with Lizzard, Dunlop and Benton from Second, all of them in the Third Platoon. The air was cool a gentle rain falling coalesced into large drops falling off the broad leaves above, splashing on the men whenever a breeze came through..

Flowers figured his main job was to get the group through the night alive, and the best strategy would be to have them all go to sleep as soon as possible, avoiding any possible contact with bad guys. Sergeant Dennis Hargrove from First Platoon had wanted to come along, but Flowers politely declined his offer of help. Hargrove would never have gone along with Flowers' plan to scam the ambush. He was known for taking great pride in his kills and some even said he kept physical evidence of his deeds, like severed ears and scalps. Flowers wasn't sure about the sack of body parts Hargrove kept, but he knew he didn't want him along tonight.

"Hey Turk, you want a hit?" Lizzard extended his arm with a heroin-soaked Marlboro cupped in his hand.

"No thanks, man." Flowers sat with his poncho pulled down over his knees and his M16 resting on his shoulder, the barrel sticking out past his helmet. "I'm going to try and stay awake tonight, let the rest of you dudes sack out."

Flowers had been a popular young worker at a Cleveland, Ohio scrap metal mill for eighteen months after high school until, as expected, his draft notice had arrived. His coffee with cream complexion, square jaw and the dapper Clark Gable mustache had earned him the nickname "Turk."

Flowers went through the usual sixteen weeks of training, then received orders for Vietnam. His approach to the Army was similar to the way he had handled himself at the scrap mill; he worked hard and got his job done. He was fair with his buddies and, in return, well-liked and respected. An optimist at heart, he believed in God and country and fully expected to follow in his dad's footsteps and lead a decent, satisfying life.

After a few months in Vietnam, Flowers felt a growing sense of futility about the war. Which led him to a cynicism about his current life in the Army very unlike the positive state of mind he had long prided himself on. He found very little evidence that Americans were welcome in Vietnam. Accordingly, he decided to concentrate on keeping himself and his men alive, while doing as little damage as possible to Vietnam and the people who lived there. The interrogations at Ak Minh disturbed the young Sergeant considerably, leaving him even more uneasy about the war.

"Suit yourself," Lizzard said and took a long toke, inhaling deeply. "But I'm going to celebrate the end of this bullshit patrol, man." He spoke through gritted teeth, holding back his exhalation for maximum effect until, as if on cue, a cup-size splash of rainwater tumbled off one of the leaves directly overhead, soaking the front of his shirt and dousing the smoke.

Dunlop, Benton and a couple of Third squaders enjoyed a good chuckle at Lizzard's expense.

"Hey, I knew the Nam shits on you, but look at Lizzard. It just pissed all over him." Spec IV Raymond Balder, from Los Angeles, captured the moment well, as he often did.

Following a robust round of jokes and laughter, the men got down to serious partying. They passed their doctored cigarettes around, with fireballs glowing in cupped hands as each GI inhaled deeply and then handed off to the guy next to him.

"Uck ooo."

"Who said that?" Benton asked.

General chuckling at the question rolled through the group.

"That's a 'fuck you' lizzard, man." Flowers turned toward Benton, keeping his arms and legs under his poncho.

"Uck ooo, uck ooo."

"Aw, man, you're shitting me, right?"

"Naw, they're everywhere in Nam. They go around saying fuck you all the time."

"I don't think they like us very much," Dunlop commented in-between drags.

"Uck ooo."

"Hmm. I'll be goddamned."

"Go to sleep, Benton. And that goes for the rest of y'all," said Flowers.

"Uck ooo, uck ooo."

After a few minutes of quiet, some of the men had started to sleep. The Prick-25 phone squeaked like a rude visitor, signaling a message from the company. Balder, who was carrying the radio for the night, began to reach for the phone but before he got to the handle, Flowers whispered, "Balder!"

then waved his hand and pointed to himself. Recognizing the wisdom of Flower's decision with a nod, Balder laid back on the ground, wrapped himself in his poncho and waited his turn for another toke. The phone squeaked again as Flowers picked it up and heard Sgt. Moore address the CO in the same groveling tone he used whenever he spoke to one of his superiors.

"Captain Welby, Lieutenant Winston's got 'em on the horn, sir."

Lt. Winston handed the phone over to Captain Welby who turned the volume up so Winston could hear his conversation with Flowers.

"How's it going out there, Sergeant?" Welby spoke in more of a whine than a command. This childlike tone of voice, together with his youthful and unbearded face, had earned him the nickname of "Boy Wonder" among the troops.

"OK, sir. Haven't seen anything yet, but we just got here a few minutes ago."

"And your men are prepared for the enemy, I assume."

"Yes sir. We got our claymores out and I've positioned the men in twos on one side of a trail down here in the valley. I figure we're about eight klicks out from the company, sir."

"Eight klicks, uh, that's fine Sergeant." Welby spread his feet and hunched over like a quarterback bracing for an onrushing defensive lineman. "We've had some reports of activity on our perimeter, about two hundred meters out. Lieutenant Winston thought one possible explanation could be your ambush group got lost out there and maybe doubled back close to us without realizing it. Any chance of that Sergeant?"

"No sir, uh…, I don't believe so. We climbed down the canyon and followed the river quite aways."

"Fine, Sergeant. You keep your men alert tonight, and I wish you good hunting."

"Yes, sir. Thank you, sir."

"Shit!" Flowers placed the telephone back in its cradle. "Balder, help me wake these guys up." A tone of near panic was in Flowers voice. "We gotta move fast!"

Balder rolled over, barely awake. "Whas' up, Turk?"

Flowers reached over and shoved Balder on the shoulder. "Ain't no time for whas' up, bro." Flowers was crouching on his feet now. "Everybody got to wake up right away and we gotta stay quiet like we dead, or else we might be. Then, we got to get the hell outta here." He duckwalked among the men, shaking each one awake, and then shushing them with a finger to his lips. *Dear Lord, help us through this one*, he prayed.

Captain Welby handed the phone back to Lt. Winston, who set the instrument into its cradle. "Sergeant Moore, alert the rest of the perimeter, then have position one open up with a ten second burst from their M60, with tracers, two hundred meters out and dead in front of them. Then have one, two, and three give it everything ..."

"But sir!" Winston interrupted. "What if the ambush is really out there at two hundred meters and Sergeant Flowers is either confused or maybe just faking it?"

Welby turned toward Winston, his jaw set, his excited eyes lit up behind his oversized, black-frame glasses. His pink boyish face made it hard for Winston not to laugh at him. "Body count, Lt. Winston, body count. I have an enemy force moving on my perimeter and I intend to kill them. If Sergeant Flowers was lying to us about his patrol's position, then may God have mercy on him and his men, because I certainly won't."

What an asshole, thought Winston.

"Everything they have Sergeant." Welby turned back toward Moore, who was breathing heavily and looking a little frightened. "Numbers one, two, and three, their 60s, 16s and 79s for a full minute, right after the initial burst."

"Yes sir!" Moore took the radiotelephone and spoke softly into it, warning the rest of the company to expect firing on the southern side of the perimeter. He took his red filtered flashlight from his belt, and flashed it twice toward position one. A stream of fire leapt from the barrel of Brubaker's machine gun, taking a certain and deadly path to the hiding place of Flowers and his men.

Without waiting for the end of Brubaker's initial salvo, the others in the three firing positions opened up-three M60s, six M16s, three M79 grenade launchers and Rick Shawnasee in position two, who concentrated on firing his favorite L.A.W. anti-tank rockets. The darkness of the night exploded into flames in front of the perimeter. The noise was so overpowering that it was impossible for the men to concentrate on anything except their own weapons and ammunition, and the baseball diamond-sized patch of jungle two hundred meters in front of them where they firmly believed a deadly enemy lurked. Lethal rounds pored onto the area in a blazing sheet of hot lead for a full minute. Just before they stopped shooting, the inner plungers could be seen through the metal of the barrels, pounding back and forth like pistons from hell. It seemed to Winston that it would be hard for even an ant to survive the barrage, let alone a human being.

"Cease fire! Cease fire!" Moore boomed. He took it upon himself to time the fire and stop the men at the one-minute mark set by Welby. His order was echoed by soldiers from each of the engaged positions who called out, "Cease fire!" The M60s with their long ammo belts, had neared their limit for continuous fire as the chambers glowed red and translucent.

As the last couple of rounds were squeezed off by one of the M16 riflemen, Bellucci, the third radioman of the patrol, rushed over to Lt. Winston and handed him the phone. Bellucci stood ashen-faced as Winston listened in horror to Sgt. Flowers' description of the carnage.

"Winnie, we got seven guys down and I'm pretty sure four of 'em ain't gonna make it!"

"What the hell's going on, Flowers?" Winston yelled into the mouthpiece. "Did you guys get hit by NVA, or what? And give me your exact position so we can get you guys some help!"

"We're right in front of the company," Flowers spoke in a low monotone, trying to contain his panic. Winston could hear moaning from the wounded in the background. "Guys weren't in any shape for another ambush tonight, so I took 'em out about two hundred and fifty meters and told 'em to sack out." There was a brief pause, "You guys just… hit us."

"Oh my God," Welby muttered, and wandered off to the other side of the perimeter. He sat down by himself, well away from the command post.

"Sit tight, Flowers. We're getting the medic out to you guys right now, and we'll have the dustoffs in as soon as we can." Winston motioned at different soldiers to come over to where he stood. He placed his hand over the mouthpiece. "That's Flowers out there, right in the middle of that piece of jungle we just fired up." Brubaker and the three others standing in front of Winston looked stunned. Waving his arm in the direction of the stricken ambush group, Winston yelled, "Get out there as quick as you can and see what you can do to help until the choppers get here!" The men responded immediately, running full-tilt toward Flowers and the others. Winston turned his attention back to the radiotelephone. "Just tell everybody to hang in there, alright?"

"Right sir," Flowers answered quietly, before clicking off.

Lt. Winston handed the phone to Belluci. "Get me division." He turned toward Miller, who had run over from his position on the other side of the perimeter. "I guess the CO finally got his body count."

Miller, who had not volunteered for the ambush because of an upset stomach, looked at Winston with wild eyes. Winston shook his head in disgust.

The day after the ill-fated ambush D company returned to Fourth Division base camp at An Khe. After jumping off the slicks the troops walked in small groups toward the company tent area. No one looked up as they passed brigade headquarters with the Ivy Division colors hanging proudly next to the Stars and Stripes. Normally, there would have been a brief assembly for the brigade commander to congratulate the men before releasing them for a few days' rest at base camp, but this was hardly a normal return from a normal operation. Delta Company's men were dragging ass today.

Peterson and Dunlop walked slowly down the dusty path toward Third Platoon's tent. They were still weighed down by the equipment they carried on the patrol, including their weapons.

"We can check in the claymores and grenades after lunch," Peterson said.

"Where'd they take Benton?" Dunlop asked.

"They fly the dead guys to division and log 'em in there. Then they stick 'em in bags and send 'em to cold storage in Saigon until there's enough to fill a plane for Travis in California." They came to their tent and Peterson pulled back the door flap. Both men retreated from the blast of hot air coming from the oven-like interior. "Shit, they really oughtta' leave these flaps up when we're out in the field." The two soldiers stepped inside the tent, walked over to their squad area and laid their gear on their bunks. Peterson sat down and took a long drink from his canteen, then looked over at Dunlop. "Benton's probably in a cold stack of bags at Tan San Knat, waiting for a plane. One sure way outta this shithole, I guess."

Dunlop sat down gingerly on his bunk, across from Peterson. He nodded, keeping his mouth slightly open and squinting with his one good eye. The other eye was nearly swollen shut, along with much of the right side of his face. A bloody bandage on his left arm protected a flesh wound he had sustained the previous night.

"Hey troop, you look like dogshit," Miller said as he strode into the tent, followed by Lizzard.

"Yeah, Spiderman, you best get over to the Aid Station." Lizzard tossed his gear on the dirt floor and collapsed on his bunk. He made it through the previous night's events unscathed, adding to his already considerable reputation for good luck. He had a boyish, handsome face and, except for the nervous and darting eyes, the guy seemed impregnable. "Man, you'll come down with an infection, sure as hell, you don't get some antibiotics, and soon." Peterson nodded in agreement as Lizzard spoke.

"I guess you guys are right." Dunlop stood up, patting his pockets to look for a smoke. "I'm gonna go check on Flowers, then I'll get on over to the Aid Station and have 'em take a look."

Peterson took an open pack of cigarettes from his shirt pocket and held it out toward Dunlop. "Keep 'em." Dunlop took the pack and Peterson folded his hands beneath his head for a pillow. "Flowers is gonna get busted back to Spec IV."

"Figures," Miller said, a note of contempt in his voice.

"I stopped at battalion on the way over here." Peterson's eyes were closed as he spoke.

"What'd ya find out, Pete?" Miller propped himself up on an elbow.

"Well, the CO just went straight to his room and shut the door. I guess he's off the hook. You know, honest mistake and all that." Peterson grunted slightly and cleared his throat. "The company lost five guys-three dead and two on their way to Japan for surgery." Peterson took a deep breath and let it out. " Benton got shot in the head, and Third squad lost Wallace and Huffaker. Hillman and Grabowski from First squad are the ones headed for Japan. Word is they'll both make it, but won't walk again. Grabowski'll probably end up blind." He paused for a moment. "We're fuckin' lucky that Turk moved everybody just before we opened fire. Before they got hit, they'd managed to get to the edge of the kill zone. If they'd stayed where they were, probably they'd have all been dead."

"Son-of-a-bitch," Lizzard said quietly.

"Other than busting Flowers, it looks like they're going to sweep it under the rug, make like it was a real firefight." Peterson fell silent for moment, staring at the tent ceiling. "And you want to know something really weird? Flowers is gonna stay in charge of Third squad."

"No shit?" Said Dunlop.

"Yeah, word is that Winnie insisted on it. Said he was the best man available for the job."

"That fuckin' Winston is okay, you know?" Miller said. "

Dunlop gently probed his swollen face, a smoldering Marlboro between his fingers. "I guess I'll see you guys at dinner, unless they keep me at the aid station."

"Don't worry about your shit, man. We'll take care of it if you gotta stay over there." Lizzard said.

"Hey, thanks."

The three wished Dunlop good luck. He walked over to Third squad's area, and past Flowers who was stretched out on his bunk, deep in the sleep of physical and spiritual exhaustion. He hadn't even bothered to unlace his muddy boots. Dunlop ducked as he left the tent.

CHAPTER XI

January 10, 1970

"YOUR PUNISHMENT IS, YOU GOTTA GO TO VIETNAM"

PFC TOM KELLY STOOD WITH HIS HANDS AT HIS SIDES IN A CASUAL approximation of the attention position, along with four of his fellow soldiers at Fort Lewis. The expressions on the GI's faces gave away little of what was on their minds. They had been told at morning formation to be in their CO's office at the end of their work day and Kelly figured he and the others knew pretty much what was up.

Kelly was starving and exhausted from a heavy day's work at the Logistics Center. He felt rumpled and dirty in his GI fatigues, a marked contrast to the crisp and authoritative appearance of his commanding officer. He decided to concentrate on looking as unconcerned as his four black friends.

Captain Wilcox was pissed off. He stood behind his desk and studied a sheet of paper that seemed of great importance to his command, the 543rd supply company. Finally, he looked up and fixed his gaze on the five silent soldiers in front of him.

"You men have made a giant mistake with this, this...."

"Petition, sir," Kelly interjected.

"Yes, ah, petition." Wilcox swung his gaze onto Kelly. The Captain's pale pinched face was expressionless, except for his upper lip, which curled slightly. "That's correct, Private Kelly," he said slowly.

Wilcox returned his attention to the other four men. "This paper may seem innocent enough to the casual observer." Wilcox raised his fist to his mouth and cleared his throat. "One might even say that there is some merit to the opinions stated," he continued, hitting his stride like an angry minister in the middle of a sermon. "I'm sure that you four men had honorable motives for promoting this...this document." His body language made it clear which men he was addressing now, and Kelly could see that he was not one of them.

Kelly knew the other soldiers on the carpet with him were just as responsible for the success of the petition as he was. All young black fellows, they felt strongly about a punishment that had been slapped on one of the brothers in the company. It was unjust and unnecessary, and typical Army harassment with an added racial twist.

Private Daniel P. Wilson had not cleaned a toilet to the satisfaction of one of the lifers. When the Sergeant discovered Wilson reading a book instead of cleaning the toilet for a third time, Wilson was assigned to a humiliating punishment detail that extended well beyond the day he was supposed to get out of the Army.

The absolutely worst thing that could happen to any GI was to have his E.T.S. (estimated time of separation) date extended, especially when he was short, like Wilson, with only a month to go. That was a big mistake on the part of the Army.

The petition had been Kelly's idea and Gunner Fernley, one of the four guys now in the Captain's office with him, had run with it. Fernley quickly wrote a statement and organized a dozen GIs, all black, to take copies around the fort and ask their fellow soldiers to sign them in support of Wilson. Kelly had not expected much would come of his petition, but he thought it was worth trying. For Kelly, it was mostly something to brag about at an upcoming Progressive Labor Party meeting for local GI members. Nobody was more surprised, or worried, than Kelly once the ball got rolling. Theoretically, they could all go to jail for a long time.

Altogether, one hundred and nineteen signatures were collected over four days. At the headquarters building, the same five young men gave the petitions to Major Hadley, their battalion commander. Wilson's punishment was rescinded the following morning.

"But despite the obviously good intentions in this statement," Wilcox went on, "I wonder what you would say if I told you that one member of this group in front of me is neither a good soldier, nor a good American." He looked slowly at each of the first four, avoiding Kelly, then placed the petition on his desk. The faces of the enlisted men on the carpet remained blank. "As a matter of fact, I have received reliable information that Private

Kelly, here, has joined his country's enemies and become a communist." Wilcox uttered the last three words in a slow whisper then he smiled slightly.

"What do you say to that, Private Washington?"

"I don't know about communists sir," Washington answered, "I was mostly worried about Wilson."

Silence for a few moments.

"What about you, Gallon, anything you'd like to add to what Washington just said?"

"No sir." Gallon's lips hardly moved and his eyes appeared fixed on an object behind and slightly to the left of Wilcox.

"Fernley?" Wilcox seemed a little less sure of himself now.

"No sir." Fernley looked straight ahead respectfully. "We was wantin' to help Wilson, sir."

"And you, Private Thibeau." Captain Wilcox set his jaw and leaned forward toward Michael Thibeau from Louisiana, his thumbs and fingers pressing on his desktop, "What do you think about the fact that Private Kelly is a self-proclaimed communist?"

Kelly closed his eyes and tried to concentrate on what Becky had fixed for dinner the night before-cheeseburgers, his favorite.

Thibeau switched his hat from one hand to the other, sniffed, and said, "Well sir, I guess I would say that if all communists do like Kelly, then I'm probably one myself."

Wilcox slipped a little on the desktop, then straightened up and set his jaw. The five men stood around the Captain in silence.

Kelly was talking on a pay phone outside the barracks at the Fort Lewis Vietnam Replacement Center. It was after midnight on a cold and wet January night. The rain was constant, but not heavy. A steady drip had formed off the brim of the bush hat he had been issued that day, and his new jungle fatigues were feeling cold and damp after twenty minutes of standing outside next to the unsheltered telephone.

"So, everybody gets off okay except for you, and your punishment is: you gotta go to Vietnam. Is that about it?" Kelly found it incredibly comforting to stand there in the damp and cold and listen to Becky talk. To him, her voice had a rich and sincere feminine quality, like a gentle Aretha Franklin song.

Becky had been at work when he got home from the fort the previous evening. By the time she returned to their apartment, he had already fallen asleep. This was their first chance to talk about the events of his day leading up to the phone call from the Vietnam Replacement Station.

"Yeah, I guess that's the deal." Kelly kept his hand over the mouthpiece and spoke in a soft voice to avoid being caught by the guys on guard duty. He wasn't supposed to be making a call at this late hour.

"I snuck out early this morning, Beck. I hope I didn't wake you up."

"I slept 'till nine. Never heard a thing when you left. Thanks HB."

"I was early for morning formation, so I got a chance to check on the guys."

"Everybody OK?" asked Becky.

"Yeah, everybody was there with the usual blank stares. You know, another day in the Army." Kelly cleared his throat. "Like... ho-hum."

"That's good, Tom."

"For sure. Maybe no repercussions for anybody."

"That would be just fine," said Rebecca.

Kelly sighed. "Yes, but five minutes before it was time to climb on the trucks and head for our jobs at the Log Center, I got called to the CO's office and handed my orders for Vietnam. Wilcox gave me the papers personally, with a snide grin on his face."

"Oh...," said Becky.

"Yeah, and then he says, 'I hope your commie friends take good care of you over there, you miserable traitor.' I just stood there motionless for a second while it felt sorta like my entire insides had vaporized."

"My God, what an asshole!" said Becky.

"You got that right, Beck," Kelly said. "And dammed if I was going to show any fear in front of that bastard." Kelly chuckled. "And so went the day for your favorite PFC," he said. "Lots of paperwork, waiting, inoculations, waiting, getting jungle fatigues and boots, waiting, and then more waiting." He stopped talking for a moment and lit a cigarette.

"Jesus, Tom," Becky said. "This is all really happening, isn't it?"

"Yeah, babe," he took a drag on his smoke. "Seven pm, I finally got to the Replacement Center." He chuckled and added, "Missed dinner."

"Oh, Tom, you're hungry, aren't you?" Becky said. "I hope you can get some sleep tonight."

"Don't worry, Beck," Kelly said. "The center's got a late hours snack bar. I grabbed a cheeseburger and a beer, then I went over to the dayroom." Kelly laughed quietly. "Just a bunch of GI's in jungle fatigues waiting to go to Vietnam. Spent the evening watching Star Trek reruns and shooting pool until it was time to call you, sweetie."

"So what happens next, HB?" Becky asked.

"Well, every couple of hours or so they announce a new bunch of guys for a flight. My name went into the hopper tonight at about eight o'clock, so I'll probably be on a plane by noon tomorrow."

"Oh...."

"Yeah, I know," Kelly replied. "I'm sorry, babe, but I don't think we'll be seeing each other till I get my R&R over there." He stretched his neck with the phone still at his ear.

"What's R&R, Tom?"

"Rest and recreation, it's where they give you a little break from the war. A lot of the married guys meet their wives in Hawaii for a few days. How does that sound, sweetheart?"

"Hawaii, huh? Well, if you're going to be there, I guess I could manage to squeeze some time away from my busy schedule. But you gotta promise me, big guy, that you'll arrive in one piece, okay?"

"I promise." They both fell silent for a moment, and then Tom said, "Hey, you're going to finish your nurse's training, aren't you?" Becky had been accepted into a Licensed Practical Nurse school soon after arriving in Tacoma. She had eight months left to complete her program, and they had both agreed that it would be a valuable skill when she was done. "Don't worry," Kelly said, "I'll send you my pay. I hear there aren't too many exciting things to spend it on, anyway." They both chuckled, each of them aware of the stories of cheap sex and drugs for sale to the GIs in Vietnam.

"I guess I can stick it out." Becky's voice sounded a little down, "But I might try to visit my mom next month. I bet I can talk them into a week or two off, given the circumstances."

"That would be a nice break for you, babe."

"So HB, what's going to happen when you get there?"

"From what Frank said in his letter, you hang around Saigon for a few days, then they send you to a line unit and you start humping the jungle for a year. When I get to the Replacement Depot in Vietnam I'm going to try and talk them into sending me up to Dunlop's unit."

"That's a great idea!" Becky said, as her spirits seemed to brighten. "And Tom, you gotta promise me, the war is not your personal responsibility. Just be careful, and leave the petitions to us over here, okay?"

"Hey, they're going to call me get-a-long Kelly." He smiled. "I'm gonna let the Vietnamese fight their own war and just keep my young ass out of the way."

"HB, I really have to get some sleep now, and so do you."

"Yeah... okay, babe."

"Keep your eyes open and your head down over there, big fella."

"I will, Beck. Goodnight."

"Goodnight, sweetie."

Chapter XII

One Way to Get Out of Long Binh Jail

"I WANT THIS FOOL OUTTA MY JAIL!" MAJOR THELONIUS WATKINS' strident voice was surprisingly high for such a large and fearsome looking man. He had worked hard throughout his eighteen years in the Army and had done well for a black soldier. He had risen from the ranks to his current post as Commander of the US Army Stockade, Vietnam, located near Long Binh-known among the troops as Long Binh Jail or LBJ. A stay at Major Watkins' facility was considered to be about the only thing in Vietnam worse than humping the boonies with your unit.

After nearly a month at LBJ and the previous week in solitary, Pvt. Willie Tuggins was thinking that he just might be glad to get back to a line unit. Judging by what was being yelled in front of his cell, he figured his jail time would be coming to an end soon.

"But sir, we're looking into some very serious charges against this prisoner." First Lieutenant Darryl Johnson was red-faced as he spoke to his commanding officer. The anxious prisoner watched the two officers argue over his fate through a small window in the cell door normally used for passing meal trays. Only a thick metal door separated the three of them. Tuggins bent over to look out and turned his head from one side to the other to follow what was being said.

"Sir." Johnson's voice shook as he spoke. "I have two of my best men in the hospital from beatings that I believe this man encouraged other prisoners in this facility to administer."

"That's exactly my point, Lieutenant." Watkins' words were slow and precise, his expression a glare at the young lieutenant. The veins in his temples looked ready to pop out of his head. He was a large and powerful man, who reminded Tuggins of a massive bull named Bill that his father had purchased for breeding when he was a small boy. "I want this asshole outta here! And until that happens, you know as well as I do that this facility is going to be less and less under our control."

"He's right, you know." Tuggins interjected and both officers turned toward the prisoner for a moment with surprise and contempt curling their lips and distorting their faces. Tuggins smiled, trying to look as pleasant and respectful as he could.

"Sir, I cannot accommodate your wishes at this time, sir!" Lieutenant Johnson nervously fingered the large brass key ring hanging from his black leather military-policeman's belt. "If I were to do so, I don't believe that I would be in compliance with the code, sir," referring to the Uniform Code of Military Justice, the legal bible for military policemen.

This current uproar at LBJ began about a month before in a sleepy Mekong Delta village. Pvt. Willie Tuggins had the temerity to interfere with a couple of his fellow Ninth Division soldiers who, according to their account, were in the process of searching a peasant's dwelling. Tuggins marched them out at gunpoint and brought them to his CO, accusing the two soldiers of attempted rape of a civilian non-combatant. This had not been the first occasion when Tuggins' views had come into sharp conflict with others in his unit. This time he had received a three-month sentence to LBJ for his efforts.

For the first two weeks his stay in the notorious military prison had been largely uneventful. He had worked hard at blending in with the other prisoners. Wake-up was at 0500, for an hour of morning exercises under the watchful eyes of spit-shined guards who doled out verbal abuse while the prisoners sweated and strained. The rest of the day consisted of boring and repetitive work assignments. Scraping old wax off a floor with a dull razor blade for thirteen hours, or maybe cleaning toilets in the Officer's Quarter's with a toothbrush were common jobs. The food was much worse than what the soldiers received in the field. Meals were only a chance to sit for a while; no conversation allowed.

At first, LBJ seemed like a more regimented Basic Training, awful, but survivable. But then, Tuggins learned about beatings of prisoners, especially by a couple of vicious guards who worked the night shift. What appeared to trigger the extreme punishments was anything other than groveling respect and obedience toward the guards. So Tuggins organized the guys in his barracks to resist the beatings by administering some of their own.

The plan worked fairly well. The rough treatment ended for the most part, and the two worst offenders were put in the hospital. They served as an example to other guards that they were dealing with human beings and not animals. To no one's surprise, Tuggins was removed from his barracks and placed in a vacant wing of the facility, used for overflow solitary confinement when the main "hole" was full.

But then, a letter arrived from a South Carolina congressman, with a copy to Willie, inquiring about Pvt. Tuggins and urging Major Watkins to take steps to ensure fair treatment and safety for this prisoner. Pvt. Tuggins, the congressman wrote, was the son of the Reverend Joseph Tuggins, an important community and church leader in his South Carolina congressional district.

The letter concluded with a paragraph informing the major of an upcoming congressional vote on a military funding bill and suggested that "by a generous interpretation of the section TIME OFF SENTENCE FOR GOOD BEHAVIOR in the UCMJ, Pvt Tuggins could well be released and back to his unit before this important vote."

Willie figured that Major Watkins could take a hint, so he watched the argument between the two men in front of his cell with just a touch of humor. He was fairly confident that the outcome would be in his favor.

"Lieutenant Johnson, what I'm suggesting here is in full compliance with the U.C.M.J." Watkins spoke so quietly that both Tuggins and Johnson had to strain to hear his words. He thrust a thick paperback book toward Johnson. "According to my reading, this prisoner is due for release today under provisions of the section in the manual regarding early release for good behavior."

Johnson turned away from Watkins and took a step toward Tuggins' cell door. As he sorted through the keys on his ring he said, "Sir, I believe that under your interpretation we would release Ho Chi Minh himself, if he were a prisoner in this cell today." He inserted a key into the lock and swung the door open. Watkins stood a few feet away with his arms folded across his broad chest.

Tuggins stood at attention in the open doorway with a grin on his face. "Lieutenant, sir, I believe Ho Chi Minh died last fall," he said as politely as he possibly could, "so you really...."

"That's enough, private!!" Johnson moved closer and positioned himself so that his nose was almost touching Tuggins' face.

Major Watkins bowed his head, brought a hand up to his forehead and muttered, "Jesus Goddamn Christ!" He spun around and marched crisply back up the hall toward the main prison, carrying the U.C.M.J. manual still open to the good behavior section. It's pages fluttered like a butterfly. "He's outta my jail by 1600, Lieutenant!" the major's voice echoed through the building just before he slammed the door shut.

Tuggins felt the spray of the Lieutenant's vituperation on his face as Johnson yelled, "Just shut the fuck up, until I can get your sorry ass processed out of here!" Johnson moved closer and banged his nose into Tuggins' right eye, "On the other hand," he reached to grasp the eighteen-inch nightstick attached to his belt, "just give me one more piece of lip, asshole, and I'll consider it an invitation to make it so that nigger father of yours won't be recognizing you for a while."

Tuggins blinked repeatedly as he replied, "Yes sir!" and struggled to restrain the grin on his face. "I mean, no sir!" He paused briefly to consider his words. "I mean, yes sir, I will cooperate with whatever you want me to do today." He then took a half-step back and gave Johnson the most ingratiating and respectful smile he could summon.

The lieutenant stood with his hand massaging the club. His slender fraternity-boy's face was twisted in rage and beet-red from his starched shirt collar to his crew-cut blonde hair. He breathed slowly and deeply as he glared at his prisoner. Pvt. Tuggins stood still, politely waiting for instructions.

CHAPTER XIII

In Country

IT HAD BEEN THREE HOURS BEFORE DAWN ON JANUARY 14, 1970 when Kelly and the rest of the sleepy replacement soldiers arrived from Hawaii at Tan Son Knat Airport, just outside Saigon. The stars were out on a lovely tropical night as the young men filed down the stairs from the plane. It was not possible to see much of Saigon through the wire mesh grenade barriers covering the windows of the military bus as it wound its way through darkened streets to the US Military Assistance Command Replacement Depot. The darkness mirrored Kelly's feeling of mystery and foreboding.

But in the mid-morning sunlight and two days after his arrival in country, Kelly was fascinated by the view through the wire mesh on his way to the airport where he would catch a plane north to Pleiku, and be processed into Frank Dunlop's battalion in the Fourth Infantry Division. It had not taken much talking to persuade the clerk at the Repo Depot in Saigon to change Kelly's original combat assignment to Third of the Eighth. The clerk told him that Dunlop's battalion had lost a few guys that week and needed replacements.

Must be at least ninety degrees, Kelly thought. The air was still, and smoky from outdoor cooking fires and the exhaust of thousands of darting motor scooters. *So humid, it's kinda hard to breathe*, he added to himself. People were speaking in an indecipherable, for Kelly, language constantly punctuated by loud laughter and movements of slender arms and hands.

Most striking to him were the young women lending their gentle beauty to the crowded cityscape as they rode about on their motor scooters. Most wore traditional black pants with a shirt extending to the ankles and then split to the waist on both sides. Conical peasant hats rested casually on their shoulders, held by drawstrings, and their blazing black hair bounced as they navigated the bumpy streets. To Kelly they looked like angels, riding invisible currents on their flowing gowns; beautiful, alluring, and modest, all at once.

It was difficult for Kelly to connect this fascinating city on such a fine morning to the brutal war going on not far away-a war he would be a part of all too soon.

The bus driver was a lucky Spec IV who had been assigned to Saigon for his tour of duty. He called out to Kelly, his only passenger, without taking his eyes from the murderous traffic. "That's the American Embassy on your left." The young driver honked his horn angrily at one of the ubiquitous pedicabs blocking their way. "And that corner over there is where that Gook got his brains blown out during Tet '68. You probably seen it on TV back in the world."

Kelly looked out through the wire mesh at the six-story glass and stucco embassy as they slowly drove by. A huge American flag on the roof drooped listlessly in the heat. He wondered what it had been like when Viet Cong fighters entered and almost seized this towering symbol of American power during the big Tet offensive.

Kelly mused about his connections with Progressive Labor Party as his military bus drove on toward the airport. They were kind of goofy, and a little cocky, and seemed to believe that they had the world's problems figured out. *Not likely*, he thought. Still, he really appreciated that PL insisted the anti-Vietnam War movement was open to working people, not just the privileged student elite.

During his layover in Hawaii, Kelly talked on the phone with John Diaz, an older member of PL. *Diaz was a nice guy*, Kelly thought. Diaz urged Kelly to keep his goals modest with regard to any anti-war organizing while in Vietnam. "Basically, Tom," Diaz said, "your main goal should be to try and survive the year, like everybody else over there." He went out of his way to wish Kelly well, and urged him to be cautious. Unlike some of the brash student types he encountered around PL, Diaz had been in the Army during the Korean war, and tried to organize his fellow GIs under actual combat conditions. He had been around the track enough times to know what a difficult and dangerous situation Kelly faced.

"If something comes up, and you feel comfortable about being able to protect yourself and the guys you're working with, go ahead and give it a shot." Diaz said "Just don't think you can pull off something like stopping the war by yourself, okay?" He concluded; "By the way, that business about your black friends up at Fort Lewis sounds like pretty good work, Tom." Kelly had thanked him and the two said good-bye.

Kelly's bus turned onto the long straight road that ran northwest from Saigon's central area to the Tan Sun Knat Airport. *Won't be long now*, Kelly thought, as the little van sped up.

Willie Tuggins sat on a bunk in an empty company tent and looked around, calm and satisfied. It looked like brothers slept here. Pinned to the cloth wall of the tent were girlie photos from Jet magazine and, as far as he could tell, every black Playmate that Playboy had published since 1965. One of his arms rested on his full duffle bag as he scratched the back of his head. *It's really fine to be out of jail*, Tuggins thought, *even if it is ninety degrees in here.* The tent smelled like damp canvass and the bunks had more rust than metal in their springs, but he didn't care. Nothing could possibly be worse than solitary at LBJ.

Roman Lister, the company clerk, stood at the tent opening. "That one you're on now, that's Flowers' bunk." Lister rested his clipboard on his leg. He pointed to the bunk across from Tuggins. "That one there belonged to Wallace. Why don't you grab it?"

"Wallace done with it?"

"Yeah."

"He go home?"

Lister shook his head

"He ain't gonna make it home?"

Again Lister shook his head. His expression was somber.

"Well, I guess he won't mind if I put it to some use...." Tuggins stood and lifted up his duffle bag.

"Right on, bro." Lister nodded, a faint smile appeared on his face. "Look." He glanced at his watch. "There's a couple hours before chow. Why don't you and me take a tour around camp?" When Tuggins didn't reply right away, Lister added, "Ain't much else for me to do, with the company out in the field and Brigade getting a new bird later this week," he referred to the spread-winged eagle insignia worn by full colonels.

Tuggins set his bag upright. "Give me a few to unpack."

"Great!" Lister raised his arm and pointed to a large, open-walled tent, fifty yards away. "I'll meet you over at the Mess Hall in half an hour."

"Right on," Tuggins grinned and brought his clenched fist toward his heart and tapped a couple of times.

Lister nodded, then set off in an easy athletic stride, tapping the clipboard against his leg rhythmically as he went.

Tuggins removed a pad of paper and a pen from his bag. He set the paper on his lap, snapped open the ballpoint and took a deep breath. He sat motionless for a few seconds then began to write.

Dearest Dorthy,

Well, your lonesome fella is out of LBJ! I guess that means I'm half-free. Oout of jail, but still trapped in the green machine. (smile) I got assigned to the Fourth Division, up in the northern part of Vietnam. The plane from Saigon went up the coast most of the way, and Dot, you would have loved to see the beautiful country. Long, white, sandy beaches and mountains that come right up out of the surf, with their tops covered in misty clouds. And God almighty, there's jungle everywhere, girl!

I hear that Fourth Division is a pretty good place for a brother. Of all the outfits over here, they're about the least gung-ho. I just met the company clerk and he's a bro from Durham. Imagine that! All the way over here and I start running into fellas from home. He's going to introduce me to some of the other guys this afternoon. I'll write to you and describe everybody I meet, you know I will. (smile)

I don't think it's too awful dangerous over here any more. My new outfit, (D company, Third Battalion, Eighth light Infantry Brigade) hasn't seen any serious fighting for almost a month now and from what I hear, it's the same all over the Central Highlands. But don't worry! I promise to avoid scrapes, battles, combat, etc. I ain't gonna play no hero, only survivor.

I think of you all the time, Dot. You are my inspiration when things look bad over here. I can't wait till we're together in our own home, with all this war stuff behind us.

I love you more than words can say.

Yours forever,

Willie

P.S. Can you believe what Daddy did with that congressman to get me out of jail? I'm sure I don't know the half of what went on, but I'm humbly grateful to a father who looks after his children like one of the Lord's angels.

As they walked past the D company mess tent, a pair of senior sergeants cast a furtive glance upon the eight black enlisted men standing together in front. It had been easy for Lister to assemble a group of black soldiers, cooks and clerks, to welcome Tuggins into the battalion. Word had gotten around that this was an LBJ veteran with a few stories to tell. *They must be worried that we're planning something*, Willie thought. He turned his attention back to the soldiers. "Bro, LBJ is most definitely a bitch," he said in reply to a question from one of the GIs. Finishing another story he said, "So we kicked a little ass on the screws, and they quit all that shit. But then they stuck me in solitary."

"How'd you get out so soon, Tuggins?" Lister asked.

Willie explained about the letter from his congressman and the scene in front of his cell with Lt. Johnson. He had them all laughing pretty hard as he tried to imitate Johnson's contorted facial expressions.

"Hey, man, I gotta go and catch up on a couple of things before time to eat. I'll see you all at chow." Lister started to walk away, but Tuggins raised his arms over his head and started some Dap. The other guys followed his lead of arm waving, hand slapping, and fist shaking that left everybody in a jovial mood as they dispersed back to their various work areas.

✶ ✶ ✶

"So they give you KP over here too, huh?" Tom Kelly and Frank Dunlop sat together on a wooden bench outside the kitchen area of the Mess Tent. Dunlop was wearing standard jungle pants, an olive drab (OD) t-shirt and a floppy bush hat. The front of his shirt was soaked with soapy water and grease, and his hands were clean and wrinkled. A small towel was draped over one of his shoulders.

"Shit, we wouldn't want the Army to lose money on us for the day, would we?" Dunlop picked something from his teeth, then spat.

"Your hands look like they been in greasy Army dishwater for a while, Frank." Kelly glanced at his friend. "And the rest of you don't look so good, either." He studied Dunlop's head. "What happened to the side of your face, man?"

Dunlop proceeded to tell the story of the ill-fated ambush at the end of the last patrol. "And that's about it," he concluded. He flipped his cigarette onto the ground and said, "They kept me here when the company went out this time, but the doc says I can go and meet up with 'em tomorrow." He stood and stretched his back. "Hey, why don't you come along? The other new guy that came in on your chopper from Pleiku, what's his name?"

"Tuggins, I think."

"Yeah, he and I are gonna catch the supply run in the morning. I'm sure they'll be glad to have another body out there, and it would give you a chance to meet everybody."

"Hey," Kelly smiled, "I don't even know where I'm gonna sleep tonight. And besides, you think I'll be ready for the war tomorrow?"

"We got plenty of room at our end of the tent. That Tuggins guy grabbed one of the empty bunks and you can have one of the others. We'll let em know in the morning where you're sleeping." Dunlop looked over his shoulder at the other KPs then glanced at his watch. "Don't worry about tomorrow; nobody is ready when they first get here. We'll get you set up first thing in the morning. The slicks leave at eleven, so we'll be out there in time for lunch."

"Sounds okay, I guess." Kelly laughed and shook his head, a little dizzy at the pace of things. "But what about your crazy CO? What do you guys call him, 'The Boy Wonder'?" Kelly shook his head again. "He sounds kinda dangerous."

A look of contempt came over Dunlop's face. "Don't worry about him. The L-T runs the company." He adjusted his bush hat. "Lt. Winston's okay, really. He's from your area, man. Went to college in Santa Clara."

"I'll be damned," Kelly said.

"Look, I'll be done here in about an hour. Why don't you go cruise around camp a little and meet me back here at 8:30? I'll get you set up and then tomorrow we can fly off on our big adventure."

Kelly looked over his shoulder to make sure nobody was within earshot. He wrinkled his brow, "Uh, when I caught the chopper in Pleiku, I mentioned your name and told the door gunner that you and I were buddies at Fort Lewis."

Dunlop's face was blank. "And?"

"Well, the guy got this big grin on his face and told me that my financial worries were over." Kelly folded his arms across his chest. "Now, what did he mean by that, bro?"

Dunlop looked down at his wrinkled fingers as he chuckled and shook his head, "That was a guy named Swartz you talked to."

"Yeah, I remember his name tag"

Dunlop pulled out a cigarette, placed it between his lips and lit up. "Swartz needs to learn to keep his fuckin' mouth shut." He inhaled deeply and continued, "I know I can trust you, Kelly. But Jesus, Swartz can't be goin' around telling everybody about our little business. Loose lips sink ships, you know?"

"Business?" Kelly now had a knowing grin.

"Er, yeah, business." Dunlop played with his cigarette. "I'm into high-end clothing sales, you might say."

"No shit?"

"Yeah," Dunlop said, "guys going home want to look good on that first date, so I got this arrangement with some fellas in the PX system. They order really fine stuff from Italy and then we steal it and sell it for half of what you'd have to pay at the PX. Works out great, man." He smiled. "I got $18,000 put away in a stash box."

Kelly's eyes widened. "Whoa!"

"You want in, man?"

Kelly nodded. "Sure, but look, I gotta go and finish taking care of some stuff."

"Okay, but be careful around a guy named Vandyne. We all call him Lizzard and, believe me, that's what he is." Dunlop took a draw on his smoke. "He's in our tent, so watch out if he tries to pump you for information about me. One of the clerks, a guy named Lister, told me he saw Lizzard and a couple of officers from Saigon in a meeting with the Boy Wonder. According to Lister, they were very interested in yours truly." Dunlop pointed to his chest with his thumb and smiled.

"Hey," Kelly said, "is it okay if I leave my bag here for a while?"

"Sure," Dunlop said.

Kelly leaned his duffel bag against a bench, and then wandered off into the warm evening, taking in the sights and sounds of a division-sized military camp at war in Vietnam.

As he strolled thru the rows of large canvas tents, daylight softened into evening. GI's loaded and unloaded supplies, choppers spooled up their engines in the landing area, and diesel trucks roared. Everyone he saw was dressed exactly alike in the same loose-fitting jungle fatigues; thin pants with plenty of pockets, shirts worn as jackets, with sleeves rolled up just past their elbows, and floppy hats that reminded Kelly of his uncle's fishing cap. These guys served as a constant reminder of the place and situation. *This is it pal, the Nam*, thought Kelly.

Kelly worked his way through the morning chow line, looking for something good to eat. He was surrounded by the sounds of clanging pans and cooks shouting at each other as they brought huge steaming trays and pots to the serving line. The throaty murmur of a dozen animated conversations reverberated in the Mess Tent along with occasional bursts of laughter from the different tables. The smell in the tent was a pleasant mixture of cooked bacon, potatoes, coffee and cigarette smoke.

As he moved past the servers, Kelly skipped the congealed mass of yellow goo that was supposed to be scrambled eggs and stopped to request a large bowl of oatmeal from the KP. Down the line he picked up a cinnamon roll and a cup of coffee. To finish off, there were brown sugar and raisins for the oatmeal. *Not bad*, Kelly thought.

Dunlop was already seated at a table, forking his food down like it would be his last meal for a while. The other new guy, Tuggins sat next to

Dunlop staring sleepily into his coffee cup. Kelly pulled a chair out and sat down. "Morning, men," he said.

Tuggins looked up from his coffee just long enough to give Kelly a slight nod and went back to staring sleepily into his cup. Dunlop stopped eating for a moment, took a drag on a cigarette and nodded, then returned his attention to his food.

Tuggins finished his last swallow of coffee. "Well, if you gentlemen will excuse me, I got some things to take care of before we leave this morning."

"If you run into any problems," Dunlop said as he wiped his mouth, "talk to Bailey, over at supply. He'll help you out."

"Yeah, right. I remember you saying something about him yesterday," said Tuggins.

"Don't bother with Wilbik over at the Weapons Room." Dunlop took a final drag on his smoke. "He's short and he don't give a shit."

Dunlop turned toward Kelly. "How'd you sleep, man? You were stacking some pretty good Z's when I got up, so I figured I'd let you zonk a while."

"I appreciate the hospitality, Private Dunlop," Kelly said in between mouthfuls of oatmeal. When both were done eating and lit their smokes, Kelly said, "Say, what's this third squad or second squad stuff about?"

Dunlop sputtered in his coffee as he chuckled. "They had me in Peterson's squad at first. That's the second. Now they got me in third with a squad leader named Flowers. It's the same platoon, with this lifer named Croix for platoon sergeant and Bill Winston, everybody calls him Winnie, our L-T. He's the guy I told you about from Santa Clara."

"Oh yeah."

"I was gettin' along fine in second squad, when this asshole lifer from First Platoon, Sergeant Moore, caught me with a doobie just before the company left on patrol." Dunlop leaned back in his chair and stretched his arms. "He said he was putting me in third squad so I wouldn't contaminate any of the real soldiers around here."

"What did he mean by that?" Kelly was curious now.

"Well, third is where most of the brothers in the platoon are." Dunlop took a drink of coffee. "Didn't bother me, though. Hell, I always seem to wind up with the bros, anyhow."

"Don't you think it's kinda racist for that sergeant to say something like that?" Kelly asked.

"Don't sweat it, man," Dunlop chuckled. "Third squad is cool. We've got a great guy in charge, and everybody just wants to cut a low profile and get out of this motherfucker alive. You'll fit in just fine, Kelly. You and all your politics-bullshit." He smiled briefly as he pushed back his chair and stood up.

"Sounds good to me," Kelly said.

"Come on, troop." Dunlop said, "We got a bunch to do this morning before we mount up."

CHAPTER XIV

January 17, 1970

ON PATROL

THE SUPPLY-RUN HELICOPTER ROSE FROM THE PAD AT FOURTH Division Base Camp with a roar so loud that the soldiers in the slick had to yell to make themselves heard. When they gained sufficient altitude, the pilot tilted the big bird's nose slightly downward and they swept forward in a graceful arc up and over the jungle and across the Song Ha River to their rendezvous point where D Company had set up it's mid-day perimeter. Kelly got his first real taste of GI Vietnam helicopter travel.

He had flown on a chopper the day before, out of Pleiku, but was too inexperienced and frightened to enjoy the flight. He sat scrunched against the thin aluminum skin of the war bird for the forty-minute flight to An Khe. Today was different. Dunlop and Tuggins demonstrated the fine art of sitting in the doorway of the cargo compartment, legs outside with their feet resting on the skid. There was just enough room for the three of them to squeeze into the opening, with the door gunner's M60 sticking out between Dunlop and Tuggins. Flying at three thousand feet and one hundred and twenty mph, cool air washed over the three young men as they were rushed to war.

Twenty minutes into the flight, Dunlop hollered at the other two and pointed downward. About a thousand feet below, an enormous jungle parrot soared on unseen air currents, and casually flapped its huge powerful wings. Kelly could not make out much detail, but he marveled at the bird's stunning colors. Its size was much bigger than any bird he had ever seen flying in California.

Minutes later, Dunlop called out again and directed their attention to a red flare descending slowly in the distance. Kelly looked questioningly at

Dunlop, who nodded and motioned that they were going in for a landing. *Well, here goes,* Kelly thought, as he glanced nervously toward the pile of weapons and ammo they had brought along.

Several of the soldiers from D company's Second and Third Squads had positioned themselves in a tree line for lunch break. Since the company had halted in a relatively safe area along a ridge, with plenty of cover and good downslope visibility front and rear, only moderate precautions against attack were deemed necessary. This afforded the men the opportunity to get the latest base camp news from Dunlop, and to meet the two new members of the company, Kelly and Tuggins.

The hungry grunts concentrated on eating for the first few minutes of the rest stop. The only sounds were p-38s opening c-rations and the gentle clink of spoons against the cans. Fast Eddie Miller had reaped a bonanza from the supply helicopters; a whole box of beans and franks along with two boxes of pound cake, twenty-four cans in each box. Some of the pound cake would be saved and used for barter later in the week with villagers, or maybe with guys from Second Platoon.

"That cake'll bring a good price in cigarettes or dope." Dunlop explained the fine points of the c-ration economy to Kelly.

Miller finished eating, leaned back against a rock and lit a cigarette. "So Spiderman, looks like you brought us a coupla FNG's".

"Well, one FNG. This here is Kelly, a buddy of mine from Basic and AIT. He just got to Nam." Dunlop looked at Kelly, "Ten days ago, right?" Kelly nodded. "And over here, we have our latest LBJ graduate, Private Willie Tuggins." Tuggins nodded and smiled.

"What they have you there for, bro?" Flowers asked.

"Well." Tuggins looked around, avoiding eye contact with the other GIs. "There was these two guys trying to rape this girl and I... I turned 'em in."

"And they put you in the 'J' for that, huh?" Flowers took a large bite of pound cake. "What happened to them other two fellas?" he said as he brushed crumbs from the front of his shirt.

"Nuthin'." Tuggins shrugged his shoulders and glanced away from Flowers. He looked as though he would just as soon get on to another topic.

"Figures," Lizzard spoke. "Green Machine always seems to get it just right, don't it now?"

"So, Tuggins, you have any good time over here yet?" PFC Steve Gage asked.

"Tuggins, Kelly, allow me to introduce Professor Steven Gage," Flowers said.

Gage was a black Third Squad guy whose regular assignments on patrol were storytelling and carrying the M79 grenade launcher. He had been an English major in college before being drafted, and his memory of the stories in the books he had read was truly astounding. He had lucked out and stayed back in the perimeter on the night of the ill-fated ambush at the end of the last patrol. This fortuitous circumstance had resulted in more than a little good-natured ribbing. He was known by the nickname 'Professor' because he wore metal-rimmed glasses and always carried a novel with him. He had a handsome, kind face and was considered a little on the serious side.

"I was in country for about three weeks, down in the delta, when I got busted." Tuggins answered Gage's question.

"Ninth Division?" Gage asked.

"Yeah." Tuggins nodded.

"I hear that's some shit down there." Lizzard was sitting and rocking on his helmet as he spoke. "All them rice paddies and all them fuckin' vills. I hear they get a lot more action than we do."

"You heard right, Liz." Flowers said, pushing his helmet up on his forehead, "You thinking about asking for a transfer?"

"Hell no, man." Lizzard smiled and shook his head. I'll take the good ol' Third of the Eighth do nothings any day."

"You guys seen much since you been out this time?" Dunlop asked, looking over at Flowers.

"Quiet as a mouse fart inside a wall, Spiderman," said Flowers.

From up ahead in the company, the sounds of soldiers getting ready to move out filtered back to the group around Kelly; canteen belts buckling, rucksacks swinging onto shoulders. Peterson got Flowers' attention and motioned with his head to indicate it was time to leave.

Flowers said quietly, "Let's mount up, guys."

As the group on the ridge stood and adjusted their gear, Kelly had a queasy feeling in his stomach. Dunlop walked over next to him.

"Just stay about ten feet behind me and do whatever the rest of us do. You'll be okay." Dunlop started off and Kelly fell in.

Peterson had been placed in charge of the ambush for the night. Nine soldiers from Second and Third Squad were positioned along a small stream with about a hundred meters of jungle to their rear and what appeared to be a little-used trail following the opposite side of the stream in front of them. According to Dunlop, there wasn't much chance they would be seeing any bad guys. "It would be way too open for them to come deedy-boppin' up that trail, over there", Dunlop said quietly to Kelly. "But then again, the fuckers never seem to come along where you expect to see them, so...."

"Hey." Peterson's voice was a loud whisper from the other end of the group. "Let's keep it quiet over there, Dunlop. You guys are advertising."

Dunlop lowered his voice. "That's Peterson, my old squad leader. He's cool. Winston put him in charge tonight on account of what happened a couple of weeks ago." He changed his position slightly and pushed a large dripping leaf from his line of vision. "I guess Flowers is gonna be in the CO's doghouse for a while."

"Hey, man, we're all gonna be in the shithouse pretty soon if you don't shut the fuck up!" Flowers whispered from Dunlop's other side. Dunlop smiled broadly and shook his head.

Silence fell upon the young men like a shroud. Kelly felt an uneasy loneliness, lying on the damp jungle floor with his rifle aimed and waiting for someone he prayed would never come. He tried to force himself to think of pleasant things from his past. Becky, other girls, sports, parties; nothing worked. Every shadow across the stream took on the form of a Viet Cong soldier, getting ready to shoot him. What a bitter irony to be killed by someone that he believed, in his bones, was in the right.

After about an hour in the damp silence, Peterson crawled over to Flowers' end of the ambush line. Kelly was startled when the squad leader suddenly appeared in front of them, seemingly out of nowhere. "Not much, huh?" Peterson squatted in front of Flowers and spoke barely loud enough for Dunlop and Kelly to hear.

"Looks like a lotta nothin' to me." Flowers answered as he sat up and pointed his M16 up and away from Peterson.

"Well, I was hoping it would be kinda quiet here." Peterson glanced back over his shoulder toward the trail on the other side of the stream. He turned toward Flowers, rubbed his chin, and then said, "Look, what the fuck do we care about Welby's body count?" He spat on the ground next to his boot. "What do you say we leave two guys awake at a time, two hour turns."

"That's fine with me, Pete." Flowers said. "But what about Hargrove?"

"Don't worry, I'll take care of the ol' Cong Killer. He owes me from a deal a few weeks ago, and besides, even Hargrove needs to sleep sometimes."

"Alright, man." Flowers chuckled. " Let's see if we can't get a little shut-eye then."

"Right, now let's make sure it's guys next to each other, so both will stay awake." The Sergeant turned toward Kelly.

As Kelly looked at Peterson in the murky light, he thought of pictures he had seen of the famous Mexican bandit and revolutionary, Pancho Villa. Same fierce black mustache, dark brown eyes and an air of danger. *Only this guy Peterson would eat Villa for breakfast. He's huge!* Kelly thought.

"Troop, you ready to watch our young asses for a couple hours tonight?" Peterson asked.

"I'll be okay," Kelly answered. He sat up when Flowers did.

Peterson cradled his M16 across his lap and turned toward Dunlop. "Alright, Spiderman, I'm countin' on you to keep the new guy awake." He rose to a crouch and began to move back toward his end of the line, then stopped and turned back to Kelly and Dunlop. "Flowers and Gage go next, and so on up the line, until Miller and me. That should get us close enough to first light, and then we'll shove off." Peterson unslung the radio-telephone from his shoulder and set it down in front of Dunlop. "Pass this along to the guy after you, just in case the company calls again."

"Right," Dunlop nodded.

"And Dunlop, no fuckin' smoke tonight. No tobacco, no horse, no nuthin." Peterson stared at Dunlop until he nodded assent.

"That's no bullshit, man," Flowers added. "I don't want to be sleeping next to no fireballs tonight."

"You guys get some rest," Dunlop said. "Kelly and me'll hold the fort."

Peterson quietly disappeared, back to his position at the other end of the string of soldiers. Kelly and Dunlop made themselves as comfortable as possible, sitting against a large tree. Their backs were slightly toward each other, so that their combined field of vision would take in the greatest possible portion of the surrounding jungle.

"So how's Rebecca?" Dunlop whispered. The two men had been silent for a few minutes to allow the rest of the guys time to fall asleep.

"She's doing okay." Kelly thought he saw movement across the stream out of the corner of his eye. He jerked his head around and stared in the vicinity of the motion, but saw nothing more.

"See something?"

"Nah, I'm just imagining things." Kelly brought the barrel of his rifle back upright and relaxed against the tree. "You know me, just itching for a fight." Kelly kept his eyes toward the patch of thick brush on the other side of the stream. "Becky's gonna stay in Tacoma and finish her nursing program. By the time she's done, I figure it'll be close to my R&R, so we're gonna try and spend a few days together in Hawaii before she goes back to San Jose and gets a job."

"Sounds bitchin."

Kelly heard a match flame, but saw only the briefest flash as Dunlop fired up a doobie.

"Hey Frank, you sure that's such a good idea?"

"Ah, nobody's gonna see nuthin'." Dunlop let out a large, satisfied exhalation. "These fuckers are all out for the count, and it don't look like the bad guys are too interested tonight."

A few minutes later, Kelly asked, "What about Elena? She have the baby yet?"

"Two days after Christmas."

"Man, that's incredible! Boy or girl?" Kelly scooted around and looked at Dunlop.

Dunlop took a deep drag, concealing the fireball in his cupped hands. "Boy, six and one-half pounds. I was in the field and didn't find out until three days after we got back to base camp."

"That's tough, Frank."

"Yeah, she wrote me this letter where she seemed all bitter about some stuff, and then told me about the baby toward the end. You know, "Oh, by the way...""

The two young men stopped talking and Kelly stared out at the menacing night forest. The only sound was the babble of a little creek. Every shadow seemed to be alive, taunting the young men. Finally Kelly thought, *What the fuck, I might as well relax.* He began to feel sleepy but the thought of nodding off on guard duty terrified him. He went back to wide-awake and scared.

A few minutes slipped by, then Dunlop elbowed Kelly without speaking. Kelly looked at Dunlop, who was pointing to the same area where minutes before Kelly had noticed something suspicious.

"You see that?"

"Oh fuck...." Kelly was able to make out the distinctive shapes of numerous helmets. It looked like thirty to forty of them, spread out in the tree line on the other side of the stream.

"I was hoping that maybe I was hallucinating from the smoke."

"I'm afraid not, old buddy." Kelly took a deep breath, "So what do we do now?"

"I guess we just sit here and pray." Dunlop paused for a few seconds, breathing heavy and fast. "Whatever you do, don't move your gun around. They're probably just as scared as we are."

It looked like they were facing about fifty unmoving enemy soldiers across the stream. And those were just the ones they could see. Flowers was snoring away next to them. *This is truly incredible*, Kelly thought, *our one hope is that they might laugh themselves silly over how stupid we look.*

After a few minutes of staring across the stream, Kelly began to think they might not die that night, maybe only get captured, as long as nobody woke up and did something dumb. *God, if only I had learned a little Vietnamese*, he thought.

Suddenly, numerous bright lights flashed onto the D company soldiers. Kelly squinted from the light in his eyes.

"What the hell is going on?" Dunlop sounded bewildered.

"American soldiers!" A voice boomed from a loudspeaker behind them. "Why have you come to our country to kill and destroy?"

Flowers woke with a snort and sat up with one hand shielding his eyes, the other reaching for his rifle. "Hey Spiderman." He stopped to clear his throat. "This a dream, right?"

"Flowers, I'm sorry, man, but this definitely ain't no fuckin' dream."

"I was afraid you'd say that...." He took his hand away from his M16.

"American GIs! For twenty-five years the glorious Vietnamese People have fought bravely for peace, land and the independence of our beloved country!"

The other soldiers woke up and sat in stunned, terrified silence as the voice over the loudspeaker thundered on.

"GIs, there is nothing for you in Vietnam! You should be home with your wives and sweethearts!"

"Oh, yeah." Dunlop muttered quietly.

"American soldiers! You must hurry and return to your beautiful homes before you are dead in Vietnam, where no one knows you!" The loudspeaker crackled for a moment. The sermonizing voice seemed to be weighing its next words. "You are very lucky Americans tonight. We will give you one last chance to save yourselves."

"Okay fellas, here's the deal we can't refuse," Flowers said softly.

"All Americans must lay face down with arms in front. Now!"

The men complied with the voice and lay down onto the moist jungle carpet of rotting leaves and dirt. Miller reached over and shook Hargrove, who had, so far, managed to sleep through the excitement.

"What's happening?" the startled Hargrove called out as he reached for his M16.

Miller grabbed the weapon at the same time as Hargrove. "Cool it, man." Miller's voice was commanding, allowing no room for opposition from the overly eager soldier. "Now let's just do like the man says and lay down."

Hargrove looked pretty silly. His face was painted with camouflage and he looked like he was ready to go out trick or treating. Kelly noticed that he stuck out like a sore thumb; *Poor, dumb Hargrove*, he thought.

With the GIs on the ground, several Vietnamese soldiers moved among them and quickly collected their weapons and ammunition. All the while, the voice from the loudspeaker kept up a steady barrage of exhortations to the prone D company troopers. Occasionally, the voice warned them not to move, but Kelly figured there wasn't much chance of that.

Kelly looked at Dunlop and mouthed the word, "Who?"

Dunlop responded by moving his lips silently, "N-V-A."

Kelly rolled his eyes, and looked away.

For two hours the ambush group lay still next to the little stream. The only sounds were the water gurgling and the many night jungle creatures. The NVA lecturer had warned them not to move for an hour, and Peterson doubled that, just to be sure. They had no weapons or ammo, but nobody expressed much concern about taking precautions against attack.

"Alright," Peterson said. "That's long enough. Everybody up now." The rustle of the guys getting up, along with a few coughs and curses, followed Peterson's order. "We gotta come up with a plan for gettin' back to the company," he said.

"Ain't that the Goddamndest shit you ever saw?" Lizzard said. "I mean, the gooks just walked right in here and picked us clean." The moon had risen, providing enough light to see Vandyne shake his head with a lit cigarette in his hand as he scratched his nose. "As long as I live, I ain't never gonna forget what happened here tonight."

"I tell you what," Hargrove spoke in his Tennessee twang, "I'm looking forward to my next chance. I get a hold of that little fucker who was hollerin' at us while we was on the ground, I'll cut his throat and give him a little talkin' to while he chokes on his own fuckin' blood."

"Aw, c'mon, Hargrove. Have a sense of humor, man. They coulda just shot us, you know?" Dunlop said.

"Dunlop, don't give me none of your pussy talk."

"Hey, man, you probably wouldn't be too hospitable either, if it was those guys settin' up an ambush somewhere in Tennessee," said Tuggins.

"Now listen to this," Hargrove rose to the bait, "We got Ho Chi Minh over here, tellin' us what's wrong with the good ol' US of A."

"That's enough!" Peterson spoke up. "Look you guys, we got enough trouble without taking off after each other." He paused for a second. "Now, here's the plan. We got a clear night with a nice moon, so we can get going right away." He paused again. "The Gooks trashed the radio, so we're in basically the same spot as a few weeks ago, only a little worse. If we just walk right up to the perimeter, Welby will think half the NVA is coming and you guys know what that means."

"Yeah, Welby, the fucking Boy Wonder," added Dunlop.

Grunts of agreement and a few muffled curses came from the group.

"So what can we do, Pete?" Fast Eddie Miller said.

Peterson Looked over at Miller. "That's where you come in, partner."

Miller raised his eyebrows and nodded. He brushed his brown hair out of his eyes. He looked at Dunlop, winked, and then said to Peterson, "Whatcha got for me tonight, boss?"

Peterson went on. "When we get within a couple clicks of the company, we send Miller in by himself. Meantime, we sit down and wait, in total silence." He looked directly at Dunlop for a second, then back at Miller. "Miller, when you get to within hollering distance, just call out and explain the situation." Peterson started laughing, at first nervously, and then from his belly. He was soon joined by most of the others.

General agreement with the sergeant's plan was expressed by most of the group, and then Peterson turned back toward Miller. "Okay with you, Eddie?"

Miller shrugged his shoulders. "Sure, Pete."

As the GIs set off in the moonlight Kelly stopped Dunlop. "Why'd Peterson pick Miller to contact the company?"

Dunlop chuckled. "Cause he's Fast Eddie." He hoisted himself up over a rock, following Gage, who walked just in front of him. "If we had a thousand like him," he turned back and offered Kelly a hand up, "the war would probably be over in about a week. Don't worry, he'll get us back in."

"You fellas better pick it up," Flowers said to Kelly and Dunlop. "Y'all keep stopping every couple minutes, we could be in a worlda' hurt when we gets back to the company."

"But, Turk, what if I gotta pee?" Kelly asked.

"Kelly, ain't nobody ever showed you how to pee and keep walkin'?" Flowers unbuttoned his fly and proceeded to urinate no-handed, without stopping on the trail. "No hands is important 'cause then nobody can tell what you're doin'."

"Aw, shit," Miller said from in front. "Turk's just showin' off how long his hose is."

General chuckling came from the whole group, even including Hargrove.

Fast Eddie went on, "White dudes should never try that, cause they sure gonna spray the front of their pants if they do."

The ambush patrol erupted into general laughter and cat-calls. So much for hiding from the enemy.

CHAPTER XV

January 27, 1970

BASE CAMP BUSINESS

"AH-TEN-HUTT!!" THIRD OF THE EIGHTH BATTALION SERGEANT Major Lawerence Grimley boomed over the loudspeaker to the assembled men who had just returned from their latest patrol through Vietnam's Central Highlands. Soldiers barely moved in response to Grimley's command and remained in scruffy formation.

On a temporary speakers' platform arrayed before them, Grimly, a major and the new brigade commander stood smartly. Kelly noted the crispness of their uniforms and the shine on their boots, and then looked at himself. *What a bunch of grubs we are*, he thought.

"Dissssss-missed!" Grimley announced, and the ranks immediately dissolved into a pulsing flow of young men moving toward hot food, showers and bunks.

"Colonel's talk was kinda stupid, don't you think?" Kelly asked Dunlop and Flowers. They walked together off the parade ground and into the sea of tents that led to D Company's area.

"Stupid is going a little easy on the man," Flowers said. "You ask me, the new bird's dumb as a fence post and not nearly as handsome."

"Shit, you guys see the stomach on that motherfucker?" Dunlop held his hands out in front of him and puffed up his cheeks. "I was afraid he'd fall over on his face when he tried to stand at attention." The three men laughed. "Actually," he said, "I was starting to feel kinda sorry for him."

Miller, Vandyne, and Peterson fell in with Kelly's group, Gage and Tuggins came along with another new guy, Raymond Green, from Detroit.

As a black man, Green's assignment to Third Squad a few days before hadn't surprised anyone.

"Man, I can't wait to take a shower and slide in between some clean sheets tonight," Vandyne said as he bounced along with a grin. "Only thing would make it better is if somebody sweet was there to share the experience."

"Now don't be asking any of us to help with that, Lizzard." Dunlop cracked.

The Second and Third squadders were weighed down with packs, canteens and the M16s they had been re-issued since losing their old ones at the ambush. Their gear clanged and clopped lazily as they walked along.

"Making us hump for a day without our guns. That was kind of weird, don't you guys think?" asked Kelly. His jungle fatigues were filthy with sweat and dirt and torn at the knees. His bush hat shaded his eyes at a jaunty angle. He was proud of the veteran infantry soldier he had become in the last ten days.

"Fuckin' Boy Wonder, was afraid to ask for our replacement weapons, 'cause he woulda looked stupid back at Battalion," Peterson said. "We were just lucky that Winnie kept us outta harm's way 'till he came up with a story that Welby went along with."

"That bullshit about us losing our gear in a river crossing, right Pete?" Miller said.

"Yeah, that's the story." Peterson turned toward D company's tent.

Flowers, Gage, Dunlop and Kelly followed him in, along with Wilson and Green.

"Anybody seen Dunlop?" Kelly said, as he came to Third Squad area at 0800 hrs, the morning of January 28th, 1970.

"You're up bright and early, troop." Vandyne layed down his Batman comicbook on his chest. "I bet Spiderman's out at the wire." He folded his hands under his head. "I heard he met this little honey from An Khe when he was hanging around base camp last month."

"Uh, what's the wire?" Kelly said. "Dunlop mentioned it a couple weeks ago, when I first got here."

Vandyne chuckled. "Forgot you were still pretty new." He sat up and rubbed his head. "It's the outer boundary of the camp. It's what keeps the Gooks out and us in." He tossed the comicbook aside on his bunk. "People from the village come up to the wire and sell shit. You know, sodas, gum, cigarettes... Anyway, there's this chick from the village comes every morning and she and Ole' Spidey seem to hit it off." He had the look on his face that had earned him the nickname Lizzard, a cross between a grin and a leer.

"No shit?"

"Yeah, why don't you go check 'em out?" He pointed to the walkway in front of the tent. "Follow that path out past the Mess Tent, then just keep going 'till you see a big ol' barbed-wire fence. I bet they're out there."

"In this rain?"

"Hey, you know what they say about love conquering all."

Kelly chuckled and nodded a couple of times, then set off from the tent. It felt good to stretch his sore muscles as he walked. Like most new infantry soldiers, Kelly was astonished that he could endure tramping for hours with sixty pounds on his back. Walking without the pack made him feel pretty light on his feet, and he began whistling a popular Beatles song, 'Sergeant Pepper's Lonely Hearts Club Band.' It made him think of times in San Jose when the smells of incense and marijuana mingled as girls in short skirts offered him tokes on their doobies. *Sweet times*, he thought.

It had started to rain the night before and had continued into the morning, cooling off the air to a pleasant seventy degrees. The path out to the wire was a soggy mess. Kelly slogged along wrapped in his poncho. The mud clung to his boots as if it tried to suck him into the earth with each step.

"Hey, Spiderman, what's goin' on?" Kelly said as he walked up to Dunlop, who was standing at an eight-foot-high barbed wire fence talking with a young Vietnamese girl who stood on the other side.

"Hey Kelly, I want you to meet Tuyen." Dunlop extended his hand toward the girl through a section of the barbed wire. She was short and thin by American standards, but lovely, with a beautiful face and a warm smile.

Dunlop's lady friend wore traditional loose-fitting black pants, white blouse and broad-brimmed conical hat. She held a metal tray supported by a strap around the back of her neck. The tray displayed Marlboros, chewing gum, and American candy bars.

"Hello, Tuyen," said Kelly. The young woman turned her head toward him, but kept her eyes facing downward. Kelly tried to meet her gaze, without success.

Tuyen reached through the wire as she looked back to Dunlop and grasped his fingers. A smile spread across her face, framed by the rainwater dripping from the edge of her hat.

"Tuyen beaucoup wet, cold." Dunlop said slowly, smiling at the girl. "Maybe go home, come back tomorrow?"

Tuyen laughed warmly and then looked at Dunlop with a sparkling gaze. Kelly wondered whether she had understood anything he'd said. "Oh, Jesus." he muttered, wondering just how far this friendship had gone. Tuyen released Dunlop's fingers and turned to leave, stepping carefully around water filled shell holes.

"Guess we should get out of the rain, huh?" Dunlop hunched himself up in his poncho "Want a Hershey?" He brought his hand out of the armhole and extended a chocolate bar toward Kelly.

"Thanks." Kelly accepted Dunlop's offering and they set off toward their company area, plodding along through the mud,

"Really," Dunlop said. "it's just a friendship." He sat on his bunk with his bare feet resting on a wooden pallet that Kelly had salvaged from the Mess Hall supply area the day before. "Hell, I'm a married man with a kid, right?" Dunlop rubbed his wet hair with a towel. "Besides, Tuyen is just a kid."

"Sure man. She might be all of two, three years younger than you." Kelly said. Several of the Second and Third Squad guys had gathered at one end of the D company tent, out of the rain. Flowers was cleaning his rifle and looked at Dunlop with a sly grin. "You telling us you haven't even had so much as a notion toward that girl? Cause, if that's what you're saying, we's a little worried about you, Spidey."

General laughter.

Dunlop picked at his toes pretending not to hear.

"Hey, Pete, when you figure we're going out again?" Miller asked.

Peterson sighed. "Now that you mention it, I was supposed to let you guys know that they're planning on taking us out day after tomorrow."

Groans came from several in the group. Kelly felt a sinking sensation in his stomach.

"Shit." Van Dyne looked up from his comicbook, "I got a shipment coming in a couple of days."

"Don't worry, Liz," Flowers said. "I'm sure the cooks'll take care of it for you."

"Yeah, that's what I'm afraid of."

Dunlop looked at Kelly. "Lizzard here is quite the aspiring businessman." He shifted his gaze toward Vandyne, "He seems to have a pretty good source for Bong Son Bombers, among other things."

"Bong Son Bombers?" Kelly wondered if they might be some new weapons he hadn't heard about yet.

"Imagine a great big Havana stogie. " Miller held a hand up to his mouth like he was smoking. "Only no tobacco, just the most powerful weed you ever had, rolled up like a cigar." A satisfied grin spread across his face as he exhaled.

Quiet descended on the group of young soldiers. Kelly realized that surviving one patrol was not really much of an accomplishment. He began to feel trapped, along with a mixture of fear and panic. *The worst part of it is,* he thought, *we're all gonna go out and hop on the birds and just do like they tell us.* He felt a strong urge to run away or maybe fake an injury, anything to avoid the coming mission. *Fuck heroism, and fuck doing the right thing for world peace or the people of Vietnam.* All he could think of now was avoiding the knot in his stomach he lived with on the last patrol.

"Hey you guys, what if we just said 'fuck it' this time?" Kelly looked around the group. His jaw was set tight, his eyes intent on each man. The group remained silent.

"What's wrong Kelly?" Flowers examined the chamber of his M16, pulled the bolt back, and let it slide back into place. He aimed the rifle at an imaginary target on the ceiling of the tent. "Don't you appreciate the opportunity Uncle Sam is providing you to defend the free world?"

"This Commie-assed motherfucker here, my good pal Kelly, thinks there's nothing wrong with our situation here that a nice little revolution wouldn't fix," Dunlop said.

"Whoeee!" Flowers exclaimed as he clicked the firing pin forward.

Vandyne lit a cigarette. "Man, I got ninety-four days to go. I ain't doing or saying nuthin' to fuck myself up. They tell me to open fire, I just ask where."

Peterson raised his voice. "No point in goin' on like this, guys." He looked over at Kelly. "The Lifers hear you talk like that, troop, they'll have your ass in LBJ so fast your head'll spin."

Tuggins sat on the bunk next to Flowers looking serious. Kelly raised his eyebrows and shrugged his shoulders, then looked away from Peterson.

Dunlop caught Kelly's eye, and motioned with a nod for Kelly to follow him outside.

"Grab that other box, Kelly," Dunlop said. "C'mon, man, we gotta move fast now. You sure you want to do this with me?"

"Hell, yes, I want to do it," Kelly said as he picked up the box and walked over next to Dunlop, who was standing at the doorway of the Mess Storage tent.

"Looks like the coast is clear, but we gotta hurry down that walkway," Dunlop said. "I figure no more than ninety seconds between here and Rutherford's tent, OK?"

"Yeah, sure," said Kelly, "but what's in these boxes, who's Rutherford, and what's the big hurry?"

"You're about to deliver $500 worth of Italian clothes. Rutherford's goin' home in a couple of days. It's only gonna cost him a hundred bucks," Dunlop had a giant grin on his face. "But that's fifty bucks each for you and me," he said. "We gotta hurry cause I'm pretty sure the CID (Criminal Investigation Division) is onto my little business and I don't want to give those rats, especially Lizzard, a chance to fink us out." Dunlop raised his eyebrows toward Kelly. "Can we go now?"

"Lead the way, Private Dunlop."

"That's a nice roll you got in your shirt pocket, Spiderman," Kelly said as he and Dunlop headed back to their tent. Rutherford had purchased a few additional items, including a pair of Italian shoes. "Now, what are we gonna do with all those bucks?" he asked.

"Well, first thing, we gotta change it to big bills. Then, we stash it in this box I got by my bunk." Dunlop pulled out a Marlboro. "We can keep your share there, too," he said, "if that's OK with you."

"Sure, man," Kelly said. "I trust you."

"Then when we go out to the boonies, we can divide it up and keep it in our rucksacks." Dunlop drew deeply on his smoke as they walked. "If we left it here, I'd be afraid the CID might find it. They've already searched our tent a couple of times." Dunlop stopped for a minute and took a deep drag. "I betcha they're onto us," he smiled. "It's pretty much just cat and mouse, know what I mean?"

CHAPTER XVI

Rice or Noodles?

DAYS TURNED INTO WEEKS, AND WEEKS TURNED INTO MONTHS. It was now mid-March in the Central Highlands. Fourth Division troops tramped up and down mountains and river valleys, without encountering much. The going for the grunts was hot, wet, and very, very boring as the monsoon set in.

Rumors of the war winding down were flying around like swallows at sunset. Word was that several Ninth Division Battalions had been pulled out of their camps in the Delta and sent home. Everybody had their fingers crossed.

Down south in Saigon's Chinese district, it was a filthy, sticky and suffocatingly hot night at the Quang Pho Bat Cafe, or the Bat, as it was called. Spider plants hung still in the open windows; no breeze tonight.

Service at the Bat was notoriously lousy, but the food was wonderful. The little restaurant served only three things: delicious noodle soup called Pho, Vietnamese tea, and a remarkably potent rice wine that was rumored to come from Hanoi.

A scattering of Vietnamese intellectuals made a show of smoking their American cigarettes among the world traveling hippies, semi-peaceniks, wire-service stringers and a few sleazy CIA-types. The café was full.

Big Steve Beltzer covered his cup of wine with one hand and smiled as he shook his head at the waitress. She pretended not to notice him and headed lazily toward another table with her plastic pitcher. Beltzer looked around. *Wonder if anybody's here to keep an eye on us,* he thought. Seated at the tiny table with Big Steve, New York Times reporter Fred Greenburg belched and chuckled, "Had enough, have you?" Greenburg asked.

"That stuff will definitely alter your consciousness," Beltzer said as he stretched his long legs into the aisle. The waitress walked up to where Beltzer's legs were blocking her and looked sternly at the tall American. Realizing his error, Beltzer grinned sheepishly, quickly curled his legs up under the table again. His gaze fell upon a Vietnamese man sitting alone at a table on the Bat's terrace. *He might be the one,* he thought.

"See something?" asked Greenburg.

"That guy on the terrace, sitting by himself."

"Umm," Greenburg grunted as he looked over Beltzer's shoulder.

"He's turning up a lot lately," Beltzer said and scratched his chin whiskers. "Could be my new little friend from the National Police, keepin' watch on me."

Greenburg sipped his rice wine and raised his eyebrows. "Could be," he said.

Beltzer was a freelance journalist from San Jose, California. He was called up for the draft, but then received a 4-F classification—physically unable to serve; the answer to every young American male's prayers at his induction physical. This made Beltzer even more interested in Vietnam, now he wouldn't have to carry a gun. So, he journeyed to Saigon and began filing stories about the war and the people affected by it. Beltzer was a geeky guy. His slender, friendly face would never be described as handsome. He wore an unkempt goatee and glasses thick enough to make his eyes appear to be bulging. He walked with the awkward gait of an Ostrich with sore knees. He always had a tattered notepad in one hand and several pens in his ink-stained shirt pocket.

"So what's up in the Highlands?" Greenburg casually lit a cigarette and exhaled the smoke slowly, looking at Beltzer.

"What about the Highlands?" Beltzer pretended not to know what Greenburg was asking about.

"Oh, c'mon ol' buddy." Greenburg put on his most ingratiating smile. "I know you're on the plane for Pleiku tomorrow."

"How'd you know that?" The hair on Big Steve's neck stood up.

"I got my sources."

Beltzer sipped at his empty wine cup and set it down slowly. "Thought I'd spend a few days in Dalat; get out of the heat for a while."

"So why Pleiku?" Greenburg flicked ash from his cigarette into his half-full bowl of noodle soup. "There's a daily up to Dalat, right after the Pleiku flight."

"I'm meeting this girl in Pleiku and..."

"Yeah, sure you are Beltzer." Greenburg glanced across the room toward an American seated at a table to his right. The man had been staring in their direction, but looked away when Greenburg seemed to catch his eye. "CIA pricks," Greenburg grunted.

"No, really..." Beltzer began.

"Look, big guy." Greenburg took a drink of his wine, "You've acquired something of a reputation around here for being in the right place at the right time, know what I mean?" He cleared his throat. "That piece of yours in the New Yorker last month about the village that wasn't exactly pacified-that turned a few heads."

Beltzer shrugged his shoulders and smiled a little.

"And everybody's been saying something big is about to happen up north. You know, all that bullshit coming out of Washington about VC sanctuaries." Greenburg waved his cigarette as he spoke, and slurred his words a little. "A friend of mine at Fourth Division says they're moving a lot of heavy stuff toward the Cambodia border."

"So?" Beltzer stood up and began to count his money to pay.

"So, give me a holler if it looks like something is about to break up there, will you?" Greenburg said.

"You take care of yourself, Fred." Beltzer dropped a handful of piasters onto the table, saluted Greenburg, then turned and walked out of the cafe, ducking down at the doorway to avoid bumping his head.

Nobody knew how Steve Beltzer got away with the shit he pulled, but he had a knack for convincing people to trust him and do him favors. At the Pleiku airfield he showed his tattered American Embassy press credential, now three months expired, to one of the Huey pilots, and asked if he could hitch a ride to Qui Nhon. "Why the hell not?" came the reply from the young warrant officer to the towering reporter with the lopsided grin.

Beltzer arrived at the bustling seaport town of Qui Nhon on the back of a truck loaded with ARVN rangers from a South Vietnamese Army camp on the northern edge of town. The ARVNs enjoyed his company immensely, constantly mentioning (in Vietnamese, of course, which Beltzer understood perfectly) his towering height and speculating on what affect it might have on his sexual prowess. The group was evenly divided. Half thought he must be an incredible lover, the other group thought most women would be repelled by such a huge fellow.

In 1970 Qui Nhon was a lively town of 150,000. It had been founded several hundred years earlier as a tiny fishing village and then slowly grown into a busy Asian seaport serving the central Vietnamese coast and points inland.

Qui Nhon's harbor was a favored inlet for smugglers of every stripe, including drugs and contraband weapons. Two years before the mayor turned his official residence into a high-end massage parlor catering to American soldiers who roamed the streets when on pass.

The truck dropped Beltzer a few blocks from his destination in the heart of the city's large and bustling red light district. He adjusted his rucksack as he walked along the busy market street. Many people gawked at him as he lurched along. In Vietnam, the seven-foot-tall Beltzer was accustomed to amused giggles wherever he went.

He ambled through a little gate under a sweet smelling, climbing jasmine arbor and up to the front door of the well-known Madame X's. He pulled the cord next to the door and heard a set of soft chimes ring inside. Moments later, a lovely young woman greeted him with a warm smile and beckoned him to enter. He looked nervously behind himself, out toward the street, but saw no one who seemed to be following him.

That same March day a jeep of happy GIs drove into Qui Nhon from the airport. Tuggins, Miller, Dunlop and Kelly had wangled permission for a quick jaunt to the coastal city, supposedly to pick up spare parts for the Mess Hall. The truth was that Dunlop had received word of a shipment of valuable watches. Lt. Winston went to Captain Welby about the trip. Only after each man swore in blood to be back the next day, did the CO reluctantly agreed to Winston's proposal, insisting that Sergeant Hargrove go along in charge of the detail. It seemed, the Captain had said, like a good idea to get a few of the troublemakers out of the area while they were getting ready for their next operation.

Staff Seargent Dwane Hargrove from Tennessee was an Army "lifer" who rather enjoyed his time in Vietnam. At twenty-six, he had been in the Army for eight years and was on his third tour in the warzone. It was rumored that Hargrove had barely escaped charges for the grisly execution of five Vietnamese peasants, who, it turned out, had been considered quite friendly to the Americans. According to Miller, he was "not the brightest bulb in the lamp."

The five men from Delta Company flew in on a supply chopper. At the Qui Nhon airfield, Miller struck a deal with a couple guys he knew from the 179th Aviation Brigade. He would get the use of one of their jeeps for two days in exchange for a half-dozen Bong Son Bombers and a carton filled with opium-dipped marijuana cigarettes.

The jeep drove slowly through the heavy traffic toward the center of Qui Nhon. Kelly drank in the sights as the jeep rolled along. Everyone seemed to be out moving around. The produce stands were well stocked and the fish stands had creatures on display from the South China Sea that he had never seen and would not have thought edible. One fishmonger walked over toward the GIs when they were stopped for a moment. He carried an enormous fish, which he proudly thrust toward the jeep while shouting something that must have been an exhortation to buy the dead monster. Kelly shouted "No way!" The others laughed heartily.

They stopped at an intersection. "I'll jump off here, Eddie." Tuggins called from the back.

"You'll what?" yelled Hargrove.

"Sure thing, Tug." Miller turned around with his hands still on the steering wheel.

"I'll meet you guys at that restaurant, over there," Tuggins pointed to a small cafe near them with an unreadable name and a group of older Vietnamese men talking and smoking out front, "at 8 o'clock tonight."

"But..." Hargrove sputtered as Miller stepped on the gas. "You guys could get me in a hell of a lot of trouble, you know?"

The other three laughed uproariously as the little jeep sped along. "Don't worry, killer." Miller shifted gears and took a deep drag on his hand-rolled cigarette. "We'll be back in time to report when we're supposed to." He tossed the cigarette into the muddy street. "Now, what was the name of that place you were telling me about? The Blue Rat, or something like that?"

"The Blue Rabbit," Hargrove said, somewhat dejectedly.

"That's it!" exclaimed Miller "Next stop, it's the Blue Donkey!"

"Fuckin' A!" shouted Kelly and Dunlop, almost in unison.

The jeep left a trail of whoops, catcalls, and ribald laughter as it zipped along toward its new destination. Hargrove hunched over looking angry.

Fast Eddie took out a twenty-dollar bill and extended it to the gnarled old woman. She stuffed it into her shirt pocket, looked at Miller. "More GI want boom-boom today?"

"Not today, mama-san." Miller adjusted the 45 caliber in the holster on his hip. "But mama-san, please, make sure that GI has number one boom-boom, okay?" He pointed toward a curtain of beads where Hargrove had just disappeared

Oh, yes, yes!" the old woman said, smiling with what remained of her teeth.

"Mamma-san, please tell GI, tonight, nine o'clock, right here." He pointed at the floor forcefully. "We come back, get him."

"Oh yes, yes. You come back, get GI, nine o'clock." She smiled, nodding her head, proud of her comprehension. "Number 1 boom-boom till nine o'clock!"

Miller gave Dunlop and Kelly the thumbs up, then strutted out the door. He hopped into the driver's seat of the jeep and before Kelly got settled, he gave it full acceleration, wheels spinning and swerving, leaving a plume of mud and exhaust in his wake. Kelly fell into his seat, and then reaching for his jungle hat, fell onto Dunlop in back.

"Hey, fuckhead, sit in your own seat!" Dunlop laughed, pushing him back toward the front.

A few minutes later, Miller pulled the jeep off the road and onto a bluff above rolling surf and a white sand beach a couple of miles out of town. "Well troops, it's only eleven-thirty." He hiked back his jungle cap and brought his hand up to shade his eyes while he surveyed the water below.

"Way I see it, we can do whatever the fuck we please this afternoon."

"Man, that was absolutely, far-fucking out, the way you got rid of Hargrove," Kelly said.

"Shit, they'll have him so whacked out on pussy, weed, and whiskey, he won't even know we took off." Miller looked at the other two, grinning and nodding his head.

"Hey, guys, we gotta remember to pick up those watches," said Dunlop.

"No sweat, Spiderman," Miller said as he set the jeep's hand brake. "We got you covered, troop."

Kelly took a deep breath of the sea air. It was so far from the rotting smells and cold terrors of the jungle trails the company had humped over for the last two months. It seemed like an eternity had passed since he had felt this good. "Becky and I used to go out once in a while to a beach kinda like this, near Santa Cruz."

"Oh, shit," Dunlop laughed, "next thing you know he's going to be blubbering about home. Ruin the whole goddamn day!"

"Best way to start off a fine adventure like this is with a swim." Miller climbed out of the jeep, took off his shirt and hat, and tossed them onto the driver's seat. "You dickheads comin'?"

"Eddie, you sure it's safe down there?" Kelly asked, a little worried.

"Yeah." Miller turned toward the beach and swept the horizon with his arm, "We're basically surrounded by friendlys here. ARVN's a half mile north, and Americans just the other side of town. We're talking some pretty big shit too, you know: air, tanks, artillery." He turned back around toward Dunlop and Kelly. "Besides, VC don't want to pull nuthin' around here. This place is too important to them as an arms smuggling port-of-entry." He placed a boot up on the fender of the jeep, stretching his back. "Shit, if we're lucky, we'll see some of the nurses from that big American hospital just down the road."

"I guess I'll stay up here and watch our stuff," Dunlop said and pulled a heroin Marlboro out of a small tin in his pocket.

"Aw, shit, man," Kelly said, and looked away toward the waves breaking on the beach.

"Still into them horse nails, huh?" Miller said to Dunlop.

"Every once in a while." Dunlop replied.

"Well, look here." Miller unbuckled his holster and handed the gun to Dunlop. "You can't watch nuthin' when you're asleep, like on the ambush a couple months back, right?"

Dunlop nodded, taking the 45 and setting it on the seat next to him. The heroin cigarette dangled from his lips and his eyes were hidden behind dark aviator sunglasses. *A real picture*, thought Kelly

"So promise me you'll only do half. No more-right?" Miller stuck his hands on his hips and looked intently at Dunlop's sunglasses.

Dunlop nodded again.

"Okay, troops." Miller swung back toward the beach. "Here's the plan. We get in a swim. Then, we wander up to where I seen them nurses." He shaded his eyes and looked up the beach, toward a group of swimmers some distance away. "Maybe get some dates for tonight. Then we go check out 'ole Tuggins at Madame X's. I don't know if I believe that shit about him meetin' some guy or not. But if he's got something going there, I say he ought to spread it around to his buddies." He turned back toward Kelly and Dunlop. "Am I right, gentlemen?"

"Right on, shit yeah!" exclaimed Kelly and Dunlop, on a roll now.

"After we check out Tuggins, we go police up Hargrove, rent a room and stuff him in bed for the night. Then troops, we get down to some serious partying." Miller had the same impish grin on his face that he always seemed to have when he was about to get away with something. He started walking down the small path that led to the bluff. Kelly followed along, stopping every few feet to take in the scenery, and check for any bad guys lurking in the bushes. When he reached the beach, Miller jumped out of his trousers, kicked off his boots and socks and ran full speed into the surf, with Kelly close behind. Kelly tumbled into the warm waves and let the sea surround him like a giant womb.

The chimes at Madame X's rang a third time. Kelly, Miller, and Dunlop stood impatiently outside the door. "What do you guys think?" Dunlop asked, taking a deep drag on his cigarette. "Maybe everybody's fuckin', nobody left to answer the door."

"I wonder what they charge," Kelly said, trying very hard to seem nonchalant.

"Down boy," Miller said. "Ain't no time for that right now."

"Hey, I wasn't saying..."

Just then, there was a sound from inside of a bolt sliding back. The door opened and the same smiling young woman who had greeted Big Steve Beltzer earlier in the day stood in the doorway. Kelly felt his pulse quicken and he started to breathe a little more deeply.

"Please to come in, GIs." Her heavily accented voice was light and musical, but she spoke slowly and Kelly understood her with ease. "My name Lan Tho Giao." She said as she stepped back from the doorway and bowed her head ever so slightly. The three soldiers stepped through the doorway and into the parlor.

There were two bamboo couches and a chair set around a large bamboo round table. There were no windows in the room, so the only light came from a dim electric bulb inside an ornate paper shade next to the chair. A wide assortment of Playboy magazines and other girlie books were scattered on the table.

"GIs please to sit down." Lan Tho Giao clasped her hands in front of herself and nodded.

She's about nineteen, Kelley thought. *Doesn't seem like somebody'd you'd find in a whorehouse. Innocent looking, but man, what a babe!* She didn't appear to be wearing any make-up. Her long black hair was pulled back from the sides.

"GI's like to see girl today?"

"Well..." Kelly stammered, unable to assemble his words.

"Actually, Mam," Miller cut in, speaking with a deference Kelly had not heard him use before. "We've come to find our buddy."

She smiled demurely. "GIs want to see buddy today?"

"Well, not exactly like that." Miller held his jungle hat in both hands, spinning it as he talked. "What I mean is, we left our buddy here a few hours ago. He's a little shorter than me, but bigger, uh, muscles, and black hair..." She waited calmly for Miller to finish, giving him her full attention. "And he's a black guy." Miller smiled and nodded his head, exhaling deeply.

"Oh, black GI, this morning." She nodded and smiled broadly.

"His name is Tuggins, and we really do need to talk to him, okay?"

The young woman straightened up, dropped her hands to her sides and said, "One moment please." She disappeared down a hallway, trailing her white Ao Dai. After a couple of minutes, she then re-emerged. "GI"s to follow please."

They followed her down a long hall, past several closed doors. Two women stood in an open doorway, leaning casually against the bamboo frame. They both wore skimpy lingerie, and displayed a generous amount of silken skin. *They're very pretty ladies, but a little too made-up*, Kelly thought. Lan Tho Giao stopped to talk with the two girls and the three soldiers gathered around. Kelly stared at one of the girls, but became embarrassed and turned away when she looked at him and giggled. *Jesus Christ on a goddamn bicycle,* he thought.

The hostess seemed to be making an elaborate explanation, pointing first at the three GI's, then to a door at the end of the hall. When she was finished, the two women looked at each other and laughed with hands covering their mouths. Lan Tho Giao turned and said, "Come please."

Tuggins was seated in a chair across from the entry with a cup of tea in his hand. He acknowledged his three buddies as they came in, nodding to each of them in turn. Sitting next to Tuggins was Big Steve Beltzer. Beltzer clutched a dog-eared notebook in one hand and a pencil in the other.

A woman was seated on Tuggin's other side on a red velvet couch, who in Kelly's opinion, did look like she belonged at Madame X's.

She's about 40, thought Kelly. *Between all that hair piled up and the makeup caked on her face, it's a wonder she doesn't just fall over forward. Look at the silk robe, complete with a fire-breathing dragon! And those bright red fingernails, man, they're long enough to stab a guy.*

Tuggins stood, "Fellas, I'd like you all to meet Chau Thi Te." He extended his hand toward the aging Asian princess. "Otherwise known affectionately throughout the Central Highlands as Madame X."

The three newcomers stood with their hats in their hands and murmured greetings toward the woman, who nodded slightly in return, not changing her expression.

"And this here is Steve Beltzer, a newspaper guy from New York."

Beltzer stood up, "Actually, California," he said, smiling a little. He shook hands with Kelly, Miller, and Dunlop and sat down again.

Tuggins turned to Beltzer. "We 'bout got it wrapped up then?"

"Yeah, this is great!" Beltzer reached down and stuffed the notepad into his pack. "You think of anything else, just get a hold of me in Saigon, or you can reach me through Madame X here." He pulled a business card out of his pack and handed it to Tuggins.

"I just might do that." Tuggins placed the card in his shirt pocket. He turned toward his three buddies. "Where's Hargrove?"

"Long story, man." Miller answered. "You ready to split?"

"Well, not exactly, fellas," Tuggins said. "Chau Thi Te, here, has prepared a dinner for us and she says there's plenty for you guys, too." He spun his bush hat around with one hand. "Whadaya say, huh?"

"Hey, sounds good to me," Miller answered with a smile. "Okay with you guys?"

Kelly and Dunlop nodded enthusiastically

Nine diners sat around the grand table normally reserved for the wealthiest and highest-ranking visitors to Madame X's. Kelly turned to Tuggins, seated next to him, and asked about a small, elaborately-decorated piece against the wall close by.

"That's an altar to their ancestors, man," Tuggins answered. "Most Vietnamese homes have one, if they can afford it."

Kelly looked around the colorfull room and thought, *really nice.* "I bet they spent a little money, doing this place," he whispered to Tuggins.

"Yeah, probably." Tuggins said smiling across the table at Lan Tho Giao.

Hmm, wonder if that means anything? worried Kelly.

"Lan Tho Giao tells me General Westmoreland ate here one time," Tuggins said.

"No kidding," Kelly said. "Might have sat right here, huh?" He looked down at his seat and chuckled. "I wonder what else he did while he was here, eh?"

"Hey, take some of that in front of you and pass it on, ok?" Tuggins said

"What is it, man?"

"That, bro, is a bowl of glazed pumpkin cubes," Tuggins said. "They got caramel sauce and sesame seeds on 'em. Go ahead and try some."

Kelly dug in-there was poached snapper in peanut sauce with rice paper, lemon grass tofu, sticky rice, noodles and lotus green tea.

"Which you prefer, Mr. Kelly," Lan Tho Giao asked. "Rice or noodles?" She looked at Kelly. "Chau Thi Te want to know."

Kelly was surprised to be addressed directly by the lovely Vietnamese woman. "You can call me Tom, ma'am." He thought for a moment. "I guess I'd have to say noodles."

Big Steve Beltzer grinned and suppressed a chuckle while Lan Tho Giao spoke to Madame X in Vietnamese. Chau Thi Te and the two young women on either side of her covered their mouths and laughed demurely.

"Chau Thi Te laughs because rice means prefer wife, and noodles, prefer mistress."

Kelly's face turned a little red as he struggled with his chopsticks. "I guess I'll have to check with my wife on that one."

"So, Steve is it?" Kelly directed his question to Beltzer.

Beltzer's mouth was full of a large piece of snapper. He raised a finger, chewed and took a sip of his lotus tea. "Most people call me Big Steve, but I answer to almost anything."

"I was just wondering how you heard about Tuggins, here," Kelly said.

"I've been working on a piece for the New Yorker about the experiences of black GIs over here." Beltzer put down his chopsticks and wiped his mouth. "I managed to wangle a couple of interviews with guys at Long Binh Jail and they couldn't stop talkin' about this guy." He pointed at Tuggins.

"So," Kelly said, "What do you think of the war, as a whole?"

Talk at the table stopped. Everyone waited for Beltzer's reply.

"I think it sucks, Tom."

Lan Tho Giao spoke rapidly and quietly to Chau Thi Te.

"But," Beltzer said, "I'm sure you know more about that than a geeky writer, like me."

Tuggins said, loud enough to be heard by all, "The point ain't that it sucks. The point is what we gonna do about it?"

Everyone seemed to talk at once for a few moments, in English and Vietnamese.

Dinner proceeded, with everyone in good spirits. Conversation was mixed English and Vietnamese, with Lan Tho Giao frequently translating from one to the other. When all had finished eating and a languid quiet of satisfaction had settled over the group, a Vietnamese dessert of strong coffee pored over ice with a layer of condensed milk at the bottom of a small glass was served.

"We better be movin' out, troops," Miller said, setting his empty coffee glass down on the table.

"Yeah, you right, Eddie," said Tuggins, as he leaned back in his chair and placed his hands on his stomach.

"Don't forget, we gotta police up Hargrove over at the Blue Mule," Dunlop said, as everyone got up. The four GIs offered profuse thanks for the wonderful meal and headed for the door.

"So what the fuck was going on back there with the fancy dinner and that big guy, Tug?" Kelly leaned forward from the back seat of the bouncing jeep.

"My Dad got introduced to the guy. He's a writer for some magazine back in New York." Tuggins looked straight ahead as he spoke, his right arm resting on the door of the jeep. "They set up a time for him to ask me a few things when Beltzer could be in Qui Nohn."

"What'd he want to find out, Bro?" Miller asked while steering the jeep around a corner. "Coordinates on our position for the next VC mortar attack?"

"Nah, nuthin' like that." Tuggins looked over at Miller, smiling. "He just wanted to know my opinion on the role of black GIs over here."

"Well," Dunlop said, "I hope you told him everything was fine as long as the white dudes took care of burning shit and pulled all the KP."

General laughter sounded as the jeep sped along the muddy highway.

"Dinner was just their way of being friendly, I guess," said Tuggins.

Moments later, Miller pulled off the road next to a fruit and vegetable stand. He walked over to the proprietor, then came back to the jeep and passed around a bag. "Mangoes," he mumbled with his mouth full and juice dribbling down his chin.

"Hey, man, didn't you get enough at dinner?" asked Dunlop with a smile.

Miller's face took on a serious expression. "Look here, guys. We need to make a plan for tonight." He wiped his mouth with his sleeve.

"Alright, Eddie, let's hear it." Kelly didn't look up from his mango, he was having a little trouble getting it peeled.

Grunts of agreement from the other two.

"Okay, now. We got to get Hargrove, but that's no sweat cause he's gonna be so spaced out, we'll just dump him in bed somewhere and lock the door."

"That's cool." Kelly said, finally taking a generous bite of his ripe fruit.

"Then I'm gonna take you guys to this restaurant I know and we'll meet up with them nurses I talked to this morning and have a couple of drinks with 'em."

Silence followed. Kelly felt a little uncomfortable, thinking how Becky might feel if she found out he had gone on a date. Tuggins looked a little worried too. Dunlop was inscrutable behind his sunglasses.

"Well, don't everybody thank me all at once for lining up some chicks for tonight." Miller looked from one to the other, confused at their reaction.

"It's nuthin' against what you did, man." Tuggins said. "It's just that us three are kind of spoken for, as far as women are concerned." He fingered the mustache he had grown since being released from LBJ. "You know what I mean, right?"

"Actually, Tug," Dunlop said, "I'm not so sure about that, for myself, anyway."

"What do you mean?" Kelly looked at Dunlop.

"Shit, I got a 'Dear John' last week."

Silence for a few moments.

"She moved in with some fucker in Sacramento and says she wants a divorce."

"Oh man..." Kelly shook his head.

"Hey," Miller brightened, "That sets you up for tonight, don't it?"

Dunlop was quiet.

"Well, there is that little Vietnamese honey he meets out at the wire." Kelly raised his eyebrows a couple of times. "Maybe there's more to that situation than our good buddy has led us to believe, eh?"

Everybody chuckled, ribbing Dunlop a little.

"I told you guys." Dunlop sounded frustrated. "We're just friends."

"Oh sure, sure," from the other three, having a laugh at Dunlop's expense.

"Besides, she ain't been at the wire since last time we were in for stand down." Dunlop continued, "Haven't seen her in more than a month now."

"Well, anyhow, I know I can count on you guys to be friendly to these lonesome American ladies tonight," Miller said as he hit the starter button and put the jeep in gear. "You don't have to do nuthin' to mess up your marriages, so no sweat." He grinned, revved the engine and popped the clutch.

"Jesus, that's really nice, isn't it?" Kelly said, inspired by the view from three thousand feet. Miller had talked the chopper pilot into swinging out over the South China Sea for a couple of miles before turning back towards An Khe. Dunlop sat in the open door of the aircraft with his feet on the port side skid. Kelly and Tuggins sat next to him, with Miller squatting behind, holding onto a dangling strap. Hargrove was sound asleep in the seat.

"Hey, Tug," Kelly shouted so everybody but the snoring Hargrove could hear him. "You think Madame X is VC?"

"Probably." Tuggins shrugged his shoulders and kept looking down at the expanse of water below them.

"Man, that gook lady?" Miller reached with his free hand to search for his lighter. "She's so VC, you'd have to check her pussy for booby traps before you boned her."

General laughter.

"Shit, Miller," Kelly smiled and shook his head. "You do have a way with words."

"Spiderman," Miller called out, how much you figure those are worth?" He pointed to the two medium-sized boxes against the wall of the chopper, across from the open doorway.

Dunlop looked around, cigarette dangling from the corner of his mouth. "Retail, they'd go for about $8000, I guess."

"Wow!" the other three said, almost together.

"We'll probably get about half that. Everybody wants a nice watch to wear goin' home." Dunlop nodded at Miller with a satisfied grin, then turned back to the rolling South China Sea a thousand feet below

"Hey, Fast Man." Tuggins looked back at Miller, "You take good care of those two nurse ladies you left with last night?"

Miller grinned and puffed on his cigarette as the helicopter swung around and headed west, toward An Khe.

"Yeah, what happened after you guys took off from the bar?" Dunlop asked Miller. "You poke both of them babes?"

"Francine and me took Connie back to her quarters," Miller answered. "Then we got a bottle of Seagram's and went to this nice little place and rented a room."

"You tell her you're not an officer?" Dunlop asked.

"Yeah, I told her. " Miller said, "But after we did it."

Chuckles from the group.

Miller raised the smoke to his lips. "I don't think it bothered her none." He inhaled deeply, then furrowed his brow. "Me not being an officer, that is."

"Francine, huh?" Kelly said.

Miller nodded his head and looked down toward the receding coastline. The helicopter streaked out over the jungle, hurrying the young soldiers back to the war.

CHAPTER XVII

Tough Going

IT WAS NOW APRIL 19, 1970 AND D COMPANY HAD BEEN HUMPING for five weeks straight, the longest they had been out since Kelly arrived in Vietnam. The soldiers were getting pretty short-tempered. A fight broke out the day before between Third Platoon's Ray Green and one of the white guys from First Platoon who made a reference to Green's body odor, which everyone agreed was pretty bad. Green was an intense nineteen-year-old from Detroit who was always ready with a Black Power salute and often overreacted to comments made in casual conversation. He went after the guy with his fists. It took Peterson, now Third Platoon Sergeant, Miller, leader of Second Squad, Third Platoon, and Sgt Hargrove, now First Platoon Sergeant, to break up the melee. Another black guy, PFC Darryl Gormick, had initially tried to stop the tussle and wound up with a broken wrist for his efforts.

"Man, if I see another can of fruit cocktail when I'm back in the world, I think I'm gonna puke." Kelly tipped the open can up to his lips for the last few pieces of fruit.

"For somebody who hates C's so much, you sure do a good job of cleaning out them cans," said Dunlop.

"Yeah, you probably got a point there." Kelly tilted the can and checked one last time to make sure it was empty.

Kelly, Miller, Dunlop, Tuggins, and Flowers were finishing breakfast behind their defensive position from the night before and facing another grueling day in the dense jungle of the Ca Lui river basin southeast of An Khe. As usual their assignment was to flush out any enemy troops in the area. The bad guys, however, had not been cooperating much, remaining well-hidden and out of the reach of the heavily-armed Americans.

"Hey, guys." Peterson squatted down, holding his rifle between his legs for balance, "Everybody ready to go?"

"About as ready as we were this time yesterday morning," Miller said with more than a tinge of sarcasm in his voice.

"Eddie, you better go check on Second Squad," said Peterson.

"I was over there about five minutes ago." Miller looked in the direction of his squad. "We're set."

"Pete, what's that stuff we heard this morning about Hargrove not making it back last night?" Dunlop asked.

"Six guys came in from ambush early this morning, but Hargrove and Stinson weren't with 'em." Peterson reached up and lifted up his bush hat and ran his fingers through his hair.

"Stinson...," Dunlop paused for a second, "he's that First Platoon guy from Wisconsin isn't he?"

"Yeah," Peterson replied. "The others said they just couldn't find him or Hargrove, so they came on in. They're all pretty fucked up about it over there." He turned his head in the direction of First Platoon.

"Didn't Stinson's wife just have a baby?" asked Kelly.

"Don't know," said Peterson. "Hopefully they just wandered off and got lost. There'll be an air search, probably have 'em both back before lunch." He pulled his hat back on. "Well, Third Squad has lead today, so I figured I'd let you guys decide who's gonna take point." He looked at Flowers. "We'll be mountin' up in about five, Turk. Can you have everybody in position by then?"

"Sure thing, boss." Flowers grinned at his friend and stood up to stretch.

Peterson addressed the group, "Remember to keep your spacing today, alright? Let's have another really boring day."

Flowers turned toward Kelly, "Hey Irish, you want point today?"

"Shit man, if you think I'm ready...." Kelly hesitated for a moment. Afraid of the idea of being out in front, he decided it probably was his turn, and besides, it was something of an honor to walk in the lead position. Flowers wouldn't have suggested it if he didn't feel Kelly had earned his grunt boots. "Sure, I'll be alright."

"Oh no, we got slow Joe from Kokomo out front today." Dunlop said, laughing.

"Don't worry, Spiderman," Flowers said, "Kelly makes such a big target, we'll get a nice loud warning when he hits the ground after they shoot his ass." Flowers looked over toward Miller, "Right, Fast-Man?"

"Sounds okay to me. He'll take good care of us." Miller winked at Kelly. "Hey, did you guys hear about that girl Hargrove was bragging about from the ambush a couple of nights ago?"

"No, man," Kelly said. "What'd the fucker do this time?"

"Well," Miller chewed on a long stalk of grass. "He got his usual three kills, of course. But he said that he and another guy raped a girl from the village they went into that night." He tossed the grass onto the ground. "He swore she looked just like some gook chick he seen selling stuff at the wire in An Khe." He looked at Dunlop, whose face was expressionless behind a dangling cigarette. "That wouldn't have been that little friend of yours now, would it?"

"No way, man." Dunlop shook his head. "We're too far from An Khe, out here. Probably just someone looked like her."

"Anyway," Miller said, "I was thinking maybe ol' Hargrove finally pulled one stunt too many and somebody decided to track him down last night."

"It's a thought," Flowers said as he adjusted his pack straps.

Kelly had never been so scared in his young life. He was ten yards in front of the next man in line, walking point for D company. At first his legs felt almost detached from the rest of his body, and the constant pulsing of adrenalin in his veins made his sixty-pound rucksack barely noticeable. He knew enough to stay off the trail where all the booby traps would be, but he was stumbling over creepers and rocks more than he actually walked. He couldn't see more than twenty feet ahead.

Every plant and shadow looked like a booby trap, ready to explode. Every step felt like it would lead him straight into a pit with poison tipped punji stakes waiting to impale his foot. His heart was pounding like a sledgehammer and his mouth felt like it was full of used sandpaper.

Flowers had given Kelly a machete to clear a trail as he moved along, but he could only take two or three steps at a time before having to stop and whack away at the jungle. His M16 was slung across his back and over his pack to leave his arms free for breaking trail and wiping the sweat from his forehead. His thoughts wandered. *Maybe that's my problem, a lack of ambition- Fuck getting ahead, fuck politics, fuck everything, come to think of it.*

After about half an hour of squishing through the soggy undergrowth Kelly became tired enough to relax. *Why not calm down*, he thought. *There's an end to everything, so maybe they'll take me off this point shit pretty soon.*

He jumped a small stream and then hoisted himself up the steep bank with some dangling vines. As Kelly reached the top of the bank and raised his head to scan the jungle beyond, the first thing he saw was one very dead GI. "Stinson," Kelly muttered as he was overcome by a wave of nausea.

Moments later, Gage poked his head up over the stream bank. "Hey man, I heard you puking up here." He climbed to the top of the bank and scooted over next to Kelly, "And now I see why."

Stinson had been shot in the head and lashed to the trunk of a small tree. His boots dangled sadly just above the ground. A large amount of blood had congealed on his face and shoulders, and another dark bloody patch spread out on his trousers below his crotch. The man's penis had been cut off and then stuffed into his tightly closed jaw. He looked like he was biting on a large, shriveled hot dog. "Well, I guess we can safely say that Stinson wasn't Jewish," Gage said

"Huh?" Kelly looked up vomit dripping from his chin.

"Foreskin." Gage pointed to a piece of flesh protruding from the end of Stinson's penis.

"Oh yeah," Kelly said, bending over to retch again.

"We ain't got a lotta time here, fellas." Flowers had made it up the stream bank and stood with a hand on Kelly's shoulder. No one could take his eyes away from Stinson's mangled corpse. "We got to check it for booby traps real quick." Flowers slung his rifle over his shoulder and stepped over to the tree. "Then get it down and get our young asses the hell outta here." Gage helped Flowers examine Stinson's body for trigger wires, a favorite trick of the Viet Cong.

Soldiers continued to appear at the top of the stream bank. Six men were now bunched up staring at the body and making a fine target for an ambush. When all the men from Third Squad had gathered, Miller came along at the head of Second Squad. Fast Eddie quickly sized up the situation and walked over to Flowers.

"You guys okay gettin' him down?" Miller said.

"Yeah, we'll be alright," Flowers continued to examine the body and the rope lashings, probing gently at suspicious areas.

"I'll take point from here. You guys can fall in after my squad goes by." Miller looked over at Kelly. "Hey troop, mind if I borrow that machete?"

"Sure." Kelly held the big knife out to Miller, "glad to get rid of it."

"Just keep everybody moving." Miller slung his rifle over his shoulder. "No rubberneckin', okay?"

"Got ya, Eddie," Flowers answered. "Hey Irish," he called to Kelly.

"Yeah?" Kelly was sitting on the ground with his head leaning on his knees, but looked up when Flowers spoke.

"You in charge of the trail," Flowers said as he looked closely at the ropes around Stinson's knees. "Keep 'em movin' as they come up over the bank. All they gotta do is follow where Fast Man's breakin' trail, okay?"

"Yeah, right," said Kelly weakly.

Three hours later the men stopped for a breather and refueling. The two bodies had been carried on poles as the company continued its' march. The men's ponchos served as shrouds. Two soldiers carried each body. Return cargo for the noon chopper.

"Demonstration purposes," Miller explained in between mouthfuls. "They were watchin' Kelly make his way, and they picked a place to hang the body where they was pretty sure he'd run into it."

"What about ol' Hargrove?" Kelly asked. "Why didn't they string him up too?" Hargrove was found about thirty yards from Stinson, his throat cut and a bullet in his stomach,

"Ran out of time, Bear," Miller said. "You were just too damn quick for 'em."

General laughter.

Kelly had earned this nickname when Gage remarked that walking behind him looked like a movie he had seen of a papa grizzly bear on a trail in Alaska. Kelly became Papa Bear, Bear for short. And occasionally 'Irish.'

"But why Stinson?" Kelly wondered out loud. "From what I heard, he was the last guy who'd be messin' with some girl out here."

"Hargrove probably took Stinson with him into the village. He always made sure there was somebody to watch his back while he was havin' his fun," Miller said. "The Gooks probably didn't know which one did it, only that they was both in the vil that night."

"Hey, I think they're moving up front," said Dunlop. The usual clinks and clanks of soldiers getting ready to move out were discernible to the Third Squad guys.

"Fuck, why don't we just hang for a while?" Miller said. "The company'll eventually figure out we never left and come look for us, what do you guys think?"

"Yeah but just think about all that fun, travel and adventure we'd miss for the next few hours." Flowers spoke as he stood and began arranging his pack straps while the others followed suit.

An hour later, several members of Third Squad stopped for a moment, crouched behind the cover of tree branches and looked out over a large meadow with a trail winding through it. The elephant grass on both sides of the trail was about six feet high. The tops of the tall green strands hung over, unmoving in the breathless afternoon heat.

"Over there, bro." Flowers pointed to the dense growth around the edge of the meadow. "That's where you're gonna take us, alright?"

Green held the machete and nodded as he looked over where Flowers was pointing. Green was small, but he was among the fastest point men in the company. A regular GI jungle-clearing machine, he had been given the nickname Black Power by Flowers.

"What are you men doing all bunched up here?" It was the new Second Platoon Lieutenant Dillard Whalen, fresh from Officer Candidate School.

Flowers looked up, "I was showin' Private Green a safe route for the company, around the meadow, sir."

Whalen was one of those wet-behind-the-ears 2nd louies who had arrived in-country convinced that the trouble with the American Army in Vietnam was not enough determined officers like himself. He had been at war all of three weeks now, having arrived via chopper during the current patrol, and had already acquired what Flowers called the L-T butt strut; he walked like a horny rooster, parading in front of his hens. He had a pudgy face with more acne than whiskers. At this very moment he appeared to be about to take command of the situation and validate his momma's belief in the overwhelming, natural superiority of her only son.

"Sgt Flowers, I want you to send your point man through that meadow, on the trail we all clearly see, right over there." Whalen pointed to the path and smiled.

"Sir, I seen the trail when we first come up." Flowers was squatting next to Whalen, leaning on his rifle. "But that's what makes me kinda nervous about goin' thataway." He shifted his weight and looked back at the meadow. "Charlie figures we gonna want to take the easy way, so he'll leave somethin' there for us that'll ruin our whole day, right on that path, sir."

"That's nonsense, Sergeant Flowers." Whalen smirked. "If there's a mine or something like that out there, we'll just have to be extra careful as we make our way, won't we? Our main problem is that we're going too damn slow, always whacking through the bushes." He took off his steel pot and wiped his brow. "Now, there's three other companies heading for the battalion rendezvous tomorrow. I don't want everybody there waiting on us. Do you understand what I'm saying, Sergeant Flowers?"

"Well, sir, I suppose my main thought is to get these guys there in one piece." Flowers spared no effort in caution since the ill-fated ambush three months ago. He looked Whalen directly in the eye as he spoke.

"Sergeant, I'm giving you a direct order to send your man out on that trail over there."

"Hey, what's the problem?" Rollie Peterson walked up to the tree line where a dozen members of Second and Third Squad were gathered, listening intently to the whispered argument between Whalen and Flowers.

"There's no problem here, Sergeant Peterson," Lt. Whalen thrust out his jaw and puffed up his chest. "I just finished explaining to Sgt. Flowers, here, the proper route across that meadow."

"Pete," Flowers stood and pointed at the trail, "Lieutenant Whalen says I should send Green onto that trail. He's thinkin' about being late for the meetin' tomorrow and I'm more concerned with gettin' my man blown to kingdom come." He looked back at Peterson. "Just look at that damn trail, Pete. You know it's a trap."

Peterson nodded and placed a hand on Flowers arm, then turned to Lt. Whalen. "Sir I'm afraid I have to agree with Sgt Flowers on this one. It looks pretty scary...."

"Sgt Peterson, I'm not asking for your opinion here. I am issuing a direct order to you and to Flowers to send your point man down that fucking trail! Now, enough of this GI bullshit, we're going by the book this time."

"But sir," Peterson waved his hands to emphasize his point, "we've already lost two wounded to mines on this patrol."

"Alright, for Christ's sake!" Whalen pulled on his pack straps and picked up his M16. "I'm gonna take fucking point!" He stepped out toward the meadow, then turned around to address the assembled group. The sun beat down on him, outlining his body against the blue sky and the bright green elephant grass. "Would you gentlemen be so kind as to follow me across this field?"

"Right, sir!" Peterson answered smartly.

"Power," Flowers grabbed his volatile squad member by the arm as he whispered. Green smiled and shook his head, "you go next, but keep plenty of distance from that crazy fucker." The two men watched Whalen march off toward the trail like he was on parade.

"I swear to God, Turk, I'm gonna frag that motherfucker!" said Green. "I'm gonna frag his ass tonight, see if I don't."

After Whalen had gone about thirty yards, Green fell in behind him, stepping cautiously, like on a frozen pond early in the winter. One after another, the Third Squad troops left the shade and safety of the trees and followed Green. Kelly noticed that Whalen and Green had disappeared around a curve. The searing heat jumped at him along with the sound of the cicadas singing in the grass. *Probably celebrating how they don't have to fight the war*, he thought. *Damn bugs, just watchin' us go by.*

It wasn't very long before the meadow exploded. The line came to a halt, and two medics carrying a stretcher hurried to the front of the column. A few minutes later, the medics came back with Whalen, now missing most of both legs and bouncing on the bloody stretcher with the rhythm of the two men as they carried him. When they passed Kelly, he noticed that Whalen was shaking uncontrollably. The jagged ends of his shattered leg bones were poking into the air like bloody, broken sticks. Minutes later, the rest of Third Squad filed past, back toward the tree line.

"Fall in behind us, man," Flowers said as he went by Kelly. "We goin' back to where we shoulda been the first goddamn place." He looked back at Green, who was coming up behind him. "Looks like ol' Charlie took care of the new L-T for you, Power."

"Man, this sure has been one fuck of a day." Vandyne fell in with Third Squad painstakingly making its way around the large meadow.

"You got that right, Lizz." Kelly turned around and whispered loud enough for him, Dunlop, and Tuggins to hear. Kelly came to a large fallen tree stopped for a second. "Did you guys see those bones stickin out and all that blood?" The other three waited for Kelly to move ahead.

"Yeah, and just think, ol' Whalen has to go through life with his right leg shorter than his left," Vandyne said.

"Actually, Lizz, I think it was his left that was the short one," Dunlop said, nodding his head with an air of gravity.

"Naw, Frank." Kelly placed his rifle up on top of the tree and climbed over, "Lizzard's right, it was the right that was the itty bitty one."

"Hey Tug," said Vandyne, "what do you think, right or left?"

"Tell the truth," Tuggins said, "I don't s'pose it much matters."

"You guys better shut up and get your goddamn spacing," Flowers said. "We don't need no more shit this trip, okay?"

"All right, all right," Dunlop said humorously. "We're comin'."

CHAPTER XVIII

April 27, 1970

RIDE THE MAGIC BUS

GREEN RAISED HIS ARM AND SLAPPED THE THREE OF CLUBS DOWN onto Peterson's king of hearts.

"That's trump, Pete," Tuggins said as he pulled the three of hearts from his hand and laid it on the pile.

"Clubs are trump?" said Peterson. He looked over Tuggins, then back at his hand. "Aw, shit."

Kelly spun his five of hearts into the pile of cards on the bed in front of him. "Yes, Sergeant Peterson," he looked at Peterson with a triumphant grin, "I do believe clubs are trump."

Green scooped up the cards with a flourish and added them to his stack. After returning from evening chow the four soldiers were using a bed as a makeshift card table. "That makes our bid, Papa Bear." Green pulled the queen of clubs from his hand and snapped it down with authority. "The rest is gravy, my man." Green nodded rhythmically with a satisfied grin on his face.

Miller and Dunlop entered the tent and walked over to where the others were playing cards. "Hey, Bear," said Miller. "Spiderman and I were talkin' at dinner and we thought we'd ask you somethin', if it's okay."

Kelly looked up at Miller, "Sure, what's up?"

"Well, we was wondering if you ever looked where you're shootin' during a firefight. We both noticed last patrol that you always seem to have your eyes closed or somethin', just stickin' your rifle out in front of you pointing up in the air and lettin' her rip."

"Yeah, I guess you're right." Kelly paused for a second. "Man, I don't think I could ever shoot people because they're standing up for their country." He looked around the group of young soldiers for their reactions to what he had just said. Everyone, including Flowers and Gage who had just walked in, were looking at Kelly in stunned silence.

"Look," Miller said, "you didn't ask to be here, and neither did anybody else in this tent." Most heads, including Kelly's were nodding. "But that don't change the fact that even though the gooks might have a point, they'll fuckin' kill us, just like they did Stinson, if we don't kill them first. Know what I mean?"

"Yeah, I know," Kelly said with his head bowed.

"He's right, Tom," Dunlop said.

"Next time," Miller was looking right at Kelly as he spoke, "I want to see you look where you're shootin'. At least point the fucking gun at 'em. Don't worry about the gooks, they can take care of themselves. Your job is to protect the guys you see here."

"Okay," Kelly said softly.

"Hey, who's got winners?" Green asked jovially.

"Brother Gage and I would be pleased to jump in and show you all how to play some whist." Flowers said.

"Well, Turk, don't just stand there," said Green. "These two losers were just getting up." He gestured toward Peterson and Tuggins, who made way for the two newcomers.

Flowers picked up his cards and began to sort them. "Pete, the Professor and I were over by the main gate a while ago and you wouldn't believe the shit they got movin' out there."

"Yeah, and it's all heading west," said Gage. "Tanks, artillery, most of the trucks in the division, big cloud of dust. We counted twenty Chinooks out at the airfield, all loaded up, ready to go."

"Somethin's comin', Pete," said Flowers.

The company had flown back to base camp three days after the battalion rendezvous on the twentieth. This was their fourth day back in camp, an unusually long time out of the field for D company.

Peterson nodded and said, "Yeah, we're going out again in a couple a days."

"Where to this time?" Miller asked.

Peterson looked at Miller. "Sorry Eddie, but I'm not supposed to say."

Silence descended on the group for a few moments.

"Hey Pete," Flowers said, "what did those two captains I saw you talking to yesterday want?" Flowers spun a card onto the playing surface. "They looked like they came from somewhere safe, you know, clean fingernails."

Peterson raised and lowered his eyebrows. "CID, from Saigon."

"Whoa!" said Miller. "Now what would the Criminal Investigation boys be interested in at Third of the Eighth?"

"Checking into the movement of a large volume of contraband merchandise through An Khe."

"Drugs?" Dunlop asked casually, his face inscrutably blank.

"No," Peterson answered, a smile spreading across his face, "believe it or not, this time it's clothes." He stroked his mustache, "They said it looks like maybe a quarter of a million dollars worth have been ripped off from the PX system."

"Your play, Gage," Dunlop said.

"Oh, yeah." He took a card form his hand and dropped it down.

Slap, went Green's ten of diamonds. "What you got for me, Papa Bear?"

"Huh?" Kelly was thinking about the coming operation. "Oh yeah." He brought his attention back to his cards and considered his next play.

"C'mon Kelly, it won't hurt to try it just this once" Dunlop said as he raised a warm cup of cherry cool aid to his mouth. The whist game and associated party had gone on for several hours beyond taps the night before. Finally, around 0200, everyone had collapsed in their bunks and gone to sleep. In the morning, the D company heads--potheads--and brothers had come out to formation at 0700, and promptly stumbled back to their tent to try and stack a few more Z's.

It was supposed to be Peterson's job to make sure everybody was up and working on some useless project or other, but he had partied pretty hard himself and had announced in the morning that he felt no great desire to play platoon sergeant just then.

As Kelly scanned the noontime mess hall, he noticed that the entire gang had awakened in time for lunch. He looked back at Dunlop and said, "Man, I really thought this fuckin' thing was winding down." He felt scared and a little nauseous about the operation starting the next day. When he first sat down he had eaten a chocolate donut, but then promptly lost his appetite to a queasy feeling in his stomach. He was wondering if the coming action might turn out to be the last one for him. Try as he might, he couldn't get the thought of Whalen, lying legless on the stretcher, out of his head. What would it be like if that happened to him? Would Becky want to stay with him? He pushed his tray to the side still full of food and lit a cigarette to go with his coffee.

"See, there you go again." Said Dunlop as he spread mustard, catsup and relish on both of his hot dogs. "You're always trying to analyze everything too much." He took a big bite out of one of the dogs and then a sip of koolaid. "How many days you got left, Kelly?"

"What do you mean, in Nam?" Kelly shrugged his shoulders, "I'm not sure." He looked at the ceiling for a moment, "Let's see, I flew in to Saigon on January 14 and today's April 27, so that's a little more than three months...."

"Man, I can see half your problem already." Dunlop set his food down, "You gotta keep track of your days, man. Me for instance, I got two hundred and twenty-six to go." He popped the end of the first hot dog into his mouth and chewed for a minute. "Now, that doesn't sound so groovy, until you consider how much better it is than three hundred and sixty-five." He grinned and brought his hand up with his thumb and forefinger about an inch apart, "I'm getting a little short, man."

"I think I see what you mean," Kelly said.

"Sure, now all you gotta do is subtract the number of days you been here from three hundred and sixty-five and then keep track of it, just like we used to do in basic."

Kelly counted in his head for a few moments. "I think I got two hundred and seventy-two days left."

"Great!" Dunlop smiled. "Now doesn't that make you feel a little better?"

"I guess so."

"Especially when you think about all those poor fuckers over three hundred."

"Hmmph." Kelly knocked the ash from his smoke onto his food tray, "It'll be a whole lot better when it gets into single digits."

"You got that right," said Dunlop and picked up his second hot dog. "So, why don't you come and take a ride on the Magic Bus today? I guarantee you won't be disappointed." He took another bite and sat there chewing.

Kelly considered Dunlop's suggestion for a moment. "What the hell? At least there'll be some entertainment watching you guys get stoned out of your minds," he said, took a deep drag on his cigarette.

"And get to hear some of the finest fuckin' rock 'n roll tapes this side of Saigon, don't forget." Dunlop stood and picked up his lunch tray and jungle hat. "Let's go, man." He looked at his watch. "Bus leaves in about ten minutes."

"Where's it going to?"

"It don't go nowhere," Dunlop said and laughed. "Just rides around base camp with music humming and smoke rollin'." He flashed his winning smile. "You're gonna feel a lot better. No shit."

Kelly gathered up his things and followed Dunlop over to the kitchen window to hand in his tray to the KP. The two walked into the street, headed for the division dispensary. There, they found the Magic Bus with its engine running, ready for the afternoon tour.

"Sit here, man," Dunlop said. The thirty-man bus was full. Kelly's and Dunlop's were the last two seats.

Kelly looked at Dunlop with his lip curled and a thumb pointed at the GI sleeping in the seat next to him. "Is he gonna puke on me or what?" Kelly whispered to Dunlop

Dunlop laughed, "Nah, man." He reached into his pocket and produced a small plastic bag filled with dried green leaves. "That's Samson," he nodded toward the snoring fellow. "He's too fuckin' short to stay awake." Dunlop sprinkled some of the potent marijuana onto a cigarette paper and rolled a fat doobie. "He's goin' home in about a week, he won't bother you."

The door closed and rock music began to blare from the elaborate speaker system, the bus rolled slowy away from the dispensary. As the GI's started their journey around Fourth Division Camp, the Magic Bus filled with a light blue, pungent smoke.

Dulnop lit his joint. He inhaled deeply and held his breath for a moment. A look of contentment spread across his face and he exhaled grandly. "Take a toke, bro." Dunlop reached across the asile with the smoldering doobie.

"I dunno, man." Kelly looked worried.

"Oh c'mon." Dunlop reached a little further toward Kelly. "Nobody's gonna tell on you to your commie buddies."

"Aw, what the fuck," said Kelly. He took a draw and handed Dunlop's doobie back to him.

"You see that guy sittin' by himself in the second seat?" The scruffy GI Dunlop pointed out raised a joint to his lips and took a drag. "He's CID, man. Steer clear." Dunlop raised his eyebrows, smiled, and nodded at Kelly.

"So Brother Tug, you say they ta-takin' us out tomorrow for some k-kinda invasion?" PFC Gormick from D company's First Platoon, stood with his feet spread. His hand had healed up from the fight on the last patrol. Gormick looked down at the shorter Tuggins from his six feet three inches. The light, skinned black man spoke with an occasional stutter. He kept his hair as bushy as he could get away with and wore large, Army issue black-rimmed glasses. He was not what anybody would call handsome, but from what people said, he did okay with the ladies, back in the world.

Tuggins looked up at Gormick and nodded, "That's right, bro." He folded his arms across his chest and waited for the next question from the group gathered around him in front of the Mess Hall. There were a dozen black soldiers, standing in a circle with Tuggins in the middle. He had mentioned to a couple of the guys during lunch what he knew about the coming operation. He first had led the group in an elaborate version of Dap, to bring the guys together, but also to keep the lifers away. They didn't like to be around much when the bro's were doing their Dap.

"So Tug," Gage said, "how'd you find out about all of this invasion stuff?"

"For the last few days, everybody been talkin' bout all the heavy shit we got moving west, toward Cambodia," Tuggins began.

"That's right," and "Right on," came from several in the group.

"So, I called this guy in Saigon who writes for a couple of newspapers back in the world." Tuggins took Steve Beltzer's card from his pocket and handed it to Gage, who passed it around for the others to examine. "He told me that the President wants to clear the NVA out of Cambodia, and guess who gets to go do it for him?"

"They sendin' the Fa-Fearsome Fourth out, to take care of business, huh?" Gormick said.

Sarcastic chuckles and guffaws came from several of the assembled soldiers.

"Yeah, and they got units from the 101st, 82nd, the 1st Cav, and the 11th Armored Cav goin' in, too. Not to mention a whole bunch of ARVNs." Tuggins looked from person to person as he spoke, "Thirty, maybe forty thousand troops altogether."

"Damn, Brother." Gage shook his head as he spoke. "I got fifty-two days left in Sheeitnam. I'm supposed to get married two weeks after I'm back home. Ain't this a bitch? "

"When's this bullshit goin' down?" Gormick asked angrily. "They just ka-keep on finding ways to throw our young asses into the fa-fire."

"And every time they do, a few more of us don't make it out," Tuggins added.

CHAPTER XIX

April 29, 1970

0630 HOURS

INVASION

PETERSON ROSE IN THE DARK TO BEGIN PREPARATIONS FOR THE day's operation, then woke up everyone else so they would be ready for the 0600 formation. One lantern cast a dim, flickering glow, a soft breeze whispered through the rolled up doorway of the tent. The men were quiet as they stuffed their rucksacks with gear for a day out on the killing trails of Vietnam, each lost in his own thoughts.

Kelly looked up from his rucksack to see Dunlop bristling with grenades and M16 magazines, and extending a new deck of playing cards toward him. "Thanks, man." He glanced at the girlie pictures on the back of the cards, smiled at Dunlop and placed the cards in his shirt pocket.

"That'll give you something to remind you of home." Dunlop picked up his steel pot and placed it on his head. "Besides, you like to play solitaire so much I figured you could use 'em when we get really bored out there."

"Yeah, sure," Kelly said. "Maybe we can get a little whist game going during the first firefight."

"Here, Kelly," Dunlop held out a paper lunch bag. "stick this in your rucksack, OK?" Kelly shoved the bag down to the bottom of his pack. "There's about twelve grand in there," Dunlop whispered. "Try not to lose your pack."

Kelly was stunned. He couldn't think of anything to do but nod.

"We sold a few watches, man," Dunlop whispered. He nodded at Kelly, then turned around and walked back to his bunk. He hoisted his full rucksack to his shoulders, slung his rifle over his shoulder and walked back toward Kelly's bunk. "You ready?"

Kelly groaned as he rose from his bunk, pack already on, and leaned over to pick up his rifle. A grinding fear had formed a lump in the pit of his stomach soon after he startled awake. *What the fuck was Cambodia anyway?* He wondered. *Talk about injun country!* "Motherfuck it, man. Let's go get 'em."

The men of the Third Squad strolled onto the parade ground where the battalion was assembling. Twin rows of two-and-a-half ton troop-carrier trucks hunkered down, their motors idling in a rumbling diesel chorus. The lights of the trucks shone through the blue exhaust, lending an eerie quality to the scene. Kelly and Dunlop lined up, then Tuggins, Miller (newly demoted back to Third Squad for his excessively shabby hair), Lizzard, and Gage. Flowers, Peterson and Green brought up the rear. Kelly watched Flowers step between Peterson and Green, as Green waved his arms and looked agitated.

Kelly looked out over the seven hundred members of his Battalion, the Third of the Eighth, as they stood in the field waiting for the order to climb aboard the rumbling trucks. Guys were poking each other, sharing cigarettes and a few off-color jokes. Despite Kelly's misgivings over where they were headed that day, he felt a sense of pride and belonging. The Third of the Eighth was an outfit with an awesome amount of power at its disposal. Most of the men had been tempered in the fire of combat. They were a hardened veteran group.

Likely as not, they would be moving under the cover of the full might of the US military-helicopter gunships, fighter bombers from aircraft carriers lurking off the coast, and maybe B-52s with their mind-numbing five-hundred-pound bombs.

But somehow Charlie always took his calculated gambles and made the American grunts pay the price. American casualty totals on the news were all that anybody cared about back in the world, and Charlie was always aware of that.

When all the soldiers were present and accounted for the Major in front bellowed, "Let's mount up!" Immediately, the men climbed aboard, urged on by their sergeants and lieutenants. As the first deuce-and-a-halfs sped away, the drivers waiting in line anxiously goosed their engines until it was their turn to leave.

Third Squad stood waiting.

"Hey Spiderman!" a voice called out.

"Three guys in suits are lookin' for you back at the tent, man."

"They say what they want?" asked Dunlop.

"Just you, troop."

Dunlop turned to Kelly, "I'm gonna get up on the truck now, man." He grabbed his rifle and pack. "If those CID guys come over here lookin' for me, just tell them I went on sick call, OK?"

Kelly nodded.

A few minutes later the rest of Third Squad hopped on the truck. Kelly wound up at the end of one of the benches, scrunched up against the truck wall. Gormick sat next to him and took up a lot of space with his long legs and linebacker shoulders. Along with the sixty-five pound rucksack on Gormick's back, his helmet and rifle, plus a few Laws he had slung over his shoulders there just wasn't a lot of room left for Kelly.

Gormick bounced down onto Kelly each time the speeding truck hit a hole in the road. Gormick bellowed a good-natured "Sorry, man!" every time, until the other guys joined in like a chorus. Kelly wasn't so sure how funny it was.

After about forty-five minutes, the convoy turned onto a smoother road and the group in the truck fell silent. Everybody assumed a blank, "let's get it over with" expression, and after a few minutes, several guys even looked like they might be asleep.

"I know we headed west now," Flowers said later, as he looked up at the pale-blue morning sky and then at his watch. "We goin' to Cambodia, Pete." Flowers sat three men down from Peterson, and he spoke loud enough for everybody on the truck to hear.

Peterson nodded, looking at the floor.

"Shit, you guys," Vandyne called out from Kelly's end of the truck. "what the fuck's in Cambodia?" Lizzard looked around the group.

"Nuthin' but a whole lotta trouble," Tuggins said.

"I was afraid of that," Lizzard answered.

"So what we supposed to do about it, huh?" Flowers seemed a little peeved.

"Shit's got to stop somewhere, Turk," Tuggins said.

"Oh, yeah." said Flowers as he pulled his helmet over his eyes and leaned back against the side of the truck.

Kelly relaxed and dozed off after calculating his odds at surviving the day at a little better than fifty to one. *Not bad*, he thought.

* * *

Everything was delayed at the moment for Third of the Eighth's part of the Cambodia invasion. They waited near the border. A field kitchen was set up to give the troops a hot meal before taking them across that border and throwing them into the soup.

Kelly reached for the last dirty lunch tray in the dishwater pot and let out a "finished at last" sigh. It was hot as a motherfucker and he couldn't distinguish between the sweat and the greasy water soaking his OD t-shirt.

The mess sergeant walked down to Kelly's end of the line and told him to head back to his platoon. "Okay, Sarge," said Kelly. It didn't take much convincing. He dipped his hands in the rinse barrel, shook off the water, and set out to find his squad.

The Battalion fanned out around the small grove of banana trees where the kitchen/eating area and the command center had been set-up to take advantage of a little shade from the burning mid-day sun. Alpha, Bravo, Charlie and Delta companies were positioned at each end of a fifty-yard spoke radiating from the hub at the banana grove. D company had the worst spot of the four, up on a dusty rise with almost no shade. All there was for the soldiers to do was lay around with helmets over their eyes and try to get some sleep while they waited for the helicopters. The battalion area was secure with a huge chunk of the American Army patrolling nearby and more air traffic than an international airport at eight on a weekday morning. Fighter-bombers and gunships were all streaking around, looking for something to kill.

As Kelly strolled past the command post he noticed a group of six officers standing in a semicircle, talking to each other in muffled tones with their hands on their hips and looking at something near the base of a banana tree. He decided to walk over and have a look.

"Holy shit!" Kelly said under his breath.

Seated against the trunk was Private Raymond Green. Black Power had his M16 at the ready with his finger around the trigger.

Kelly walked over next to Lt. Winston.

"Winnie," Kelly whispered, "what the fuck is going on, man?"

Winston looked over his shoulder, back toward Green. "Shit, Kelly," he was shaking his head "nobody knows nothing for sure, except Green here's locked and loaded, and he's not talking."

Kelly looked at Green's expressionless face. His eyelids were drooping so low his eyes were almost shut. That is, until Captain Welby moved slightly toward him, and Green brought the barrel of his gun around directly aimed to Welby's belly-button. Welby froze, the color completely draining from his face, then raised his hands slowly in surrender and took a few steps back.

"Fucker means business." Winston turned his back toward Green and folded his arms. "You gotta give him that much."

Kelly put his hand on Winston's shoulder. "So what are they gonna do?"

"I don't know, man." Winston took his steel pot off and rubbed sweat from his forehead. "CO put in a call to division. We're waiting to hear back from them." He spat on the ground.

Kelly took a few steps toward Green. "Hey Power, what's up, man?"

Green swung his rifle around toward Kelly and slowly shook his head.

"A bunch of people have tried that Kelly. He just isn't interested." Winston took Kelly by the arm as he spoke and pulled him back, away from Green and the group of officers.

"Well, I guess I'll be taking off now." Kelly said.

Winston nodded at him with a smirk and Kelly set off for the dusty plateau where he figured he'd find the other guys in Third Squad. Maybe they'd know something about what Green was up to.

As Kelly approached the group of troopers on the rise he noticed that there were guys from all four platoons, all fully armed for combat.

"Now they want to send us into another country; Camfuckinbodia! Where's this shit gonna end?" Miller was speaking. "I tell you what. Before they're done, they'll have us fighting in ten goddamn countries, all at the same time!"

"Right ons" and "yeahs" came from the group, which looked to Kelly like it contained about half of the Brothers and Heads in the company. The talk seemed to be either about what was going to happen to Green, or whether they should refuse to go into Cambodia, or both.

"Look here," Van Dyne began, "they could shoot each and every one of us for this shit." Everybody fell silent in order to listen to the Lizzard. "And I know there's guys here that're short enough to not want to spend the next eighteen months in LBJ."

Three helicopters, two transport hueys and and a medivac, streaked overhead and then landed near the battalion command post.

When their engines quieted, Tuggins said, "Don't have to be short, Bro, to want to stay out of LBJ." He stood up and scanned the group as he spoke

Lizzard chuckled. "Yeah, you're right about that, Tug." He shrugged his shoulders. "I know you're talking from experience."

"So, dig, you guys," Gramercy, a Second Platoon new guy from Pittsburgh spoke, "If all of us decided to take the day off here, what could they do, send us to Nam?" Spirited agreement came from many in the group, with little dissent.

Dunlop stood up. "Hey, let's hear from the company Red." He turned toward Kelly, seated next to him. "C'mon pappa bear, give us your take on this shit."

Scattered applause, some hoots, and a few boos came from the group. Kelly stood up, leaning his rifle against his pack on the ground, so his hands would be free while he spoke.

Fuck, he thought, *this is a little different from talking to college kids about kicking Dow Chemical off campus.* He took his steel pot off and set it on his rifle. "Lizzard's right, we all could get in a heap of shit for even talking about this, let alone doing it." He paused a moment to swallow. "It looks like ole' Tricky Dick wants to try and close down the Ho Chi Minh Trail. And I guess if he could actually do it, the war would probably stop and we could all go home next week."

Solid cheering about "going home next week."

"But you guys know how the VC and NVA can take enough casualties to have every mommasan in Vietnam crying her eyes out, and the next day they always come back for more, and the next and the next...." Kelly glanced at Tuggins, who was standing on the other side of the group with his muscular arms folded across his chest and nodding his head. Kelly continued, "If we all stick together, I don't think they can make us fight today." He took a deep breath. "Tell the truth though, I'm not sure what they'll do. But I guess it's worth a try."

The brothers were very concerned about Green, and the heads were scared about the potential consequences of standing up to the Army. Peterson sided with Lizzard and warned the group about the possibility of hard prison time. Everybody said the war sucked, and some guys told stories about buddies who had been killed or gravely wounded.

Right after Rollie Peterson finished talking, a short series of shots rang out from the vicinity of the command post.

Peterson motioned to Miller to come with him and headed toward the gunfire. Tuggins caught up with them and the three soldiers hurried to find out what had happened.

Just about everybody had spoken their piece, and the group fell silent.

Minutes later, Peterson, Miller and Tuggins reappeared with Lt. Winston, all looking grim. Tuggins looked at the brother's in the group motioning for them to follow him. The twenty two black guys all walked with Tuggins about fifty yards away, where they gathered around him and did some Dap.

From where Kelly sat, the brothers appeared pretty serious, but words from across the field were unintelligible.

Kelly walked over to Peterson and Winston. Dunlop and Miller came over and joined them. Kelly nodded to Winston and said, "So what happened with Green back at that tree?"

"It went pretty quick, according to Top. Division sent in a Medivac and a couple of choppers full of MPs to arrest him." Winston looked over his shoulder at the group with Tuggins and returned his attention to Kelly. "The MPs set up a perimeter around Green with their 16s locked and loaded." He lit a cigarette and took a couple of deep puffs. "Then somebody, Top's pretty sure it was Captain Welby, shot Green and he collapsed. A couple of the MPs shot at him too, but quit when they saw how bad he was hit." Winston took another deep drag on his Marlboro. "Green squeezed a burst off on his way down, but it went wild. Then he dropped his weapon and just laid there."

"Was he breathing when they took him away?" Dunlop asked.

"Looked like it to me, but he was a bloody mess. Hard to tell for sure," Winston answered. "After the choppers left, Top went over to Welby and took his rifle and smelled the chamber. The little cocksucker swore he didn't fire first."

"Oh, sweet Jesus!" said Kelly. Discipline was beginning to unravel in the company. This is just what he and all his anti-war and socialist pals in PLP had fantasized about. This was his chance to really stick it to the Army and the whole war effort. So why was he confused as hell with a burning dread in his gut? *It's weird,* he thought, *but going into Cambodia looks simple compared to this.* "Sweet Jesus!" He said, again.

"Here they come!" Van Dyne stood up and pointed across the field at the group of black soldiers with Tuggins. They were moving together, across the field and toward the group of Heads on the rise. When the groups were a few yards apart, Tuggins stepped in front and set his rifle at his side, holding it by the end of the barrel and letting the butt rest on the ground. The other black guys gathered close behind him.

"Fellas," Tuggins addressed the heads, "we goin' home." It was a simple statement and Tuggins said it like he was standing in his Daddy's pulpit, greeting the congregation.

Murmurs arose from the heads, a few "Goddamns,"and then Kelly said, "What do you mean Tug?" He took a step forward. "What's going on?"

"We talked it over, and here's how we figure it." Tuggins used his free hand to emphasize his points. "They shot Green like a dog."

Several "Right ons" and "Yeahs" came from the brothers.

Tuggins went on, "The Army and the government are going to just keep this shit goin' 'til somebody makes 'em stop."

"Sorry Tug," Miller spoke from where he was seated, "but are you saying you guys can make them stop the war?"

Several heads laughed at that, but none of the brothers did.

"Naw," Tuggins replied. "But we are saying it's time for us to quit helping 'em keep it going." Tuggins turned toward Miller.

Fast Eddie chuckled. "Yeah, I see your point there, Tug." Miller scratched his goatee. "But look, man, don't you think they'll just shoot you guys like they did Green?"

"Not if we can get a few of you white boys to come with us." He spoke to the group of heads. "What about it, y'all?" He broke into a winning smile.

Dunlop took a step toward the brothers. "This company would be pretty fuckin' boring without you guys." He picked up his M16 and rested it on a shoulder. "I'm in." Then he turned to Tuggins, "So where we going?"

Tuggins smiled and said, "Saigon, Spiderman, we're gonna sit in front of the embassy till they send us home. We ain't lookin for a fight, but we'll protect ourselves if we have to."

Expressions of surprise and disbelief arose from the group of heads.

"What you think, Bear?" Gramercy whispered to Kelly with an intensity that revealed his fear and confusion. He was, after all, still a fucking new guy.

"I'm goin' with the brothers, Gramercy." Kelly put on his pack and picked up his M16. "Why don't you c'mon with us, man? It's probably safer than goin into fuckin' Cambodia." Kelly smiled broadly as Gramercy picked up his things. They walked over and joined Tuggins and Dunlop.

And then, one by one, the heads rose and walked over to stand with the brothers, everybody but Winston and Peterson, who walked over to Miller.

"You going with these guys?" asked Peterson.

"Can't miss this one, Pete," answered Miller. "What are you going to do?"

"Oh, somebody's got to stick around and try to keep things from getting out of hand." He tapped Miller on the shoulder with his fist. "You take care of yourself, Eddie."

Peterson nodded at Miller and then was joined by Lt Winston. The two walked slowly back toward company headquarters.

◑ ◑ ◑

"Alright, every man make sure your extra canteens are full and you got all the c's you can carry." Tuggins looked around at the group, his confident manner as important as the words he spoke. "Everybody best get over to those pallets of c-rations and load up before the Boy Wonder figures out what's goin' on."

"Make sure you grab all the pound cake and fruit cocktail." Miller added as he set off toward the supply area, followed by a dozen of the others.

"You guys be back in fifteen minutes," Tuggins called out, "We got to get moving if we're going to cover some ground before nightfall."

CHAPTER XX

Which Way to Saigon?

THE MOTLEY CREW OF RELUCTANT REBELS SET OFF ON A ROUTE THAT took them away from the D Company command post and up toward the same ridgeline where helicopters from division disappeared minutes before. The journey was a daunting one, certain to be full of terrible dangers and nearly insurmountable obstacles. The jungle, the Viet Cong, the NVA, and now the American Army could all be expected to make life difficult for the Delta guys.

"I bet Tuggins wishes he had Green along to break trail," Gage said, managing to look professorial as he hefted his M60 machine gun and walked along the trail.

"Shit," Kelly replied, "I wish we had Green here, too." Kelly walked next to Gage, keeping himself just behind his shoulder to avoid the barrel of the big gun. "If ol' Power was here, maybe we'd all be back at the LZ, taking naps, waiting for the choppers."

"What's this?" Gage turned toward Kelly and smiled. "Do I detect a note of uncertainty coming from the company dissident extraordinaire?"

"Naw." Kelly shook his head as he ducked under a low vine. "I was just thinking about how life can push you in certain ways, whether you're ready or not, know what I mean?"

Gage gave Kelly a nod of assent as the two moved along with the others, their weapons on safety.

The first troopers in the column neared the top of a ridgeline. Kelly counted their helmets as they bobbed along the trail behind Tuggins and Dunlop.

"Looks like about twenty in front, fifteen or so here in the middle group, and maybe another twenty just behind us with Gormick and Lizzard," said Kelly.

" I guess we picked up a few guys out of Charlie Company before we left. That's fifty five of the toughest soldiers this army's ever seen. Can't imagine anybody getting in our way, can you?" Gage looked down to step over a large boulder. "This kinda reminds me of a book I read about these medieval knights who were out on their own one time and..."

"Oh fuck." Kelly came to a ready stance with his M16 in both hands, across his chest. Gage bumped into Kelly's ass with his head down, and interrupted his story of the Middle Ages in mid-sentence, then looked straight ahead following Kelly's gaze.

Everybody in front of them had stopped and bunched up with Tuggins and Dunlop looking across a twenty-yard clearing at approximately thirty soldiers facing them silently.

The group was led by the hotshot West Pointer Third of the Eighth Battalion Commander, Major Norman Whitley, out on his first operation. It was believed by the Delta troopers that he had been instructed by his superiors to re-instill some form of military discipline in them, and his first challenge looked to be a tough one. Whitley was a big, handsome man with a build similar to Peterson, who stood next to him, with his feet spread and a perplexed look on his clean-shaven, youthful face.

On Whitley's other side stood First Sergeant Potter, then Captain Welby and Lt. Winston. The others with Whitley were mostly sergeants, drawn from the other three companies in the battalion.

When Gage realized what he saw, he pulled the slide back on his machine gun without hesitation and let it slam forward, jacking a shell from the belt into the chamber of the M60. This sound signaled a clear threat; he was now locked and loaded. Immediately, several of the soldiers on the other side of the clearing locked and loaded as well. Captain Welby drew his 45 and aimed it at Tuggins.

Tuggins slowly laid his rifle down and walked back to Gage. A jungle bird screeched a mournful cry, and then there was dead, cold silence in the clearing.

Tuggins slowly raised the barrel of Gage's machine gun until it pointed safely into the air. Very softly, he said, "Bro, we just want to be on our way here, without any unnecessary casualties. Know what I mean?"

"Gotcha, Tug," Gage replied, keeping his eyes on the group at the other side of the clearing.

"Now, here's what we gonna do." Tuggins took a deep breath and glanced over his shoulder at Whitley's group. "Brother Kelly, I want you to reach over here and open the magazine on Gage's 60 and detach the belt from the round in the chamber.'" Kelly did as Tuggins instructed. "Right on. Now professor, I need you to jack that round out onto the ground."

The live machine gun round bounced off a rock and came to rest in the grass at Gage's feet. Major Whitley's group lowered their weapons, and again, silence descended on the clearing. The anxious eyes of soldiers on both sides darted back and forth under the brims of their helmets, trying to make sense of this extraordinary situation.

"Sir!" Tuggins called out, "We've decided to break it off and head home."

Whitley stood still as a statue, looking directly at Tuggins. He made no reply.

"Sir, what happened to Green was the last straw. We've taken as much as we can." Tuggins paused to pick up his M16 and looked down. "Sir, we gonna to go to the embassy in Saigon and sit down 'till they send us home." He stopped for a deep breath and raised his head. "We need to be on our way and I'm afraid y'all standing across the trail over..."

"That's enough Private!" Captain Welby raised his 45 again. "Now lay down your weapons and raise your hands over your heads! All of you are under arrest!"

"Who the fa-fuck does he think he's ta-talking to?" Gormick was standing next to Kelly. He spoke in a low voice, so only his buddies right near him could hear. "We got twice as ma-many as them, and there ain't no-nobody over there with much combat time, except for Pete, and maybe a couple of those First Platoon guys." Gormick spat on the ground. "Shit, just say the word and we'll mo-move those assholes out the way, Tug."

"Easy, Gordo," Flowers whispered from behind Gormick. "Let Preacher handle this."

Welby locked and loaded his 45, and aimed it at Tuggins. "I'm warning you men..."

Everything happened quickly after that. Welby fired, and missed. A half dozen shots rang out from the men with Tuggins while First Sergearnt.

Potter ran between the two groups shouting "Ceasefire!" Captain Steven Welby, the Boy Wonder, collapsed in a bloody heap.

Sergeant Potter turned toward the rebels, "Miller and Tuggins, I order you to take your men on that ambush I sent you on, now!" He raised his voice to maximum command level, "Let's be moving, men. Get the lead out!" Sgt. Potter pointed toward the trail over the ridge, then turned back toward Whitley, who had not moved or changed his expression throughout the entire confrontation. "Sir, we'll let them tire out a little on the trail, get hungry and thirsty tonight." He nodded at Whitley. "No point in any more damage here, sir. We can send out choppers and pick them up in the morning."

With that, Major Whitley's group parted to either side of the trail. A group of men, including Peterson, attended to Captain Welby, who was out of sight. Tuggins' group filed past them, weapons pointed up.

CHAPTER XXI

A President and his Cottage Cheese

H.R. HALDEMAN STOOD QUIETLY IN FRONT OF THE 37TH PRESIDENT of the United States, his boss Richard M. Nixon. Haldeman figured that the President was letting him squirm a little while he processed the very bad news he had just delivered. Haldeman had once been described by Nixon as "my asshole." The President had meant it as a compliment of sorts, meaning that he believed he needed an asshole to maintain control over the young punks he had been forced to hire to carry out the policies of his administration. Haldeman wedged a finger under his shirt collar, pulling it away from his neck. His usual brooding glare was decidedly uncocky at the moment.

"So we have a few niggers running around Vietnam, refusing to obey orders. That about it?" Nixon had placed his lunch of cottage cheese and ketchup on his desk, folded his hands on the cloth napkin complete with presidential seal, resting in his lap.

"Well, not exactly, Mr. President."

"Not exactly what, Her?" Nixon knew it offended Haldeman when he used this nickname, but he felt like offending someone, and Haldeman was available.

"It's not just niggers, Mr. President."

"Oh?" Nixon spooned some cottage cheese into his mouth.

"Actually, as near as we can make out it's pretty close to fifty-fifty." "You know, black and white together, as the saying goes." Haldeman forced a weak smile at his own joke, "and a few Spics thrown in as well, I understand."

"How many all together?" asked Nixon raising his napkin to his lips.

"We're not sure, Mr. President. A squad of choppers went out this morning, expecting to pick these guys up with their tails between their legs. The choppers backed off when a couple of Law rockets were fired."

"How many guys, Her?"

"The flight commander estimated about five hundred of some of our best combat-tested guys out there, armed to the teeth and refusing to obey their superiors' orders."

Nixon threw down his napkin. "So, is there anything else you'd like to tell me, Her?"

Well, yes sir." Haldeman shifted his weight and closed his eyes, half expecting Nixon to take a gun from the drawer of the enormous hardwood desk and shoot him. "General Abrams has cancelled the Cambodia thing for now."

"General Abrams did what?" Nixon screamed.

"General Abrams ordered all of MACV into defensive perimeters and demanded the pentagon get Bob Hope and his babes over there as soon as possible, Mr. President." Haldeman raised his hand to his mouth in an unsuccessful attempt to suppress a nervous belch. "There are rumors of mutinies in the ARVN. We just received a report that claims an entire ARVN brigade was surrendered to the NVA by a Colonel Trinh."

"My God, man! How can all this be happening?" Nixon began to pace. "We were going to make the Ho Chi Minh trail unusable for a while, and then get our guys the hell out of there."

"Well, Mr. President, we had all those troops massed along the Cambodia border…" Haldeman nervously cleared his throat.

"And?" demanded Nixon.

"Sir, somehow, word got around our troops and the ARVNs pretty fast about what was coming. We're pretty sure some of our black soldiers were communicating with the other side and then got word to their friends among the ARVNs." Haldeman paused for a moment, "We're looking into this 'Dap' ritual. Some of the intelligence guys think it might play some kind of role here." He cleared his throat. "Oh, and I called Hefner, and he said he'd get a bunch of bunnies together to go over there with Hope."

"Look," said Nixon as he gazed out an oval office window. "I don't care what's behind this: Dap, Dip or Dipshit." He reached under his desk and flicked a switch.

Tape's off, thought Haldeman.

"I want it handled. Total news black out till at least tomorrow..." Speaking very firmly now, Nixon brought his hand up to his chin. "There could be a battle where most of these guys got killed, couldn't there?"

"Yes sir, that kind of thing happens over in the jungle."

"Haldeman," Nixon walked over to his aide and thrust out his finger, "I'm counting on you to handle this quickly and with the utmost discretion. No fuck-ups. Remember, fuck the Gooks. Our chief concern, now and always, is the '72 election, right?"

"Right, sir."

CHAPTER XXII

May 1, 1970

"You Never Know…"

DAWN HAD BROKEN DAMP AND DRIPPING, WITH FAINT CLOUDS OF vapor rising from the men's clothing as it started to dry in the building heat. It was day three for the rebel soldier group, heading for Saigon. Tuggins increasingly came to rely on Fast Eddie Miller to guide the growing column of dissident Americans. Sometimes it seemed almost as if Miller had been born in this jungle. A dozen of the original brothers and heads gathered around him. Like just about everyone else, Fast Eddie hadn't shaved since they left camp four days before and his goatee was becoming a full beard. His pockets were crammed with rolled up maps, girlie magazines, and beef jerky pilfered from the officers' mess just before they left. He stood expectantly in front of the ragged crew of leaders of the rebellion.

"So, Fast Man, clue us in about where we are at the moment" said Kelly. They had been marching pretty hard for two days. Everybody's clothes were filthy, but their spirits were okay. The feeling of being part of a growing movement buoyed up the Irish Grizzly Bear. *Who knows*, he thought, *maybe, if we make it to Saigon, they'll have to listen to us about how fucked up the war is.*

"Sure," Miller knelt down one knee, and used a stick to draw a diagram in the sandy loam of the trail where they slept the previous night. "Pete told me all this stuff the night before the operation, and I was supposed to keep it secret, but I don't guess that matters a whole hell of a lot now, huh?"

Miller got a hearty laugh, then continued, "The deal, as usual, was the Ho Chi Minh trail." He finished his crude diagram. "We were up here west of Pleiku, near the Cambodia border." "The main action was planned for down here, just northwest of Saigon, near Tay Ninh. They threw the First Cav into the teeth of it there..."

"Poor fuckers, they always gettin' the bloody end of the stick," Flowers commented.

"Right, Turk." Miller looked back at his diagram. "This here was the objective, a place called the Parrot's Beak, where Cambodia pokes into Nam."

"Looks more like a limp dick to me, than a Parrot's Beak," Dunlop said.

Several of the guys laughed.

"I figured somebody would notice that," Miller went on. "Anyway, our job was to catch bad guys sneaking back up toward North Vietnam. Also, try and take a little pressure away from the guys in the Cav."

"So what about now, Miller?" said Dunlop and lit a cigarette. "Where are we headed, An Khe?"

"Okay. We skirted around An Khe yesterday." Miller drew a line directly east from their current position. "We're headed for Qui Nhon, over here on the coast. We're going to march parallel to Route 19, stickin' to the boonies as much as possible 'til we get to Qui Nhon." Miller reached over to the far eastern edge of his drawing. "Here. By then we figure we'll have enough guys in the column to hop onto Highway #1 and head on down the coast. We'll go through Nha Trang and Phan Thiet, then we'll follow #1 inland through Bien Hoa and on into Saigon." He looked up at his friends. "Embassy shouldn't be too hard to find, once we're there."

"Hey, man," Flowers said, "How far is all this shit? I mean, we gonna walk all the fuckin' way down there, or what?"

Miller turned toward Flowers, "Not to worry, guys." Miller's face assumed the smirk that usually signaled something good was coming. "We figure we'll get some of these transport guys to come along with their deuce-and-a-halfs out of Qui Nhon." He broke into a full grin. "After we hit the coast it'll be first class all the way, huh?" Fast Eddie pulled out a cigarette and lit it, exhaling thoughtfully. Flowers stood up and stretched.

"Sounds like about four hundred miles, give or take," said Kelly.

Gage and Tuggins stepped into the small clearing towards Miller. They had left their weapons with Flowers and Kelly an hour before and gone to make contact with new guys joining the growing column.

"Hey Tug," Kelly said as Tuggins came up and stood in front of the seated group, "What's the count?"

"We think it's pretty close to six hundred this morning, with maybe another six hundred or so making their way here," Tuggins said, a little out of breath.

"We waiting on some guys now?" Dunlop asked.

"Yeah, we sent in a couple of dudes to pass the word at An Khe yesterday, and now it looks like about half the brothers from Fourth Division are coming with us, along with a whole bunch of white guys." Tuggins leaned down to pick up his M16 and slung it over his shoulder. "I figure we'll give them a few more minutes." He looked at his wristwatch. "Then we gotta get going. Eddie says we got a hard five days 'til Qui Nhon." He looked over at Miller.

A trio of scout helicopters roared overhead.

Kelly stood up and said, "Nosy motherfuckers," loud enough to be heard over the whup-whup of the rotors above them.

"They keepin' an eye on us, alright," Tuggins added.

"So Tug," Dunlop said as the choppers receded, "You guys find out anything about ol' Welby?"

"How about Green?" Gormick said. "Anybody know if he made it?"

"Yeah, and what about the Lizzard," asked Kelly. "Nobody's seen that guy for a couple of days now."

"We talked to a couple of fellas from Third of the Eighth who just got here this morning," Tuggins said and paused for a moment. "Nobody knows about Green yet, but we found out that Welby died at the clearing."

Several gasps came from the group along with a few astonished curses.

"The Boy Wonder is no more," Dunlop said as he stood up and brushed the dirt off his pants. "I guess there's no turnin' back now."

"Nice shot, Turk," Gage said as he checked the firing mechanism of his M60, letting the slide spring forward.

"Man didn't need to be here no more," Flowers said. "He was gonna shoot Tug."

"Several guys made nice shots," Tuggins said. "We hit him half a dozen times, so we'll never know for sure who actually took him out." He walked over to Flowers, placed a hand on his shoulder and said, "Thanks, Bro."

"As for Vandyne," Tuggins continued, "he slipped away the first night and made his way back to An Khe. Those guys from Alpha Company told me they saw him scrubbing pots in the mess area."

"What a dipshit!" Kelly said. "He probably thought they would give him a promotion, and now all he's going to get is a bunch of hard time at LBJ."

"Turk," Tuggins said, "I'm putting you in charge of organizing these new guys coming in from Fourth Division, okay?"

"I best be getting on, then." Flowers adjusted his knapsack and took his bush hat out of his pocket.

"Take Gage and Dunlop with you. Have everybody form up platoons of twenty or so, then companies of about a hundred. You guys call the shots until they get a chance to vote on who's gonna be in charge."

"Alright, Tug." Flowers nodded to Gage and Dunlop and motioned with his hand to leave.

"Just a second, fellas," said Tuggins.

Everyone watched Tuggins, waiting for him to speak.

"Professor, you need to find somebody back there to carry that 60, okay?"

"Right, Tug," Gage said.

"I'll be needing you to run around a lot, so grab somebody's 16 and make a trade." Tuggins raised his hand. "Now listen up everybody, no firing any weapons except in defense of the column." He looked around the group of men in the clearing as everybody nodded in agreement.

"We was talkin' about a name for us," he went on, "and this dude suggested the Panther Division. That alright with y'all?"

Several "right ons" and other indications of agreement issued from the group in the clearing.

"I don't know, what about the 'Beavers'?" came a voice from in back, then chuckles.

"I was in 'Snake' patrol in the Boy Scouts," Dunlop said, "What about being the 'Snakes', huh?"

"Look you guys, I sorta want it to be 'Panthers'," Tuggins said. "So, unless there's any serious objection, we'll go with that." Tuggins gave the group a moment to respond. "All right then." He nodded at Flowers, and as Turk, Gage and Dunlop left, Tuggins called out, "In about twenty minutes I'll fire off three rounds. That'll be time to move out."

"Gotcha," Flowers called back as they disappeared down the trail.

Tuggins turned back to the group in the clearing. "Miller, I need you to stick pretty close to me, okay?"

"Yes, sir, General Tuggins!" Miller wisecracked.

"That goes for you too, Kelly." Tuggins looked at Kelly. "I may be interested in some of your half-assed political opinions from time to time."

"Okie-dokie," said Kelly.

Tuggins looked at his watch. "We leave in about twenty minutes. Everybody make sure your weapon's in good firing order; you never know."

CHAPTER XXIII

A Very Big Story

BIG STEVE BELTZER LOOKED AROUND THE ROOM. HE COULDN'T quite believe that he was back in Qui Nhon sitting in a bamboo chair inside Madame X's brothel. Madame X herself presided over the room from her red velvet couch wearing makeup that would shatter if she smiled and just about the biggest hair he'd ever seen. A painting of a cherry tree in full blossom hung on the wall behind her. A large ceiling fan bravely stirred the stifling air, thick with the sweet fragrance of incense.

Across from Beltzer sat Lan Tho Giao, the young brothel hostess he met on his last visit. A Vietnamese man with a severe, withdrawn expression on his face sat next to her. Beltzer felt a little uncomfortable and took a sip of the subtle tea they had all been served..

Lan Tho Giao's duties at Madame X's were only a cover for her position as principal aide to the local commander of the North Vietnamese Army. She smiled at Big Steve, "Thank you so much for coming today." she said. "How was flight from Saigon?"

"Bumpy," Beltzer replied, "If you want to know the truth. I had to pull in every favor owed to me from here to Saigon." He clutched his ragged notebook. "There's a weird feel to things, like we're on the verge of chaos. I don't know....One of the chopper pilots I rode up here with was smoking weed and wasn't taking any of the usual precautions. As we flew in, it looked like there were hundreds of GIs out on the beach just laying in the sun enjoying themselves." Beltzer took his pencil from behind his ear and stretched out his long arms. "What the hell's going on? Is the war over, or what?"

"Actually, Steve Beltzer," Lan Tho Giao folding her hands in her lap. "We were about to ask you a similar question."

"Who's we?" asked Beltzer, looking directly at the Vietnamese man.

"I am very sorry for rudeness," Lan Tho Giao said with a smile. "This," she held her hand out toward the man next to her, "is Dong Van Binh, my fiancé." Dong looked critically at Beltzer, and nodded his head slightly. Although he was dressed in civilian clothing, Dong Van Binh had the wary look of a soldier who had lived with battle and death for many years. He sat with his arms folded and his back straight, remaining stiff like a seated statue.

"General Dong is commander of the Third Army of the Democratic Republic of Vietnam. I am here to act as his interpreter," Lan Tho Giao announced. "We asked you to come today because of your connection with the American soldier, Willie Tuggins."

"Wait! Hold it a minute!" Beltzer fumbled with his notepad as he stuffed it into his backpack. "I could get in a whole lot of trouble for this." He stood up, put his arms through his pack straps and shook the pack into place. "I'm probably in violation of enough of my country's laws right here to put me away for more time than I care to think about." He started for the door, then looked back. "Be seeing you guys."

Lan Tho Giao trotted over to Beltzer, rose on her tiptoes and placed her hand on his forearm. "Please, Steve Beltzer," she said intently, "I promise, you will not be asked to violate your conscience or the laws of your country."

Beltzer looked down into the eyes of the beautiful Vietnamese woman. Lan Tho Giao gently guided Beltzer back to his seat, still holding onto his arm.

"We are very confused about the intentions of the Americans in our country, Mr. Beltzer," she said. "We are in possession of information that many American soldiers have decided not to fight people of Vietnam." Lan Tho Giao took a drink from her teacup, set it down, and continued, using her delicate hands for emphasis. "Our people tell us that all divisions of the American Army have withdrawn into defensive positions. They respond when attacked, of course, but they mount no aggressive patrols or ambushes." She halted a moment to allow time for this surprising news to sink in.

"I still don't understand why I'm here or why you are telling me all of this," Beltzer said. He reached into his pack again for his notebook and jotted down a couple of notes. "What does Tuggins have to do with all this?"

Lan Tho Giao smiled. "Our cadres are observing between three and five thousand soldiers moving in a column toward Qui Nhon. These Americans are about fifteen kilometers away from where we are seated now. After careful observation, we believe that these men are acting against the orders of their commanders."

Lan Tho Giao stopped speaking for a moment and looked closely at Beltzer. Big Steve exerted great effort to maintain his facial expression, but dropped his notebook into his lap. *Jesus fucking Christ!* He thought.

"What we are seeking from you, Steve Beltzer, is a way to communicate with these American soldiers," she glanced at Dong Van Binh seated next to her, "so that no harm will come to them from our forces." Lan Tho Giao leaned toward the general and spoke several sentences in Vietnamese. He replied curtly, almost angrily.

"We have reason to believe," Lan Tho Giao went on, "that your friend, Willie Tuggins is one of the leaders of this remarkable group of soldiers."

Beltzer's eyebrows rose as he listened closely. "Tuggins!" he exclaimed. "Well I'll be surely damned!" He scratched the three-day growth of whiskers on his chin thoughtfully. "My goose is about as cooked as it can get by now, I guess. They'll figure I helped plan this whole thing when I was writing that article on black GIs in Nam. Shit!" He turned to face Lan Tho Giao with a hint of a smile. "You might as well fill me in on what you want me to do."

"Very good, Steve Beltzer!" Lan Tho Giao smiled from ear to ear. "Tonight we will go to place where the Americans and Tuggins will be tomorrow morning. We will make contact...."

"Just hold on a second," Beltzer held up his hands. "I might be willing to work with you guys a little bit, but this sounds like suicide to me."

"Is very safe plan," said Lan Tho Giao. "Remember, all American Army units are inside defensive perimeters. We will travel under cover of darkness, taking great care to avoid any contact with anyone who might do us harm."

Big Steve Beltzer looked at her skeptically, folded his arms across his chest and made no reply. *This could turn out to be one big fucking story*, he thought.

◐ ◐ ◐

May 3, 1970

0800HRS

The going was getting slower as the days wore on. There were countless cases of blisters and foot rot, especially among the clerks and cooks who were not used to the endless plodding in the jungle. Kelly, and Gage, and those around them, perked up their ears toward the barely discernable shouts coming from ahead of them in the Panther Division column of now approximately four thousand five hundred men..

"That's Fast Eddie, ain't it?" Dunlop had caught up with his buddies when he heard the developing commotion.

"Tuggins!" the shout came through the jungle.

"Yeah, that's Fast Man alright," said Dunlop.

"Must be something going on up ahead," Kelly locked and loaded his M16, "or he wouldn't be making such a racket."

"Down, boy!" Miller said as he walked up to Kelly. He was breathing hard. "I'm just trying to get hold of Tuggins. You guys seen him?"

Kelly put the safety on his M16 and pointed the barrel up in the air. "He's about a hundred yards back, I think."

"Tell all your guys we're stopping at the big clearing up ahead, okay?" said Miller.

"Sure thing, Fast Man," said Dunlop.

"I gotta go get Tuggins so he can meet these guys from Madame X's that are wait'n up in the clearing. Tell him to meet me there, if you see him before I do."

Miller trotted off.

◐ ◐ ◐

Kelly looked around the hillside where a couple thousand fellow Panthers had gathered to smoke and joke. *What a target! If this was regular wartime, we'd be cooked hamburgers by now,* Kelly thought. It was 10 AM with heat already building, and they were taking their first break of the day. He took a long drag off his Bugler and looked out over the smiling, hopeful faces of the GIs. Their chatter set up such a racket, Kelly felt exhilarated, like he was at a college football game or a rock concert. *We'll make it, somehow*, he thought.

"Kelly!" Gage yelled from fifty yards away where he and Tuggins were talking to a tall American in civilian clothes and a Vietnamese woman about half his size.

"Hey Kelly!" Gage called through cupped hands. "Why don't you drag your lazy GI ass over here?"

Kelly flipped his smoke onto the ground and slung his M16 over his shoulder, and walked toward Gage and Tuggins. As he passed different groups of soldiers, some called out to him. "Hey there goes the bear!" and "Yeah, give us a growl, man."

"How much further to Qui Nhon, man? My feet are gonna rot off my legs if I don't give 'em a rest pretty soon."

Kelly stopped and nodded to the man with sore feet. "Let me see if I can find out something over there. I'll come back and let you know." Kelly winked at the guy, then walked over to the group with Tuggins.

"Hey Kelly," Tuggins said, "You met Steve Beltzer at Madame X's…"

Beltzer smiled awkwardly and pumped Kelly's hand.

"…and this here is Lan Tho Giao," Tuggins smiled and placed his arm around Lan Tho Giao's waist. "She's the lady who let y'all in. Remember when she asked you about rice or noodles at dinner?"

Oh shit. Kelly extended a grimy hand toward the woman, which she shook firmly. *There's something going on between those two.*

"Lan Tho Giao here has an open line to the VC and the NVA. She says they want to confirm that we aren't interested in fighting with them anymore. That way, they can let us walk through their turf without challenging us."

"Tell you the truth, Tug, it's kinda hard to imagine us being a threat to a bunch of Buddist Monks right now, let alone the VC or NVA." Said Kelly as Flowers, Miller, and Dunlop walked up and joined the group. "We got as many guys carrying their buddies as carrying guns. I know for a fact some of the white guys are talking about trying to arrange some sort of surrender. A scout chopper landed yesterday and spent a few minutes on the ground with some guys from the Americal. Nobody would tell me what they talked about, but I could'a sworn I saw Lizzard there, trying to hide his face. Everybody's tired, thirsty, hungry, and scared and we're running low on rations. Miller says he 's got a supply run arranged in Qui Nhon, but that's at least a day and a half away."

Tuggins waited 'till Kelly finished. "Um, I've got a little more bad news, fellas." He took a deep breath and let it out. "Lan Tho Giao tells me they're setting up a greeting party for us before we get to Qui Nhon."

"Hey," Gage said, "I thought everybody was stood down."

"For the most part, they are," Tuggins said. "But they're putting together a bunch of gung-ho, Hargrove-types. Only a hundred or so, but armed up the ass. The VC's pretty sure where they'll hit us." Tuggins turned toward Flowers. "Turk, can you guys be ready by tomorrow night?"

Flowers nodded. "I better get back," then spun around, walked away quickly, then stopped. He turned back toward Tuggins, "You need us, you get word to me and we'll be there, Preacher." Flowers trotted off toward a clump of trees at the edge of the clearing, where he disappeared.

"So how does the VC know about this reception committee?" Kelly asked Tuggins.

Dunlop shook his head and grinned, "Kelly, don't you know that every mama-san cleaning lady reports directly to her local VC?"

"No shit?" Kelly was genuinely surprised.

"Yeah, and those lifer-types like Hargrove are dumb enough to trust those old gals who clean up after 'em and do their laundry." Miller scratched his goatee, then leaned onto his M16 and looked directly at Kelly. "If this shit is coming from the mama-sans, you can take it to the fucking bank, man."

Lan Tho Giao nodded her head as Miller spoke.

"We better be getting back to Qui Nhon," said Big Steve Beltzer. He held out his hand to Tuggins. "I wish you guys all the luck in the world, and I'm afraid you're going to need it."

As he shook hands with the towering journalist, Tuggins said, "I want you to know how much y'all comin' out here means to us." He looked Beltzer in the eye. "We won't forget about the help you gave us today."

"Look, Willie, if I can be of any more assistance, get in touch with me thru Lan Tho Giao, at Madame X's." Beltzer thrust his hands into his pockets. "I can't guarantee anything, but I do have some connections in Saigon that might be able to get your story out, if that would help." He nodded at Gage, Kelly and Miller, then hurried off to catch up with Lan Tho Giao at the edge of the clearing. "I'm going to write up something about all this." Beltzer was walking backwards with his hands cupped at his mouth. "Okay if I get it published?" he shouted.

"Hell, yeah!" Tuggins shouted in return.

Tuggins turned back to his buddies, "Kelly, I want you to put together about ten companies into a battalion. We'll call it first battalion." He folded his arms across his chest. "Make sure you have as many guys as possible armed with enough ammo for at least a fifteen minute firefight."

"Okie Dokie," said Kelly.

"The same goes for you two." Tuggins paused as both Dunlop and Gage nodded. "Professor, yours will be second and Spiderman, you got third. Oh, and make sure you have a coupl'a shovels for each platoon." He paused for a moment "Well, let's get going, fellas."

"Hey, Tug," Gage began. "We gonna fight these guys straight up?" He cocked his head and put on a skeptical smile. "I mean, we might have the whole world down on us pretty quick." He looked up toward the sky. "I don't exactly relish the thought of being on the receiving end of one of those B-52's, you know?"

"Professor, we really think these jerks coming tonight ain't gonna get a whole lotta help. Then if we can hold 'em off tomorrow evening, news is gonna get out about what we're doing here." Tuggins stopped and thought for a second. "Then it's all gonna be politics, right?" He broke into a winning Preacher smile.

"Right," Gage answered, "and we figure to have a pretty good chance, don't we?"

"There you go, Bro," said Tuggins.

The newly appointed battalion commanders hurried off to carry out Tuggins' orders. Miller remained, looking a little unhappy. He had not been given a command assignment. "Fast Man, I got to have you next to me, help me make all these decisions, where to go, when to fight, like that, okay?" Tuggins said.

"Sure, Tug," Miller looked over at the trees where they had last seen Flowers. "So what's Turk up to over there?"

"He's organizing a bunch of Brothers into a special detachment." Tuggins grinned. "They gonna call themselves the Black Panthers."

CHAPTER XXIV

May 4, 1970

THE BLACK PANTHERS

FOR MANY HIGH-LEVEL AMERICAN MILITARY AND CIVILIAN OFFICIALS, John Paul Vann was the personification of the US war effort in Vietnam. Vann had recently been given the responsibility of general command in the II Corps area of Vietnam. This created an unprecedented situation for the US in wartime; a civilian would be issuing daily orders to all the American military personnel in the Central Highlands and the rice deltas of Vietnam's central coast area.

Vann's former commanding officer, Colonel Brighton Phillips, was a jungle fighter. He was half a head taller than Vann, with carefully applied camouflage on his clean-shaven face. He wore battle-scarred jungle fatigues and dust-covered jungle boots. He kept his M16 with him, grasped in his right hand with his finger next to the safety and the barrel pointing toward the ground. Ample numbers of extra ammo clips and grenades dangled from his blouse.

After an exchange of pleasantries between the two, Phillips was waiting to hear what his former commanding officer would have to say about the situation they found themselves in this morning in Vietnam. A short distance away, a number of soldiers were relaxing in the shade of broadleaf trees.

"I promised Haldeman I'd clean up this mess before it got leaked to our friends in the press." Vann dressed in marked contrast to his soldier friend. His clothes were civilian casual, except for a carefully knotted necktie and a buttoned up shirt. He wore a lightweight golf jacket to ward off the chill he often encountered while flying in his personal Ranger scout helicopter from one hotspot to another in Vietnam's II Corps. His upper lip was set hard and his eyes were those of a hawk observing its next meal.

"How many troops we got here?" Vann asked.

"One hundred eighteen of the finest ever assembled in Vietnam." Phillips spoke in a rich baritone, in contrast to Vann's weak, almost whiney tenor. He looked the civilian commander directly in the eye. "No officers, besides me. All NCOs with CIB's and hard core to the soles of their boots."

"Everybody fully loaded?" Vann asked crisply.

"To the rear gills, sir," Phillips answered. "Ammo, guns, water, everybody has more than enough."

"Fine. Good work, Bright." Vann shifted his weight a little and folded his arms across his chest. "What we have here ought to be plenty for the job."

"And, uh, what is the job, sir?"

"About six thousand armed cowards, deserters and drug addicts have mutinied and are attempting to make their way to Saigon, where they hope to be put on planes and sent home," Vann said.

"I figured something was up when they ordered everybody in my sector back inside perimeters." Phillips nervously rotated his rifle by twisting his wrist back and forth. "But God, six thousand traitors! What's the fuckin' world coming to, anyway?"

Vann nodded slowly.

"We can take 'em, sir." Phillips brought his M16 up across his shoulder keeping his finger near the safety and trigger. "We'll hit 'em so fast and hard, the ones still alive'll be begging to go back to their units."

"I knew I could count on you, Bright." Vann turned and pointed to a line of transport helicopters waiting behind a grove of trees. "Got you eighteen Hueys. That oughta get you in and out of there before the press catches on."

"A couple of gunships and a Cobra wouldn't hurt..." Phillips ventured.

"Sorry, Bright," Vann said, maintaining his command stance, "we gotta do this under the radar as much as possible. If the fuckin' press gets hold of this shit, we're in a world of hurt. Understand?"

"Understood, sir."

"You guys have plenty of LAWS?" Vann asked.

"Everybody's carrying at least three, some have four."

"Good," Vann said. "We'll put you in about a hundred yards from their main body. Soften them up with a barrage of half your laws, and then cut loose with your 60's and 79's for a couple minutes. By the way, how many of your guys are carrying 60's?"

"Twenty machine gunners, sir," Phillips said, "with about three times the ammo we'll need for the initial burst."

"Excellent. After the first couple minutes of fire, have your guys double time through them, shooting as many as you can and scattering the rest. We'll police 'em up in trucks as they straggle into Qui Nhon." Vann made a fist. "Take 'em from there, straight to jail. They won't be seeing their mommys any time soon."

"Think they'll put up a fight?" Phillips asked.

"This is a rag-tag bunch if ever there was one, Bright. They're chickenshits, or they wouldn't be pulling this stunt, now, would they?"

"I see your point, sir."

"I'll be surprised if they get off more than a couple of shots," Vann said. The two men shook hands.

◐ ◐ ◐

DUSK

After Lan Tho Giao and Steve Beltzer came to warn of the impending attack, Tuggins and the Panthers chose not to attempt an escape to the relative safety of Qui Nhon. They marched part of the day and then dug in across from the tree line where they had been told to expect the assault. Tuggins reasoned that it would be better to meet their adversaries in well-defended positions, than be caught out in the open. Miller agreed.

"I can't see shit over there, Tug." Miller looked through the dimming, evening light as hard as he could. He could make out very little across the two hundred twenty yards of four to six foot tall elephant grass, to where they had heard the noise of numerous helicopters landing less than a minute ago. They had good visibility over the grass, but not into the trees. Their position was in the middle of the Panther defense line.

"It's them, Fast Man." Tuggins drew in a deep breath and let it out. "I can feel it."

"Everybody where they supposed to be?" asked Tuggins.

"Professor and Spiderman are on our left," Miller spoke in a nervous whisper. "The Bear's on our right. They're all dug in pretty good, far as I can tell."

"How many guns you figure on our side?" Tuggins asked quietly.

"About five hundred guys on the line with 16's, fifteen or so 60's and maybe a hundred LAWS." Miller was silent a second while his stomach rolled.

"I figured there'd be more than that," said Tuggins.

"Me too, but most of the guys coming in the last couple days didn't bring any weapons with them."

"Lifers collected 'em all, didn't they?"

"Yeah, but we still wound up with quite a bit of hardware." Miller looked out over the field in front of them. "We got seventeen grenade launchers and about one hundred fifty boomers for 'em. The guys know they gotta wait for orders before they fire off any of those grenades."

"That's right, Eddie," Tuggins said. "Those guys are the artillery. We gotta wait and see how we're gonna use 'em."

Miller coughed to clear his throat. "Turk's got one hundred fifty rifles with the Black Panthers. They're about a hundred yards back, but he's having a hard time keepin' 'em from sneakin' up to the line. Those guys are really itching to fight."

"They're gonna get their chance tonight," Tuggins said. "How many you figure they are, coming after us?" he asked.

"I heard sixteen, maybe twenty choppers landing. There might be one hundred thirty, one hundred forty. It's hard to say for sure. But we've got plenty of ammo and I told everybody to keep their 16's on semi and not put out a stream of bullets."

"That's cool, Bro," Tuggins said. "How about the main body?"

"They're tucked away about a click back. Along with the aid station my girlfriend, Francine, and some nurses set up." Miller shifted his position a little to relieve some tingling in his foot, which had fallen asleep. "Guys are a little scared with most the weapons up here, but everybody's hanging in there. We got a group of three hundred ready to reinforce up front, if M16's become available."

"Lord, I hope there isn't too much of that," Tuggins said.

"Tug?" The darkness made it difficult to see in the foxhole.

"Yeah, Fast Man?"

"What the fuck are those assholes waitin' for?"

"Don't you worry, my man," Tuggins said. "They'll be along."

A series of loud pops went off across the field followed by loud swooshing sounds like at a Fourth of July fireworks show.

"HEADS DOWN!!" Miller screamed, a split second before the first LAW rockets hit.

Every guy on the Panther line had been through this before and knew that a rocket attack ends pretty quickly. The main event, an all out assault on their position, would almost certainly follow. But, for the time being, they were all fairly safe in their foxholes.

● ● ●

Kaboom! Kaboom! "Long as we stay down," Kelly cupped his hands to his mouth and shouted above the noise of the explosions, "we'll be okay through the barrage. When it slows down," Kaboom! "we gotta keep our eyes peeled, cause they're gonna be coming."

Kelly was in one of the foxholes, all of them dug into a rise six feet above the field. He was glad he ended up with No Nonsense Kapinski, a nineteen-year-old Polish guy from the west side of Chicago. He had acquired his nickname from his penchant for seriousness and careful attention to detail. "Nothing much funny about this Nam shit," he had said on more than one occasion. He always carried at least two full canteens of water, and if you needed a bandage or some ointment for your feet, he was the man to find.

Except for a lot of ringing ears when it was over, not much harm was done by the LAW attack on the Panthers. As things quieted a little, medics went to work evacuating the wounded. For the most part, injuries proved to be minor.

"Tug!" Kelly exclaimed, surprised to see his buddy crouching next to his foxhole, well away from his own position. "What are you doing here, man?"

Tuggins spoke quickly, "Pass the word...They'll be comin' soon, hold fire until I give the order. Then we'll open up on 'em from where I am and everybody join in, okay?"

"Sure thing, Tug," Kelly said.

"I want to get them to commit their force. Come close enough so we can do some real damage."

As quickly as he appeared, Tuggins was gone again, back toward his own foxhole.

"Hey NO-NO," Kelly spoke quietly, "Go on over to the next position and make sure everybody understands what Tug just said, okay?"

Kapinski nodded and spun around. Kelly stopped him for a second with a hand on his shoulder. "Make sure they know we gotta get the word down the line as fast as possible, all right?"

Kapinski nodded again, then climbed out of their foxhole and ran in a crouch over to the next group of defenders. Staying behind the dugouts as they ran offered good cover to the messengers racing between the twenty-eight foxholes in Kelly's First battalion.

As the last position received word of Tuggins' plan, machine guns opened up from the other side of the elephant grass. With every fourth round a tracer, it made for an impressive light show, and went on for a minute or two. But little damage was done to Tuggin's guys. The Panthers were well dug in.

"I can't believe that's Americans over there, Kelly."

"Yeah, No-No, it's a bitch," Kelly said.

"If they come this way," Kapinski said with his voice quavering, "you gonna shoot 'em?"

"Not much choice," Kelly answered. "If we don't, they're sure as hell gonna shoot us, know what I mean?"

No-No nodded.

"Besides, Tug tells me we gotta beat these guys tonight, cause the NVA is watching."

"Wha???" said Kapinski.

"Yeah," said Kelly, as he looked out across the elephant grass "according to Tuggins' friend, Lan Tho Giao, there's some in the NVA that don't believe we're for real." Kelly sighed. "They figure it might be better to wipe us out, you know, discourage folks back in the world about the war, even more than they already are." Kelly looked at Kapinski. "We gotta beat these guys tonight, or else Lan Tho Giao doesn't think she can stop the NVA from attacking us."

All four men in Kelly's foxhole trained their weapons on the tree line and made sure they were locked and loaded, safeties off.

o o o

"I see 'em now, Tug!" Miller called out. "They're comin' toward us, right over there!" Tuggins crouched next to Miller. "It's so fuckin' dark, all you can see are silhouettes. But look," Miller pointed, "there's a bunch more. You can hear 'em screaming now!"

Tuggins aimed his M16 at the second group and flipped off the safety. "Hold on...hold on...OPEN FIRE!"

Miller echoed Tuggins command at the top of his voice as five hundred rifles opened up on their attackers. Individual cracks in rapid succession blending into one huge explosion, while the distinct odor of burnt gunpowder drifted over their positions.

Tuggins' guys were all experienced troopers and deadly shots. Colonel Phillips men began to fall in the hail of fire from the Panther line. Phillips' commanding voice could be clearly heard, "Fall back! Fall back!"

The Panthers continued shooting for another twenty seconds, until nothing could be seen across the field but the dark tree line against the starry night sky.

"Cease fire!" Tuggins called out and the field fell quiet, except for the muffled moans of the wounded.

For the next few minutes, occasional fire came from the force with Colonel Phillips. Some LAWS, a few bursts of grenades from M79 launchers, but nothing to seriously challenge Tuggins' guys in their foxholes.

"Whew!" Miller exclaimed. "I guess we showed 'em, huh, Tug?"

"Yeah, Fast Man, we did," Tuggins said, wiping dirt from his face. "But man, what happens now?"

Miller said, "I don't see 'em just pulling those fuckers outta here and letting us continue on our jolly way into Qui Nhon. Do you, Tug?"

"No, Fast Man, I don't," Tuggins said.

"I figure," Miller said as he squinted out across the field "ten, fifteen minutes max."

"Yeah," Tuggins said, "If those guys are still across there calling for help, they'll bring down a whole bunch of air..."

"And blow us to kingdom fucking come," Miller said.

"Eddie, get Turk up here, will you?" Tuggins said.

Miller was out of the foxhole in a flash, and then back at Tuggins' position in less than two minutes with Flowers beside him.

"What's up Preacher?" Flowers was quite a sight. Without his shirt his muscular black arms and shoulders gleamed in the light of the newly-risen quarter moon. His M16 was draped behind his neck and across his shoulders held in place with his hands dangling over each end of the weapon. A broad, black headband was tied across his forehead and Bandoliers crossed his chest with magazines for his rifle and several grenades. Like every one else in the Panthers, he hadn't shaved or cut his hair for a couple of weeks, so he was getting a little wooly.

"That your uniform for the Black Panthers?" Tuggins asked.

Flowers smiled and nodded his head slightly.

Tuggins turned to Miller, "Get all the guys with M79's, and their grenades up here fast as you can, Eddie."

Without a word, Miller vanished.

"Turk, these guys are a bunch of gung-ho, flaming assholes acting way outside the chain of command." Tuggins leaned his M16 against the front wall of the foxhole and crouched as he faced Flowers. "If we can clear 'em outta here, the Brass'll pretend like they never existed."

Flowers nodded.

"But, if we leave 'em there very long," Tuggins went on, "they gonna come and rescue them, sure as you and I are right here talkin' to each other."

"What you got in mind, Tug?"

"I want you to bring the Black Panthers up, Turk, " Tuggins said. "We goin' over there and bust up their little party. Get 'em back in those choppers and outta here." He spread his arms and pointed to both sides of his position. "We'll put the center of your guys right here, and then bring everybody up behind the foxholes, on line and about three feet apart, okay?"

"We ready, Tug."

"When you figure you're set, sound the charge, Bro." Tuggins pointed behind him, across the field. "They're right over there, man. Won't be hard to find."

Flowers held out a fist out and did a brief Dap with Tuggins, then he was off.

Five minutes later, Flowers returned to Tuggins' foxhole, along with Eddie Miller and seventeen guys with grenade launchers. The Black

Panthers lined up, each on one knee. They were acting like racers at a speedway, revving their engines. Tuggins thought, *wonder how long Flowers can hold 'em back*. A group of the men began clapping in unison. Some of the fellows began inserting chants in between claps, syncopating the rhythm as they clapped. *CLAP!—CLAP! CLAP!—MM!!—MM!!*

"Fast man, you in charge of the artillery," Tuggins said. "When these guys take off, I want you to lay down a barrage on that tree line, yonder… about five grenades a second. That'll keep their fire down until Turk can get over there. But make sure you let up after twenty seconds, we don't want to hit any of our own guys, huh?"

"Right," Miller said, and then looked at his friend. "Tug, where do you think you're goin'?" Miller demanded.

Tuggins had taken off his blouse, tied a black bandanna around his head, and picked up his rifle. "Can't miss this one, Eddie."

"Preacher," Flowers hunched down again behind Tuggins' position, "there's really only one man we can't afford to lose here tonight, and I think we all know who that is."

"But…" Tuggins started.

"But nothin', man!" said Flowers firmly. "You stayin' right where you are and doing your job. We gonna go do ours." He broke into his most winning grin.

Miller glared at Tuggins and shook his head slowly from side to side. Tuggins looked back at Flowers.

"Don't worry, Bro, we be back in about ten minutes," Flowers said. He stood up and brought his rifle down to his side. "Those dudes over there just waitin' for us to line 'em up and fly 'em outta here. They're nothin' but a bunch of punk-ass motherfuckers." Flowers spat on the ground. "Won't be no trouble." He grinned again.

Tuggins leaned back against the wall of the foxhole, his shoulders slumping. He sighed deeply and nodded.

Miller climbed back out of the foxhole and quickly arranged his grenade launchers into four groups. Each group of four would fire together, in sequence with the other three groups, one group after the other. He placed them in between foxholes, lying prone and ready to blast away. He made sure all were within the sound of his voice. The Black Panthers were waiting just in front of the foxholes, each on one knee.

One of the Black Panthers began singing along with the clapping and chanting. "They think they're gonna kill us! *MM!!—MM!!* They say that we're no good! *MM!!—MM!!* They think they can take us! *MM!!—MM!!* But we'll see about that! *MM!!—MM!!*"

Flowers stood up, raised his rifle in the air, and screamed, "Black Panthers!" But before he could finish his command, the line of Black Panthers surged into the field and he had to yell "Charge!" as he ran to catch up.

As he ran, Flowers screamed an ancient warrior's cry and shouted encouragement to the fellows near him. Not that any of them needed urging; everybody was hollering loud enough so that no one could hear much but his own bellowing. Flowers felt like his chest might explode.

Miller's grenade launchers began their barrage on the enemy tree line. The fragmentation grenades sailed over the heads of the racing black soldiers and landed in the tree line across the field, to deadly effect. Flowers and the Black Panthers reached the tree line winded, but at close to full numerical strength. They immediately set upon the remaining men of Phillips' force, who threw down their guns and raised their hands over their heads in surrender.

o o o

With two thirds of his force killed or wounded, and a bunch of brawling, rebel GI's on top of his position, Brighton Phillips took the only sensible option. He called out for a ceasefire.

"I'll take that weapon, sir," Flowers said as he approached him. Phillips laid his M16 on the ground. "Now get your hands behind your head... please, Sir." Flowers kept his rifle trained on Phillips.

"We have a lot of wounded here, soldier," Phillips said. "They're going to need attention soon or we'll have a lot more dead."

"The sooner we can get you guys on slicks and outta here, the happier I'm gonna' to be," Flowers answered. "Why don't you get your radio man over here?"

Phillips called out to his radio operator, Flowers was informed that helicopters would return in about ten minutes to pick them up.

Flowers left Gormick in charge of Phillips and walked out among the defeated guys and their wounded. He wondered at his strong sense of pity mixed with exhilaration. He never in his life felt more completely alive than he did at this very moment.

"Hey! Hold up over there!" Ten yards from where Flowers stood a Black Panther held his M16 to the head of one of Phillips' men. The guy was obviously trying to surrender, holding his hands high in the air above his head. Flowers strode over quickly. "Bro, what's the problem here?" he asked.

"Ain't no problem, Turk," replied Sgt. Eddie Matthews from Oakland, California. "This man and I just had a little disagreement about my mama's occupation, and I was gonna settle it with him, home-style"

"Bro, we can't be pulling none of that shit tonight," Flowers said. "We in plenty enough trouble already, okay?"

Matthews lowered his rifle.

"Now, why don't you get this man over to the assembly point so we can get his ugly ass outta here?" Flowers placed a hand on Matthews' shoulder and pointed over where several dozen prisoners were now under guard. Matthews marched off with his man.

"Hey Blackjack! " Flowers called out. Pvt. Donald Blackman was nicknamed "Blackjack" because he was from Reno, Nevada. He had become a medic in the Army, and wore a red cross on his black headband.

Blackman hurried over to Flowers. "What's up, Bro Turk?"

"Blackjack, I need you to gather up our other medics and anybody else who's not busy guarding prisoners. See what you can do to help these guys with their wounded, okay?"

"Right on," said Blackman, nodding.

"There's a few of our fellas that didn't make it all the way across," Flowers said as he looked out across the expanse of moonlit elephant grass. "Make sure you find anybody who's layin' wounded." He turned back to Blackjack. "Bring their guys back here to the choppers and get our wounded back to our aid station, behind the foxholes."

Blackman hurried off to carry out Flowers' instructions. Flowers pulled a flare pistol from his pants pocket, raised it in the air and fired a high, bright red flare that illuminated the night sky all the way back to the Panther defense line: "All Clear."

Damon Flowers walked back toward the area where Gormick was assembling prisoners. As he approached the group, Gormick called out,

"Hey Turk, I got one here says he knows you from back on the block in Cleveland."

The prisoner had his hands clasped behind his head and was grinning at Flowers.

"Sugarboy," Flowers said as he nodded and grinned at Marcus Fortier. "It's okay Gormick, I know this dude, all right." He turned back to Fortier "For god's sake Bro, take your hands down! What the fuck happened, man?" Flowers asked.

"I was in prison, you know mistaken identity. I took care of a couple of dudes in prison that was beatin on a buddy of mine. Was a couple of guards just as glad to get rid of those guys, as my buddy was. One of them was a cousin to the warden." He shrugged his shoulders, "They came to my cell one Sunday and offered me a deal; three years in the Army or the rest of my dime at the big house." He pulled a Marlboro from a pack in his shirt pocket and lit it. "I took three in the green."

"Right on." Flowers said. "So how'd you wind up with these guys, tonight?"

"I was on this LRRP (long range reconnaissance patrol) team with two other fellas and they told me they was goin' with Phillips."

"That the name of that major in charge of these guys?" Flowers said. He looked at a large scar above Fortier's right eye that was new since the two had last seen one another. The scar stood out bright pink and two inches long against his dark black skin. *I wonder where he got that?* Flowers thought.

"Yeah, Major Phillips. The dudes on my LRRP team thought we were gonna fight some special commie unit, you know, save some kidnap victims, and all that." Fortier took a drag on his cigarette and looked out across the elephant grass. "I was pretty surprised when I seen you fellas coming across the field over there. I'm sorry Bro, if I'da known...."

Flowers reached over and gave his old friend a playful push on the shoulder, the way he used to when they played football together. A helicopter landed nearby and Flowers waited for the noise and wind to subside for a moment. "You wanna come with us?"

"Where you all goin'?"

"We headed to Saigon to sit down by the embassy 'till they let us go home, man."

Fortier broke into another grin and shook his head. "Nah, man, you ain't serious!"

Flowers' said, "We deadly serious, Bro."

Fortier nodded, no longer smiling.

"You can help us, Sugarboy."

Fortier's furrowed his brow and rubbed his sparse goatee thoughtfully.

"I don't like to brag, but I got a lot of responsibility here, Bro. Now, we're pretty sure they're sending spys in to fuck us up, you know?"

"Yeah, I can see that happenin', all right."

"Well, what you could do is watch my back, you know? You and me stick together and if you see somethin' comin', maybe you can get it turned around."

"And you say they gonna send us home after we get to Saigon?" Fortier asked.

"Either that or they're gonna have a whole bunch of dudes clogging up the streets around the embassy for a while." Flowers said, and put on his most winning smile.

Fortier relaxed his shoulders and broke into a grin. "Me watchin' your ass, just like football, huh?" Fortier extended a clenched fist toward Flowers and the two soldiers did some Dap, sealing the deal.

CHAPTER XXV

May 9, 1970

DAYS LATER AND THOUSANDS OF MILES FROM THE FIELD OF BLOODY elephant grass, H.R. Haldeman endured an embarrassing cussing-out from his commander-in-chief. Usually, a private meeting, or 'face-time,' with the President was a greatly coveted opportunity, but not this time.

"Just where the hell was Vann while all this was happening?" Nixon sprayed spittle as he yelled, his red face six inches away from Haldeman's. "Probably fucking his brains out in one of those little whorehouses. God-the-fuck-dammit!" Haldeman winced.

"Well, Mr. President, actually, Vann was in his helicopter..."

"That's enough! I don't want to hear any more about how that miserable puke fucked me up!" Nixon screamed, poking at Haldeman's face. "Just tell me where those traitor-coward-motherfuckers are now," he growled.

"The Panthers, Mr. President?" Haldeman asked.

Nixon leaned on his desk, then stood up and folded his arms across his chest. "For Christ's sake, stop calling them the 'Panthers,'" will you?" he sneered. "Makes them sound so goddamn noble."

"As far as we know, sir, they're in Qui Nhon, having the time of their lives," Haldeman said.

Nixon began pacing. "Please explain what you mean by 'time of their lives', Mr. Haldeman." He turned and glared.

"Well, Mr. President, things are a little confused over there at the moment." Haldeman took a deep breath. "Our forces are withdrawn to their base areas-defensive action only." He tugged on his shirt collar with an index finger. "Five divisions of the ARVN stationed in the northern half of South Vietnam, have collapsed. Roads leading into Da Nang and Qui Nhon are choked with deserting South Vietnamese soldiers and their civilian followers."

"So what about our little 'Panther' buddies?" Nixon asked.

"Apparently, Mr. President, they received assistance from some of the locals..."

"You mean Viet goddamn Cong, don't you?" Nixon interjected. "Locals, my ass!"

"Yes sir, that's probably the case."

Nixon scowled.

"The deserters made it into Qui Nhon on jungle paths," Haldeman continued, "to avoid the chaos on the main road. When they got to the city, they were greeted warmly and taken into people's homes." He pulled at his shirt collar again. "They're being treated pretty much like conquering heroes."

"Heroes!" Nixon seethed.

"Yes, Mr. President. Our people tell us that they're eating and drinking to their heart's content. Some of them are helping out with family chores, going fishing with them, that kind of thing."

"How goddamn touching, Her!" Nixon walked over to his desk, reached under the center drawer and flipped off the switch to his tape recorder.

Uh-oh, thought Haldeman.

Nixon paced back and forth, holding his finger in the air like an arrogant professor. "You're to leave tonight for Saigon, Haldeman."

"Yes, sir, Mr. President, I'll arrange for my flight as soon as we've finished our meeting."

"Right." replied Tricky Dick. "Now, when you get over there, don't bother trying to mobilize any of our guys."

"That's right, sir," Haldeman said. "The reports indicate that it wouldn't be possible to move any our units while this is going on. After those so-called 'Panthers' wiped out Vann's force outside of Qui Nhon, word spread like wildfire. I'm afraid these mutineers have taken on the mantel of a respected military force, sir."

"Good God!" said Nixon.

Haldeman went on, "The black soldiers are in almost open rebellion, doing this Dap stuff in large groups and refusing orders to stop. A lot of the white soldiers are going along with them, taking drugs and lying around listening to rock music. The First Cav tried a couple of mobilizations, and one company reported that none of the black soldiers came to formation. Most of the white guys who showed up were only wearing undershorts." He bit his lip, but could not restrain a smile.

"What you are saying is in no way, shape or form funny!" Nixon roared.

"Yes, er, no, Mr. President." Haldeman regained control. Nixon continued, "I want you to find Vann and then I want the two of you to go and see the ARVN liason officer with the First Brigade of the ROK Army's Capitol Division in Pleiku, Colonel Kim Yong Rim." Nixon kept pacing, but was relaxing into his subject now. "You're familiar with the troops from the Republic of South Korea who are assisting us in South Vietnam, aren't you, Her?

"Yes, Mr. President, I'm aware of the Korean troops that are fighting with us there against the communists."

"Colonel Kim is on our side, Haldeman, and I bet he can persuade the ROK Army commander to help us with this dirty business." He spun around toward Haldeman, and raised his clenched fist chest-high. "Those deserter cowards must be stopped before they get to Saigon!" Nixon said, almost under his breath. He held the pose for a few moments, until Haldeman looked away from his penetrating stare. "Let's see if we can't put the fear of God back into those guys, Her."

CHAPTER XXVI

May 11, 1970

IT WAS 4 PM AT THE QUANG PHO BAT CAFÉ AND TWO DAYS since the meeting between Haldeman and Nixon. The Bat pulsated with excitement as patrons raised their voices in competition creating a din of English, French and Vietnamese. A lanky, middle-aged waitress hurried from table to table slinging two large pitchers of rice wine in a futile attempt to keep up with her patrons' thirst.

"You didn't really do that, did you Beltzer?" AP reporter Fred Greenburg sat across from Big Steve Beltzer, at their favorite table next to an open window that gave them a grand view of the shabby, crowded market area of Saigon's Cholon district. Rumor was, you could buy just about anything in the booths along the market street.

Beltzer shrugged his shoulders, then held his glass out for a refill as the waitress worked her way past their table.

"C'mon Big Steve, tell me you're joking!" Greenburg held his glass toward the waitress. Next to the scruffy Beltzer, Greenburg looked like he was dressed for a morning meeting with his editors at the New York Times. He was clean-shaven and had barely loosened his necktie.

"What was I supposed to do?" Big Steve extended his arms in a gesture of wonder. This startled the customer on his right, who wondered what the seven-foot stranger's forearm was doing between him and his soup bowl. "I really like this guy, Tuggins, and it seemed like maybe I could make things a little safer for him." He pulled in his arms. "What's so terrible about that?"

"What might be a little problem is those NVA guys you were hanging around with," Greenburg set down his glass down and pulled his extra large Pho soup bowl closer. "You know, helping the enemy, little stuff like that."

"Really Fred, all I did was make it so those guys could get to Qui Nhon in one piece."

Greenburg grinned and shook his head a couple of times. They picked up their bowls and scooped noodles toward their mouths Asian-style, slurping up the zesty broth with meat, basil, fish sauce, hoisin and flaming hot sauce. They ate gluttonously, as one is supposed to do when eating Pho, especially when you're half drunk at the Bat.

Greenburg finished first and placed his empty bowl to one side. "So now what?" He took a generous draught from his glass. "I mean, those guys can't stay in Qui Nhon forever."

Beltzer raised his napkin to his mouth and belched. "Well, the political situation in Nam is working in Tuggins' favor." He stopped and cleared his throat. "They can't get any of our guys to go after the Panthers and they can't bomb 'em. What the hell would that look like back in the U.S.? Somehow, Tuggins has to figure out how to get to Saigon."

"Oh, that sounds like a great idea! That way they can fight their way through the Third ARVN division up in Bien Hoa, which just happens to be the only unit in the whole South Vietnamese Army that will put up a real fight these days. And the marine brigade in Saigon functions as a royal guard. That'll be a lot of fun for your pals, fighting those 'death before dishonor' guys from the Palace."

"Uh, you forgot the ROK Army," Beltzer said and took a drink of his wine.

"Shit, are the Koreans gonna get into this thing, too?" asked Greenburg.

"I'm afraid so," Beltzer said. "I talked to this friend of mine from Pleiku this morning, and she said they're moving the First ROK Brigade into positon to catch Tuggins and his guys on the road south of Qui Nhon and blow them all to smithereens."

"My God, Steve!" Greenburg lit a Camel cigarette. "There's ten thousand guys with Tuggins, right?" He picked up his wine.

"I think ten thousand was a few days ago, Fred," Beltzer said. "They picked up a bunch from the First Cav while they were in Qui Nhon this week. Probably more like twelve thousand, what with all the guys from the Central Highlands showing up in groups of forty to fifty at a time."

"Look Steve," Greenburg pointed with his burning Camel, "Tuggins and his boys are completely fucked! I've been to villages after the ROKs have gone through. The expression 'take no prisoners' was invented for those guys. General Choe is in command of the ROK Capitol Divison, but he likes to stick with his First Brigade. They're the ones with blood, instead of dirt, under their fingernails." Greenburg scrunched his eyebrows and looked directly at Beltzer. "Word has it that he personally awards fifty bucks for each kill, and he doesn't pay much attention to things like age, sex, or combat status." Beltzer, sat in rapt attention. "You ever hear the expression, 'Kill 'em all, let God sort 'em out?"

"Yeah."

"Well, I'm pretty sure that one originated with the ROKs, too."

"Look Fred, I've been thinking," said Beltzer. "If we could arrange for a film crew to be there when the ROKs confront Tuggins, it could hold the violence down and it would be the story of a lifetime for some eager free-lancer. They could sell it to the networks for a bunch of money."

"Are you kidding? Where are we gonna find somebody dumb enough to walk into that shitstorm with Tuggins?"

"Well, actually, I, uh, was thinking I'd get this guy I know to fly a film crew in a helicopter along Tuggins' march route."

"Beltzer! Now I know you've gone over the edge!" Greenburg cupped his hands to his mouth. "Somebody call a medic. My boy here needs drugs, right away!"

"Keep it down, will you?" Beltzer looked over the crowd in the dining room. "You can't tell who might be listening."

"Sorry," Greenburg held his hand over his mouth and belched.

"Really Fred," Beltzer reached across the table and steadied Greenburg, who had started to weave a little in his chair. "I know this pilot named Thompson who was at My Lai and kept things from turning out even worse. From what he's been telling me, I bet he'll help us out here."

"You think he's ready to throw away his career?" Greenburg asked.

"That's what I meant," Beltzer pushed his bowl aside. "He hates the way we've been fighting the war. My Lai really changed him and he'd like to do something to help these guys get home, and maybe stop the war in the bargain."

Greenburg rolled his eyes. "If he's so against the war, what's he doing over here flying helicopters for the Army?"

"He's not like some protester." Beltzer took a quick glance around the room again, then turned back to Greenburg. "He got out of the Army for a while after My Lai, but then he found that civilian life didn't quite measure up. When he went to see a recruiter, the Army offered him a deal where he could go right back to flying scout helicopters over here. The guy loves to fly. I think he figures he can prevent a lot of bad stuff if he's calling the shots. " Beltzer shook Greenburg gently by the shoulder to get his full attention. "What do you say, Fred, can you round up a film crew?"

"Sure," Greenburg mumbled drunkenly. "Why the fuck not?" He took in a deep breath. "What about you, old boy?" He coughed and cleared his throat. "You gotta get something out of this for yourself, man."

"Shit, the word's out on me, I'm afraid." Beltzer shook his head and picked up his wine glass. "Haven't been able to publish a damn thing for weeks."

Chapter XXVII

May 11, 1970

Winter Soldiers

"You sure about this, Tug?" Kelly asked his friend outside the massive tent set up for Panther Division headquarters in Qui Nhon. It was the end of a hectic day preparing for their pullout from the lovely coastal city the next morning. The Panthers were now about 13,000 strong.

The edge had dulled from the heat of the day as the sun settled behind the highlands. Just a few runners under the direction of Fast Eddie Miller were working on the final details and logistics for the departure. The Panthers would head down the coast road, and toward Saigon. The insistent sound of typewriters and shouted communications came from the tent. Occasionally, laughter could be heard in response to the seemingly endless supply of jokes that GIs always seemed to come up with.

"C'mon man, this ain't that big a deal," Tuggins responded. "She'll probably just shake hands and send me back here by ten o'clock tonight."

"But that's not why you're going, is it?"

"She's a beautiful woman, Kelly."

"Yeah, and she also happens to be an agent of the goddamn North Vietnamese." Kelly raised his hands, palms out, in exasperation. "Have you thought about what the press would say if they get hold of this shit?" Kelly looked closely at Tuggins to see if his words were having any effect. "C'mon, man!" he pleaded.

"Listen, Bear," Tuggins put a hand on Kelly's shoulder and gave him one of his finest 'Preacher' smiles. "I'll be careful. Ain't nobody gonna find out about this, I promise. Besides, Lan Tho Giao might have some information that can help us out tomorrow. Maybe that's why she sent me the message."

"Sure, Tug," Kelly sighed and lit a Bugler smoke and watched Tuggins saunter off down the road, toward Madame X's.

● ○ ●

Tuggins pulled on the chord next to the large mahogany door and heard soft chimes inside. He felt his pulse quicken as the latch on the door turned. There stood the lovely Lan Tho Giao, smiling warmly.

She took a step back and beckoned him to enter. "So please to see you, Willie Tuggins," she said as he walked past her into the stuffy receiving room.

"I didn't want to leave without saying goodbye," Tuggins said as he took off his hat.

"Tomorrow you begin journey to Saigon." Lan Tho Giao took his arm and led him down the main hall to the ornate room where he met with Madame X and Big Steve Beltzer. This time they were alone.

"Where is everybody?" Tuggins asked as he settled into the soft, cushioned couch.

"House closed temporarily due to extraordinary situation," Lan Tho Giao spoke from across the room as she poured two cups of green tea. "Girls and Chau Thi Te go to farm owned by uncle. They work hard, but have plenty to eat."

"How'd you know we were leaving tomorrow?" asked Tuggins, suspiciously.

Lan Tho Giao sat down next to him. "What Panther GIs do is very important to Vietnamese people," she said.

"So, uh, did we pass inspection at the firefight the other night?" asked Tuggins.

"General Dong Van Binh very impressed with courage and skill of Panther soldiers." Lan Tho Giao took a small sip of her tea. ""Will help Panthers reach their goal, in any way he can."

As she set her cup down and turned toward Tuggins, her arm brushed against his. "Willie Tuggins have girl back home who waits for him?" asked the beautiful NVA officer.

"It's been so long." Tuggins reached for her chin and guided her to a kiss, then embraced her as they savored each other. Lan Tho Giao rose and gracefully slipped out of her Ao Dai. She stood naked before him, smiling shyly. Her breasts were small and her nipples erect. Her hips flared gently, inviting Tuggins to satisfy his hunger.

He gazed upon her loveliness long enough to make her blush a firey crimson. This embarrassed him as well, and he looked away. Lan Tho Giao then reached down to Tuggins and took his hand leading him out of the room and down a hallway that was new to him. At that point he probably would have followed her off a cliff.

◗ ◗ ◗

Early the next morning, the two ate a quick breakfast of rice and leeks flavored with fish and more green tea to wash it down. Lan Tho Giao walked over behind Tuggins' chair, reached down and straightened his collar. "I almost forget something, Willie Tuggins." She went back into Madame X's office and retrieved a large canvas bag. "Mail was sent through Red Cross in France." She handed the bag to Tuggins and smiled. "French ambassador in Saigon thought Madame X good place to find Panther GIs."

"I guess he figured right." Tuggins flipped the bag over his shoulder. "Guys'll be glad to see this."

"Willie Tuggins, you must know there is great danger for you and your friends on road to Saigon," said Lan Tho Giao.

"Yeah, Lan Tho Giao," Tuggins chuckled. "I'm sure you right about that."

The lovely woman smiled demurely. "Willie Tuggins should say 'Em Giao' to Lan Tho Giao." She placed a hand on Tuggins' chest. "Our people tell us that American government making new ambush, only this time with large army of Korean soldiers." A look of worry crossed her face.

"The ROKs, huh?" Tuggins shook his head in consternation. "Seems like we get through one thing and they just throw somethin' else at us!"

"Korean soldiers very powerful, Willie Tuggins. Our sources say Koreans wait for Panthers just north of Nha Trang." She unfolded a piece of paper with an image of the Panther march route along Highway #1 toward Saigon, similar to Fast Eddie Miller's drawing more than a week before. "Here Nha Trang," she pointed to the map, "and here Korean ambush place." She moved her finger slightly. "Panthers must stay on road because of river and mountains."

"Man, I don't see how we're going to get around them on this one. We've got a lot of guys, but half of them can hardly walk. We expect a lot of ARVN's and their families to be on the road with us, slowin' things down. No way we can take to the jungle again, Em Giao." Tuggins shook his head and followed her as she traced his predicament with her finger on the map.

"Koreans have at least one thousand soldiers, Willie Tuggins. Many tanks, mortars, and artillery." She looked at him. "What will Panthers do?"

"I gotta admit that's a tough question." Tuggins took his loose-brimmed jungle hat from his pocket and placed it on his head. "And I better be getting back." He picked up the mail sack and reached to open the door.

Lan Tho Giao placed a hand on each of his arms, stopping him for a moment. "Be careful, Willie Tuggins." She stood on her tiptoes and kissed him on the cheek. "Goodbye, Willie Tuggins."

"Goodbye, Em Giao." Tuggins stepped through the doorway into the early-morning light of Qui Nhon. As he strode toward Panther headquarters area, two tears fell slowly down his cheeks.

◑ ◑ ◑

"All right, fellas, listen up." Tuggins stood in front of the assembled leaders of the Panthers. For the most part, they were the same group that set off from the clearing where Captain Welby died ten days before. "Here's the deal." Fast Eddie walked up next to Tuggins with a three-foot-square version of the map Lan Tho Giao drew for Tuggins earlier that morning. "This is us, here in Qui Nhon." Tuggins pointed to the map as he spoke. "And here's sweet home, Saigon. Between these two places is about four hundred miles of hot, miserable hoofin'." He turned back and pointed at the map. "And here, in Nha Trang, they're preparing another little party for us just outside of Qui Nhon." Groans and curses came from the group.

Tuggins went on, "Fellas, this time they're gonna throw the ROKs at us, 'cause none of our guys'll fight for 'em against the Panthers."

"The ROKs!" Dunlop threw his cigarette to the ground. "You gotta be shittin', Tug!"

"Fuckin' Koreans'll shoot us down like dogs, man," said Gage.

"So what do you guys think we should do?" Kelly directed his question to Tuggins and Miller.

Miller looked at Tuggins, "Preacher?" Each man directed his full attention to Tuggins.

The young man from South Carolina took his hat off and placed it in his back pants pocket. He drew in a deep breath and exhaled slowly. "We got a ways to go before Nha Trang, guys. I figure about one hundred and forty miles. If we make twenty miles a day, that will put us there in seven days, that is if nuthin' goes wrong, which is one hell of a big 'if'." Tuggins folded his arms across his chest. "A lot can happen in a week, so we'll just have to play things by ear. Fast Eddie, Turk and me are workin' on something but a lot's gonna depend on what some other folks can come up with." He held his hat in both hands. "This ain't gonna be like those jerks we beat that came with that Colonel Phillips guy. The ROKs are a no bullshit bunch of stone killers, and there's gonna be a whole lotta them. But listen, we gonna, all of us, make it home. That's my promise to you guys, and I want you all to spread that word. Every Panther needs to keep the faith."

Miller stepped up. "Alright you guys, how ready is everybody to blow this town."

Dunlop led off. "Forget it man, no way we're leaving today." He lit the cigarette that was dangling from his lip. "My guys' blisters are just starting to get better, and for the most part they've been enjoying themselves here." He flicked the ash from the end of his smoke. "I'm starting to pry 'em loose, but it's a struggle. A lot of them think they're in love and want to take the girls with them."

"We can't be havin' that, Spiderman."

"I know," Dunlop replied. "They've all been getting fed pretty good and they hate to give that up for what's facing us. I'd say Wednesday, maybe Thursday. We'll be ready by then."

"Anybody got anything else?" Miller asked the group.

"Spiderman has it right, far as I can see." Gage said as the rest of the group indicated agreement with nods and "Right on's."

"Eddie, why don't you give the guys a report on transportation arrangements?" Tuggins suggested.

"Okay," Miller stepped forward again. "By last count, there's about thirteen thousand five hundred of us here in Qui Nhon."

Expressions of surprise and delight came from the group. "That is one hell of a bunch of dudes!" Flowers said.

"Man, you got that right," Miller said. "We got about thirty guys from the 179th to bring their trucks over, but that'll only be enough for the guys who really can't walk. And keeping that many vehicles gassed up from here to Saigon will be a logistical nightmare. I put this guy, Plummer, from the 179th in charge of the trucks. He's their best mechanic." Miller turned around and looked at the map, which was leaning against a tree. "Right now we should have enough C-rations to make it as far as Nha Trang." Loud groans arose from the group. "Yeah, I know you guys are getting used to all this home cooking, but I'm looking forward to some good ole pound cake and fruit cocktail! Know what I mean?" A round of laughter rolled through the group.

"One more thing before everybody takes off," Miller went on. "Tug brought a bag of mail back from a meeting he went to last night." A few chuckles and whistles came from the group. "We divided up the letters by battalions, so make sure you pick up what came for your guys."

The meeting broke up and everybody went for the stacks of mail arranged on a table.

"Hey Tug!" Flowers called out. "Here's one for you, man. This was in the Black Panthers' stack." Flowers handed a wrinkled dirty envelope to Tuggins who shoved it into his shirt pocket. 'Dorothy' was written on the corner of the envelope.

◑ ◑ ◑

"You get something from your girl back in the world?" Kelly asked. Tuggins sat hunched in the shade of the headquarters tent wall reading a letter. "Hey man, are you crying?"

"Yeah, I guess so." Tuggins wiped his face on his sleeve and looked up at Dunlop and Kelly. "I sure do miss her!" he sighed.

Dunlop smiled, "Don't sweat it, man. All we gotta do is figure out some way around the ROKs, then it should be pretty easy-going the rest of the way to Saigon. Hey, she'll probably meet you at the embassy."

"The ROKs," said Tuggins, shaking his head.

"Don't worry, Tug, you'll think of something," Kelly said.

"Yeah, something...." Tuggins said. "Hey fellas, Dot says I'm a father, by the way."

"A father!" Kelly exclaimed. "Tug, that's great!"

"Yeah, all we gotta do now is figure out some way to stay alive long enough for me to see my little boy. Ain't this a bitch?"

❍ ❍ ❍

Kelly distributed the mail in his battalion and then settled back into the shade of a tree. He read a letter from Becky:

May 7, 1970

Dear Tom,

What in the world is going on over there? I'm terrified something has happened to you. The news is full of crazy stories about peace negotiations, and they're claiming they've stopped all the bombing in Vietnam. God, it's so wonderful, if it's true!

I called your division headquarters and asked what was happening and they were really evasive. I talked to some creepy Major who's the information officer or something like that. He finally told me that you and Frank were on some kind of special mission where you couldn't get any word back to the States for a while. It seems like weeks since I've heard from you! I pray to God you're okay. Write to me as soon as you can, okay?

Things are pretty wild here. There's a national academic convocation (really a student strike) scheduled for next week. Down in the Bay Area, people are talking about shutting down the Oakland Induction Center for the week.

Rumors are flying that there's a big troop rebellion going on. You wouldn't know anything about that, now, would you? First they announced this huge invasion into Cambodia, and then the next day they just pretended like they hadn't said anything about Cambodia at all. The talk on all the news programs is about these new peace negotiations and maybe the war ending. That would be so great!

Aside from all the political earthquakes, life is pretty normal here. I tried to get your sister to come up to Tacoma for a while, but she chickened out at the last minute. I think she was worried that she would have to stand on her own two feet a little up here. You know what a manipulative daddy's girl she can be.

I can't help thinking that maybe this will be over soon. Get word to me as soon as you can, okay? We'll have a huge party when you come home. I can't wait!

All My Love,
Becky

❍ ❍ ❍

"Nha Trang, huh?" Fred Greenburg said to Big Steve Beltzer.

"That's what it looks like, according to my sources," Beltzer said.

"Sources." Greenburg scowled as he looked at Beltzer across his bowl of noodles.

The two American journalists were seated on a park bench not far from the Quang Pho Bat Cafe. Beltzer felt their conversation might be overheard inside the Bat, so they purchased bowls of noodles and tea at an outdoor stall.

"Remember my friend up in Pleiku? I talked to her again, and she told me a couple of ROK Army Corporals heard about me interviewing black GI's up there for an article, and they figured my friend could get word to me."

"So, these ROK Corporals," Greenburg lowered his bowl of soup, "What did they have to say?"

"They said that some of the ROK soldiers are pretty disgusted with the way they're being used in Nam, but there's not much they can do about it. You know, orders and all that."

"Yeah, then what?"

"Well these fellows really admire Tuggins and his guys, and they wanted to get word to them about the ambush at Nha Trang." Beltzer took a sip of his tea. "They're really afraid there's gonna be a massacre."

"So, Big Steve, old buddy, just what did you do with this juicy little bit of intelligence?"

"I got word to this woman up in Qui Nhon who's an undercover NVA major or something."

Greenburg coughed and spit out a mouthful of his soup.

"Look Fred, all your film crew has to do is take a little ride up to Nha Trang, wait around maybe a couple of days, then fly over Highway 1 and film Tuggins and his guys trying to get past the ROKs," Beltzer said.

"And you think just because we're overhead with cameras everybody's going to keep their weapons on safety?" He slurped down another mouthful of noodles. "Fat fucking chance!" said Greenburg.

"No, but I do think it might help prevent a slaughter when Tuggins and his guys surrender."

Greenburg's face looked worried, "So you don't think they can make it to Saigon?"

"C'mon, Fred," Beltzer pushed in a mouthfull of noodles, then swallowed, "the Koreans won't hesitate to cut those guys to pieces if they don't give up. You know that."

"Yeah, I guess I was just hoping that somehow they'd figure out a way. It would make a great story. You know, those crazy Panthers marching into Saigon and surrounding the Embassy." Greenburg sighed, "Jeeze," he said.

"Yeah, and that's exactly why the US government will never allow it," Beltzer said and looked around them. "They'll work out a deal with the North Vietnamese, stop the war, pull out of Vietnam and all that," he stopped to drink his bowl dry, "but they're not going to let it look like they were forced to leave by a bunch of scruffy, insubordinate GIs. Man, I sure wish there was a way to get something published about Tuggins and his guys!"

"Yeah, I suppose you're right about how the US government will react," Greenburg said.

"Fred, will you do it?"

"Goddamnit Beltzer, yeah, I'll do it." Greenburg put his bowl down on the bench and covered his eyes. "And I can kiss my career, and maybe my young ass, goodbye."

"Nah, Fred," Beltzer put his arm around Greenburg's shoulder, "this is going to be a great story, man. You'll probably get a Pulitzer!"

Greenburg kept his hand over his eyes and lowered his head. "Oh yeah," he groaned.

o o o

"Sir, are you telling us that if we go with you now, all would be forgiven?" 'Professor' Gage directed his question to the man standing with Tuggins facing an audience of twelve hundred black soldiers. Major William Stroud, West Point '65, was currently assigned as a battalion commander in the 1st Air Cav. A black man from Tennessee, Stroud was on a fast track for promotion as the Army cast about for a way to cope with the increasing dissent among its black soldiers. A gentle breeze came off the blue water to cool the soldiers as they listened to Stroud. The last rays of gentle light from the setting sun shown on Stroud's face as he listened to Gage.

"That's right, soldier," Stroud spoke into a megaphone. "The President has authorized me to offer amnesty to any man who reports to me tomorrow morning for reinstatement to his unit." His voice was clear and strong, and he spoke without hesitation. "I'll be in this same spot, at 0600 tomorrow. If you want to do something to show all America that black folks will do our part to defend the country, you'll be here tomorrow."

"Major!" Damon 'Turk' Flowers called out and stepped in front of the group to speak. One of the men in the crowd holding a bullhorn rushed to hand it to him. "You come to talk to us this fine evening about what we oughtta do from here, and we thank you for that." The tall sergeant with the black bandanna around his forehead cut a figure equally impressive to Stroud's. "The way I hear what you're saying, is that you'll let all of us, including the white guys, go back to our units if we report to you tomorrow morning. That about right, Sir?"

"That's absolutely correct, Sergeant."

"No punishment for the last three weeks, right?"

"Right, Sergeant."

Flowers looked at the faces of the black soldiers in the crowd near him. What he saw was a mixture of hope and defiance. He spoke into the megaphone again, "Major Stroud, some of us been here quite a while. Our year's almost up." Words of agreement came from many present. "There's others got a ways to go, and even a few FNG's still wearing their combat diapers."

Laughter and chuckles came from the group on that one, along with a few "right on's."

"What we all got in common," Flowers went on, "is that we've had enough of this fuckin' bullshit over here!"

An eruption of applause and catcalls followed Flowers' last statement, and other soldiers began shouting out grievances and demands for answers. "I lost enough brothers over here" was heard along with "What the fuck happened to Green?"

From the other side of the crowd Gage rose to speak. "Sir, this place doesn't feel right to a lot of us." He held his torn jungle hat in both hands. "You get up in the morning and you're drenched in sweat inside an hour. Major Stroud, it was sweltering hot on Christmas day. Maybe if you all get us into a war with Canada, we'll think about that. Maybe you could say we're winter soldiers, Sir. Maybe that's why it's not goin' so good for us over here." He paused a second and placed his hat on his head. "I guess that's it, Major." Applause, whoops and 'right-ons' followed his speech.

Amidst the general uproar, a chant started from some Third of the Eighth guys, "We're sick of this shit! Hey! We're sick of this shit! Hey,..." Flowers remained standing and waved his arms in rhythm with the chant, egging the guys on.

Stroud stood at attention and absorbed the crowd's indignation, his face impassive, his hands at his sides. When the group finally quieted, he raised the megaphone to his mouth. "I'll be here at 0600 tomorrow. We will arrange transport for all who show up." With that, he handed the bullhorn to Tuggins, spun around and walked briskly away from the assembled black Panthers toward a waiting jeep. He climbed into the jeep to head out.

CHAPTER XXVIII

May 13, 1970, 0800HRS

HUMPIN' DOWN HIGHWAY #1

TUGGINS, MILLER, GAGE, DUNLOP, FLOWERS, FORTIER, AND KELLY sat together on a hillside watching the scruffy troops of the Panther Division as they clogged the road leaving Qui Nohn. At last count, one thousand five hundred and eighty guys in Kelly's First Battalion were leading off the big trek to Saigon,

"You did a nice job gettin' your guys ready, Kelly," Tuggins said as he watched the First Battalion march past.

"I sure hope so," Kelly said, looking out over the men entrusted to him.

Some of the men wore bright colorful shirts or conical hats like the peasants in the rice fields. Some carried cloth sacks filled with rice. All proudly displayed the evidence of affection from the people whose homes they shared for the past week. Only a scattering carried rifles slung over their shoulders.

For the most part, the Panthers were in fine spirits, smokin' and jokin' as they walked. Only a few were limping a little, evidence of Fast Eddie's provision of transport for the truly lame.

Most everybody had a full rucksack stuffed with clean, if frayed, clothing and a share of c-ration cans. Miller had scored big in a Vietnamese Army warehouse, finding enough food to last the division about a week. Everybody had at least three full canteens of water and enough cigarettes to last a few days.

Not marching in step, but still somehow together, every soldier moved rhythmically with the thousands of others before and after him. *These guys look pretty confident*, thought Kelly. *Things worked out for us pretty good, first winning that fight in the elephant grass, and then getting the great week in Qui Nhon.*

"Hey, anybody know what happened with that fucker Stroud?" asked Miller. "Any guys show up to go back to their units this morning?"

"I went over there to check it out," Gage said as he grabbed a stem of grass to hold in his teeth like a cigarette. "There were a couple of dozen guys, mostly from the 1st Cav."

"I figured there might be a few from that bunch," Tuggins said.

"Yeah, and you guys will never guess who else was there." Gage put a big smile on his face and waited for them to guess.

"Aw, c'mon now, Professor," Flowers said, "have mercy on us!"

"Well, you put it that way, I guess I can just tell you." Gage took a breath and raised his eyebrows. "When I got to the pick-up point, bigger than dogshit was one Private William 'Lizzard' Vandyne, standing at the head of the line to get on one of Stroud's trucks."

"That dumb fucker!" Dunlop said as he exhaled a cloud from the roll-your-own smoke Miller had just handed him. "He acts like he was raised in a damn barn. What's he think they're going to give him, a battlefield commission for deserting twice?"

Flowers pretended to looked concerned, "Maybe that boy was raised behind the barn, out with the hogs." The group on the hillside chuckled over the misadventures of their erstwhile buddy from Third of the Eighth.

◖ ◖ ◖

"Hey, anybody seen Spiderman?" While the Panthers were eating their evening meal, Kelly walked back to Third Battalion's area to find Dunlop. "No-No, you seen Spiderman?" Kelly called out to Kapinski. They were now four days march out of Qui Nhon, about half way to Nha Trang. The column had grown to over fifteen thousand. Trailing the Panthers were approximately fifteen thousand Vietnamese refugees who feared the collapse of American power in South Vietnam. The civilians kept ahead of General Dong Van Binh's Third NVA Army, which was moving south along the coast road, consolidating power as the South Vietnamese Army collapsed and fled.

Things had settled into something resembling a rhythm. Besides the endless plodding toward Saigon, the troops were cooking, cleaning, and helping their buddies when needed. Lan Tho Giao had organized the local peasant associations along the way to provide a warm evening meal at the end of each day's march. After dark, guys either stood guard or tried to get some sleep.

"Say Kelly, you see those two guys over there, behind the serving line?" Kapinski said, as Kelly walked over to him.

"Yeah, No-No, what about 'em?"

"Well," Kapinski said, as he sucked some noodles off his chopsticks, "I thought you might be interested in that side arm one of 'em has."

"No-No, that's a Russian military pistol, and I'm pretty sure the guy wearin' it's VC."

"Shit, Kelly."

"No-No, who do you think's organizing all this chow for us?"

Kapinski shook his head. "Fuck, man."

"Don't sweat it, No-No." Kelly stood up. "They want us outta here even more than we do. They figure if they organize the locals to feed us, we'll be gone that much quicker." He cupped hands to his mouth. "Spiderman, where you hiding?" Kelly called out. Kapinski went back to his noodles.

"Dunlop's over there," said a fellow seated on a large hardwood log, eating the meal he had been served along with the rest of the Panthers by Lan Tho Giao's volunteers. He pointed toward a clump of bushes on the other side of the road.

Kelly shaded his eyes from the setting sun and trotted over.

"Hey Frank," Kelly called out, "you got somebody asking for you."

Dunlop pushed his penis back in his pants and buttoned his fly. "What you talkin' about, Kelly?" Dunlop stood there with a Marlboro dangling from his lips.

"Remember that chick you used to hang out with at the wire in An Khe?"

Dunlop raised his eyebrows and took the cigarette from his mouth. "Course I do," he said.

"Well, I think she might be one of the servers up in First Battalion."

"Nah, man." Dunlop raised his smoke to his mouth for a drag. "Probably just somebody looks like her."

"Well, she's asking about some 'Spiderman GI'." Kelly had a shit-eating grin from ear to ear.

"Fuck, I don't believe it." Dunlop tossed his cigarette to the ground and crushed it underfoot. "You mind goin' over there," he pointed to the group of soldiers on the log, "and tell those guys I'll be back before dark?"

"Sure, man." Dunlop was off in a flash, headed for the First Battalion dinner line. Kelly walked back toward the fellows on the log. *Just friends, ha!* Kelly thought.

❍ ❍ ❍

Tuyen looked up from the ten-gallon pot of noodle soup, ladle in hand.. "Handsome GI want more soup?" She beamed up at him.

Dunlop stood transfixed, with a face-cracking grin.

Lan Tho Giao walked up and stood next to Dunlop. "So, this is famous Spiderman GI," she said, holding out a hand to Dunlop.

"Oh, yeah," Dunlop grasped Lan Tho Giao's, the two smiling broadly as they shook.

"Tuyen work very hard on English," Lan Tho Giao said. "Spiderman think so?"

"Huh? Oh yeah, definitely!" said Dunlop, looking at Tuyen as she smiled. He kept pumping Lan Tho Giao's hand.

"Hey, what's the fuckin' hold up?" came a voice from the line behind Dunlop.

Lan Tho Giao stepped back and called out "Thanh, come please!"

Dunlop dropped Lan Tho Giao's hand and watched a young Vietnamese woman approach the serving line.

Lan Tho Giao said something in Vietnamese to the young woman and turned back to Dunlop. "Time for Tuyen rest. Maybe you help with English, Spiderman." Thanh stepped around the soup pot.

"Uh, yeah. Great idea!" Dunlop said.

Tuyen took off her apron and came around to stand with Dunlop. She kept her eyes on the contents of the pot, but stood close enough to touch the trembling Dunlop.

"Good!" Lan Tho Giao placed a hand on each of their shoulders. "All girls must return to me," Lan Tho Giao looked at Dunlop, "before dark. Okay, Spiderman?"

"Yeah, dark." Dunlop nodded vigorously.

Lan Tho Giao smiled and directed her attention to the chow line. Dunlop said "C'mon, I'll introduce you to some of the guys." They walked off together in the general direction of Third Battalion.

◐ ◐ ◐

MAY 16, 1970, 1900HRS

The packed dining room of the Quang Pho Bat Cafe vibrated with its usual frenetic energy. "Reverend Tuggins, I'd like you to meet a friend of mine." Big Steve Beltzer extended his hand toward the man approaching the table where Beltzer sat with the Baptist minister from South Carolina. "This is Hugh Thompson, the helicopter pilot I mentioned to you."

"I am honored to make your acquaintance, Mr. Thompson," the Reverend said, rising from his seat and reaching across the table to shake hands with him. "Mr. Beltzer has been telling me of your courageous stand at My Lai. You should know, sir, that all America owes you a tremendous debt of gratitude."

Thompson smiled at the Reverend and then looked down at the table as he removed his sunglasses and baseball cap. He placed the cap upside down and set the glasses inside. The colorful patch of Thompson's unit, the 179th Aviation Brigade, was visible on the hat. He wore his pilot's jumpsuit with, as he liked to say, "enough zippers, pencils, patches, and weapons to keep the MPs busy while you swallow the evidence." His face had a new wrinkle or two since My Lai, and the expression of a man with much on his mind. Thompson reached into one of his pockets and pulled out a pack of Camel cigarettes and a zippo lighter. He lit a smoke and inhaled deeply. He nodded toward Reverend Tuggins and said quietly, "Thank you, sir."

Thompson turned and glanced out a window at the Cholon District market-street. He looked back toward the two men at his table and jerked his thumb at the window. "It's bloody hell chaos out there." He took a drag on his cigarette. "I was walking over here and this guy comes up to another man on the street, and shoots him, point blank, in the face. Then just walked away." He drew deeply on his Camel. "It sure is nice to be here at the good ol' Bat with you all, and I'm very pleased to meet you, Reverend."

"I thought you would enjoy meeting each other." Beltzer said as a waitress came up to their table. Beltzer said something in Vietnamese to the waitress and signaled three with fingers and drew his hand in a circle around the table. The waitress nodded without smiling, briskly placed three plastic glasses on the table and poured rice wine into each of them.

"Reverend Tuggins here, is wondering if he could ask a favor of you, Hugh," Beltzer said.

"Sure, but first I'd sure like to know how he managed to get here. I've heard that Tan Son Knat is shut down tight. Nobody in or out." Thompson looked at Reverend Tuggins and waited for his answer. Reverend Joseph Tuggins looked his sixty-two years. The combined effects of the last year's worry over his son Willie, and the arduous trip he had just completed, had left him somewhat haggard. Uncharacteristically, he had not shaved for a couple of days and the short-sleeved white shirt he wore looked lived in.

"Fred, over here!" Beltzer called out and waved his arm at his journalist buddy, Fred Greenburg. The reporter from the New York Times saw Beltzer and headed toward their table. Conversation stopped for a moment while Greenburg sat down and was introduced around.

"Mr. Thompson had just asked me to relate the story of my coming to Vietnam when you arrived, Mr. Greenburg," Tuggins said..

"In Hampton County, we are blessed with a fine representative to Congress." Reverend Tuggins said as a waitress placed steaming bowels of noodle soup on the table. "The honorable Lewis Willard, Jr. is the son of a fellow Baptist Minister whose church is located in the county next to ours. Representative Willard is the first member of our Black community to enter Congress from South Carolina since reconstruction, and we are all very proud of him."

"When I learned of my son's current adventures, I placed a call to Representative Willard's father and explained the situation as I understood it."

Greenburg interrupted, "Excuse me sir, but it's my understanding that there's a total news blackout back in the states on the situation over here."

"A young white gentleman came to my door four days ago." Tuggins gently waved his hands for emphasis. "His name was Denny Dixon and he said he had come to see me as a representative of the Progressive Labor Group from California. He told me that a friend of Willie's in Vietnam had written letters home to his wife in which he spoke highly of my son. This man's group has embarked upon an effort to establish contact with a large group of American soldiers my son is apparently leading here in Vietnam." He spooned a taste of the broth in front of him into his mouth and swallowed. "I believe these boys my son is traveling with are calling themselves the Panther Division, but I'm sure 'division' would amount to a considerable exaggeration of their numbers."

"Actually, Reverend Tuggins," Beltzer said between slurps of noodles, "they might be the biggest American division in Vietnam right now. Hugh and I did a fly over yesterday, and we're thinking fifteen to twenty thousand. Not counting the Vietnamese fleeing the NVA advance right behind them."

Reverend Tuggins paused for a moment and raised his eyebrows and cocked his head. "Well," he continued, "the day after I spoke to Representative Willard's father, the Congressman telephoned me from his office in Washington DC. We talked for quite a long time. When I finished explaining the situation to him, he offered to arrange a trip to Vietnam." Reverend Tuggins attempted, without success, to get some of the slippery noodles to stay on his spoon long enough to get them into his mouth.

"So, this Dixon fellow," Beltzer interjected, "what's the deal with him, Reverend?"

"Oh, he's back at the hotel with Congressman Willard and his aide," Reverend Tuggins said.

Beltzer and Greenburg exchanged glances. Beltzer raised his eyebrows and shrugged his shoulders.

"At any rate, Mr. Thompson, we made it here against the odds, and I'm afraid that I need to ask a fairly large favor of you."

Thompson dropped his cigarette onto the floor and crushed it underfoot. He folded his hands on the table in front of him and looked at Reverend Tuggins.

"We brought five hundred American flags with us and I was hoping you would agree to take us out to this Panther group so that I could deliver them to my son."

Thompson raised his eyebrows and smiled. He looked away from the table for a few seconds and then looked back toward Reverend Tuggins. "The flags are a great idea, Reverend, but I don't think it would be possible to take you out to the Panthers. To tell you the truth, I expected to get shot down myself by now, with all the craziness out there." Thompson stretched out his legs. "I'm flying without anybody's permission, most of the guys still in the control towers are stoned." He took a pen and notebook from his zipper pocket. "Why don't you give me the info I need to find those flags and I'll see that your son gets them."

Reverend Tuggins gave him the name of his hotel. "I'll tell the management to expect you. The flags are in two boxes in a storeroom behind the registration desk."

"Great, I'll grab 'em tomorrow morning," Thompson said as he stood up to leave. "We were gonna take a run up that way anyhow." Before Thompson could leave, Beltzer pulled on his sleeve and said a few quiet words to him. Thompson nodded in agreement and strode out of the room.

"Now, Reverend," Greenburg said, "I want you to pick up your chopsticks and hold 'em like so...."

Reverend Tuggins awkwardly attempted to follow Greenburg's instructions, while Big Steve Beltzer looked on with a large grin.

○ ○ ○

MAY 18, 1970

The sun rose over the blue curls of the South China Sea. The Panthers had stopped for the night along a beautiful stretch of Highway #1 where the breakers could be heard in the quiet. No-No Kapinski pulled guard duty in First Battalion, the 0200 'til dawn shift. He liked the time slot because it afforded him the best chance to get an unbroken stretch of sleep before the division set off on it's daily trek, at about 0900. No-No reached for his cup and took a long drink of the tea he had saved from the night before.

As he inhaled a deep breath of sea-scented air, he heard a faint rumbling coming from the jungle on the other side of the road. *Shit! Sounds like tanks*, he thought. No-No quickly drained the cup, held his M16 in a ready position and called out to the guards on either side that he would go and have a look. He broke into a trot, first crossing Highway #1, and then heading up an overgrown hillside road, into the jungle.

As he neared the top of the hill ten minutes later, the powerful diesel engine of an American M-48 'Patton' tank roared less than thirty feet away jumping into view from the opposite direction. Exhaust smoke enveloped him as the behemoth 'Jungle Buster' came to a branch-crushing, skidding halt, it's treads locked in place.

"Hey man," came the voice of the soldier standing in the open hatch of the tank's turret, "What the fuck do you think you're doing?" The tank commander removed his leather gloves and shook them at Kapinski. "Hey man, you know we almost fuckin' ran you over?"

"Uh, I have to ask you to identify yourself before I let you go any further," Kapinski spoke with a quavering voice. He remained in the tank's path, holding his M16 across his legs with the barrel pointing off to the side, away from the tank.

The tank commander chuckled and said, "My name's Dennis O'Connor and I'm looking for a buddy of mine from AIT." He wore thick-lensed, Army issue glasses and was covered in freckles.

By now, four more tanks had pulled up behind the first one, all of them revving their diesel engines.

"You know a guy named Tom Kelly?" asked O'Connor, raising his voice to be heard over the roar of the tanks.

"Yeah, sure," Kapinski said, resting his rifle butt on the ground. "He's still asleep about a hundred yards back thataway." He motioned with his head back toward the road.

"Kelly's here," he leaned down and spoke to the driver inside the tank. "What's your name, fella?" he asked Kapinski.

"Larry, but most of the guys call me No-No."

O'Connor chuckled again, then said, "How'd they come up with No-No?"

"Stands for No Nonsense."

"I guess that's a compliment, then." O'Connor looked back over his shoulder and surveyed the other four tanks as a shepherd would his flock. "Well No-No, why don't you climb up here and take us to where old Gas Man is getting his beauty rest."

"Gas Man?"

"You ever try to sleep in the same barracks with Kelly?" O'Connor said as Kapinski nimbly climbed onto the tank and sat down on the turret, resting his rifle across his knees.

"Can't say as I ever did."

○ ○ ○

"Really, Dennis, it's great to see you. We figure the more the merrier, know what I mean?" Kelly said to his old infantry-training buddy from

Fort Lewis. A crowd had gathered around the five tanks across the road from the First Battalion mess line. While O'Connor and Kelly talked, the crews on the other tanks smugly answered questions from the grunts about fighting in the iron monsters.

"The more the merrier," O'Connor said, "'cept, we gotta leave our machines here, huh?"

"Well, like I said, I checked this out with Tuggins and Miller..."

"Who's Tuggins and Miller?" O'Connor asked.

"That's them over there in the mess line." Kelly pointed toward where Miller and Tuggins were standing in line waiting for their morning oatmeal. By some miracle, Fast Eddie had provided enough fresh milk for everybody that morning. "The black guy and the white guy with the goatee, standing together."

"But, what if some bad guys come along and use our tanks to come after us?" O'Connor said.

"We'll drain the fuel, so they won't be able to drive 'em right away." Kelly saw Miller walking toward them with a bowl in his hands. "Fast Eddie, here, will be most grateful for the gas. We can sure use it for the trucks. And besides, the bad guys aren't gonna do anything to interfere with us making it to Saigon. All they want is to see all of us on boats, waving goodbye."

"I don't know, Kelly...." O'Connor looked back at the tanks under his command as Miller walked up to the group.

"Look," Kelly said, "we can disable them so nobody can use 'em for a while, right Eddie?"

"Sure," Miller spooned cereal out of his bowl as he stood with Kelly and O'Connor. "Plummer'll make sure they just sit there until somebody can get some cranes in to move 'em." Miller turned to O'Connor, "We can really use your fuel, man. Whaddaya say?"

"Well," O'Connor began, paused for a moment, "as long as we get to be in Kelly's bunch here." He paused for a moment again, "Somebody's gotta keep an eye on this commie goofball, maybe I can help out with that part."

CHAPTER XXIX

May 22, 1970, 2000HRS

NHA TRANG

"WELL, FELLAS, HERE WE ARE AT THE LAST BIG HURDLE, Y'ALL might say." Tuggins spoke softly to the battalion leaders of the Panther division assembled in the bivouac area. It was nearly dark and no fires were allowed, no clanging pots and pans. Orders had gone out for everyone to stay under the cover of the forest canopy, away from the road. Nha Trang was just three clicks away, and scouts had brought news that a powerful enemy army awaited them just outside the little fishing town.

Much as Lan Tho Giao had predicted, the blocking force of ROK Army veterans, about one thousand troops plus thirty tanks were positioned a few hundred meters back along a ridgeline on either side of the road. If the Panthers tried anything like the Battle of the Elephant grass, they would be cut down quickly in a murderous crossfire.

"So what now, Preacher?" Dunlop said as he looked at the three foot diagram that Miller held for the Panther leaders to study. "That map don't look too good for our side. Maybe we should call this whole thing off and beg for mercy. They can't put twenty thousand guys in LBJ, huh?"

Nervous chuckles came from the group.

Tuggins smiled. "Nah, Spiderman, they can't put us all in LBJ. But hey, I'm still thinkin we can make it to Saigon, without giving up."

"But Tug," Dunlop said, "we can't fight these guys. They'll blow our shit away so fast, people will forget we ever existed."

"Really, man," Tuggins said, "we been workin' on this plan. Miller, Flowers, and me think it has a good chance of getting us past these guys up ahead."

"Okay, Tug, what you got in mind?" Gage asked. "It kinda looks like they got us outgunned this time."

"They always got us way outgunned, Professor." Tuggins studied the ground in front of him and rubbed his chin for a few seconds. He looked up and took a deep breath, "I'm sorry fellas," he shoved his hands into his pants pockets, "but if this thing stands a chance of working, we're gonna have to keep it a secret from those ROK guys up by Nha Trang. Only four or five of us are going to know the whole plan." He took his hands out of his pockets and folded his arms across his chest. "I'm gonna have to ask everybody to trust me on this one."

A pensive silence settled on the group. Tuggins stood quietly, awaiting reactions from the Panther battalion leaders. Guys made eye contact with each other. Finally, after what seemed like several minutes, Dunlop spoke again.

"Well, Preacher, we've come a ways trusting you, and I guess if you say we can make it to Saigon, we'll just carry on." Dunlop cleared his throat as nods of agreement came from the other battalion leaders. Several 'right ons' were added by Gage and others, with no indications of opposition from anyone present.

◐ ◐ ◐

MAY 23, 1970, 0700HRS

"I don't know about this, you guys." Dunlop spoke to a group of six Panther leaders. Like most of the rest, he hadn't shaved since they had left Qui Nhon. For Dunlop, not shaving wasn't quite as big a deal as for some. What had appeared on his cheeks was not much more than a golden fuzz.

Like many of the men, Dunlop had taken to wearing a large blue headband with a peace symbol in front. His blond hair was getting pretty scruffy, so the band helped to keep hair out of his eyes. His dirty jungle fatigues had been cut off to make shorts and he'd taken off his shirt.. He wore two canteens of water on his belt, but carried no weapon or ammunition.

"I haven't run in a race since high school, senior year."

"That's not that long ago, man," Kelly said.

"You got any idea how many cigarettes I've smoked since then?" Dunlop asked Kelly, sounding a little irritated. "And that isn't even bringing up all the other shit I've been smoking over here." Dunlop smiled and looked around the group for support, which wasn't exactly forthcoming.

"I heard about your running times in school, Spiderman," Tuggins stepped forward. "Look at you now, boy, ain't a ounce of fat on you." Tuggins grabbed Dunlop by the arm and shook him a little, which caused everyone to laugh. "Really, Bro, we need you to do this. The whole plan rests on us letting Beltzer know exactly when we're going to leave the tree line and come under those guns tomorrow."

"But what the fuck's Beltzer got to do with it, anyway?" Dunlop said.

"We been all through that, Bro. We can't tell you everything, 'cause you might get caught." Tuggins grabbed Dunlop's other arm and looked directly at him. "When you get where you're going, you'll see what Beltzer's doing for us, and then you give him the code about tomorrow's time and answer any of his questions." Tuggins released Dunlop's arms, "Whaddaya say, Spidey?"

"Shit." Dunlop nodded without smiling, "You fuckers know I'll do it."

The others in the group broke into applause and began patting Dunlop on the back so much he started coughing.

"Right on, Spiderman!" Gage said. "And don't worry man, we'll take good care of your little girlfriend while you're gone."

"Gee, thanks, Professor. I'll try and return the favor some day. If I'm still alive, that is."

"Eddie, fill him in, okay?" Tuggins said as the group broke up and headed back to the encampment.

◑ ◑ ◑

"This here's Bui," Miller said to Dunlop, gesturing toward a slight Vietnamese man who walked up as Tuggins and the others left.

"Bui what?"

"Beats me, man." Miller shrugged his shoulders. "They just told me Bui."

The man extended his hand toward Dunlop. "Hi, mafuka!" His face was set in a warm, engaging smile as he pumped Dunlop's arm.

"Uh, Bui's English ain't so good." Miller shrugged his shoulders again. "He thinks we all call each other motherfucker. Bui here, is one of those tough little VC fuckers who can run all night on a bowl of rice and a cup of tea. He's promised to go slow enough so you can keep up. All you gotta do is follow him to Beltzer's chopper."

"Chopper?"

"Uh, yeah. I wasn't exactly supposed to tell you about that."

"Well, just how far is this chopper I'm not supposed to know about?"

Bui stood with Miller and Dunlop, smiling and nodding in an engaging manner. He constantly shuffled and tapped his feet. The man seemed to be overflowing with energy.

Miller cocked an eyebrow and scratched his beard. "It's about eight clicks the other side of Nha Trang. That's eleven altogether." Miller pulled a pack of Bugler from his pocket and began rolling a cigarette. "We figure you can make it by two this afternoon, then get back here just before nightfall." He gave the first smoke to Dunlop. "Here's the shit you'll need when you get there." Miller said as he handed Dunlop a piece of paper. The date and time, 24 May (the next day), 1500 hrs was written on the slip, together with a combination of 4 colors and 2 numbers.

Dunlop started to fold it and stuff it into his pants pocket when Miller stopped him.

"Nah, man. You gotta sit down and memorize what's in this." Miller pointed at the coded combination of colors and numbers. "Then you give it back to me and tell me what's on it without looking. Then I burn it, okay?"

"Sure." Dunlop chuckled, sat down, and began to study the paper. Miller lit his cigarette and started to stroll around the clearing, smoking his Bugler and trying not to bother Dunlop.

○ ○ ○

"You think he'll make it?" Gage asked as Flowers, Tuggins, and Miller stood watching the bouncing forms of Bui and Dunlop disappear into the jungle two hundred meters away.

"Yeah, they gonna make it," Flowers said. "The man's impressed me. No dope since before Qui Nhon, nuthin'. You guys'll see, he'll be sloppin' noodles with us tonight."

"I hope you're right, Turk," Gage said. "But this right now is the toughest run that boy ever had in front of him. Up and down those fucking hills, jungle vines tripping him, heat and humidity enough to turn a guy into a prune, I don't know..."

"We'll just have to wait and see, fellas." Tuggins took his jungle hat from his pocket and pulled it onto his head. "Meantime, we best be getting' back. It's really important that we give everybody a feeling of confidence today. They all know we're out-gunned so much we might as well be a bunch of Boy Scouts. Top of that, it's gonna be hot and boring as hell today."

"Speaking of hot and boring, Tug," Miller said. "I got an idea."

"Okay, Fast Man, let's hear it," Gage said.

"Well, me and Gormick was out exploring by the river after dinner last night and we came to a pretty nice pool created by this big bend." Miller turned around and pointed toward the river, drawing a crescent in the air with his arm and finger. "It's a really nice spot and we was thinking that we could let each battalion take a turn and have a swim." Miller looked at Tuggins and waited for him to respond.

"Sure, why not?" Tuggins broke into a broad grin. "They know we here, all those scout helicopters overhead. No use trying to hide any more. Only make sure we maintain normal discipline, okay?"

"Of course, Tug," Miller said.

"Make sure you position strong swimmers up high on both sides of the river, so they can keep an eye on everybody. Ten lifeguards on either side with a couple of skiffs to haul guys out, if the need comes up." Tuggins thought a second. "I'll ask Lan Tho Giao if she can find a couple of little boats we can borrow for the day."

Miller quickly set off to organize the festivities, and before long the huge pool in the river was full of swimming, frolicking Panthers.

○　○　○

Dunlop's lungs were on fire with each breath. The two runners had covered approximately three quarters of the distance they had to run. "Hold...it...a...second... Bui, will ya?" Dunlop bent over and braced his hands on his knees as his chest heaved with every breath. The world was looking a little dark to him, and he began to think he might faint. He felt a gentle tug on his right arm.

"Hey mafuka!"

Dunlop looked up at Bui, who stood there with a big smile holding a hand up making a "V" peace symbol with his fingers.

"Goddamn! All right already!" said Dunlop. He launched himself down the trail, determined not to stop until they reached their goal. Bui raced past the plodding Dunlop and resumed his position in the lead.

o   o   o

"Yes, Mr. President, that's correct," H.R. Haldeman shouted into the radio-telephone. His brow was furrowed as he stared at the ground, trying to hear what Richard Nixon was saying to him from Washington DC. "Yes sir, I agree. We shouldn't attack them while they're playing in the river. And it is terrible that they're having such a good time when they should all be sitting behind barbed wire."

"That's right sir, everything is ready here. There's no possible way they're going to get past General Choe's force." Haldeman looked across the patch of trampled grass toward General Choe Yong Ho and his staff. The Korean officers waited calmly for him to finish talking to the President. Choe was in front with his interpreter, talking quietly and using hand gestures. Like the rest of his senior officers, Choe was dressed in crisply-starched American jungle fatigues with shirtsleeves rolled up just past his elbows, shining American jungle boots and a jaunty jungle hat.

"Yes, Mr. President," Haldeman said loudly. "Good bye, Sir." He clicked off and handed the phone to the man standing next to him, who hurriedly placed it back in its cradle. Haldeman walked briskly over to General Choe. He noticed a large dark tattoo on Choe's right arm depicting a person impaled on the bayonet of a thrusting soldier, complete with drops of blood from the hapless victim. Haldeman felt a cold shiver in the small of his back, then smiled broadly.

"President Nixon sends his greetings, General Choe." Haldeman said to the interpreter.

Choe nodded, then answered in Korean.

Haldeman puffed up a little and addressed Choe again through his interpreter. "The President wants me to tell you that he has absolute confidence in you. He thanks you for coming to the aid of your close ally, the United States of America, in her time of great need. He wants me to assure you that this act of great courage and generosity will not be forgotten." Haldeman paused. The interpreter fell silent. The Korean general stood with his hands at his sides and looked coldly into Haldeman's eyes. Choe didn't crack even the smallest of smiles as he waited for Haldeman to get down to business.

"The President has ordered me to delay any attack on the mutinous Americans." Haldeman nervously cleared his throat. Almost imperceptibly, Choe nodded while the interpreter continued.

"I am to set up a blockade on the road beneath your positions on the ridges, General." Haldeman cleared his throat again. "President Nixon asks that soldiers of the Army of the Republic of Korea help us stop any mutineers that attempt to break through our roadblock." Haldeman stood silently. Slowly, a small smile came to the hard Korean general's face.

Haldeman extended his arm toward Choe and the two men shook hands. Terms understood, deal done.

◑ ◑ ◑

Hugh Thompson was truly in his element. He stood with one foot resting on the left wheel strut of his bubble helicopter, and one elbow resting on his flexed knee. His eyes were hidden behind dark aviator sunglasses as he lazily puffed on a camel. He was the picture of a military leader, exuding a quiet confidence. Hugh Thompson usually didn't have much trouble getting his orders followed. But today was going to be a little different.

Thompson told the members of his team all about his arrangement with Tuggins and the Panthers, and asked for their help. Warrant Officer Steve Roberts wished him well, but declined to participate in the mission. This left Thompson with only one gunship piloted by Warrant Officer Nathan Rawlings of Chattanooga Tennessee, to cover his bubble's dash across the road at Nha Trang.

Thompson looked at the small clearing he selected for an LZ (landing zone.) Rawlings had just brought his gunship down about fifty yards from where Thompson stood by his helicopter. The powerful rotor on the Huey Gunship, though slowing, still blew down hard enough to flatten the tall grass near Rawlings' ship. When Thompson caught his fellow pilot's eye behind the plexiglass windshield of the cockpit, he placed his camel between his lips and gave his buddy a firm 'thumbs up.' Rawlings was a relatively new pilot, one of the few blacks in the squadron. Thompson never missed an opportunity to teach, especially when the chance to offer encouragement presented itself.

On the ground, the crews from the two war birds busied themselves checking their machines, instruments and weapons. Downtime between flights was always used for careful scrutiny of the choppers and their guns. Hugh Thompson was a real fanatic about maintenance.

When his rotor stopped, Rawlings climbed down from the Huey and walked over to Thompson's chopper.

"Think they'll show?" Rawlings asked as he walked up.

"You got me, Nate." Thompson smiled slightly. "I got 1420," he said as he looked at his watch. "I figure we can stay here about an hour before they start looking for us. We best be somewhere tucked in for the night by 1530."

Rawlings thrust his hands in his pants pockets and nodded agreement. Two men guarded either side of the clearing. The rest of the crew methodically went over the two helicopters, taking their time at it, since it looked like they would be on the ground for a while. Thompson and Rawlings smoked while they scanned the jungle for any sign of Dunlop approaching.

"1515," Hugh Thompson said to Nate Rawlings and yawned as he looked at his watch.

The crew-members had completed their chores and sat in the gunship's doorway with their feet resting on the skid. Two guards were doing stretching exercises, trying to stay alert.

"Hugh, over here!" Thompson's crew chief, Armando Alvarez, called out from behind the bubble. Everybody, except the two guards, hurried to have a look where Alvarez was pointing.

Sure enough, about two hundred meters down a ravine, two figures were climbing toward them. One of them, a Vietnamese, carried a large white flag. The other, the American, Dunlop, appeared to be struggling to keep up.

"I'll be damned," Thompson said to no one in particular. Alvarez waved both arms back and forth until he was sure the two runners had seen him.

Minutes later, Bui and Dunlop stood in the clearing with the two helicopter crews. The runners heaved with each breath as sweat ran down their faces. Thompson and his crew stood silent, waiting for the men to gather themselves.

"My name's Dunlop," the runner from Sacramento said, in between breaths. "Where's that Beltzer guy?"

"I'm Thompson," the pilot said. "That's Beltzer, over in the other chopper." Thompson pointed to the ungainly journalist, as Beltzer struggled to get his long legs out the door of the helicopter." He grinned at the sight of Beltzer's efforts. "Take your time," Thompson said to Dunlop. We got a few minutes here."

After a brief pause, Dunlop continued. "This here's Bui," he said as he pointed to the now broadly smiling Vietnamese.

Thompson nodded toward Bui, who immediately raised his hand to his forehead in military salute while maintaining his gleeming smile. "Hi, mafuka!" Bui said, to Thompson.

"Uh, Bui here don't speak much English," Dunlop said.

"I can see he's learned the most important words," Thompson said, returning Bui's salute. The group surrounding the runners had a good laugh.

"Sir," Dunlop began.

"No need for formalities here," Thompson said, "name's Hugh." He extended an arm toward Dunlop and they shook hands.

Beltzer walked up to the group and shook hands with Dunlop. "Steve Beltzer," he said.

"Well, Hugh, Mr. Beltzer, here goes." Dunlop took a deep breath before he continued. "24 May, 1500 hrs. Brown, blue, yellow, green, 38, 2."

"Green, huh?" Thompson said.

"Yeah, green's the last color."

"Okie dokie." Thompson nodded. "Can I give you fellas a lift somewhere?"

"Man, that would be great!" Dunlop thought a second, then continued, "How's about you drop us about a half mile east of the river, maybe a mile above our camp." Dunlop looked at Thompson hopefully, "Know where that is?"

"No sweat, boys." Thompson pointed toward Rawlings' gunship. "You all climb aboard with Nate and his guys." He turned toward Rawlings, "It's about twenty minutes from here. Just follow me, Nate."

Rawlings and his crew trotted back to their Huey.

"Let's mount up!" Thompson called out.

In less than a minute, the two choppers had spooled up, with Thompson lifting from the ground first and Rawlings close behind.

o o o

MAY 24, 1971, 1100HRS

"Spiderman, you say you left those guys about a mile upriver yesterday?" Tuggins pruposefully asked in front of the assembled Panther battalion leaders. He wanted word to get around that there was a plan for the confrontation today and the Panthers could expect some help from people connected to the outside world.

"Yeah, I figured we shouldn't get too close to Nha Trang cause somebody might see Thompson and put two and two together. You know, all those fuckin' geniuses in military intelligence." Dunlop said, and received a hearty laugh from the eleven Panther battalion commanders present at the meeting.

"Good thinkin', Spidey," Tuggins said

"I think they were going to spend the night in this nice, covered area we found," Dunlop said. "They're probably still up there where me and Bui left 'em."

"Uh, we best forget about Bui, Spiderman," Tuggins said looking at Dunlop. "You get my drift?"

"Yeah, sure. No sweat," Dunlop answered.

"And I'm pretty sure they're gone by now, cause they was goin' to pick up some folks early this morning in Pleiku," Tuggins said.

"Hey, Mighty Preacher, you mind lettin' us po' ignorant folks in on all this stuff you and Fast Eddie got cookin'?" Gage said.

"I'm sorry Professor, but I got to keep it to a minimum number of guys knowing what's up 'till the very last minute. You do need to know right away, so I want you and Spiderman to stay after the briefing. Eddie'll fill you guys in, okay?"

"All right," Gage said.

Miller stepped up next to Tuggins holding a large, detailed map of the day's battlefield. Tuggins stooped and picked up a stick to use for a pointer.

"Hey," Tuggins called out, "everybody get enough to eat this morning?"

Groans and catcalls came from the group in response to Tuggins question about breakfast. Kelly spoke up, "Sure Tug, fruit cocktail and noodle soup. A real hungry man's meal."

Scattered laughter responded to Kelly's quip.

"Anyway, fellas," Tuggins chuckled, "here's where we are right now." Tuggins pointed to a forested section of the map, in between Highway #1 and the big river bend where the Panthers had gone for a swim the day before.

"Now along these ridges, that's the ROK's set-up."

Uneasy murmurs came from the group about the ambush waiting for them. "Jesus, man. Those fuckers have been up there for, what, three days now?" Gage said. "You'd think they'd get bored and leave, or something."

"Sorry Professor, they still there. Anyway, like I been sayin', there's about a thousand of 'em, and they're heavily armed. Thirty tanks, right about here." Tuggins pointed to a spot on the map. "Some American civilians, probably CIA, got a roadblock set up in easy gun range of the road. It looks like their plan is to give us a chance to surrender at the roadblock, and if we don't, cut loose on us about here." Tuggins pointed to a section of the road just beyond the CIA checkpoint. "That way, they probably figure the guys that haven't passed the roadblock yet will get discouraged and give up."

"Looks like they got a pretty airtight plan, Tug." said Sgt. Armand Henry, formerly of the First Air Cavalry, and currently Ninth Panthers Battalion commander. "I don't see much chance for us to slide through on this one, Bro."

Tuggins and Miller stood silent before the group for a few moments, Tuggins said, "Look, we got a plan that they ain't ready for." Tuggins puffed his chest a little and set his jaw. He looked over the assembled Panther leaders. *As fine a group of fellas as I could ever hope to be part of,* he thought. They were a motley crew, hardly recognizable as soldiers anymore. Cutoff pants, no shirts, hairy as a bunch of cavemen, all were wearing headbands, black for Flowers, Tuggins, and Gage, blue or red with peace symbols for everyone else. "We gonna surprise 'em this afternoon, and then we'll all be eatin' dinner tonight in Nha Trang." Tuggins broke into his best politician's smile. "Lan Tho Giao's gettin' the food all ready for us and I'm askin' you guys to have faith today. We gonna get past these guys. We gonna make it to Saigon. I promise y'all, we goin' home."

Nary a word was spoken. Everyone sat still in front of Miller's map, studying the drawing. A few guys chewed on long grass stems, others smoked quietly.

"Now, here's what I need you guys to do today," Tuggins began, smiling as he talked. His words were forceful and intended to build confidence as much as inform. "As soon as we get done here, everybody needs to start getting ready for this afternoon. Make sure your men all carry plenty of water. It's gonna be hot as a fryin' pan out there and we don't want anybody collapsin' from thirst." Tuggins looked over the group, and pointed on the map to the edge of the forest, about six hundred meters from the barricade on the road. "Everybody needs to be on line here by 1430, so let's get started no later than 1330. We'll be ten guys deep, and all eleven battalions across. Turk, the Black Panthers will be here." Tuggins pointed to an exposed spot about twenty meters in front of the others.

"Everybody keep a close eye on Turk's group. I want you all to do exactly what the Black Panthers do, okay?" Tuggins looked from man to man, satisfied to see people nodding. "When Turk starts to run, it'll be a slow, double-time at first. That's y'all's signal. Get your guys double-timin' up close behind Turk. Every swingin' dick's gotta be movin' smartly for this to work. Anybody can't run needs to stay back here with Eddie, till the ROKs leave. Gradually, the Black Panthers'll speed up till they hit the road-block at a dead run. Everybody's runnin' for all they worth now, and don't nobody stop 'till you get behind this hill," he pointed to a spot on the map, "here. That's safe from the ROKs." Tuggins took a deep breath. "After that, we just cruise on into Nha Trang. There, we pick up some trucks in town, then double back and pick up Eddie and the guys that couldn't run with us today. Everybody got it?"

Gage stood up. "No point in hanging around here. I'm going to go make sure eveybody in my bunch has full canteens."

"Uh, Professor, I need you here for a few minutes after the meeting, okay? You and Spiderman," Tuggins said.

The rest of the group got up and left the meeting area headed for their respective battalion areas. Gage, Kelly, and Dunlop huddled with Tuggins.

• • •

Tuggins, Miller, Flowers, and Kelly stood together, looking out over the open stretch of road in front of them that wound its way up to the CIA roadblock, a little over a quarter mile away. It was 1300 and blazing hot, even in the shade of the forest canopy. Twenty to thirty men could be seen at the roadblock, milling around in civilian clothes, with rifles slung over their shoulders. On the ridges, the ROKs were sitting tight, with only occasional movement visible among the Korean troops. The thirty ROK tanks sat together in the middle of their eastern ridge position, with cannons pointing down at the road ready to slaughter Tuggins and his men should they try to pass the barricade.

"Eddie," Tuggins said while turning toward Miller, who was gazing intently toward the road past the blockade with a hand on his forehead to shade his vision. "We get the flags passed out?"

Miller took his hand down and turned toward the others. "Your dad sent us six hundred flags, Tug. The guys found some branches to use for carrying poles, and we got 'em distributed evenly among all the battalions. Turk's got one hundred for the BP's." He pulled out a package of Bugler and sprinkled some onto the cigarette paper he held in his hand. "It's gonna look like a fuckin' 4th of July parade out there, Bro.

"That's what we want, Eddie," Tuggins said, and then turned to Kelly. "Bear, I want First Battalion right behind the Black Panthers."

"Yeah, Tug, we figured that." Kelly pointed to the ground, about six feet in front of them. "I'll be right there, in about twenty-five minutes, with my eight hundred guys spread out on either side of me."

"Ten deep, man, with your flags in front," Tuggins said.

"No sweat, Preacher." Kelly smiled broadly, "We'll be there."

"Kelly, you think this is gonna work today?" Tuggins looked at the Panthers dissident-in-chief more seriously than Kelly had seen his friend's face.

"Yeah, I do." Kelly took a deep breath. "I talked to Denny Dixon last night, on a radiophone Fast Eddie found somewhere. Denny thinks it's a sound plan, especially with Beltzer and those guys." He wiped his brow with an arm. "He says support for the war is crumbling back in the world. There's all kind of fuckin' rumors flying around, and half of 'em are about us. Nixon's trying to keep a lid on things, but word's getting out." Kelly grinned. "I don't know about you, but I'm looking forward to Lan Tho Giao's dinner in Nha Trang tonight."

"Well, my commie-ass Bro, I hope your commie-ass buddy knows what he's talkin about." Tuggins said and turned to Flowers; "Where's the Professor? He okay with everything?"

Miller spoke up. "Prof is fine, ready to go. I seen a few of his guys coming up to the line already, over yonder." Miller pointed to a position about at the far left of the forming Panther Division line. The ever-affable Gormick was cheerfully placing men as they arrived.

"Very good," said Tuggins. "What about Sugarboy, Turk? I seen him with those three bodybuilder friends of his this morning."

"I sent Sugarboy and his guys to guard the halt and lame, back in the rear. Those Special Forces guys love to strut around with their M60's across their chests, so they didn't complain about not bein' in the charge today. Just made me promise to save some food for 'em in Nha Trang."

"Kelly, where's your buddy, Spiderman?" Tuggins said, a strong note of tension coming into his voice. "Everything okay with his guys?"

"Tug, for Christ's sake!" Kelly said, a little exasperated. "Frank is fine. He's doing a great job with his Battalion. Look, over there," he pointed to the right side of the Panther line. "Those guys are part of the Third and they're formin' up already."

"Turk, you think you could get the Black Panthers up here a little early?" Tuggins asked softly.

Flowers began chuckling, signaling the others to join in. Finally, with everybody laughing out loud, Tuggins joined in too and let his hair down a little.

"Sure, Preacher," Flowers said between chuckles, "I'll go get 'em now." Flowers and the others set off each for his respective group. Time was getting tight.

o o o

"What can you make out, sir?" said Haldeman's aide, who was standing next to him on the ridge near General Choe's tanks. Peter Grassley was from Minitosh, Wisconsin and had graduated first in his class the year before. Like many young Americans, Grassley harbored questions about the war, but he kept his doubts to himself on his new job, preferring to take advantage of the opportunity that had practically fallen in his lap. He was something of an idealist, but mostly an opportunist.

"Take a look, Grassley." Haldeman extended his binoculars to him.

Grassley pointed the binocs toward the tree line where the Panthers were assembling. He swept them back and forth across the tree line. "Looks like they're getting ready to do something, sir."

"That would be my guess, son," Haldeman replied, a little sardonically.

"And would you look at all those flags, sir!"

At the mention of flags, Haldeman's interest was piqued. He raised one eyebrow slightly higher than the other and reached out to take the field glasses back. "Grassley!" he called out.

The young aide had not heard his boss. "Sir, a bunch of black guys are coming out in front of the rest. God, they look like a bunch of pirates, except for all the Stars and Stripes. Man, I've never seen so much red, white and blue!"

"Grassley!!" Haldeman yelled, "give me the goddamn binoculars, now!"

Sheepishly, the young fellow complied. Haldeman immediately brought the binocs up to his face. "Well, I'll be a son of a bitch," he said as he scanned the scene. Haldeman trotted over to General Choe, who was standing with his interpreter. Grassley followed closely behind him.

"General, would it be possible to lay down a barrage half-way between the road block and the front line of those black troops over there?" Haldeman pointed to Flowers' men, in front of the tree line.

As the interpreter translated Haldeman's request, a smile came over Choe's face. When the interpreter was finished, Choe gave his reply, pointing to sections of the field in front of him.

"General Choe says that your idea is a good one, Mr. Haldeman," the interpreter said. "He suggests firing in rounds of five, three seconds apart, until all the tanks have fired once.

"Please tell the General that will be fine," Haldeman said. He scratched his chin for a moment, then added, "Tell the General we want to be cautious to not hit any of the American soldiers, yet."

Choe nodded as the interpreter spoke. When he was finished, Choe looked over at Haldeman, then strode over to one of his colonels and issued his orders.

o o o

A salvo of thirty tank cannon rounds is nothing to sneeze at, even if the shells all land fifty to a hundred meters in front of you. The Black Panthers, along with the rest of the Panther Division, got themselves as close to the dirt as they could.

"Whaddaya think, Preacher?" Flowers yelled to Tuggins, who was six feet from where he lay.

Tuggins wiped dust from his mouth and eyes, then cupped his hands around his mouth and yelled, "It's just a warning, Turk."

Boom! Boom! Boom! On went the demonstration of the awesome kill power facing the Panthers.

"Otherwise, we'd be getting' a lot more than dirt on us right now," Tuggins called out.

"Where the fuck's Beltzer?" Flowers shouted, over the noise of exploding shells. "Ain't they sposed to be here by now?"

"Give 'em another five minutes," Tuggins said as he looked at his watch. "Don't worry, he'll be here," he yelled. Then he looked back upfield, toward the flying dirt and debris of the barrage, which seemed to be coming to an end.

"Everybody up!" yelled Flowers. The field and road in front of them had fallen silent. The air began to clear. Slowly, the Black Panthers rose and brushed themselves off. They reformed their lines with weapons and flags at the ready. The fellows all had their game faces on now. Whatever Tuggins and Flowers had in mind, they would do their utmost to carry it out.

From the roadblock, a voice came over a loud speaker; "Gentlemen, it's time to end this foolishness before many of you are killed!" The voice reminded Tuggins of drill sergeants in basic and the guards at Long Binh Jail. "The best thing for you to do is surrender at once. You...."

The man with the loudspeaker interrupted himself as he and everybody else on the road outside of Nha Trang directed their attention to the sky above them. Two helicopters, a scout and a huey, flew up over the east ridge and out above the road, circling between the Panthers and General Choe's force.

The choppers were quite a sight. Two huge American flags flew from the skids of the scout and two large signs were affixed to either side of the Huey. One of the signs said 'TV' and the other said 'U.S. Rep Louis Willard'. The flags and signs were clearly visible from the ground to the Panthers, and to General Choe's force. Slowly, the aircraft circled at about two hundred and fifty feet, just high enough to clear the ridges, where Choe's forces waited for additional orders.

A roar of approval rose up from the Panther lines. Whatever happened here today would be filmed and shown to the world. The Panthers might die on the road in front of them, but their story wouldn't.

"Kelly, you see that?" Dunlop had come over to the left end of his group, from where he could call out to his friend in First Battalion. "That's Thompson up there. Fuckin-A, man!"

"Yeah," Kelly said, "and it looks like he's got a damn film crew with him, just like Tuggins said he would." Kelly walked over toward Dunlop. "Now, keep your eyes on Turk's group. You're really gonna see something," he looked at his watch, "in about thirty seconds."

o o o

"Shit." Haldeman pulled down his binoculars and looked at Grassley. "This is all I fucking need." He chewed on a middle fingernail for a second. "Get me the White House, now!" he commanded.

Grassley sprang into action, ran to pick up the telephone on his prick-25 and cupped his hand around the transmitter as he struggled to reach the President.

General Choe and his interpreter hurried over to Haldeman and Grassley. "Sir, General Choe wishes me to inform you that it would be a simple matter to shoot down the two helicopters." Choe looked at Haldeman expectantly.

Haldeman shook his head for a moment, then took in a deep breath and let it out. "Shit. There's some goddamn congressman up there, General. I can't shoot him down without orders from my President." He turned back toward the road and raised the binoculars to his eyes. Grassley kept shouting into the phone at unseen tormentors, who apparently did not understand his need for instant connection to the President.

o o o

"Black Panthers, Atten-shun!!" Flowers called out.

"ONE-TWO!!" came the shouted response from five hundred scruffy black GIs, standing tall in their unkempt splendor. They were backed by eighteen thousand buddies, ready to follow them home. The Panthers wore torn, filthy, and makeshift uniforms, but their hearts were as one. Quiet came to the little patch of ground outside of Nha Trang, except for the lazy whir of the circling helicopters. A stiff, hot breeze blew across the road, unfurling the several hundred flags the Panthers were carrying. Muscles rippled and jaws were set in grim determination.

One man in the front row of the Black Panthers began clapping in rhythm to a chant he called out. "Who are we?"

"Panthers!"

"What Panthers?"

"Black Panthers!"

"Who are we..."

It took only a couple of repetitions until many in the Battalions had joined in the rhythmic clapping, filling the little valley with drumming energy.

"Guess it's time to go, Preacher!" Flowers called out as he lustily brought his hands together in time with the others.

"Guess so, Brother Turk!"

The two men walked out in front of the line of chanting troops, then turned and faced the guys. Each raised the M16 he carried, high over his head, then placed it on the ground in front of him.

"Hurry now! Pile 'em up right here! Make a stack so high, they'll see it all the way back in the world!" Flowers called out.

A couple of the guys brought their weapons forward and dropped them on top of Tuggins' gun. Then a couple more, then a rush of men with weapons flying onto the piles. The other battalions took up the activity with gusto, disarming themselves while keeping up the clapping and chanting. Beltzer and his film crew hovered over the Panthers, the filming cameras in the helicopter doorways visible from the ground.

After the guns were piled up, Flowers stood ramrod straight and called out over his shoulder to the men assembled behind him. "Black Pantherrrrrs, double-time, HO!"

And, so, the first five hundred went, clapping in unison and running in step toward the roadblock. As they neared their goal, they picked up speed until they were about a hundred yards from the barrier in the road. There, they broke into a full run. An exuberant yell emerged as the charging mass of rebel GIs approached their adversaries at the roadblock. The weapons of the CIA men were pointed directly at the onrushing hoard of five hundred disarmed soldiers and the eighteen thousand screaming Panthers running just behind them. There wasn't a weapon in sight among Tuggins' guys.

○ ○ ○

"Shit!" a disgusted H.R. Haldeman spat out as he studied the road near the roadblock. His eyes were glued to his field glasses while he moved his head and arms back and forth, seeking any evidence of arms being carried by the Panthers.

"What do you think, sir?" asked Grassley, in a tentative, almost confused voice.

"The way I see it, son, we can't kill the Congressman. And we sure as hell can't shoot a bunch of unarmed American soldiers while cameras are filming the whole damn thing." Haldeman took the binoculars down and grimaced. "Looks like that Tiggins, or Jiggins, fucker, whatever his goddamn name is, has us over a barrel, and it doesn't look like he plans to use any jelly."

"Shall I inform General Choe, sir?"

"Yes, I suppose." Haldeman brought the binoculars up to his eyes again and pointed toward the road. "Choe is waiting for my go ahead, so we don't really need to worry that he's going to open up before we want him to." Haldeman swept his field of vision from one end of the Panther line to the other. The first group was past the roadblock now and most of the ragged mass of GIs had slowed to an easy trot. The far ends of the line were blending together on the road behind the barrier, forming one long column again.

"Go ahead Grassley. Tell General Choe that we won't be requiring his services today." Haldeman sighed.

"Yes sir, right away." Grassley hesitated a moment, then said, "Mr Haldeman, what did you mean about us being over a barrel?"

"Well son, here's how things stand right now." Haldeman let the binoculars fall on their strap and rest against his belt. He faced Grassley, "All over Vietnam, we can hardly get enough men to turn out for unit formations to fill the front row, let alone the ranks. The colored soldiers are in open rebellion everywhere. They're refusing duty, dressing like goddamn Africans, and doing that Dap stuff 'till they're blue in the face. It's totally out of control." He took a deep breath and exhaled. "We are in command of only about one-third of our airfields and we've got sizable elements from three divisions in the Southern Highlands ready to join these guys as they leave Nha Trang. Down in the delta, they tell me that half of the Ninth Division is headed for Saigon to meet up with them and help surround the embassy."

"The South Vietnamese Army is in a complete state of collapse. After what happened here today, they'll all figure their best chance at survival is to just get rid of their uniforms and blend in with the refugee crowds heading south." Haldeman glanced back toward the road below, shook his head, then returned to Grassley. "You might say we're totally fucked and there's not a damn thing we can do about it." His face assumed a quizzical expression. "You ever get through to Washington?"

"No sir, but we're still trying."

CHAPTER XXX

So Long ...

"WHERE'S FAST EDDIE? ANYBODY SEEN HIM TONIGHT? AND WHERE the hell's Sugarboy?" Tuggins scanned the small restaurant. A steaming bowl of noodles sat untouched in front of him while he thought of one problem after another and demanded answers from the assembled Panther leaders. The battalion commanders gathered around a large circular table that occupied an entire room of the only restaurant in Nha Trang. Hundreds of exhausted and happy troops were milling around just outside the nameless three-room building without even a sign in front. They all seemed to be working on bowls of noodles filled by smiling Vietnamese women, most of whom were carrying guns in the jungle not a month before. Lan Tho Giao had organized food for thousands, with serving stations from one end of town to the other.

"Sugarboy is in line, getting some soup, Tug," Flowers said. "Miller brought down the rest of the guys and he's checking his trucks over yonder and puttin' out guards for the night. He'll be along in a few minutes."

"Well...." Tuggins trailed off, looking worried.

"Well what, Preacher?" said Flowers with a beaming smile. "It's party time, Bro!" He raised both of his clenched fists, just above his head. "Tug, we made it!"

◦ ◦ ◦

May 29, 1970

"Hey look," called out Kelly, pointing with his bush hat about fifty yards off from where he sat with Dunlop, Tuggins and Sugarboy Fortier in front of the American Embassy. "That's Lizzard over there." The four began waving, to gain Vandyne's attention.

"I'll be dammed!" said Dunlop, "I never thought we'd see that fucker again."

"Here he comes," said Fortier. "He sees us now. Who's that with him?"

"Oh, my God," Kelly shouted, in amazement. "That's Black Power!"

"Power, over here!" Tuggins called out to Raymond Green. Green walked up with Vandyne, and Tuggins was so happy to see him, they hugged and did elaborate Dap. "Man, we thought you was gone for sure!" Tuggins exclaimed. "How you doin'?"

"I'm still pretty sore," he patted his stomach gingerly, " but I guess I'll live."

"You're comin' home with us, aren't you?" Dunlop asked Green.

"Sure, man," said Green, "but since I got shot, you guys gotta catch me up on everything."

"Hey, fellas," said Lizzard, smiling slyly and with a nervous tic in his left eyebrow.

"Where the fuck you been, man?"

"I been with you guys, all the way since An Khe," Lizzard lied. His eyes darted back and forth.

"Sure you were," laughed Kelly

"Look, I gotta be goin', fellas," Lizzard said and lit a cigarette. "I'm supposed to hook up with this guy named Stroud." He took a deep drag on his smoke and exhaled nervously.

"That the same fucker who tried to talk the brothers into deserting the Panthers, back in Qui Nohn?" Fortier asked.

"That would be one and the same, Sugarboy," Dunlop said.

"Shit!" growled Fortier.

"He's gonna take a few of us back to the world for a press conference with the President," Lizzard said, a note of pride in his voice.

" Well, I'm sure you'll ably represent the Panthers, Lizzard," Kelly said with a deadpan expression on his face.

"You guys can count on that," Lizzard said, tossing his cigarette on the ground then spinning around and leaving the four Panthers to wonder about their messed-up old buddy. "Great runnin' into you guys," Lizzard called out over his shoulder. "Be seein' you, Power." Then he disappeared into the crowd

o o o

MAY 31, 1970

A large group of GIs gathered around Tuggins to hear what he was saying to Kelly, Dunlop, and Fortier. Fast Eddie Miller and Turk Flowers stood on the edge of the gathering since they had been present for the morning's meeting between Haldeman and Tuggins inside the embassy.

"So, what's the scoop, Tug?" said Kelly.

Tuggins smiled, "Good news, fellas." Applause and cheering broke out from the five hundred or so GIs within earshot. For most of them, this was their third day outside the embassy. Tuggins waited for the hooting and whistling to subside, "They want us outta here, as soon as possible. They afraid the news guys are all gonna start showin' up and broadcastin' what's goin' on here."

Tuggins held up several papers stapled together. They flapped in the hot breeze a he waved them above his head.

"This here's a list of ships in the South China Sea heading this way right now. They put out a call to our allies to help get us outta here. Looks like it shouldn't take more than a week or so, and we'll have everybody on board something or other, and gone from here, for sure."

"Hey Tug!" a voice came from the crowd.

"Yeah, Bro." Tuggins respectfully directed his attention to the questioner.

"The Army gonna get us home, or what?"

Tuggins chuckled, "Last count, there was three hundred eighty thousand troops to load up. If we wait for the Army, it'll take 'till next year to get everybody back to the world." Tuggins pointed to the list. "There's eighty-two ships from thirty countries headed for Saigon. Some are already in the river, a few will be here by morning." He dropped the list to his side.

"Which brings up something." He waited till the crowd was a little quieter. "Might as well start moving away from the embassy. We'll set up kitchens at the docks."

Kelly looked out over the sea of young men. Thousands of guys in every variation of uniform he could imagine with even more creative touches than when they were out in the boonies. They were milling around, trying to get out of the sun, and drinking water passed around by Lan Tho Giao's girls, and generally having a pretty good time, now that they weren't going to die in Vietnam. *Reminds me of those guys just back from Nam the day we picked up our uniforms for basic training,* Kelly thought.

"Bear, c'mon over here," Tuggins said to Kelly. He pointed to a vacant spot under the vines that ran along the fence in front of the embassy.

"What's up, Tug?"

Tuggins spoke in a low voice. "You and Spiderman got your deal set up?"

"Yeah," Kelly nodded, "Sugarboy's a full partner now, too." He raised his hands and shrugged his shoulders a little. "We're ready to go, as soon as we know which boat we're getting on."

"There's a Spanish ship, the Cosita Mejor, gonna be at Wharf #3 tomorrow morning, about 1000 hrs." Tuggins raised his eyebrows "Can y'all have your stuff down there by then?"

"Don't see why not, Tug."

"Okay, cause I want you guys on that boat." Tuggins looked over Kelly's shoulder for a moment, then said, "They're talking about bringin' a couple of news crews on board to film some interviews. You up for that?"

"Sure," Kelly said, "Why the hell not?"

○ ○ ○

"Oh my fuckin' God!" Tom Kelly scanned the enormous warehouse and the rows of ten-foot shelves, filled with thousands of cameras, stereo systems, watches and every marketable consumer item imaginable. "This stuff is all ours?" he asked the grinning Dunlop and Fortier.

"All we gotta do is get it on the boat." Dunlop said and pointed to Fortier. "I think this man, here has it pretty well planned out."

Sugarboy Fortier cleared his throat. "MPs are gone, man. Took off their arm-bands when we got to Saigon. US civilians used to work in this place all flew outta here. I gots thirty men that was together in LBJ gonna be here soon as it's dark." Fortier thrust his hands into his pants pockets. "They all got M16s and at least ten mags. Most of 'em were with Turk's Black Panthers."

"I thought those guys gave up their guns back at Nha Trang," said Kelly.

Fortier smiled broadly, "Nah, man," he said. "Rolled up a bunch in ponchos and kept 'em back with the guys couldn't walk."

"Goddamn, you guys...." Kelly said with a smile.

"About 9 tonight, I got eighteen deuce-and-a-halfs showin' up. Everybody gonna pitch in and load. There's a connex on every truck, and we'll just put em up on that freighter Tug told us about." Fortier smiled. "Any questions?"

"Yeah," said Kelly. "How much you guys figure this stuff is worth?"

"I figure it'll take about six months to fence it all in California," said Dunlop. "Conservatively, we got a cold $650,000 here, Bear." He exhaled a deep drag of smoke, "I think we'll have enough to pay off Sugarboy's crew, give all twenty of us about $20,000 each and cover any odd problem that comes up. That's enough to get started back in the world, huh?"

0 0 0

Surgarboy Fortier bent over the railing of the Spanish freighter and hung on for dear life, as he tried his best to empty his stomach into the Saigon River.

"I can't believe the man has anything left to puke," declared Flowers, shifting on the gently bobbing steel deck of the ship taking the American soldiers home.

"Maybe he's trying to fish," Eddie Miller suggested and took a drag on his Bugler smoke. "They call it chumming. You spread lots of bait on the water and then you grab anything that comes up."

"Agghhh" retched Sugarboy, catching himself as he almost fell over the rail.

"Hey fellas," said Tuggins, "let the man suffer in peace, okay? It's not his fault he's never been on a boat."

Eight hundred American soldiers crowded the deck of the Cosita Mejor as it made its way down the Saigon River toward the South China

Sea. Eighteen metal packing boxes were stacked, two high, in the main cargo hold. All the boxes bore proper-looking import slips with a San Francisco destination. The water was smooth, and the blue sky shimmered against the dark green of the surrounding jungle. The light brown river rolled gently under them. Groups of homebound GIs played cards and some slept. Several circles of guys sang, chanted and clapped, "Who are we?...Black Panthers!"

"So, Bear," Flowers said, "what you gonna do when you get back to the world? You said something about law school, didn't you?"

Sugarboy turned away from the railing. His face was as green as one ever sees on a dark skinned black man. "Somebody say lawyer?" his eyes were barely open. "I could use a good lawyer."

"Go back to your business, Sugarboy," Kelly said as Fortier weaved and caught himself. "I don't know, Turk. First I gotta get a B.A. in something or other. What about you?"

"School, I guess."

"What about you, Tug?" Kelly said. "You gonna follow in your Daddy's footsteps?"

"I don't know," Tuggins answered. "I been thinking maybe medical school."

"That what the rest of you all are thinking 'bout doing, school?" Flowers asked.

Dunlop, Miller, Blackjack, Gormick, Green, Kapiniski, O'Connor, and Gage, all nodded. The group was leaning against a rusty metal wall that offered a bit of shade.

"Hey Tug," asked Miller. "You get a chance to say goodbye to Lan Tho Giao?"

"Nah," said Tuggins. "Last I saw her, she was going into the National Palace with that General husband of hers. Gonna be mayor of Saigon or something. What about that nurse you was with?"

"Yeah, Francine." Miller took a long toke on his Bugler. "Well, we're gonna meet stateside," Miller said. "She and her friend Connie wanna be the last ones out of Saigon."

Tuggins nodded and smiled. "Them and their nurse friends were a lotta help, setting up all those aid stations."

"Sure enough, Preacher," Eddie said.

"Hey, Spidey, what's gonna happen with that girl from the wire at An Khe?" asked Flowers.

"I promised Tuyen I'd be back for her," Dunlop said. "I told her it might take a year or so. We're gonna live in Sacramento, ain't that somethin'?"

"How much you have to give those guys at the docks to get our boxes loaded, Spiderman?" asked Tuggins, grinning.

"Lucky thing I had some cash with me, huh?" Dunlop said. "Took about $5000. I had to pay off a couple dozen guys."

"You gonna take that off the top when you sell the stuff," asked Tuggins, "ain't ya?"

Dunlop nodded, and lit a Marlboro. "What about ol' Hugh Thompson and that congressman what's his name?" Dunlop asked Tuggins.

"Name is Willard," Tuggins said. "Thompson grabbed a Huey and flew my dad, Willard and that Dixon guy out to Bangkok to catch a commercial flight back to the States." Tuggins shifted his position a little. "Ol' Beltzer is on board the Cosita. Gonna interview us for some big article he's finally gonna get into his magazine." He turned toward Kelly. "Bear, what you think is gonna happen with the election next year?"

"I talked to Becky night before last. She says Nixon is coming out of this smelling like a fuckin' rose." Tuggins chuckled as Kelly reached for the Bugler roll-your-own Miller passed to him. Kelly went on, "He's taking full credit for ending the war. The VC are letting him off the hook by arranging an interim government to oversee arrangements for gettin' us outta Nam, and he's gonna present himself as the man who brought our troops home. Probably win in a landslide, no matter who the Democrats put up."

Flowers shook his head in wonder, "Tricky fucking Dick!" he uttered softly.

"Hey guys, look at that tower over there," Miller called out and pointed to a tall white steeple rising above the passing jungle off the starboard side of the Cosita.

"That's the last we gonna see of the Nam, fellas," Tuggins said. "The spire of the National Cathedral, in Saigon." He wiped his brow and gazed, along with his buddies, at the receding tower as the Cosita headed for the mouth of the river and into the open sea.

Quietly, Kelly said to himself, "So long, Vietnam."

ACKNOWLEDGEMENTS

As with any book worth reading, the contributions of many people other than the author were large and valuable beyond measure.

During my hitch in the Army, I talked with many American soldiers recently returned from Vietnam, who generously shared their wartime experiences with me and truly made this book possible. Two buddies of mine deserve special mention here. Don Fancher was really in the Fourth Division and on the dusty plateau along the Cambodia border where the meeting of Bros and Heads took place that formed the basis for this book. Don was at the meeting, said his piece, then went into Cambodia with his buddies. Steve Morse was an anti-war pal of mine who was, like me, a member of Progressive Labor Party. He risked a lot to try and organize his fellow soldiers against the war. One morning Steve was pulled out of a cell in the Ft. Lewis Post Stockade at about 2 AM and wound up behind a 50 cal machine gun on an apc heading into Cambodia for the invasion. Years later, he was of tremendous help to me finishing this book. Steve's a great editor.

Speaking of editors, I want to express eternal gratitude to Teresa Selfe, the principal editor of this book. Teresa is a highly skilled and generous person, and a great teacher. About Teresa and a few others, I have to say: "couldn't have done it without her."

Minh-Hoa Ta, Ed. D. is Dean of Instruction at City College of San Francisco. She is a friend of Steve Morse's, and he asked her to help me with Vietnamese names and language that I used in the book. Boy, was I glad to hear from her! Thank you, Minh Ta, for helping me make this book more authentic.

I was able to use the picture on the cover because of help from two really good guys. David Zeiger of 'Displaced Films' is the writer and director of 'Sir! No Sir!' described very aptly on their website as a "Long suppressed story of the GI movement to end the war in Vietnam." He directed me to the writer, James Lewes, who had the image he believes comes from an anti-war newspaper, 'Liberated Barracks.' James Lewes has written 'Protest and Survive: Underground GI Newspapers during the Vietnam War.'

My son, Jeremy, kept telling me the book was worth reading and encouraged me a lot over the years. He and his wife, Allison, my wonderful daughter-in-law, truly cheered me on.

Most of all, I want to acknowledge the critical role played by my wife, best friend, and editor, Paula Jane Yeghoian King. She was with me every step of the way and took over during the final editing. Without Paula, there would be no *So Long, Vietnam*.

Brian King
8/20/13

ABOUT THE AUTHOR

BRIAN KING is a sixty-seven year old writer and political activist. He lives in Seattle, Washington with his wife, Paula, and very near his son, daughter-in-law, and two grandchildren. He retired six years ago after working thirty-five years as a Respiratory Therapist.

Brian was born in Chicago, Illinois, and went through grade school there, and high school after he and his family moved to California's Santa Clara Valley. During the summer of 1965 he went to the South and worked in the Civil Rights Movement on voter registration campaigns. Upon returning to California, where he was a student at San Jose State college, he became deeply involved in the movement against the War in Vietnam.

A year after receiving his draft notice for induction into the Army, with the FBI hot on his trail, Brian decided to report for training in the Army. Many of his friends in the anti-war movement agreed with him that he could organize more important opposition to the war as a soldier than as a prisoner, had he refused induction.

Brian's time in the army provided him the material for *So Long, Vietnam*. The Army decided not to send him to the war, but many of his friends told him their stories of their experiences in the combat zone. These stories exerted a strong pull on Brian until, twenty years later, he decided to write his book.

You can e-mail Brian at *bking@solongvietnam.com*

24756940R20177

Made in the USA
Charleston, SC
06 December 2013